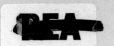

FRIDAY THE 13TH

HATE-KILL-REPEAT

Six feet: the distance that separated Norwood Thawn and Jason Voorhees.

Norwood was desperately trying not to show it, but he felt unnerved. Perhaps it was Jason's unearthly countenance. Or the way his rock-like fist grasped the blood-caked machete. It was hanging by Jason's side, but Norwood knew this could change at any moment.

Still, he had faith. Both spiritual, and in his own ability to sway others.

"What say you?" he said, careful to keep his voice steady. Perhaps this giant was like a dog. He might smell fear. Maybe that's how he operated. "Will you join us?"

Norwood swallowed hard. Was Jason Voorhees really like them?

His own concealed blade felt cool and sharp against his wrist. He really hoped he wouldn't have to use it.

FRIDAY THE 13TH

HATE-KILL-REPEAT

A NOVEL BY
JASON ARNOPP

BASED ON CHARACTERS FROM THE
MOTION PICTURE FRIDAY THE 13TH
CREATED BY VICTOR MILLER

BLACK FLAME

Dedication: For Mum, Dad, Uncle John, Sarah Corby, Ray "Which one is Jason Voorhees, again?" Zell, Rebecca Levene and everyone else who suffered regular updates about how many words I'd written.

A Black Flame Publication
www.blackflame.com

First published in 2005 by BL Publishing, Games Workshop Ltd., Willow Road, Nottingham NG7 2WS, UK.

Distributed in the US by Simon & Schuster, 1230 Avenue of the Americas, New York, NY 10020, USA.

10 9 8 7 6 5 4 3 2 1

ISBN 13: 978 1 84416 271 0
ISBN 10: 1 84416 271 0

A CIP record for this book is available from the British Library.

Printed in the UK by Bookmarque, Surrey, UK.

ONE

Kitty-Lou was about to die. Oblivious to this fact, she felt great.

Every muscle in her body was supremely blissed-out; multiple orgasms tended to do that for a girl. Sure, she was pushing fifty, but Kitty-Lou Maynard could still attract the guys, yes, sir. Men swarmed around her and her show-stopping chest like moths to two big flames. To prove it, there she was, lying on a bed between a pair of sleeping studs.

She turned her head on the pillow and gazed past Bud's unshaven face to see that it was 2.23am. This small room might only cost twenty-nine bucks a night—the Eight-Ball was the kind of joint which also offered an hourly rate, for the benefit of hookers and their clientele—but at least it offered a bedside clock with green, luminous digits. Not bad for a shit-heap on the outskirts of Rochester, New York. She doubted the water pressure would be too great in the shower but, hey, she had certainly enjoyed herself so far.

Bud and Kyle. She'd met them that night at Dolly's Dive, downtown. At first, Kitty-Lou had wondered if they were queer, as Bud was a big, hairy growler and the smooth-shaven Kyle seemed more effeminate, especially for a black guy. Naturally, it didn't take much drinking or raucous, bar-slapping innuendo for Kitty-Lou Maynard to decide that they were good ole hetero boys. Once they got her inside this room, the fact was conclusively proven. Repeatedly. She smiled and ran her hand lightly over Kyle's muscular thigh, noticing thin cords of light, which snuck past the graying net curtains. Outside, she vaguely remembered, lamps were dotted around to help guests stagger to their allotted ten by ten foot room.

Sudden noises made her shiver. Someone out there sounded distressed. She heard a cry of pain and her eternally overactive imagination insisted on constructing a scenario whether she liked it or not. A lone woman had been attacked. Raped. Slashed. Out there in the courtyard, decreed the creative side of Kitty-Lou's brain, this woman lay on her back, half-dead in the middle of a metallic graveyard of still, silent automobiles.

Stop it, Kit, she told herself. Go back to sleep, hon.

She closed her eyes, only to hear footsteps. Feet were striding toward their door, she was sure of it. Perhaps more than one pair. She inhaled sharply, the breath suspended in her lungs.

Four firm knocks nearly ensured that she never breathed again. Who the hell could this be, in the middle of the night?

Aw, come on, her rational mind jibed. It's some beery jackass, who thinks he's in our room when he's got his key fob the wrong way up and he's actually in room six. Or it's a crack whore desperate for a few dollars to pay her man.

Or was it the woman she had imagined, battered and bruised with her torn underwear hanging from one ankle?

To her left, Bud was stirring. The smell of his alcoholic namesake emanated from him like nobody's business; was he only called Bud because he drank the stuff? She didn't care. She just wanted him to answer the damn door.

"Was that knock on... ours?" he mumbled, his eyes shut.

"Yep," she said, extending a hand to ruffle his short, gel-spiked hair. "Be a doll and see who it is, would ya, sweetie?"

Bud groaned, swiping her hand away. She remembered that she didn't know him from Adam. She knew his dick far better than his brain. Still, in all likelihood they were the same thing.

"Go on, Bud," said Kyle to her right. "Do the right thing, man." He chuckled into the pillow.

Bud exhaled heavily as he sat up, muscles pulsing as he rotated on the bed. "Why me, dude?"

"You're nearest to the door," came the muffled reply. Bud grunted, then slapped his feet on the floor, pulled his jocks back on and yanked a T-shirt over his head.

Four more knocks on the door. Louder.

"Jesus," said Kyle.

"I'm coming!" yelled Bud, for the third time that night. Yelling way too loudly, he was clearly a man with a hair-trigger temper. Kitty-Lou didn't like that quality in a man these days, it reminded her too much of Jerry. Hadn't she finally left *that* punchy bastard, to live the free and easy life she'd always dreamed of? Oh yeah, guys were always sweetness and light when you met them in a fucking bar, but as soon as they'd parked their pork mobile, it was a different story.

Bud was standing, his Lakers shirt hugging him in a most complementary manner, Kitty-Lou couldn't help but notice. Again.

He grabbed the door chain and slotted it into the latch.

As the door opened, a six inch strip of light shot across the floor and part of one wall. Kitty-Lou couldn't see who was out there, just one side of Bud's disgruntled face.

Bud didn't like the look of these people at all, even if they *did* look terrified. They closely resembled the kind of highfalutin folk who had looked down their noses at him his whole life. Was it *his* fault that he couldn't read or write? Nope.

They both looked about forty, he judged. The guy had receding blond hair, his tanned forehead beaded with sweat. He was all clean looking and cultured, wearing a spotless suit like some kind of swish encyclopedia salesman or cocktail bar faggot. The lady with him? She wasn't too bad a piece at all, Bud considered, briefly flicking his eyes up the length of her. Blonde, dolled up to the nines. Very glam, or she would be, if pain and fear weren't etched across her face like tattoos.

"I'm so sorry to bother you," said the man, sounding as posh as Bud had figured, "but this is an emergency. We're being chased by a m-m-maniac. He attacked my wife."

The stutter surprised Bud. This guy looked pretty self-assured. The woman winced as she presented her left shoulder, which had hitherto been concealed by her right hand.

Blood. The material of her white summer dress had been hacked open, the flesh below red and wet.

Behind him, Bud could hear Kitty-Lou and Kyle asking what was going on. He had no time to explain. Even if these visitors weren't his kind of people, the bastards clearly needed help. Why did they have to pick *this* room?

He glanced back inside. "Cover yourselves up."

Yanking the chain out from across the door, he stepped back to grant the couple entry. Once they were inside, he swung the door until it was almost shut, sticking his head out through the gap. The motel's sparsely populated parking lot looked like an oil painting. After running his eyes around its entirety, paying special attention to the patches of shadows, which lurked between vehicles, he closed and locked the door.

"Oh my," said Kitty-Lou. "But why didn't you guys go to the front desk?" As she spoke, she wondered why the pair looked vaguely familiar.

"We didn't see it," said the woman, her delicate features taut with pain as her husband tenderly examined her arm. "We're not staying here. We were attacked in our car, out on the freeway."

"This guy came out of nowhere with what looked like a sword," continued her husband. "When he went for Penelope, I managed to fight him off and we just ran b-b-blindly over here."

Bud furrowed his brow and leant against one bed-post. "Did he follow you?"

The husband shook his head. "We didn't look back."

"Oh my fucking God," breathed Kyle. As he said this, both of the newcomers turned their heads to face him. They were glaring. He involuntarily dropped his jaw, amazed that they could find time to be offended by profanity at a time like this.

"It's 911 time," said Bud, reaching for a chunky telephone on one bedside table.

"Sure," said the husband, finally breaking his gaze away from a bemused Kyle. "I'll do it. I... I know what happened." His eyes were glazed, as though focused on nothing at all. Kitty-Lou thought it looked like shock.

The room's occupants sat in silence as the man whom they quickly came to know as Norwood Thawn got past the operator and briefly outlined the situation. Then he gave them the Eight-Ball's address.

By that point, Kitty-Lou had almost entirely dressed herself. As much as she loved men in uniform, she didn't want to be naked when the cops arrived. Truth be told, she was afraid that they might assume she was a working girl, spending the night here with two guys. Typical, her first three-some and *this* shit went down.

As she bent down to tie her shoelace, she noticed the condom. There it was, sitting on the floor in plain sight, used. Looking up, she saw that Norwood had followed her gaze and was looking at the amorphous blob.

"Hey," she smiled at him. "At least we're safe, right fellas?"

Behind her, Kyle nodded awkwardly, wiping the sleep from his eyes. Bud just stood there looking at Norwood and Penelope, his arms folded defensively. The faintest hint of a shrug rippled across his broad shoulders.

Kitty-Lou sensed an atmospheric shift in the room. Sure, Norwood and Penelope had suffered a traumatic incident and she was trying to cut them some slack. Yet there was something about these people that was starting to chill her, deep down in her craw. *Where* had she seen them before?

"So what have you been up to tonight?" Norwood asked Kitty-Lou. His face was ambiguous, suspended halfway between nudge-nudge amusement and something altogether more... serious. Judgmental, even.

Kitty-Lou laughed, but it felt forced. She glanced nervously at Bud, who was still staring at the increasingly steely couple. "I think you should leave," he said, after Norwood's question had hung in the air for a few pregnant seconds. "Why not head over to the front desk and wait for the cops?"

Norwood was still looking at Kitty-Lou. "Did you have sexual relations with both of these men tonight?"

Kitty-Lou swallowed hard. Then something in her head snapped, something which reminded her of the day she decided that she'd finally had enough of Jerry. "What the hell does it have to do with you, mister?"

Norwood chuckled. "Hell, indeed. Hell, my dear, is where you and your partners in disgusting filth are headed." As he grimaced, Kitty-Lou remembered: these people had been at Dolly's Dive.

Bud took a few steps toward Norwood, only to see that Penelope was holding a gun in her right hand, using the arm which had supposedly been injured. The fire which danced in her eyes was the most frightening thing he had ever seen. It would also be the last thing he saw. Penelope pulled the trigger.

Any noise the gun might have made was muted to an innocuous *phut* by its suppressor attachment. The result, however, was no less devastating. Bud staggered backwards, half his head vanishing in a red mist. Blood splattered the wall behind him as he slumped to the carpet, his shirt blooming red.

As if anticipating Kitty-Lou's scream, Penelope leveled the gun at the older woman and fired again. A ragged hole appeared above her right breast and she toppled off the bed, slamming hard into the floor, gasping incredulously.

Kyle made a bolt for the door, but Norwood darted into his path, punching him in the face and dropping him. Straightening his shirt collar, which Kyle had blindly tugged, Norwood sighed as though dealing with a difficult child. He crouched and sat astride the man's chest.

Penelope tucked the gun back inside her handbag and entered the cramped, damp riddled bathroom, rolling up her dress sleeve and scrubbing red gunk from her shoulder. When she emerged, Kyle lay still on the carpet. Her husband had removed the man's eyeballs and was holding them aloft on his flat, bloody palm as though presenting her with the finest caviar.

"Do you know, my dear," he said. "I think they've seen the light."

Then he turned back to look at Kitty-Lou. The woman was still breathing, down there by the bed.

He undid the buckle of his ornate belt and turned to Penelope.

"Get the whore back on the bed."

Silence hung over the waters like a cloak. At that time, almost three in the morning, even nature's own creatures succumbed to the demands of darkness and held their peace. Only the occasional lamp, a token gesture for campers foolhardy enough to pitch their tents at Crystal Lake, punctuated the gloom. Various outbreaks of mass murder had led to the area's name changing several times over. At one point it was called Forest Green. At present, it was Clear Waters. Yet, as with any attempt to reinvent something age-old, the locals still referred to the place as Crystal Lake. Some more morbid souls insisted on calling it Camp Blood.

That evening, an expensive looking tent sat a short distance from the bank where black waters hungrily lapped the shore. Bobby and Gina had pitched it near one of the lamps, but the light somehow didn't seem to reach them.

"What are you doing?" said Bobby.

"I'm putting my bra back on," came the reply from his otherwise naked girlfriend. "I got nipples like frickin' champagne corks."

Bobby chuckled, manhood in one hand. "And what's wrong with that? C'mon, Gina, take it off. You'll be putting those panties back on in a minute."

She threw him a withering look. "Are you psychic? Christ, why did we come *here* to camp, when we could have stayed in Orlando?"

Bobby sighed. "Because this is a cool place, Gina. This is where Jason Voorhees is supposed to have killed all those kids."

Gina gave him the same scared look he'd seen upon his every mention of Voorhees's name. "I must be insane for being here," she said, tugging her black lace underwear back over her shapely behind. "It's frickin' freezing and we might get killed at any moment."

"First of all, why do you always say 'frickin'? Why not try 'fucking'? Specifically, why not try fucking me? That's what we're here for, right?"

Gina folded her arms and angrily examined the goosebumps. "Call me freaky, but the constant threat of murder doesn't do much for my libido."

"What's a lib-eedo?" frowned Bobby.

Gina merely raised her eyebrows. The nineteen year-old made a good quarterback, but he wasn't the brightest light. Gina cast her eyes over his taut six-pack stomach, then his rough-hewn face, and tried to remind herself why she was here; mainly to annoy the other cheerleaders, in truth. She'd loved Mary-Beth's expression when Bobby had announced he was taking her, Gina, away on a camping trip.

Right now, though, the glow of that point-scoring triumph was starting to fade.

"Look, Gina. I'm only messing with you. Jason Voorhees is past tense, if he ever existed at all. Did you hear about the last people to supposedly face him?"

Gina shook her head, unsure if she wanted to hear more. She flinched as an owl's hollow call broke the silence outside.

"One of them was a girl called Tina, who supposedly had tele... psy... uh, special mental powers. She was in therapy at the lake when a whole load of kids and a couple of adults got iced. When the police arrived, she and her boyfriend were the only survivors."

"So where was Jason?" asked Gina, ashamed of herself for becoming interested in the story.

"Well, that was the problem. He was nowhere to be found. Tina claimed that her own dead dad had risen from the depths and dragged Jason down, wrapping chains around his neck. Of course, that's when they knew she was wacko. She and her boyfriend ended up in custody, from what I heard, and Tina did time in a fucking madhouse! Chances are Jason had nothing to do with those killings."

Gina nodded. "So he really is just a legend?"

"Maybe so. Now, how about I warm you up a little?"

"Ah, what the hell." she smiled, crawling back inside the sleeping bag.

* * *

Down in the waters, deep down, it was another world entirely. Fish floated serenely above the lake's bed, effortlessly negotiating their way through both nature's obstacles and man-made debris.

To them, it was like any other expanse of water.

Apart from the breathing. The low, rhythmic evidence that a heart pumped somewhere within this labyrinth.

Inhale...

...exhale.

There was an edge to it. A dark, foreboding temperament, like a bulging boiler ready to explode.

Inhale...

...exhale.

The sound buzzed sluggishly through the water, giving every sentient life-form pause for thought. An alien was living in the center of their kingdom. Some of the lake's creatures were smart enough to register its location, judging by the sound waves, and give it a wide berth. Others were brainless, careless or both, so traveled wherever their fancy took them.

These latter creatures would venture into the intruder's vicinity and momentarily sense the all-consuming throb of death and decay. Then they would twitch gently as they sank to the lake's base, weighed down by evil's crushing might, landing on top of a pile of equally dead acquaintances.

Sitting amid many such rotting flesh-heaps was the source of this malevolence. From a distance, it looked like just another bump on the lake's floor.

If you were in a position to look closer, you would observe that the bump looked very much like an upright head. Or, at least, it appeared to have eyes and a mouth.

Closer still, you would see that the face was uglier and more twisted than you could have dreamed.

Dangerously close now, you would look at the single eye; that wide, furious eye, twisting next to a dead socket.

Then you would turn and frantically swim for the surface, the thing's breathing now seeming to rattle around inside your own skull.

Inhale...

...exhale.

Inhale...

...exhale.

Inhale...

...exhale.

Halo Harlan's gaze burned into the ceiling. Tears clung to her cheeks. To her left, Trey lay shrouded in deep sleep, aided by far too much alcohol.

For the first six months of their relationship, Halo had thought that the booze was a calming influence. That it somehow tamed the beast within him. After all, he always seemed happy with a beer in his hand.

But she was starting to wonder. The last few times Trey had raised fists to her, he had been drunk. Tonight was the worst example yet.

They had finished eating the dinner she'd cooked. A special treat: hamburgers made from real ground beef, topped with onions and served in slightly toasted buns. The trailer didn't offer the greatest of cooking facilities, but Halo liked to think she made the most of them. Just the way her poor mother raised her.

By the time their plates were emptied, six or seven empty beer cans were cluttering the table, only one of which she had personally drained. Trey was slumped back on his chair, having seemingly enjoyed the burgers. Yet there was that terrible look in his lazy, glazed eyes. A stomach churning combination of paranoia and supremacy. Halo was never too sure if Trey actually *liked* women—that was to say, respected them—but at times like this it was obvious that he had issues.

Still, Halo told herself most days, very little about her was worth respecting. What had she done in her nineteen years on this planet, to earn respect and love? If her own father couldn't see any worth in her—and he had made those feelings perfectly clear by leaving the family shortly after her arrival into this world—then how was the rest of mankind supposed to spot any redeeming qualities that he'd missed? She knew that it wasn't strictly rational, to assume that her dad, a man she knew only from photographs, had flown the coop because of a newborn child he hadn't even laid eyes on, leaving her in the care of her older sister, but it was how she felt nonetheless. She couldn't help it. That sense of futile worthlessness had stayed with her for as long as she could remember and showed no signs of receding. Maybe that was why she was proving so slow to make something of herself and get a job. Maybe that was why she was forced to live with a man like Trey.

"What are you fucking looking at?"

She would have placed a ten dollar bet on Trey saying those exact words, when his mouth finally opened. For some reason, the sentence seemed hard-wired into his brain, whenever one of his dark moods came on. He was her third boyfriend overall and the first with whom she had cohabited. He was not, however, the first to become aggressive with her. She was starting to believe that there was a simple reason for this: she was a naturally annoying person.

"Wow," he said mockingly. "You can cook. Well, ain't you just the saint, Halo? Sometimes, you're just way too damn smug."

Smug? As far as Halo was concerned, she had been fighting a losing battle to avoid registering fear, let alone looking smug. Her voice trembled as she spoke.

"Darlin', I'm not smug, baby. Maybe you've had too much to dr—"

"Drink? Is that it? Well, fuck you." With that, he pulled the trucker's cap off his head and hurled it at her. It had bounced off her empty plate and caught her under the chin. It was painless, but she knew there was more to come. A sudden instinct told her to run out the door. There were two problems with that idea: she had nowhere else to go and her feet were bare. Like Trey was going to politely stem his rage, while waiting for her to dress for escape.

Instead, she placed the cap on the table beside her plate. "Trey, darlin', don't be this way. We're going camping tomorrow, isn't that a good thing?"

"Yes, darlin', it is," he said, in an ambiguous tone. Was it sincere? Was it sarcasm? The boundaries blurred horribly when Trey was like this. "It sure is. I just wish..."

As she waited for the rest of the sentence, Halo listened to her own heart beating one, two, three, four times.

"...you wouldn't think I was so fucking stupid."

He stood up, the feet of his chair rasping back across the cheap tiles. Gulping hard, Halo followed suit, backing into the kitchen. "Trey, darlin', what's the matter?"

Then, a terrible grin was upon his face. The grin which oh so cheerfully announced, "You're going to get it, bitch". Strangely enough, his regular smile had been one of the things, which initially attracted her to him. When Trey looked genuinely happy, his sky-blue eyes danced and he looked like a movie star. Albeit one playing a heavy metal lumberjack in a low budget flick.

"I saw you looking at Duke today, when he came over," Trey hissed. "I fucking saw you, Hayley."

Halo shook her head. Common sense screamed at her to tell him that it was actually Duke who was always coming on to her. She had been dying to blab for weeks now, but she knew that either pandemonium would result, or Trey would brand her a liar, rather than believing that one of his best friends would try and bone his girl. Anyway, they were going camping tomorrow with their friends and she didn't want to screw it all up.

"Oh God, Trey. Please don't hurt me again." She held both hands out to protect herself, but these were roughly slapped away. His next strike caught her full across the right side of her face. As was Trey's way of doing things, this was no palm slap. He hit women with the same flying fist as men.

She'd heard him joking with the boys that it was his contribution to "sexual equality".

Her scream cut off as stars flashed before her eyes and her brain struggled to process the sense data. For a few seconds, the pain was like a tidal wave flooding into a teacup.

Then she was on the floor, trembling in a fetal position, waiting for him to take his hatred one step further and kick her to death. Get it over with.

Instead, he lightly prodded her waist with the tip of one boot, as though inspecting a corpse.

"Come on, darlin', get up. Reckon you've had what was comin' to you. Won't happen again, right?"

She knew by the tone of his voice that he was already sorry for the punch—he always was—but wanted to maintain his macho stance, to make his point.

He helped her stand, then leant in toward her face, holding her tight as she tried to push him away. Then he planted a kiss where he'd struck her.

"Right?" he repeated, looking her in the eye. She saw that he had sobered up, as though the adrenaline rush and its accompanying shame had boiled away the booze.

She nodded contritely, even though she'd rather die than do anything with Duke and his greasy, hairy arrogance.

"Good," he said. "Now let's watch some TV."

The silence of the trailer park came as a blessed relief. It allowed Halo Harlan no distraction from her latest injury, but did buy her time to think.

She had lived in trailers her whole life. Wasn't quite born in one, but apparently came close enough. If anyone ever asked what it was like, living in one of those things, Halo found it difficult to answer. After all, she had nothing to compare it to. So she always just laughed and said, "It's great. You don't get neighbors on the other side of your wall." This was true enough. Having said that, the park where she and Trey presently lived often saw its share of noisy disturbance. The night before last, a couple had the mother of all arguments, with the woman loudly threatening to stab her man. Thankfully, this didn't happen. When Halo walked past them the following morning, they had been very much back together and very much hung over.

Right here, the most noise was inside her brain. They were due to head off for Clear Waters at midday tomorrow. That gave her just enough time to go and see Doctor Pryor.

She felt confident in Pryor. Rest assured, he would prescribe something to stop her from throwing up every morning.

TWO

Sleep wasn't coming easy for Edward Daimler. Maybe it was the blustering white noise of the small hotel room's air conditioning—he never understood people saying that it helped them doze off—or more likely it was the murder scene, which he and van Stadt had witnessed the previous day.

When the phone rang, it shook him out of a terrible dream in which he had been smoking crack cocaine with those five addicts of mixed race, the ones who were just about to be murdered. He had been as high as a kite, passing around the druggy paraphernalia and feeling on top of the world. Even though Daimler had never actually done crack, his brain seemed to be doing a fine job of simulating its high. Then the door had burst in and two shadowy figures arrived. He couldn't make out their faces, but they had guns and knives, and clearly didn't intend to join the party amiably.

The phone's insistently shrill ringing wrenched him away from the scenario, just as the newcomers started to draw blood. The screams of panic and terror were still echoing in his inner ear as he yanked the plastic receiver from its cradle and held it to his head.

"Daimler," he said, wiping perspiration from his brow.

He spent the next sixty seconds listening to the latest information salvos. The killers had struck again in the New York State area, this time in Rochester. Three dead in a scuzzy motel room, seemingly swingers.

Daimler listened to a few more details, then put the phone down. Yesterday, the press had grabbed this case by its lapels and shook it hard. These unknown subjects—or UNSUBs, in his abbreviated terminology—were traveling across America on a deadly road trip and the whole country was waiting for the FBI to crash their party. During the Eighties, the Bureau's profiling methods had earned them some confidence among the public, but this didn't stop the pressure piling on like a motherfucker every time the latest killing machine ran amok.

The slaughters had started two weeks ago, in Ohio. They had started in style, too: taking out an entire orgy of fifteen people in a dungeon basement. The murders had clearly been the result of a frenzy: repeated stabbings and hammer blows, along with some horrendous sexual mutilation. It was a mess.

It had only been in the last week that the FBI had started to link further homicides, which had taken place in different states. The connection was made on the basis of the similar MOs, brutal assaults on people who could be seen to deviate from societal norms: S&M fans, drug users, swingers. At times, though, the UNSUBs had demonstrated an even less liberal streak, offing couples who had enjoyed sex before marriage...

He dialed the number of van Stadt's room. She answered her phone before the second ring. "What's happened?"

Her voice was precise and energetic, but robotic. It was 6.30am, yet you'd swear van Stadt had been awake for hours. She sounded fresh as a daisy and he imagined her standing at her window, fully dressed, polished gun sliding suggestively into her shoulder holster. Daimler had only met this girl yesterday when they both arrived in upstate New York, having been assigned to this field case. Already, he had formed an impression, a profile, he thought to himself, that she was part of Quantico's new breed: hungry, efficient and eager to demonstrate their skills. Nothing wrong with that, he told himself, even if his own personal prejudices dictated that women weren't cut out for the rigors of this job.

She listened silently as he told her about the new killings.

"So we head off to Rochester now?"

"Uh, yeah," he said. "But let me get myself together first. I'll call you back."

His mouth tasted foul. As the receiver went back down, he eyed the open bottle of Scotch with disgust. His workload was getting on top of him; this, he knew. He always regretted the drinking binges come the morning, but at night they tended to work. A couple of hours spent slugging down the fire water generally meant a night's peace, even if he paid for it in the morning. Tonight, though, he'd slept fitfully *and* woken up feeling like shit.

He knew he'd become a walking cliché, the law enforcer turning to drink, but he also knew that clichés happened for a reason. Most days in this job, he saw murder scene photographs of butchered and/or raped men, women and children. There had to be a safety valve. If you didn't naturally have one in your life, you installed it yourself.

Rolling off the bed, he padded over into the bathroom and spun both shower taps. Water hissed down from the nozzle in concentrated, disparate streams.

Damn fancy shower head, he thought. This fucker'll take half an hour to get right.

Twenty minutes later, he persuaded van Stadt to join him for a quick raid on the breakfast buffet. He piled eggs and grits onto his plate, watching with barely concealed amusement as she opted for cereal and yogurt.

She was a looker, no doubt about that. Dirty blonde hair, just long enough to be tightly pinned at the back of her neck as it always seemed to be. Pure blue eyes, cold and analytical, but still damn sexy. Fit little body, no doubt partly gained from her Quantico training. She had been with the Bureau less than a year, whereas he had served twelve. He tried to remember how he felt when he was in her position, back when he had a marriage and a fire in his belly.

His wife had tried to kill him five years ago, when she sensed that he was considering a divorce. She'd wanted to end up the wealthy, pitied widow, but her plan badly backfired. Despite being his wife, she underestimated his instinctive powers. She did time in jail, along with the jackass she'd hired to run his car off the road.

As for the fire in his belly, well, that was still there, but it was generally down to whiskey. Nothing some antacids wouldn't cure.

"So who are the new victims?" she asked him, scooping milky cereal from her bowl.

Daimler put the coffee cup down, welcoming caffeine into his system. He sighed. "Sounds like it was a three-some. One middle-aged woman, two younger guys."

He watched for a reaction and saw nothing. Weirdly, he couldn't imagine Melissa actually having sex. God knows, he had tried.

She dug her spoon back into the health gloop. "So it definitely sounds like their handiwork?"

"Oh yeah. I think it's our guys. Still don't know how many of them there are, though. I'm starting to see them as a couple."

"A couple? Man and wife?"

He shrugged. "Maybe. Would make sense, seeing as they seem to have an extreme sense of moral out-rage. If they adhere to their own code, they would have to be married."

Van Stadt pondered this for a while, as they sat in silence, the breakfast room's background noises lost on them.

"Could two people really do all this stuff?" van Stadt finally wondered aloud. "I mean, physically take these people, guns or no guns. Fifteen people in Chicago? Five crack fiends here?" She finished her bowl and sat watching Daimler.

He still couldn't quite read her. Was she waiting for some wisdom from him? Or was she looking at him, as though the answer was obvious?

"Maybe they already knew their victims," Daimler offered. He stared out of the window, watching a bellboy greet some newcomers at the front of the hotel. The kid dashed toward them, all fake smiles and outstretched palms.

"That's it," he said. "Maybe they join in."

Van Stadt raised a painstakingly plucked eyebrow, but Daimler didn't seem to notice. His eyes darted around, focusing on nothing.

"They detest what these people are doing," he continued, by way of explanation, "but they make a show of being into it. They gain their trust and get them high on whatever: drugs, sex, good conversation, I don't know. They're deceptive."

"Fair enough," said van Stadt, as if generously considering his ridiculous ideas. "You ready?"

She stood up and walked away, without waiting for an answer.

Daimler watched her go, draining the rest of his coffee. He wasn't at all sure how he felt about this newbie. She was way too big for her boots.

Great ass, though.

Halo froze solid, halfway across the road. A car horn's frantic blare, coupled with a screech of brakes, told her that she had badly screwed up and could well die within seconds.

She had been lost in her own thoughts, devoting all her energy to mental processing with her body set on autopilot. As her legs handled walking along a leafy green path, heading back from the surgery to the trailer park, she dimly stared at her new thrift-store sneakers as her brain contemplated about a million worries and possibilities.

So she was pregnant. There it was: worry number one. The big Kahuna. It hadn't taken Doctor Pryor very long to work this out. Straight off the bat, he had enquired about symptoms she might have been experiencing.

Were her breasts feeling more sensitive than usual? Now he came to mention it, yes they were.

Did she have a metallic taste in her mouth? Yep, sure did.

With a knowing, but not judgmental nod, he had sent her to a room along the corridor, where a stern nurse asked her to pee into a cup. Ten minutes stretched by, feeling more like days. Then the results came back; Halo Harlan was in the club. You could have knocked her over with a feather.

How could she have been so naïve? She had felt even more embarrassed when Pryor asked whether she and Trey had been using condoms or other contraception. Trey had worn condoms at first, sure, but then the usual stupid stuff happened. For some reason, people always thought that their partner couldn't possibly be HIV positive, after having been with them for a few months. Then the rule "no glove, no love" was promptly disregarded. The rubber gloves came off. It was a dangerous kind of make-believe, Halo now realized. Furthermore, she had actually believed Trey, when he told her that the rhythm method was "ninety-nine point nine to infinity percent effective".

Of course she was pregnant. It all seemed so obvious now, yet so damn premature. Halo had yet to figure what life was all about herself, let alone being able to reassure a kid about the world's unforgiving, random ways. That aside, what was Trey going to think? She believed that he loved her, despite all the unpleasantness, and she loved him too. Didn't she? So he would be pleased they were having a kid.

Or would he react like her own father and run for the hills? There were so many questions that needed to be answered. All Halo wanted was to live her own little, quiet, insignificant life, to be happy, then this had been dumped on her doorstep. Still, she did love babies.

It was at that moment, as Halo Harlan thought about cute little babies while crossing a narrow country road, that the rapidly approaching car blared its warning siren, three times, in quick succession.

Halo opened her mouth, but the expected scream didn't emerge. The car was coming straight at her.

She was stock still in the road, like a burglar startled by house lights. The vehicle screeched and groaned, the driver trying to prevent the terrible impact.

The car finally swung ninety degrees, but kept moving in her direction, sideways. Halo truly thought it would hit her, until it came to rest mere feet away, dust rising from its wheels.

Halo was trembling, adrenaline pulsing through her. She couldn't believe that she had nearly died, especially so soon after her big news.

Tears soon followed relief, as she waited for the verbal abuse which would inevitably follow. Sure enough, the car door popped open at speed, but the driver wasn't quite what Halo had anticipated. Large black ladies weren't uncommon around these parts, but this one looked like she was from further afield. She wore a big floral dress, matched by an elaborately thick headband which barely kept her rampaging dreadlocks in check. Various pieces of wooden jewelry danced around her neck.

The woman ran toward her, arms outstretched.

"O'er here, girl, are you all right?" Her voice revealed a foreign accent: South African, perhaps. Maybe "O'er here" was, like, "Oh my God" in some other language.

Halo struggled for breath. She had learned that she was pregnant and suffered a near-death experience within the space of fifteen minutes.

The woman's face was etched with concern as she looked Halo over, as though measuring her up for a coffin. "I didn't hit you, right?"

Halo shook her head and instinctively embraced this complete stranger. There was something motherly about her that suggested she was safe, certainly safer than wandering across roads like a blind jackass.

Suddenly, the woman stiffened. She stepped back from Halo, eyes the size of pool balls. It was difficult to know what to make of her facial expression.

Fear? Suspicion? Compassion? All three and then some?

"Girl," she said. "We need to talk."

"Where shall we go next, darling?"

Norwood Thawn pursed his lips, as he always did when giving things calm consideration, then blew a thin plume of cigarette smoke out from between them. He glanced at the woman occupying the passenger seat, who was looking as gorgeous as the first day they met.

"Wherever our work is needed, my dear. We're gaining speed now. Our time is at hand."

"You think the FBI is close behind us?"

"Oh, I would imagine so. They'll be 'profiling' us now. Trying to work out what's going on up here." He raised a forefinger to his right temple and twiddled it.

Penelope stifled a giggle. "Behavior equals personality? Isn't that their motto?"

"Something like that, I believe. But I'd like to think that they'll be able to see what's happened at every stage of our trip, filthy sinners tempting us at every turn."

Penelope nodded. All around their Pontiac Grand Prix, stolen two zip codes back, commuter traffic jostled for pole position. She watched a few of the drivers: listening to music, looking at their watches, undoing their ties as the stress kicked in.

"I'm confident," she said, "that whatever the FBI think we'll get the public vote when the time comes. This is all long overdue."

"It is," said Norwood, checking his rear-view mirror as they switched lanes. "Such a shame, though, that we have to sully ourselves in order to carry out the work. I feel... unclean."

"Poor darling." Penelope blew him a kiss and returned her oddly piercing gaze to the road that flashed beneath them.

Halo helped the woman, whose name was Denzela van der Westhuizen, push her car off the road. Then they sat inside the vehicle. Through the windshield, they could see only the woods, where a thin morning mist still hovered in sheets.

At first there was an uneasy silence. Halo broke it. "Ma'am, do you want me to sign something legal? To say it was my fault?"

Denzela's pensive expression momentarily lifted and she looked amused, shaking her head as though Halo were a naïve, innocent child. Halo didn't *feel* that way; after all she was already a pregnant teenager with an abusive boyfriend. But life admittedly puzzled her, much of the time. The world was a jigsaw and she only held a few of the pieces.

"No, dear. I don't want you to sign anything. First, let me tell you what I do for a living. I'm a psychic. I read people's tarot cards. You know what those are?"

Halo nodded, feeling slightly patronized now, but trying not to show it.

"Of course you do," said Denzela. "Ha! You can never hide anything behind those eyes. Your heart is truly on your sleeve."

Halo stared back out at the woods. "So, do you want to give me a reading? I don't have much money."

Denzela shook her head again. "I don't need the cards, dear. And you don't need money to hear what I'm going to tell you. I had some very strong feelings when I came near you a moment ago."

The two women's eyes met for a second. "And no," said Denzela, "I'm not a lesbian."

Their faces dissolved into laughter, diffusing some of Halo's tension. Then Denzela's face hardened again.

"I have to warn you that when we touched I momentarily *became* you, feeling what you will shortly feel. And the emotion was fear. A storm is coming... It will take the shape of three people, but one man in particular. He..."

Denzela frowned, as though unsure of herself. "He felt to me like a man-child. An angry child in a man's body. He is evil personified, girl. When you see him, run."

Halo's stomach had been clenching throughout this woman's prophecy. Was she talking about Trey? If so, he was already with her.

"So evil is coming," said Halo, anxiously wringing her hands. "Sounds great. What will happen to me?"

"I can't say," admitted Denzela, "because I don't know."

She paused for a moment, then offered her big palm. "Give me your hand."

Halo did so and watched as Denzela closed her eyes. It was creepy to think that this woman might be mainlining into her soul.

"The wings of destiny," said Denzela. "The wings of destiny will save you when the time is at hand. There'll be a wonderful new arrival, but you'll also suffer great loss."

Halo placed her free hand on her flat abdomen. She knew what one of those predictions meant, but didn't like the sound of the great loss.

"Beware the mask," Denzela added. "I'm seeing masks worn by immensely dangerous people. Masks, both real and imaginary, you understand me?"

Halo nodded vaguely. Denzela regarded her with something like sympathy. "I can see that you're a very trusting person, Halo," she said. "You take people at face value, which is wonderful, but sadly leaves you open to attack in this day and age. Please, tell me that from this moment on, you'll at least question other people's motives?"

"Sure." Halo was feeling overwhelmed. "I'll do my best to be distrusting."

Denzela smiled and checked her watch. "I gotta go," she chimed. "I'm due to arrive for some tarot work in Clear Waters... in about twenty minutes." Halo grimaced, knowing that it was an hour's drive away at the very least.

Hopping out of the car, she accepted this strange prophet's business card and waved. Then she watched as the vehicle remounted the road and swiftly turned a corner, disappearing behind the woods.

Denzela's words hung on the air: "A storm is coming... in the shape of a man."

Despite the heat, Halo found herself shivering. She wondered again if the prophecy referred to Trey and what he might do when he discovered she was pregnant.

She shook her head. No use in thinking like that, especially on such a flimsy basis. Denzela had been nice, but Halo wasn't so sure that she believed in all that horseshit. She decided to tell Trey about the baby this weekend. They could all celebrate at the campsite.

Setting off along the path, once again, Halo was glad to be alive. She was also doing her best to remain alert. After all that mumbo-jumbo she half-expected deceivers and storm bringers to leap out from under the bridge that spanned the north river. No matter how she tried, the image of the storm, the man-child, lingered.

THREE

"Hey, Abe. Quit playing with yourself and listen to this: I found a fucking head down here!"

Rosen's announcement came an hour after he and Stratton had arrived at the lake. They had been dispatched down here at very short notice, having been told that this was a maximum priority job. Search the lake, they were ordered. Search it with a fine-tooth comb. Report any bodies or body parts found.

Abe Stratton had started to dread these jobs with Rosen. At first, the two police divers had enjoyed a few laughs as they went about their frequently grim work. Once or twice, they had even sunk a couple of frosty tallboys together when they were done. Recently, however, familiarity had bred contempt. Or maybe it was his injury. He'd twisted an ankle while rock climbing, changing their working relation~~s~~' Whereas they would previously take it in tur~~n~~

the guy in the boat and the guy who searched deep
waters for murder weapons and dead flesh, the past
three weeks had seen their roles necessarily frozen.
Stratton stayed in the boat, monitoring the safety line
while Rosen prowled the depths. In a way, he didn't
blame Rosen for resenting him.

It had been early lunchtime when they parked the
truck near Clear Waters' modest banks. As they
unpacked the equipment, Stratton had noticed a
lone camping tent in the woods on the other side of
the lake. He ignored it; the campers would inevitably
gather on the opposite bank and stare. Rubber-
necking was part and parcel of this job, even though
ninety-nine percent of the time there was precious
little to see.

They boarded the boat and the long, slow process
began. Rosen heaved the oxygen tanks onto his back,
half jokingly branded Stratton a "lucky fucker" and
disappeared into the calm waters with the mega powered, portable torch. Stratton had watched his
colleague's image distort and break up, until it finally
blended with the darkness as Rosen neared the lake's
bed. After that, it was a waiting game. Every now and
then, Rosen would check back in with him and they
would move the boat. They worked to a grid system,
to ensure that the whole area was covered evenly. In
between Rosen's returns, Stratton would sit back and
prop up his bad foot, trying to keep an eye on his
partner's safety line, despite the latest issue of
Playboy trying its hardest to distract him.

He hadn't expected anything to be found. This
made Rosen's sudden exclamation regarding the
head even more of a surprise.

The two men looked at each other, Rosen's scuba mask resting on top of his bald head as he clung to the side of the boat, relishing the fresh air.

"Do you think he'll live?" Stratton asked.

The two men laughed. In this job, humor helped bolster the thin wall which kept people from losing their minds.

"Why didn't you bring him up to say howdy?"

"I tried, but it's stuck in the mud. Give me something to dig with."

Stratton fished around in a tool bag and found a pick, handing it over. Rosen flipped the scuba mask back over his face and vanished back into the depths.

He'd been laughing nervously, back up there with Abe. Something about this job was freaking Michael Rosen the hell out.

At times, the watery depths seemed to play with your mind, alter your perceptions. Rosen was prepared for this and, after five years on the job, he took it into account. Realizing that underwater searches were, by their nature, disturbing experiences was part of the professional's job, just like identifying formations of rock and weed where human corpses were more likely to become snagged.

In these five years, though, he had never heard a voice inside his head.

The voice wasn't actually *saying* anything, at least nothing he could discern. It was a soft, sing-song voice, like that of a little kid. A child playing all by itself. A child forced to make its own entertainment when mother wasn't around. The other kids wouldn't play...

Jesus, he thought. Why the merry hell am I thinking like this? I've got to find a new partner until Stratton's fucking foot heals up. All this underwater work must be putting undue pressure on my brain.

He plunged, pointing the torch beneath him, until the lake floor rose up to meet his feet. Was it his imagination, or was the water getting colder?

Now, where was that head?

He turned almost a full circle until the torch beam found the hideously decayed thing, standing upright on the lake's bed, the neck buried in the mud. Rosen guessed it had been here a while. Either that, or the guy was always an ugly fuck.

The child's voice was louder, yet still indistinct.

The head opened its eye.

Rosen floated for a moment, legs flapping, staring down at the thing that should not be. It hadn't occurred to him that the apparently disembodied head was attached to anything below the lake's surface. That would be impossible, wouldn't it?

Even though he could sense something entering his body—some kind of new strength, replacing the fear he had initially felt—it didn't disturb him. He felt as though his own batteries were being recharged above and beyond their capacity. It felt damn good. There was nothing to be afraid of here. This guy was simply buried in the lake's bed; he needed help and he needed it fast. That's what guys like him and Stratton were here for.

Michael Rosen raised the pick. Then he slammed it repeatedly into the ground around the thing.

The water around him swiftly became muddied as thick clogs of dirt were freed from bondage and sailed slowly upwards into his field of vision. Yet his force and precision remained impeccable.

Within sixty seconds, he had revealed the buried man's shoulders.

Stratton watched as a dark circle formed on the surface, near the boat. It was mud, rising. He grimaced and returned to the pages of *Playboy*.

Better him than me, he thought.

"Hey, Gina. Come look. There's something going on, out on the lake."

Inside the tent, Gina had finished packing her things. At the sound of Bobby's voice, she rolled her eyes. The last thing she needed was yet another fascinating, camping related sight. This trip had already been a bust and she was supposed to be spending the rest of the weekend with this dull, if admittedly well-hung, bastard.

"What is it?" she yelled.

"Come see."

"Fuck you," she murmured, continuing to pack.

Rosen was hacking two, three feet beneath the lake floor. While the water naturally filled any hole he created, he was making good progress. The figure was almost half free of the sediment. Rosen could see a loop of chain, which hung around the man's neck.

The eye was fixed on him. Rosen maintained contact with it as he frenziedly carved at the sediment.

While some deep part of him, a part which had somehow been smothered, knew that this thing was unadulterated evil, he didn't feel afraid in the least.

He slammed the pick into the ground, again and again and again. Sweat was forming condensation inside his mask's visor, but he seemed able to continue using instinct alone.

What was happening to him?

Best not to think about it. Keep working. Free the poor guy.

The black circle was thick and spreading. Huge slabs of mud were rising to the surface. Stratton began to wonder whether Rosen was all right. Why all this work, to free a head from the mud? He leaned over and tugged on the safety rope. Then he waited for the tug back. Nothing happened. He tugged the safety rope again, harder this time.

The giant was almost free. Rosen felt victorious as he hacked at the final pieces of mud holding the man's huge feet in place. He hadn't seen much of the giant's body during this operation, due to the black water, which surrounded him. The diver was practically inverted, his head and upper body dipping into this hole of his own making. It was over six feet deep.

Had he enjoyed full control over his mind, he might have vaguely anticipated what would happen next. Two strong hands grabbed his legs, exerting a painful iron grip. One of the giant's feet tore free of the sediment below and kicked Rosen squarely in the face, smashing his scuba mask and reducing his nose to pulp. Water began to flood into his suit.

Amid his sudden panic, Rosen felt the giant's body rising beside him, while those hands simultaneously forced him further down into the hole. His own hands thrashed madly, but failed to make any purchase on the slick, crumbling walls. Black, foul water pumped down his throat, leaving him bug-eyed and praying for air that would never come.

The last thing Rosen felt was sheer, claustrophobic terror as a pile of mud was forced down around his head and shoulders: the very same earth that he had hacked loose was being kicked back into the hole.

Jason Voorhees stood on the lakebed, watching the upside-down man who was embedded up to his waist in filth. Only when the rubber clad feet stopped kicking and twitching, did Jason release the legs. They floated lifelessly in tune with the lake's current.

Jason looked at them. He wore clothes that appeared blackened and burnt. His spine, ribs and other bones were visible through what remained of his flesh.

He cocked his head upwards, sensing something. Noise. Movement. Life.

A rope was being tugged from above.

Jason's broad shoulders angrily rose and fell. Then he bent down and snatched the pick from Michael Rosen's right hand.

The *Playboy* magazine splayed open on the floor of the boat.

Stratton was fumbling around in the bag, looking for various component parts of the second diver's suit. Why did this have to happen? Mike had *never* gotten himself into trouble during the sixteen months they had worked together.

Something registered in the corner of his eye and he turned his attention from the bag, following the source of the distraction. His breath caught in his throat.

Standing on the lake's bank, maybe twenty, twenty-five feet away from him, was a tall, well-built man, wearing a hockey mask. He stood motionless, hands by his side.

He was holding a small axe.

Stratton knew that in this kind of situation, people tended to disbelievingly rub their eyes, or blink several times. Yet he was a man who always trusted his perception: what he saw was what he saw, and that was the end of it. His up close and personal encounters with grim chunks of human anatomy, floating deep down for all the fish to feast on, had strengthened this straightforward conviction.

The man on the bank remained still, staring out at him.

Stratton tugged harder on the safety rope. If this really was Jason Voorhees, then it was time for he and Rosen to get the hell out of here. Call the local cops, let them deal with it. He was a diver, not a law enforcer.

Still no response from down below. Something must be really wrong. Tearing his eyes away from the figure on the bank, Stratton yanked the second wetsuit from the bag.

Bobby bent double, laughing quietly with the glee of it all. He knew this was wrong, maybe even a felony, but it sure was funny.

He turned away from the lake, the sun glinting on his hockey mask. Then he headed back to the tent, to tell Gina all about it. She'd pee herself.

Back over his shoulder, across the lake, a large shadow climbed onto the boat.

Stratton felt the vessel's balance shift dramatically. He was in the wetsuit and only had the mask to go. But had Rosen clambered back on board behind him?

He turned, just in time to receive a pick in his left eye. The tool slammed against his head, bursting the orb and splattering his face with vitreous fluid. With his one remaining eye, he saw a vision of hell and knew, in his last seconds, that the real Jason Voorhees had dispatched him.

Jason released the pick. Stratton fell backwards, over the rim of the boat and plunged into the lake.

"Hey Gina, I think we'd better go," chuckled Bobby, the mask sitting on top of his head as he re-entered the tent. His girlfriend sat cross-legged, all packed and ready to leave, filing her immaculate fingernails.

"No kidding," she said. "And we're not going to another campsite. We're going home. Or, at least, I am."

Bobby's laughter lines faded. He had been about to tell her how he just fooled some diver into thinking he was Jason Voorhees, but that seemed fairly unimportant. "What do you mean?" he frowned.

Gina locked eyes with him contemptuously. "I'm bored. You're a boring little boy, Bobby. I'm going to go home and find me a real man, a man who doesn't think camping is, like, really exciting. Oh, and for your information: watching a man chop wood for one whole hour isn't remotely erotic. It's screamingly tedious!"

Bobby opened his mouth to speak, but said nothing. Being spurned by a woman was a new experience for him and his brain didn't have a stock response. So he turned and walked out of the tent.

"Where are you going?" cried Gina after him. "You've got to take me home, dickwad!"

Bobby walked blindly back toward the lake, his mind a blur of confusion and rage. That girl must be—*had* to be—a lesbian. His grip tightened on the ax.

Suddenly, his path was blocked by a man-mountain, a good foot taller than him. One malevolent eye fixed on him as the figure pulled back a slimy, black-clad fist.

Bobby's scream was cut short as Jason's blow powered through his face, emerging through the back of his skull, coated red and clutching shattered chips of bone. His eyes momentarily crossed, gazing down at the fist, which had ruined his nose, his mouth and everything down to his chin. Then they rolled up into their sockets.

The corpse sank to its knees and Jason stooped slightly, his arm remaining inside the boy's head. Then he yanked upwards, snapping the skull loose from the neck.

Jason examined the cranium, which was sitting halfway, up his forearm, like some grisly wristwatch. A flicker of recognition crossed his eye as he saw the mask, which still remained strapped to the top of the boy's head.

He tugged it loose and swiftly used it to cover his own face, tugging the straps into place behind his putrid skull. He stood there for a long moment, as though momentarily relieved in some small way. Picking up the axe, which the boy had dropped, he tested its weight in one hand, then resumed his purposeful stride into the woods, his home from home.

It wasn't long before a tent stood out among the trees. Someone was inside. A girl. Calling out to him.

"Oh, you'd better be coming back, Bobby Johnston. Take me home, goddamit!"

Jason walked straight for the tent, then trod over it, homing in on the human inside.

Gina's voice swiftly became a blend of anger and anxiety. "What the hell are you doing? Quit fucking around, Bobby!"

She stood up. As Jason located her and tightly wrapped the yellow canvas around her, the voice became fainter, smothered, yet shot through with terror. "Bobby, let me go... Bobby... Please..."

Jason raised his right arm. For a second, the severed head of Bobby Johnston stared blankly down at the tent-wrapped figure below.

The surrealism of the scene was lost on Jason Voorhees.

He brought his arm down, smashing Bobby's dead skull repeatedly against Gina's. After six blows, the canvas was soaked with blood.

Jason carried on regardless.

* * *

It was almost 1:00pm when Halo arrived back home, and she knew what that meant. In fact, she could *hear* what that meant: Duke and the others had arrived at the park. She stood at the front gate for a while, gathering her thoughts. She was still trying to come to terms with the morning's events.

When she finally summoned the mental strength to show herself, Trey was loading their gear onto Duke's pick-up truck. Duke, a tattooed bear of a man, sat on the steps to the trailer, drinking from a beer can. Standing next to him were Basket, Duke's skinny, crazy eyed brother, whose real name Halo had never been told, and his feline girlfriend Shona.

Trey threw Halo one of his deadly looks. "Where the galloping fuck have *you* been, girl? I had to pack your shit myself."

Halo swallowed hard. Luckily, distraction was immediately provided by Basket and Shona rushing over to greet her. As she hugged Shona, Halo looked over the girl's shoulder to see Duke raising his beer to her, almost grudgingly. As usual, the mechanic's face was smeared with black grease. She gave him a token, transparent smile, then averted her gaze.

"We all done?" grunted Duke to Trey, gesturing toward the truck with his beer.

"Guess so," said Trey sourly. He leant against the vehicle and wiped sweat from his brow, his eyes burning holes in the side of Halo's head.

"Okay," she said, with all the enthusiasm she could muster. "Let's go have ourselves some fun!"

MY LIFE PART ONE:
SINS OF THE MOTHER

I was six when I saw my father kill my mother.

It was some early hour of the morning and I'd had a bad dream. Something about a demon chasing me through a forest. I was terrified and I wanted reassurance from mom and dad. Mainly, my dad. Lately, mom hadn't been much use.

Walking across the landing, I creaked open their bedroom door. The two bedside lamps were on, but the room was empty. I turned my head and saw that the stairs to the ground floor were illuminated at their foot.

They were downstairs, maybe in the kitchen.

I moved to the top of the stairs and listened hard, recoiling slightly as angry voices drifted upwards. Whenever they had arguments and fights, it made my stomach tighten like a fist. I swayed against the banister, feeling queasy.

It took me at least ten minutes to descend the staircase. Something was holding me back. Right there and then, I thought it was fear. With the benefit of hindsight, I know I was resisting destiny.

I could make out what the two of them were saying, now. And it wasn't good.

"Put that down, you stupid motherfucker," said my mom. "What are you going to do: *kill* my ass?"

"Your time has come," came the reply, his voice cool, firm and even. "It's for the common good."

I ran to the door of the kitchen, my heart pumping madly. I stared inside the room, just in time to see the carving knife sinking into my mother's heart. She was gripping my dad's arms, looking into his eyes with utter disbelief. Drops of blood fell from her mouth as she made terrible choking noises.

As she slumped to the ground, still holding on to my dad, her gaze shifted and rested on me. What I then saw in her eyes is something I've never been able to forget.

My own mother looked horrified by my complete lack of compassion. Inside, I felt bad for her. But on the outside, all I did was stand there and watch her hit the parquet tiles and struggle through several last breaths.

My father seemed to know I was there, because he slowly turned to face me. He appeared sorry for what he had done.

"Sit down," he said quietly, pointing to one of the kitchen chairs.

I did so, stepping over my mother's legs in the process.

He sat opposite me, his big eyes open and earnest.

"Do you know why your mother had to die?" he asked.

I thought for a moment, trying not to look at the corpse. Then I slowly nodded my head. "I think so, Dad."

"Why do you think it had to be done?" he asked gently.

"Because she was a bad person," I said.

Father nodded gravely. "Yes, she was. Remember how we talked before, about sinners, munchkin? Sinners have to... what?"

"Pay."

"That's right. Sinners have to pay. It's our responsibility to ensure that they do. Your mother was drinking, taking drugs. Last week, she even slept with another man."

I blinked at this revelation and my bottom lip quivered.

"How could she do that stuff, Dad?" I asked, not expecting an answer. Then I pointed at my mother's dead body.

"I'm glad she's dead," I decided.

"That's a good munchkin," said dad, rubbing my hair. "Now, I'm going to take mother down to the woods. We're going to tell everybody that she's gone away and left us, you understand?"

I nodded at him, then remained on the chair, my young legs dangling, as he dragged my mom to the family camper. I fully understood what my dad was doing and why.

The mask of deception was already sliding into place. I would wear it for many years to come.

FOUR

The sense of foreboding was intense. She was tempted to turn the car around, right there and then.

Whenever Denzela van der Westhuizen told intrigued strangers that she was a professional psychic, the same question arose with dull predictability: could she foresee bad things happening to her?

Whoever posed this question to her always believed it to be the very height of wit and hilarity. Luckily, she was able to reply that yes, she could. That always shut the skeptics up. One time, she had avoided a highway, having had a bad feeling about it. Minutes later, a pile-up had wiped out close to twenty people. She was convinced that she would have been at the epicenter of the carnage.

Ever since the "Welcome to Clear Waters" sign, a mile back, the dark feelings had begun to wash over her. There was the sense that the storm she had described to Halo was closer than she had imagined. The difference this time was that she felt personally threatened. Her throat felt dry and sore.

The road continued to rush beneath her wheels. She sighed deeply, struggling to decide. She was hardly ever wrong, so should she go back? Maybe she was just freaking herself out, but somehow she didn't think so.

If today's job hadn't been so lucrative, she would have swung around and driven out of town already. But she was due to give a tarot reading for a relatively rich couple who wanted assurance that their first-born child, due in five months, would be healthy. They were offering good money. Money that would help pay for her ticket back to Jo'burg to see the family at Christmas.

"Damn it," she spat, and stomped on the accelerator.

As the trees flashed by faster, the road narrowed. Denzela checked her watch: it was 13:13. Surely there couldn't be much further to go?

Her throat was so sore it was difficult to swallow.

She slapped one hand over it, in a vain attempt to quell the pain.

Then she saw him.

Standing in the middle of the road was a huge man wearing a hockey mask. In one hand, he carried an axe. His body language exuded power and defiance. Denzela knew he would not move to avoid the impact. She also felt the storm, washing over her in all its dark fury.

This was the man-child she had warned the girl about.

These thoughts came to her in the first second. In the next, she wrenched the steering wheel around, careering off the track and missing the hulking figure by mere feet. Speeding down a slope, her brakes proving ineffectual no matter how hard she worked them, she finally hit a tree and the engine died.

Jason appeared at the top of the slope, axe hung by his side.

He began to make his descent.

Norwood Thawn drummed his fingers on the top of the steering wheel. He had refilled the gas tank, ten minutes ago. Where was Penelope?

The woman was so impetuous, so impulsive. One minute, she was reading *USA Today* in the passenger seat, the next she had ordered him to pull over into a gas station. They had almost caused a freeway pile-up in the process, and this wasn't a prospect Norwood liked. Apart from the damage that might have been done to themselves, various innocent people might have died. He prided himself in maintaining some semblance of optimism; *some* innocent people still remained on this planet. Shame that the sinners had to go and ruin it for everyone.

He considered the vehicle for a moment. Once this tank had been used up, they would have to find another mode of transport. He favored the idea of varying the type of vehicles they drove and the accommodation they took. Over the last few weeks, they had only lowered themselves to sleep in their vehicle twice. Otherwise, they had mainly stayed in motels. Two reasons for this: such establishments allowed them to meet the kind of people who needed their attention, whether they knew it or not; also, motels accepted cash. Far more difficult to trace. They gave blatantly fake names under every roof. Those people just didn't care. You'd practically have to kill them in order to get a reaction.

He peered through the windshield, into the gas station store. Until a few minutes ago, Penelope had been standing at the desk, talking to the woman. They had been smiling. The woman had handed something over. Neither of them were visible.

Norwood frowned, drumming his fingers harder. Then he picked up the crumpled *USA Today* and spread it out over the dashboard. Frowning, he tried to work out what had excited his precious Penelope so. Was it an article about their little spree?

He zeroed in on a relatively modest-looking piece, a text-only "news bite" in a side column. He smiled knowingly.

Police had re-opened investigations into the supposed killer Jason Voorhees, it said. They were dragging the former Crystal Lake, after repeated requests from Tina Shepard and her boyfriend. The couple had survived a massacre by the lake, which many still believed they had orchestrated themselves. Both remained incarcerated, pending further investigations.

Norwood traced his forefinger down the side of the article. His eyesight wasn't quite what it used to be, and he had lost his spectacles somewhere between Chicago and here. There was a quote from a local detective who effectively said: "Once we've proven Jason doesn't exist, we can go ahead and jail these kids."

He understood. Penelope wanted to go to Crystal Lake. She had long held a fascination with Jason Voorhees, as had he to a lesser degree. The press had painted Voorhees as a moral crusader, as he always seemed to target promiscuous, drug-taking teens, an ethos with which Norwood heartily sympathized.

Movement caught his eye and he looked over to see that Penelope had reappeared. She walked swiftly around the counter, paused to pick something up—a map, by the looks of it—then she was out of the door.

Norwood glanced around the gas station, seeing that the only other customer had just pulled out. They were unlikely to have seen anything, not that any foul play had been visible.

As she climbed back inside the Pontiac, he raised a wry eyebrow. "So we're off to Crystal Lake, are we?"

She was perspiring and flushed. "Darling, I'd love to. Did you read the article? Jason may still be operating. I think the three of us would get on famously. We have the same goals."

Norwood looked at her uncertainly for a second, then nodded back toward the gas station. "What happened in there?" he asked.

"She propositioned me. With her eyes."

Norwood shook his head sadly as he started the engine. "Oh dear."

"We went into the back room and... I started to enjoy it. The temptress almost had me."

Norwood ground his teeth together. "The filthy Jezebel."

"Thankfully, I controlled myself." As they left the gas station, Penelope's hand was snaking onto Norwood's crotch, undoing his zipper.

"Tell me more about this sinner," he intoned, voice cracking.

The Pontiac was soon lost in the traffic's incessant flow.

Halo made sure she was sitting in the back. After all, Duke was driving. She knew that he wasn't beyond sliding the odd hand onto her thigh, whether Trey was present or not. If seen, he'd simply pass it off as a joke.

She was loath to admit it, even to herself, but Duke frightened Halo more than Trey did. Her boyfriend had problems, there was no denying that, but at least he was honest about them. There was something dark and conniving about Duke. By contrast, the man's brother Basket was a more straightforward soul, even if his eyes didn't strictly point in the same direction.

She had known Duke, Basket and Shona almost as long as she'd known Trey. When you started seeing a guy, you generally inherited a new circle of potential buddies, whether you liked it or not. Of course, if you ever split up with the man, they would vanish from your life like ghosts, but that was understood.

Trey had met Duke a few years ago at the auto garage where they still both worked and their macho relationship grew from there. They were all about beer, football and showing off for the alleged benefit of women. Basket had come bundled with Duke, as part of the package, even if the two brothers regularly argued like crazy. No one seemed to know what Basket did for a living, but you could rest assured that it wasn't a great deal. He was a congenitally lazy, laidback guy with a limited attention span and a similarly low IQ. Perfectly loveable, though.

Halo had been delighted when Basket met Shona, three months ago. It finally gave the group a welcome injection of estrogen. They had celebrated with their first camping trip to Clear Waters, where they'd had a fairly good time. Enjoyable, apart from Duke and Basket coming to blows not once, but twice, during their twenty-four hour stay.

So, here it was. Clear Waters, round two. Place your bets, ladies and gentlemen: who would punch whom first? She hoped the answer wouldn't be Trey, laying a good one on her.

Her man presently sat in the front of the Camaro next to Duke. He still seemed pissed about her disappearing act this morning. Hopefully, she thought, he'll cheer up when Halo told him our good news.

The Camaro was anything but a smooth ride, all five occupants bounced up and down, practically non-stop. "How long'll it take to get there?" asked Shona, seated between Halo and Basket.

"'Bout another half-hour," said Duke. "Why, princess? You getting travel sick?"

Princess, thought Halo. At least he's a slime ball with all the girls.

"Hey, Halo," said Duke. "Pass your favorite guy a beer from the cooler, would you?"

Halo was relieved when everyone, even Trey, sounded jeers of protest. "You're driving, asshole," said Basket, throwing a toothpick at the back of his brother's head.

Duke smiled to himself. "I just wanted to see if she'd do it. Reckon you've got yourself a nice little slave there, man." He was talking to Trey, who shook his head.

"Yeah, right," he said, ruefully.

"Get real, guys," said Shona, playfully pinching Basket's nose. "We're not your slaves. And you're not ours. We can walk away whenever we like. So watch your fuckin' mouths!"

"That's right," giggled Halo, hoping that Trey wouldn't get her later.

She was determined not to die. Not like this.

When Denzela left Johannesburg to spend a year touring around the States, earning money from her psychic gift, friends warned her that America was violent. To which she had laughed long and loud, considering how brutal South Africa could be; in fact, Johannesburg was one of the nation's most violent cities. She had personally lost two friends to random acts of car-jacking savagery, so America seemed... almost like home. Besides, with her two kids grown up and self-sufficient, she wanted to take life by the throat and see some of the world. Being a mother was the best job in the world, and she would happily argue the life out of anyone who debated that fact, but it undeniably pinned you down. She'd first become a mother at the relatively young age of twenty-four. The next twenty years consisted of work, stress, maternal duties and, sadly, divorce.

Still, she was free to do whatever she wanted. Finally at liberty to fully exercise the unusual abilities she always knew she possessed. So far, America had proven a very receptive country, and certainly nowhere near as intimidating as many people seemed to think it was.

Until a minute ago when it suddenly became an absolute nightmare.

Denzela pushed her car door open with surprising ease, considering that the impact had buckled it. She felt dizzy and blood was trickling down the side of her face. She must have banged her head on the steering wheel, she realized.

Jumping out of the vehicle, she hadn't paused to look back over her shoulder. Every nerve in her body was screaming at her to keep moving. Away from the storm. She could feel this man's hatred, like an eternal flame, blazing close by. He was coming for her and he would have no mercy.

She broke into a tentative canter, keen to get away as quickly as possible, but cautious about injuring herself further and becoming an easy target. Relieved to discover that her legs seemed in good working order, she quickened the pace. She started running, concentrating on maintaining a good speed, while avoiding trees and ground obstacles. Her sarong wasn't the most practical of garments for sprinting, but she bunched much of its lower half up in one of her fists. After the number of times she had scoffed at females tripping over and spraining their ankles during horror movies, it would be too horrible an irony to do just that.

The sense of foreboding was stronger than ever. In fact, her death seemed so certain that part of her was tempted to turn around and shriek: "Come on, you bastard. Take me". But she had always been a fighter. Perhaps if she knew what was going to happen, she also had the power to change it. A slim hope, but hope nevertheless.

Ahead of her, the woods showed no sign of change. They merely continued. More trees, more bushes, more stuff to run through. She tried to cast her mind back to studying the area map, but she had only been looking at her destination and the roads that led to it. She had to face facts: she had no idea where she was or where she was going.

The breath rasped in her throat and her head swam. She brought herself to a halt. The woods were silent, save for a few bird noises.

She bent and rested her hands on her knees. Seeing thick spots of blood on the ground, she quickly realized they had fallen from a wound on her forehead. She had no time to worry about this; it was time to move onwards.

With one last glance back along the empty trail, Denzela once again set off on her heels.

He was loath to show it, but Ed Daimler was fairly impressed with his new partner's professionalism.

They had arrived at the Eight-Ball motel twenty minutes ago, a mere twelve hours or so after the victims had died. The place was a dump, the very definition of the term "low rent".

The bodies had been removed, but Daimler could still detect the unmistakable reek of death in room nine. The FBI's own forensics team had muscled in. This was a job for the Bureau, given the multi-state nature of this killing spree. A specialist named Mick Dunvey was sitting down in a nearby diner with Daimler, van Stadt and local homicide detective Dino Gonzalez. Between them on the table was a folder containing crime scene photos and various forensic reports. After Dunvey talked them through the pictures, being sure to cover them every time their overly attentive waitress approached, it was time to talk theories.

Perhaps because of the hangover, which he couldn't seem to shake, Daimler was content to sit back and let van Stadt make the lion's share of observations. Which she did, piecing together a comprehensive picture of what exactly might have happened to Kitty-Lou Maynard, Bud Dyer and Kyle Coopersmith. She was wearing a pair of wire-rim spectacles, which Daimler thought made her look devilishly cute.

The motel room's door lock had not been forced, she noted, so the trio must have either known the attackers, or invited them in, believing them unthreatening. "Perhaps they might have met in the same bar where these three met," she offered, before going on to examine the wounds inflicted. "Despite the fact that the female was raped, the absence of semen suggests that the aggressor used a condom, which means that these people aren't acting on impulse. They're intelligent enough to take precautions and they don't want to be caught. I—"

"At least not yet," interrupted Daimler. "I have a feeling that they're enjoying the visibility they're getting in the press. These people have a point to make. I'm surprised they haven't already made direct contact with either us or the press."

"I don't understand," said Gonzalez. "What exactly is the point they're making? They're raping and killing people—"

Daimler raised a finger to his lips and frowned. Gonzalez had been talking very loudly and eyebrows were starting to raise among the families sitting adjacent to their table.

"Sorry," nodded the detective. "But they're doing all this shit, and you say they're some kind of moral crusaders?"

"That's where their delusion kicks in," said Daimler, knocking back the cool dregs of the day's third coffee. He was starting to crave a stronger drink. "They may be genuinely convinced that what they're doing is perfectly just."

"Is there a religious aspect here?" asked Gonzalez.

"I don't think it's religious, exactly," said van Stadt. "Maybe just moralistic. These people have a strong sense of what's right and wrong. And unlike most people, they're willing to do something about it."

"You sound as though you admire that," said Gonzalez, looking half serious. He then shuffled awkwardly in his seat. Van Stadt's only reply was a withering stare. "Do... do you think they're still in the area?" he said, turning his attention to Daimler.

"Maybe," Daimler offered vaguely, feeling wretched. At present, he really had no idea. It was a relief when the waitress brought them the check.

* * *

Daimler and van Stadt joined Gonzalez for an informal interview with the clerk who had been working at the Eight-Ball motel last night. They had no idea whether their UNSUBs had actually stayed in a room, but intended to find out.

The clerk's name was Jimmy Reeve. Called back to the motel from his apartment, he clearly hadn't been planning to do much on this, his day off. His glazed eyes positively shrieked of marijuana. They were sitting in a small, untidy office and Reeve looked terrified, drinking coffee like it was going out of fashion.

Daimler suppressed a smile, knowing just how paranoid Reeve would be feeling right now. In his mid-twenties, the guy probably expected to be booked for smoking dope or blamed for the murders. As Gonzalez and van Stadt discussed some preliminary points, Daimler leaned forward and whispered to Reeve.

"Don't worry, Jim. We don't care what you do for recreation." In Daimler's considerable experience, when innocent and potentially vital witnesses were tense their memory cells had a nasty tendency to clog up.

Reeve nodded earnestly. "Thanks, man," he muttered. "Do you guys mind if I smoke?"

Van Stadt turned to him. "I'm afraid I do."

Great going, Melissa, thought Daimler. Make the guy all nervy again, for the sake of a little passive smog.

"So you were at the front desk from ten until seven this morning?" asked Gonzalez, checking his notes.

"That's right. Killer shift, huh?" Reeve laughed nervously.

"Now, I realize this isn't exactly the Ritz," began Daimler, "but during that time, did you see anybody suspicious checking in?"

"I've been racking my brains, man. Racking 'em. Came up with nothing. I mean, it was the regular crowd, pretty much."

"So what's the regular crowd?" asked Daimler.

"Young couples. Older guys with hookers, who just want a room for an hour or two. Maybe a family on a real cheap vacation."

Daimler chewed this over. "Did you see any older couples? Anyone who might not normally stay at a roach motel?"

Reeve looked almost offended. "Oh, we don't have roaches," he protested, before inferring from Van Stadt's pointed look that it didn't matter. "Sorry. Let me see..."

Daimler watched as the inner cogs of Reeve's brain struggled to spin.

God, I need a drink, he thought. Perhaps I should excuse myself for a moment and take a swig in the restroom...

Reeve shrugged. "I'm sorry. I really can't remember anyone."

Daimler sank back into his chair and rubbed his tired eyes with two middle fingers. If it looked like a covert way of saying "fuck you" to this useless dope-head, then he was frankly past caring.

"Wait, there *was* one couple," said Reeve suddenly, his eyes widening. "At least, I thought they were a couple. It was an older guy, well, middle-aged, and a slightly younger woman. They spoke kinda..."

Daimler leaned forward, winding his hands around each other as if trying to help stimulate the gray matter. "Kinda?"

"They spoke like they were from high society. They were well-spoken people. At first, I thought it was just another old guy with a working girl, but when she spoke, I knew she was no hooker. At least, not your average one."

"Tell me more about what they looked like," said Daimler.

As Reeve spoke, Daimler began to build up a mental picture and it seemed to correspond to the vague visual profile he had established. Good-looking, well presented. Just the kind of people you wouldn't expect to commit multiple homicides.

"Okay," said van Stadt, when Reeve had wrung his brain dry. "Which room were they in?"

"Oh, they didn't get a room. They looked around the place like it was infested with roaches—which it really isn't—and left."

Daimler and van Stadt looked at each other.

Gonzalez's phone rang and he held it to his head. The room fell silent as he listened, then dropped the phone back into an inside pocket.

He gestured for Reeve to beat it, and the kid lumbered out of the door.

"Sounds like they've struck again," he said. "A gas station attendant, further upstate."

Daimler nodded and frowned at the same time. "A gas station attendant? That sounds unusual, if it's them."

"Why unusual?" asked Gonzalez.

"There must be CCTV footage," said van Stadt, quietly. "We must have them on camera."

The car had been silent for some time.

Penelope was staring into the mirror, retouching her make-up. Norwood solemnly watched the road.

"You know what you've done, don't you?" he finally said.

"Yes, dear," sighed Penelope. "I got myself on camera. But did you really think I'd leave without taking this?"

Norwood looked over and relief flooded over his face.

She was holding a video cassette.

"You beautiful thing, you," he grinned.

She could see water. In the distance, through a multitude of tall, twisted trees, Denzela could see a sparkling blue mass. She told herself it must be the lake.

She continued her pace. It was amazing, she noted, what you could do when your life was in danger. Yet she knew that safety might still be a long way off.

The water drew closer and Denzela could soon see that it was indeed the lake. The water bounced hazily up and down in her field of vision.

The axe caught her in the throat. The speed at which she was traveling worsened the impact, allowing the blade to sever the head with ease.

Denzela van der Westhuizen watched from the ground as the rest of her body ran away from her, skidding to a clumsy halt, further along the track. Then, mercifully, darkness took her.

Jason turned and made his way back along the path, the axe dripping with blood by his side.

FIVE

FIVE

Tom Sheridan wasn't so sure how he felt about this conference. He had been with Entraxx for three years now, since he was twenty-one. Coming out of college back in Philadelphia, bagging a job with this corporate giant seemed the greatest thing in the world. He enjoyed the admiration of ladies, joy and relief from his folks and envy from many of his peers. Even the latter had been welcome; at the time, he'd taken it to be an indication that he was doing something right.

The job he initially took wasn't particularly impressive in and of itself, but it was in the right place: the marketing department in Entraxx's magazine and media division. Tom soon made an impression with his superiors, not least for his ability to devise effective ideas for campaigns. He soon came to learn that most of these notions would be stolen and passed off as having originated from his superiors, but that, he told himself, was the game. The main thing was that his line managers—the people he directly answered to—knew he could deliver. The fact that they then went to *their* line managers with a supposedly first-hand idea was something he was willing to live with.

His relaxed attitude eventually paid off. Six months ago, he received the kind of promotion which just wasn't supposed to happen. He shot up from a lowly marketing assistant to marketing coordinator; the kind of advancement that it generally took ten years for people to achieve. Once again, he had encountered ripples of everything from genuine joy at his advancement to flat-out resentment.

The man he had to thank for his rocket-ship ascent was Larry Bruckenheim, the division's managing director. Bruckenheim had been in the business for over thirty years, having started at the same age as Tom, and he must have developed the second sight. Even though Tom's immediate superiors bled him dry for ideas at every available opportunity, Larry seemed to see through their thieving and recognize Tom as a creative goldmine.

Of course, the interview had helped. When the marketing coordinator position became available, Tom had decided to go for the job—and *really* go for it. With only three days to go before the interview, Tom had sacrificed sleep to prepare. Bruckenheim himself didn't attend the actual interview, but word soon got to him that Sheridan had arrived with a list of one hundred and one new marketing strategies for Entraxx Media. He'd practically written a book.

Larry Bruckenheim had apparently leant back in his legendary office, offering a one hundred and eighty degree view out over downtown Philly, and said, "That's our man." This, without even seeing the one hundred and one suggestions.

Tom could still remember the look on his friend Greg Spiner's face when he gave him the news. Greg had also gone for the job and Tom was anxious that there be no bad feelings about the outcome. Greg had made a good show of it, slapping him on the back and exuding all the expected congratulatory bluster, but Tom had noticed that the smile never reached his friend's eyes. Since that day, their friendship had changed. They still hung out together and went through the motions, but the heart and soul was missing.

Greg was sitting next to him at the wheel of the BMW. His red hair poked out in shocking tufts through his backward baseball cap, his T-shirt and shorts displaying his shamefully pale arms and legs. At least, thought Tom, employees were allowed to dress casually for the event. This was only fair, seeing as it was taking up pretty much the whole weekend. Most people in the marketing department seemed thrilled by the prospect of Entraxx's latest annual social event; cheers had actually sounded when it had been announced. Once upon a time, Tom had felt exactly the same way. He had seen the Entraxx Weekend as an opportunity to network, get to know important people on a more relaxed basis.

This was the way that Greg still saw it. So did April Mather. She was slumped across the back seats, dressed up to the nines, as though they were heading to a nightclub at midnight. April didn't *do* informal. She wanted to look great at all times. While Tom knew she was a screamingly superficial piece of work, he couldn't seem to stop himself from sleeping with her.

It had been going on for almost a month. Tom hoped that Greg was the only person within the company who knew about them. April was, after all, Tom's PA. It was textbook office sexual behavior, but Tom seemed unable to help himself.

Tom's newly acquired status wasn't the reason for the decline of his enthusiasm for the Entraxx Weekend. The corporate world was starting to grind him down. It made him feel hollow. A little wine, April and song seemed to help temporarily paper over the cracks that were forming in his mind, even though he realized that she was wrong for him. She worked for Entraxx, for one thing. She was cold as ice, too. April was pure crack cocaine, an ecstatic fix but not the best habit to adopt long-term.

In retrospect, he sorely regretted confiding in Greg about their clandestine relationship. They had been propping up a bar, nursing their sixth or seventh beer, with a totally ludicrous side shot of Jaegermeister. No wonder Tom had suddenly felt the need to blurt out the fact that he was banging his assistant. Hell, he would have told Larry Bruckenheim himself, if he'd joined them.

That was then. He, April and Greg were speeding through Crystal Lake, the chosen location for this year's Entraxx Weekend. In less than twenty minutes, Greg was saying, they would arrive at the Phoenix Heights hotel. "I checked it out on the Net," he said. "The place only opened last year. It got redeveloped on the grounds of a huge old apartment block; gutted from the base up. Let's hope they've already made their mistakes and learnt from them."

"Typical of you, Spiner," laughed Tom. "You're getting a free weekend at a luxury hotel and you're concerned that service mightn't be up to scratch."

Greg shrugged. "I very much doubt it'll be luxury. Have you looked out of the fucking windows, during the last ten minutes? This is *Deliverance* country, boy!"

"It's not that bad," said Tom. He turned to face his secret girlfriend. "What do you think?"

April pulled an indifferent face. "It doesn't exactly look like heaven to me."

"So," said Greg. Tom hated it when Greg started a sentence with "So". It generally meant that he was about to say something embarrassing. "Did you guys get one room between you?"

"No way," said April.

"Thanks," Tom mock-huffed at her.

"No, I mean we *could* have had one room, but Mr Sensitive here still doesn't want anyone to know about us."

"It's not that," protested Tom.

"No?" said April. Tom saw her wide, challenging eyes in the rear-view mirror. "What is it then, Tom?"

"Now then, you guys," said Greg, grinning. He was enjoying this. "Let's have no trouble. We're all friends here."

"Hey, slow down a little," April told him. "There's a junction coming up."

Tom peered ahead. The BMW was indeed speeding toward a spot where two roads entwined.

"We're in the country," said Greg. "Apart from us suits, they all walk, don't they? They all lope around with their fucking Rottweilers, chewing straw."

"Slow down," insisted Tom. As soon as he said this, he recognized his mistake. Giving Greg an order seemed to spark the man's resentment for Tom's superior position.

"And... we're speeding up," he yelled, stomping the accelerator. "We're not in the office now, Tommy boy. This is *my* car."

"Fuck you, Greg," yelled April. "Slow the fuck down."

Another order, badly received. Greg kept his foot on the accelerator. "Look at you guys," he chuckled as the engine roared. "Like a couple of frightened little love-birds."

"What's the matter with you?" winced Tom, gripping the sides of his seat.

"There's a junction right ahead," said Halo. As usual, she was the sensible one holding the map. As usual, she was the smallest voice in a sea of bad listeners.

"Uh-huh," said Duke in reply. "Man, we are gonna rip it up tonight!" He rocked to and fro against the wheel.

"Hell yeah!" chimed in Basket. This seemed the man's favorite expression. Whenever he was in doubt, Basket opted for a "Hell yeah!"

"Hey you guys, I can't wait any more," said Shona, her voice suddenly crackling with excitement. "We were gonna wait until we got to camp, but..." She paused, smiling as though a big announcement was coming.

Halo saw Basket's hand lightly grab Shona's arm, like a gesture of support.

"What the hell is it?" said Duke. "Would you like a drum roll?"

"Fuck that," grinned Trey, next to him. "You suck at drums. I'm the man when it comes to *that* shit." He mimed a drum roll on the dashboard.

"Hey now," said Basket indignantly. "Me and the little lady have something to tell y'all."

Trey and Duke shut up and listened.

"What is it, guys?" smiled Halo, feeling an odd tightness in her stomach. She never reacted well to tension of any kind, even if it was leading up to good news.

"We're gonna have a baby!" roared Shona.

Halo's heart fluttered.

Basket punched the air, almost catching the back of Trey's head. "Hell yeah!"

"Fuck," gasped Duke, glaring back at Basket. "How come I wasn't told about this? I'm your fucking blood, dude."

"We just wanted to tell everyone together," said Shona.

"Fine," shrugged Duke. "Well, congratulations, little brother and little lady."

"Congratulations, you guys," said Halo. Her eyes were fixed on the side of Trey's head. It was difficult to see how he was responding to the news.

Then it came.

"Well done, guys," he said, turning to slap palms with Basket and Shona. "Better you than me, that's all I can say."

Halo's heart plummeted somewhere down between her knees. Her throat went dry.

Trey threw her a glance. "No shitty diapers for us, *right*, honey?"

Halo's smile was so fake, she couldn't believe that he took it on face value. She shook her head, feeling like the bottom had dropped out of her world.

"I'm serious," said Tom, beads of sweat forming around his brow. "Slow down, Greg. Please!"

This seemed to be the magic word which Greg wanted to hear. A little bit of kow-towing from the man who was his boss back in Philly. He eased off the gas and the BMW ate slightly less road.

"Voila!" he cried. "Slower."

Tom and April breathed sighs of relief. Tom could sense that April was fuming and wanted to lay into Greg, but didn't want to risk him pulling any more stunts. He felt much the same.

Suddenly, Greg spun the wheel. The BMW drifted into the left lane. "Slower," he repeated. "But in the wrong goddamn lane. Sweet Jesus, we're all going to die!"

Tom realized that his friend had waved goodbye to all vestiges of sanity. He couldn't let this pass, even if he did fear confrontation with a passion. Reaching over, he grabbed one side of the steering wheel.

"Get the hell off," shouted Greg, eyes flashing wildly as he fought to keep the BMW in the wrong lane.

"Jesus Christ!" screamed April. "There's another car coming!"

* * *

Halo saw it first; some kind of flash car, speeding directly toward them.

At that moment, Duke and Trey were looking at each other, babbling their usual bullshit.

"Duke, look out!" The words spilled out of her mouth in a garble.

Duke returned his attention to the road. "Oh my fucking God!"

The BMW was getting bigger by the second.

Greg's face went even paler than usual as he saw the oncoming Camaro.

Tom saw the Camaro too, and let go of the wheel. He didn't know why, but the rational part of his brain must have deduced that if he and Greg continued to fight for control of the BMW, they might remain on this side of the road and hit the other vehicle full-on.

But Greg didn't do anything apart from look mortified.

"Spin the wheel!" April roared.

Greg did nothing. Less than fifteen feet separated the cars.

Duke leaned back against his seat, as though trying to distance himself from the collision. Halo had prayed that the BMW would realize its mistake and change lanes. She assumed that Duke had been thinking the same thing. But what if both drivers had assumed that the other would switch? She leaned forward into the crash position that she'd seen people adopt in airplane disaster movies.

Then the Camaro howled and lurched, as Duke spun the wheel.

"Fuck!" Halo recognized Trey's voice. She clasped her hands over her ears, for all the good it would do her.

Seeing that the other car was changing direction finally seemed to galvanize Greg. He wrenched the steering wheel the opposite way. Tom held his breath. April screamed again. The two vehicles clashed as they passed each other. There was a ragged, metallic whine.

Then the Camaro was gone. Tom surveyed the rear-view mirror: the other car was careering off the road, steadily slowing down. Greg too was piling on the brakes and the BMW soon shuddered to a halt, the engine dying.

In the back, April seemed to be in shock.

Tom looked at Greg in disbelief. The man's face was deathly white, clammy with sweat. "Greg, what is wrong with you?" he gasped.

Greg shook his head slowly. His eyes fixed on the rear-view mirror and flooded with fear. Tom looked too. The occupants of the Camaro were clambering out. Some of them were yelling abuse. The biggest among them, whom Tom recalled as having been the terror-stricken driver, was examining the side of his vehicle.

Greg's hand jittered as he reached for the ignition keys. "We've got to get out of here," he murmured.

Two of the men were walking purposefully toward the BMW.

Tom grabbed Greg's wrist as tightly as he could. "No, we won't. We'll stay right here and make sure the others are all right."

The men—who looked pisssed—were within feet of their car. Tom opened his door and stepped out. He swallowed hard, registering the fury in Trey and Basket's eyes.

"I'm really sorry," he said, holding both palms up in defense. "Are you guys hurt?"

Duke was walking toward them too, tree trunk arms bulging out of his sleeveless leather waistcoat. "My fucking paintwork!" he snarled.

Greg was still in the driver's seat. He wound down the window on the passenger side and addressed the newcomers. "Tom grabbed the wheel! The guy's a maniac!"

Trey grabbed Tom by the collar, scrunching his shirt and swinging him around. Tom was almost relieved when he hit one side of the BMW with a sickening clang. At least it had a stabilizing effect.

April cranked her window down. "You lay the hell off him," she cried. "Our driver's the fucking maniac. He's a coward, too."

Tom tried to keep his composure as he stared into Trey's beady, animalistic eyes. Their faces were mere inches apart and the guy's breath washed over him. Here was a mouth, which hadn't welcomed a dentist in years. "We'll pay for the damage," he said.

"You sure will, motherfucker," said Duke. "You're gonna pay right now."

Halo felt shaky, but wasn't about to let matters degenerate. She'd seen Trey, and especially Duke, reduce people to quivering bags of fractured bone in the past.

"Hey," she called out, approaching the besieged BMW, which had also suffered major cosmetic damage. Greg's car had lost whole chunks of its light blue finish. "Chill out, guys! We're all right. We didn't get hurt."

Duke jabbed a thumb into his exposed, hairless chest. "And who do you have to thank for that?"

"You," she said. "Thank God you turned that wheel. But don't hurt these people. It was an accident." She caught Trey's eye. "Let him go, honey."

Trey hesitated.

"Please, honey. Let him go."

Trey pushed Tom against the BMW, then released his grip. As he did so, Halo couldn't help but notice that Tom was gorgeous. Chiseled cheeks, blue eyes, good skin, not unlike Trey after a makeover and an anger management course. She brushed aside this thought in the space of a second, but it surprised her. She couldn't remember the last time she had looked at someone in that way. Perhaps it was Trey's conditioning; she had become afraid to even acknowledge another man's presence, in case he blew a gasket.

Face reddened, Halo ran a hand through her long hair. Then, seeing that the beautiful man was still in danger of assault from Duke, she gently grasped the big guy's bicep. "Calm it down, Duke," she said.

The muscle contracted beneath her palm. Duke was seething.

Luckily, Basket seemed to agree with Halo. "Come on bro," he muttered in Duke's ear, stepping between him and a perspiring Tom. "Leave it."

"Greg, give the guy your insurance details," said April. "Don't be a chickenshit."

Halo didn't like the look of Greg, he resembled a shrew. The creepy guy was making a big show of appearing victimized, but she could tell that he'd been to blame for the accident. He was the driver, for crying out loud.

Duke stomped around to Greg's side of the BMW and sternly accepted what the shrew had to offer.

Tom locked eyes with Halo. "Thanks," he said, quietly. "I was almost hamburger there."

"No problem." She momentarily wished they could look into each other's eyes some more. She wondered whether he felt the same. Still, she could already feel Trey's contempt and turned to him, wrapping her hands around his waist. That usually did the trick of placating the green-eyed beast. He protectively slung an arm around her back and stared at Tom. Halo sighed. Would she be in for the third degree, later, when he was drunk? Oh, the delights in store for her on this relaxing break.

After a few uneasy minutes, everyone headed back to their rides. Halo smiled at Tom, but they shared no further eye contact. As she climbed back into the Camaro she felt the heavy weight of disappointment, as though a door to another life had opened and abruptly slammed shut.

The Camaro resumed its journey, turning into the junction that would take it through the final stretch of road to Clear Waters.

"Can't say I feel much like having fun now," said Shona, clutching her belly as though calming her unborn child.

"Ah, that was nothing," said Basket. "Few beers, we'll be fine."

Shona punched his arm. "I can't drink anymore, dumbo."

"I know," he replied. "I said, *we'll* be fine. All the more beer for us, right, Halo?"

Halo grinned lightly. Then she began to work on suitable excuses for passing on alcohol, this whole weekend. God, this wasn't the way things were supposed to be, for a nineteen year-old. She'd barely gotten to grips with the idea of finding a job, not that she didn't want to work. She had no problem with that concept, even if she still believed that the accumulated stress of her mother's factory job helped breed the cancer that ultimately claimed her. No, it was more the fact that she couldn't believe anyone would employ her. Why couldn't she be more confident, like her big sister? She was a go-getter.

"Well, I'll be a son of a fucker," said Duke after a while, glancing into his wing mirror. "Those losers are going to the same place as us."

The Camaro was indeed on the same road now, heading in the same direction. It hung back, keeping a safe distance.

"Oh great," said Trey. He turned to Halo. "I'll bet you're *real* pleased, girl. You might get to see Mr Cute Cheeks again, huh?"

Halo feigned confusion. He scowled and presented her with the side of his head once again.

"I'm sorry, Greg. I don't care whose car it is. I'm driving."

"That's pretty obvious, Tom. No problem. Guess you guys can make your own way back to Philly, when this weekend's done."

April had been slumped in the back seat, seemingly exhausted by the events of the last fifteen minutes. At this, however, she piped up. "After this, you asshole, I'd rather crawl back. Don't talk to me again."

Greg folded his arms. "No problem, April."

Tom rolled his eyes. He knew there'd been a reason why he was dreading this convention more than ever before.

He slowed the BMW as a battered pick-up truck, which looked like it used to be blue, rolled out of a side road. For a moment, the two vehicles blocked each other's path. Tom saw that the driver was a bearded man in his fifties, with curled, graying hair and eyes like balls of hot coal. He looked like a farmer. Sitting on the seat next to him was a shotgun, propped up to point at the roof.

The man stared at Tom, agitated. He clearly wanted to be somewhere fast, but wasn't about to compromise. There was something unnerving about him, as though his humanity had ebbed.

Having had enough confrontation for one day, Tom allowed the BMW to edge back. At least it would give the Camaro a head start.

The farmer maintained eye contact for a few seconds. Then he returned his attention to the road and focused once again on wherever he was going. The pick-up truck gained speed and soon turned a corner, out of sight

"What was that guy's problem?" asked April.

"I don't know," murmured Tom. "But I sure wouldn't want it to be me."

SIX

The scene was thick with cops and officials, mostly getting in each other's way.

Hordes of disappointed motorists goggled out of their windows at the gas station, either through morbid curiosity or simply a desperate need for fuel that wouldn't be met for the rest of the day.

Katherine Banks, the gas station clerk, had once been beautiful, so it seemed to Daimler. The bullet hole that had replaced her left eye somewhat compromised that beauty. The other orb stared upwards, lifeless but questioning, as if the poor girl's last thought had been crystallized by her retina: why me?

Mick Dunvey, who had joined him and van Stadt for the ride from Rochester, was examining the single bullet that killed Banks. It had emerged from the back of her skull, hammered through a hanging calendar and lodged itself in the wall.

"The caliber of the bullet suggests that these were our guys," the specialist told Daimler. "It's the same as the one used for most of the other killings."

"They may be losing control of themselves," offered van Stadt, gazing dispassionately down at the corpse. "It's common with spree killers; they start to think that they can't be caught, that they can do anything. The cooling down period between each kill starts to dwindle. Have we looked at the CCTV?"

Daimler yelled through to a local cop he'd met, ten minutes earlier. "Sam, is there any footage?" He pointed up to the small camera housed in one corner of the station's ceiling.

Sam shook his head. "Looks like they took the tape."

Daimler dug his heels into the ground and leaned back against a wall. His eyes strayed to the rows of bottles which adorned the nearby racks. He imagined their contents flowing out onto the ground, a glorious glugging noise coming from the necks. Oh, for a sea of alcoholic freedom. He could set sail and head off to sweet oblivion. No more killers, no more profiling, no more anything.

"Ed?" Van Stadt's voice snapped him out of the daydream. He turned to see her looking oddly caring, just for a second. Perhaps the ice maiden was finally beginning to thaw.

He nodded to her, preoccupied again as his gaze lingered on the front desk. "Hey Sam," he said. "What's the last thing that went through the cash register?"

Sam looked puzzled, as though wondering why it mattered. "Uh, I don't know. We haven't looked. Should we?"

Daimler shrugged. "Can't hurt."

He turned back to van Stadt. "I wouldn't be surprised if these people actually paid for their goods before blowing her eye out. If they see themselves as good folk, then surely they might want to pay their way?"

Van Stadt nodded slowly, chewing it over. She turned to stare out of the front window, onto the forecourt, as though trying to conjure up a vision of the killers themselves. While they weren't exactly getting on famously, Daimler was coming to like the girl. She took the job seriously, a little too seriously you might argue, but it was better than some green no-mark who thought the game was just like it was on TV: all hard-jawed heroics and cold beers after a long day's work.

Oh, beer. Don't think about beer.

"Walk this way, Ed," said Sam. "We've found out what the last purchase was."

The idea struck Daimler as he was midway through a marathon swig of Scotch from the hip flask in his breast pocket. Disturbingly, the best ideas often came at such times. In his other breast pocket, he carried a handy travel-size bottle of mouthwash. Emerging from one of the restroom's cubicles, he sluiced around some in his mouth and spat it into the bowl. Then he looked his own reflection in the eye.

It was a strange feeling. While he had sufficient professional detachment to realize that he had become an alcoholic, he seemed unable to do anything about it. Wasn't even sure that he wanted to.

The test would be his judgment calls. If he started making mistakes, he might reconsider his lifestyle. Provided it wasn't too late.

"Please be right about this, you bastard," he murmured, out loud.

Van Stadt followed him as he emerged from the gas station, clutching a large map.

"What is it, Ed? Let me in on this."

"Sure. Just give me a chance, huh?"

He paused by the bonnet of a police car, looking excited. "I've got it," he said, one fist clenched. He beckoned her to stand next to him and she did so, squinting against the afternoon sun.

"This map is the last thing they bought," said Daimler. As he spoke he was unfurling the paper, spreading it awkwardly across the bonnet's hot, smooth metal. "A map of Clear Waters."

"You don't know they bought it," said van Stadt, standing with her hands on her hips. "Could have been anyone, just before Banks's murder."

Daimler ignored her. "Now, we've already established that they're heading in pretty much a straight line," he offered, tracing a rough path between the kill-spots with a bony forefinger. "But where are they going?"

His finger circled the north-east. "These people are driven by a sense of moral duty. If they aren't exactly religious, then they resemble religious folk in terms of their love of purity..."

"And complete lack of tolerance for the impure," van Stadt completed, brushing a stray strand of hair back behind one of her ears.

Daimler closed his eyes, striving to make an idea solidify in his mind. "What if they want to find like-minded souls?"

"Why would they?"

"Broaden their flock. Have their views reinforced. Strength in the face of adversity."

"So who would be a like-minded soul? You've said yourself that these people are fairly unique, in terms of established killing spree profiles."

Daimler stabbed a finger down on the map and van Stadt bent down to read the location: Clear Waters. She looked at him blankly.

"Jason Voorhees," said Daimler. "Crystal Lake's self-appointed guardian of morals. This guy, whether he actually exists or not, is supposed to be a twisted puritan, killing promiscuous teens, drug-takers and people generally having a blast. Didn't you hear that radio report earlier? The local police are dragging the lake, looking for him."

"I'm not particularly familiar with the Voorhees story," shrugged his partner.

"That's because you deal in facts," smirked Daimler. "Jason Voorhees passed into legend long ago. He's a cautionary tale to scare the kids; an alibi for every psycho in a mask. Although, when a spate of killings happened up here quite recently," he tapped the map again, "the local force refused to accept it was him."

Van Stadt shook her head. "I still don't understand the leap of faith you're making."

"Exactly," said Daimler. "It *is* a leap of faith. Our UNSUBs are not using logic as we know it. They're delusional, they think they're doing the world a favor. Maybe even that they're divine messengers. And maybe, just maybe," his eyes returned to the map around his finger, "they see Voorhees as a man after their own black hearts."

Van Stadt pulled a face. "I don't know. I very much doubt Jason... What's his name? I doubt he really existed. I *definitely* doubt he's still alive, even if he ever was."

"So do I," said Daimler. "But the only important thing is that *they* might think he's in Crystal Lake. So let's head up there. Take a risk. Frankly, Mel—can I call you that?—I'm sick and tired of always being one step behind these fuckers."

Tom was impressed. The Phoenix Heights hotel looked luxurious. The BMW had turned off the main road and was now approaching it along a drive decorated at intervals by shaped hedges and stone ornaments. The building itself was massive, wider than the average big city hotel, yet stacked high. Tom quickly counted thirteen floors. The stone architecture itself appeared ancient, like a British structure, but the fresh window frames betrayed signs of the renovation that Greg had mentioned.

Greg sat silently behind him, arms folded, not even looking at the hotel. Inside the BMW it had been frosty and subdued. Tom felt proud of himself for demoting Greg to the passenger seat; he had allowed himself to be forceful. April seemed highly impressed with his sudden display of traditional machismo, which was something of a shame, as he was starting to tire of her. No doubt she'd like that, too.

"Wow, this place is nice," she said, directly behind him. "Look at that fountain."

The fountain in question was the centerpiece of a circular driveway directly outside the hotel's reception entrance. It was the most ostentatious aspect of the hotel's grounds. Around fifteen feet across and almost ten tall, its dazzling main feature was a sizeable bird, fashioned from white metal, which looked like steel, but with a glossy, reflective finish. Its jagged wings were spread, as if the creature was taking flight.

"What bird's that?" April asked.

To Tom's right, Greg made a tutting sound, gazing sullenly at the metallic creature.

"Uh," said Tom, as kindly as he could, "it's a phoenix, April."

"Oh," she said. "What's that mean?"

"It's a mythical creature. The one that resurrects itself up from the ashes."

"Ah," she said.

There was a pause as Tom swung the BMW past the fountain. Then April asked another question. "Why did they choose a phoenix, do you think?"

Greg was unable to restrain himself any longer. "It's the name of the fucking hotel, you dumbass." His eyes threw daggers in April's general direction. "Turn your brain on, for Chrissakes."

"Hey!" said Tom, as he pulled up in front of the hotel. A parking valet was making his way over to the vehicle, as was a bellboy hungry for bags and tips. "Greg, please lay off her."

"Look at the big guy, standing up for his secret girlfriend," glowered Greg, undoing his safety belt with a clunk and opening his car door. "I wonder how much longer she'll stay secret, though, huh?"

He slammed the door shut behind him, leaving Tom and April to exhale deeply.

Tom realized he was shaking.

"Mr Sheridan!"

The exaggerated roar came from Larry Brucken-heim, who was striding across the huge, marble floored reception area to the check-in desk where Tom, Greg and April were waiting for their room keys.

Tom abandoned the signing-in form which he had been completing and shook his boss's big, pudgy hand. The grip was as vice-like as ever. Larry was a big man, but not in terms of middle-age spread. He was well built for a guy in his fifties, like a marine sergeant. He was, however, doing his best to disguise the fact that he was rapidly going bald. He was Corporate America personified, all slickly insincere charm and powerful body language.

"How the hell are you doing, Tom?" asked Larry, with his usual intensity. He turned to give April and Greg a perfunctory token "Hi guys!" Without even looking at him, Tom could feel Greg's churning resentment at not being greeted by name. Larry probably didn't even know his or April's names.

As Larry stood there, slapping Tom's shoulders and amiably grilling him about the journey here, Greg and April sloped off to the elevators, room keys dangling from their hands. Larry didn't even see them go.

Tom noticed April purposefully entering a different elevator to Greg. Good girl.

"Oh yeah, that's it baby. That's it!"

Shelley heard Clayden Heinz's words only dimly. She was more concerned with maintaining her grip on the sides of his desk as they rutted. Sweat covered her forehead, bare breasts and back; she was wearing only her short skirt and pantyhose, the latter bunched up around her calves.

She felt herself rising toward a grand climax, the kind she had enjoyed many times in the early stages of their affair, three months ago. These days, Clayden seemed less considerate. But maybe this time things would be different.

"Oh *yes!*" cried Heinz, his face red and contorted. Shelley thumped the desk in frustration as she fell short once again.

Heinz sat on the floor, breathing deeply. His buzzer sounded again, for maybe the third time in the last twenty minutes. Shelley had lost count. Once again, Heinz ignored it as he attempted to regain his strength.

"Before we... got into that," said Heinz, the red patches on his face slowly fading, "I was going to tell you something. I'm sorry that it has to be now, but it's very important."

Shelley stopped still, a sense of dread dawning on her. While she was staring directly at him, he seemed unable or unwilling to make eye contact.

"I am afraid that we cannot continue with this," he finally said, his transatlantic accent varying from American to German and back again, in the space of the same sentence. "It's not... the most professional thing for us to be doing."

Shelley felt her cheeks flush and her hackles rise. Here she was, half naked on his desk and about to be thrown aside like a fast food wrapper. "That never seemed to bother you before," she said, feeling infuriated.

Still avoiding eye contact, Heinz spread his hands wide in defense. "I was weak. You are a very beautiful woman, but this is wrong."

"Yeah, right. More likely, you've got a new girl on the go. Who is it, Clay? I'll bet it's Marissa, isn't it? Marissa from the breakfast shift. Giving you something to munch in the mornings, is she?"

She hopped off the desk and stooped down to find her blouse, suddenly feeling disgusted with herself. Just minutes ago, she had felt like a girl having a glamorous, illicit relationship with her boss. Now she was too old, cast aside in favor of a younger model. Was it her belly? God knew, she had tried to tighten it up, but once you got past thirty it was more of an uphill struggle. She wished she had exercised more during her twenties. Perhaps if she hadn't been forced to look after her younger sister for all those years, she might have had more time.

She stopped searching for excuses and turned her attention to the slimy toad that was standing before her, clearly dying for her to leave. "Fine," she said. "I'll give you exactly what you want. I'm quitting as receptionist."

Heinz was wringing his hands together. Something on the ceiling had captured his attention and wouldn't relinquish it. He nodded insincerely. "I understand."

"I'm sure you do," she said, feeling sick as she realized that she was probably number fifty-eight in a long line of receptionists that he'd used and abused. Why did she fall for such a bastard? Story of her life. "Before I go, though, I'm going to go to the bar, get drunk and fuck a guest or two."

Heinz exhaled like a prude at this, yet he didn't look too worried. "Go ahead," he said quietly. "Tell Chloe to put the drinks on my account."

Was that it? His idea of making it all up to her? "You bastard!" she yelled, shocking herself by taking a swing at him. He grabbed her wrist and they stared fiercely into each other's eyes. For a terrible second, she thought their rage was about to dissolve back into passion. But he released her and stood looking out of the window, straightening his clothes as she did the same.

Then she was out of the door, blazing inside. She would never let this happen again. From now on, *she* would do the fucking.

The pick-up truck, which used to be blue, rose and fell jerkily as it negotiated the uneven soil. At the end of this narrow drive was a modest farmhouse, which looked as though it had seen better days. The roof was in a state of disrepair, and it had clearly been years since the entire property had seen a paintbrush. It sat in the middle of green fields, but the only livestock on display were a few disheveled pigs in a compact pen. Crops, too, looked as though they wouldn't be yielding much, even allowing for the blazing heat, which had cooked the area that summer.

Farmer Jack Flanahan opened his car door, eyes fixed on the farmhouse. He planted one boot on the ground, territory that had been his for the last twenty-three years. Memories good and bad flashed through his mind. The moment when he and Dolores realized that they could sustain themselves as a business. The children being born and the heart-wrenching moments when they both flew the coop to attend college. The autumn when the storms hit and devastated much of the place. That last time, he and Dolores had just pulled it all back together and started from scratch.

It all had to end. Everything always did. The farmer leaned back into the truck and grasped his shotgun, tugging it out of the seat and the vehicle. He had parked further from the farmhouse than usual, and for very good reason.

There were lights on inside the house. This, despite Dolores having told him that she would be shopping in town this afternoon. He had known—*known*—that she was lying. Truth be told, he had known this for the best part of the year. Only difference was that this time he was prepared to do something about it. He was tired of living and tired of being mistaken for a fool. As his father once said, "Make fun of a Flanahan and you'll pay the price, sooner or later."

A gathering wind whipped leaves up around him. Flanahan hefted the shotgun's long barrels up on his left palm, comfortable as ever with the balance of its weight. This weapon had been with him so long, it was practically an extension of his arm. He had carried it through every season, wasting various breeds of unwelcome critter. One night in the early Eighties, he had almost killed a human, an intruder who was wandering around his property in the night. The rain had hammered on the windows as Flanahan crept through the house, shotgun in his hands. When he reached the porch, he'd received the fright of his life as a grizzled stranger loomed out of the darkness, rain dripping from his hat. Flanahan had leveled the weapon at this grinning old loon.

Making his way down the driveway, Flanahan remembered how close to killing the intruder he had been, how his finger had gripped the trigger but managed to sufficiently restrain itself from pulling it all the way. The figure had babbled some paranoid garbage about how only *he* knew what was going on by the lake, before Flanahan told him in no uncertain terms to go away. He later discovered, through conversations with neighbors and local cops, that the guy was a pest who was being watched by the law.

What was his name again, Flanahan wondered? The farmhouse drew closer. Ralph? Mad Ralph? Crazy Ralph? Either way, the guy had finally gotten himself murdered, only months after his appearance at the farmhouse. Flanahan had figured that the area was a whole bunch better off.

He cocked both sides of the shotgun and began to walk faster, ignoring the wind's mournful howl.

The hotel's kitchen was big. Its staff worked hard, carrying large pans around, performing a kind of impromptu ballet as they avoided bumping into each other.

"Awesome," said Tom. "I feel like I'm standing in *The Shining.*"

Larry laughed and slapped his pet employee on the back, a little too roughly as usual. One day, Tom thought, he'd just fall flat on his face as a result of Larry's overly enthusiastic bonhomie. "Haven't seen that movie," added Larry, making it clear that he didn't understand Tom's comparison in the least.

Beside him stood Clayden Heinz, his hands rubbing together in a show of greasy subservience. He had homed in on Larry the moment he saw him standing at the check-in desk with Tom and scurried over, introducing himself in a nauseating display of fake charm. Obviously, Tom had thought, Heinz knew that it was well worth massaging the bloated egos of the larger cogs amidst America's corporate infrastructure. Metaphorically jerk them off during their stay and they'd be sure to come back for second and third helpings.

This was the first stop off on the tour of the place that Heinz had offered—no, *insisted*—on giving them. The kitchens were situated on the ground floor, at the back. Windows looked out over the grounds behind the hotel, which appeared to play host to golf tournaments.

"We never fall short when it comes to customer satisfaction," said Heinz. "As you can see, we employ so many staff that we never have a situation where we can't fulfill orders from the hotel's three restaurants. I'd rather have chefs sitting around doing nothing, than have a problem with the flow of dishes out of here."

"Very commendable, Mr Heinz," said Larry, nodding.

"Please, call me Clayden."

"Okay, Clayton. I'm sure looking forward to trying a nice steak this evening."

If Heinz noticed the mispronunciation of his name, then his professional sheen didn't betray the fact. Provided Larry Bruckenheim brought this kind of business to the hotel, and Entraxx bookmarked the Phoenix Heights as one of its favorite leisure destinations, Tom doubted if Heinz would object to Larry calling him Mindy Fuckhorn.

"These chefs look quite young," said Tom.

"That's true," said Heinz, eyeing him with a look which said, "Hey, you're not nearly as important as the boss-guy here. Just enjoy the tour and spare me the observations."

He went on: "They're fresh from college, the finest in their field. I'm very excited about the new talent we're fostering here."

Tom laughed to himself, seeing how Larry was being taken in by it all. These kids probably weren't fresh out of college at all; they were more likely to be teens who were doing their best and being paid a pittance.

Heinz introduced his head chef, a stocky five-footer named Chuck Waylon. Tom couldn't help but notice that the skin around Waylon's eyes appeared twenty years older than the rest of him. Must be the late hours, he thought.

Hands were shaken and bullshit exchanged. Even Larry, a big fan of food, couldn't take more than

five minutes of chat about the finer details of cui-
sine.

"Excellent," he barked. "Where to next, Clayton?"

The door had been wrenched off its hinges and was
resting limply on the frame.

Jack Flanahan stood looking at the farmhouse's
side entrance as if trying to see through an illusion.
This was real, he finally decided. Furthermore, it
would have required some serious force. This he
knew, having built the door himself, after the storm.

Frowning, Flanahan listened hard, trying to detect
noises or movement inside the house. He could discern nothing. His home was as quiet as a crypt. All
he could hear was the occasional snort from the
pigs.

Part of him wanted to go back along the driveway
to the truck, climb in and burn rubber to the
sheriff's office. But he didn't. After a moment's hes-
itation, he realized that he was done with life and
didn't much care what happened, once he walked
through the door. He had been planning to shoot
Dolores and whomever her weasel of a lover happened to be, followed closely by himself. In the
event of anything happening to the couple, the farmhouse would be jointly split between his sons Aidan
and Patrick, so they would be fine. That was all that
mattered to Flanahan.

Tears threatened to well up in his eyes, but he
stubbornly bit his lip until it passed. What had his
father said? "A tear in a Flanahan eye is a mark of
shame." Amazing how things like that stayed with
you your whole life.

Placing the shotgun upright against the outer wall, he softly grabbed the door on either side and calmly moved it, standing it against a dresser a few feet inside. Then he picked up the weapon once again and entered the hallway.

"Mr Heinz, sir. Could I have a moment?"

Walt Bluestone was the Phoenix Heights's head of security. A barrel-chested forty-something, he exuded intimidation and never knowingly smiled. His short black hair connected with a carefully crafted beard, which looped just under his chin and had been made to look all the more menacing with carefully razored slash lines on either side. A walkie-talkie clung to his waist, as did a more cunningly concealed firearm.

Bluestone rarely gave away anything in terms of emotion, but his face was presently taut with concern.

Heinz had been leading the two Entraxx men through a wide ground floor corridor lined with mirrored elevators. Tom had yet to use any of them as he hadn't actually seen his room yet. The bellboy had taken his case up, where it presumably sat by a bed where he could be taking a rest to calm his nerves, had it not been for the slimy manager dragging him along for the big show. He felt put upon, resentful and not a little frayed at the edges from his experiences with the hairy rednecks earlier. Actually, they hadn't all been rednecks. He had wondered what the young woman had been doing amid those boneheads. She was beautiful; pure and simple. If he hadn't been preoccupied with being in imminent physical damage, he might have thought that she was giving him the eye.

"No problem," Larry was saying, as Heinz excused himself and moved over to talk to Bluestone in hushed tones. Larry and Tom then stood talking casually, both of them trying to overhear the conversation.

"Jason Voorhees has supposedly returned to the area," Bluestone told Heinz, watching his paymaster clasp one palm over his forehead in exasperation. "According to Sheriff Claymark, four people were murdered by the lake this morning. Two police divers included."

"Great," said Heinz, casting a sudden sideways glance at Larry and Tom to ensure they couldn't hear. The two men returned their attention to each other in the blink of an eye; they had indeed been listening to every word, but Heinz was none the wiser. He addressed Bluestone once again. "What measures do you propose to take?"

"I want to hire a few more men to help me and Finton cover the area. Just in case this guy, whomever he is, turns up over here. We need at least one man on each side of the hotel. I can get them here within the hour."

Heinz nodded thoughtfully. "Do it. But don't pay them the full rate. Do some kind of deal."

Bluestone sighed. "If you pay peanuts..."

"...you get good, basic security guards," completed Heinz. "Now get to it."

Murdered guests would be bad for the place's reputation, thought Tom. If Heinz could hire a couple of rejected police wannabes, then he wouldn't see the harm in doing so.

Bluestone was still hovering. "Anything else?" asked Heinz impatiently.

"Yeah, Mr Heinz. What are we going to tell guests? They shouldn't be going down to the lake right now."

Heinz shook his head as if it was supremely unimportant. "Let them listen to the radio and work it out for themselves. The cops will be all over the area, anyway. The main thing is that nothing happens *here*. Understand?"

Bluestone nodded almost imperceptibly and strode off, his back as straight as ever.

Larry and Tom briefly raised eyebrows at each other, as Heinz returned to join them, acting as though nothing was unusual. "Now then, gentlemen," he grinned. "You'll like this part. Let me show you the bar."

Flanahan's finger rested on the trigger as he stole across his own carpet. This hall cut through the middle of the house, dividing the living area at the front from the bedrooms at the back. As he walked, he glanced into rooms. Maybe, it occurred to him, Dolores really was out and there had been a break-in.

As he came to the open plan living area, which was flooded with light, the smell hit him hard. The only thing he could compare it to was Dunwin's slaughterhouse, a mile away. When he ferried livestock there to be carved up, he drove away as soon as possible, to avoid taking in that terrible, deathly reek.

He never expected to smell it *here*. Yet there it was, catching the back of his throat and making him feel ill. He was fearful.

As he peered around the corner, through the door-less doorway, the sight almost made him drop the gun.

The room resembled a vision of hell. His own personal version.

Not one wall had been spared splashes of blood.

Flanahan's jaw slackened as he took in the scene. A banner adorned the far wall, proclaiming: "Happy Birthday Dad". Lying in various contorted positions around the room were Dolores, Aidan and Patrick. Each of them was missing at least one limb, which with a little effort, could be spotted elsewhere on the blood-soaked carpet, like some sick puzzle game. Aidan, his beautiful firstborn Aidan, no longer had a head. It stared at Flanahan from the couch, where it lay on its right cheek.

Flanahan stared from one set of wide, lifeless eyes to another. All spoke of the horror his family had endured. But how could this be? His brain struggled to process the information and realized his boys had come home as a surprise. Except their work schedules meant that this was the only date they could make, two weeks before the actual event. He could easily imagine Dolores telling them that it was the thought that counted. She always said that.

The tears started to flow, fast and bitter. He no longer gave a damn what his father had always said about them. He realized, for the first time, that he had made the classic mistake of becoming his father, viewing everyone with suspicion and inventing one paranoid fantasy after another. Suddenly, the possibility that Dolores had been having an affair seemed meaningless. Who cared? He could hardly blame her, the way he'd been acting.

Practicalities gripped him. Wrenching his wet, salty face away from the carnage—his family, his beautiful boys and wife—he ran into the room and grabbed the phone. Picking it up with one hand and brushing away his tears with the back of his other, he quickly realized that the line was dead.

A door slammed behind him. He spun, his breath catching in his throat, to see a masked man crossing the corridor outside the living area, spanning it with one mighty stride. He wore a mask, through which Flanahan couldn't see the eyes, and had to bend in order to fit his head through the doorway.

Flanahan felt his feet slide beneath him. He was standing on blood, still slippery. Steadying himself with all his strength, he fumbled with the gun.

Was it a man? You could see the thing's *ribs,* for Christ's sake. Might this be some angel of retribution?

The figure remained just inside the room's threshold. Watching Flanahan. Its shoulders moved as though driven by industrial pistons.

Flanahan noticed, for the first time, that this satanic vision was carrying his buzz saw. The very saw which he used to hack down trees around the farm's perimeter, the same saw which had seemingly reduced his own flesh and blood to, well, just that.

Flanahan didn't wait for this giant to take further action. He raised the shotgun, pointed it at the thing's chest and squeezed the trigger.

The blast deafened Flanahan, the kick driving him back a pace, despite his familiarity with the weapon.

He fell backwards, tripping over a body part, one that he didn't want to think about.

Before his head struck the wet carpet, he saw that the figure had taken the blast. His aim had been true. What didn't seem true was the fact that this beast had merely stumbled two steps backwards, gripping the sides of the doorframe for support and cracking them. He was striding back into the room.

The buzz saw's hungry whir dominated the room like a wild animal prematurely woken from slumber. Flanahan could only faintly hear the sound. In his dazed state, he realized that the gun had fallen from his grasp. His hands squirmed as they desperately searched the carpet on either side of him, finding only dead meat. Flanahan looked up to see the figure standing directly over him.

The spinning saw blade lowered, carving effortlessly through his face, bisecting it from top to bottom, reducing his head to two spurting halves. Chunks of brain and bone flew up to strike Jason. One blob of cartilage hit the chin of his mask and clung there.

Jason deactivated the saw and stood in the sea of death, as the blade whistled to a halt. For a minute, it looked as though he was surveying his own personal kingdom, slowly turning his head to take it all in. If Jason was pleased with his handiwork, there was no sign.

He strode back out through the doorway, taking the buzz saw with him.

SEVEN

"What the hell is it now?"

Duke rolled down his left window. The cop who stood outside was doing his best to appear authoritative and sure of himself, but he had "rookie" written all over him. His mirror shades were far too big for his face and even Halo knew that a pair of frightened eyes was hiding behind them.

The Camaro was on a dirt track, no more than a mile from the lake. The cop had come from that direction and flagged them down. Then he had appropriated his best macho stride, as he approached the car.

"How can we help you, sir?" asked Duke, who had a knack of appearing like a big, benign angel when forces of law and order were nearby.

"You haven't done anything wrong," said the cop. "I wanna make that, uh, clear from the start. We just have to warn people against going down to the lake right now."

"Why's that, officer?" asked Shona, fluttering her eyelashes from the seat behind Duke.

"Well, we're not issuing full, official details as yet, but there seems to be a dangerous criminal on the loose in the area. There was an, uh, incident this morning."

Duke and Shona stared at the cop through their respective windows, waiting for details.

"Four homicides," said the cop. He said the word "homicides" as though this was the first time he had got to say the word in an official capacity. Halo could tell that it excited and scared him at the same time. "Four homicides, down at the lake," he repeated, warming to the sound of himself talking death. "So you'd be well advised not to head down here. If that's where you were going. The lake is all cordoned off."

"Oh no, officer," said Duke. "We're just passing through. But thanks for giving us the heads up."

"No problem. You, uh, kids be safe now."

"Thanks, officer," said Shona. "Have a nice day."

The cop smiled at her, nodded and headed back to his own vehicle. Duke and Shona rolled their windows back up.

"Shoot," said Halo. "So where do we go now?"

"Where do you think?" said Duke. "Down to the lake."

His statement triggered an immediate division between the sexes. Trey and Basket nodded, as if the idea made perfect sense, while Halo and Shona looked horrified.

"Come on, guys," Trey said to the ladies behind him. "It'll be fun. Let's live on the frickin' edge!"

"You've got to be kidding," said Shona. "Please tell me you're kidding." She looked to Basket for support, but he was simply shrugging.

"You heard what Deputy Fucknut said," laughed Duke. "The lake is crawling with cops. What self-respecting killer is going to hang around? We'll be in the safest place. We won't go all the way down to the lake. We'll camp in the woods."

"No way," said Halo. "Absolutely no way. Let's turn around and go back."

At this, Trey flipped. "Oh my God, woman. Are you intent on making sure I have no fun on this Earth whatsoever? You'll stay with us, goddammit. Drive on, dude."

Duke urged the Camaro onwards. Halo and Shona fell silent, exchanging horrified glances.

"We're gonna get murdered!" roared Duke. "We're all gonna die!"

"Hell yeah!" Trey and Basket howled together.

The Camaro picked up speed.

Officer Zeke Hollis wished he had a patrol partner. He had been given the task of driving around the area, warning locals to be on their guard. This was the first time he had been given something important to do, but he also felt vulnerable, driving around on his own, even though it was still daylight. The killer had dispatched a couple of police divers, after all, along with those young campers. Every few minutes, Hollis's right hand would almost involuntarily head down to his belt holster, to check that his gun was still in place. For the rest of the day, that Beretta would be his surrogate partner. Worst of all, these darn shades kept slipping down over his nose.

As he drove, Hollis mentally ticked off the community members whom he had already visited. Who next? He really ought to stop off at the Flanahans' farm and inform the couple what had happened.

His radio buzzed static and he spoke at it. "Hollis."

The voice was Sheriff Claymark's. "We found another body, Zeke, in the woods. Had its goddamn head removed. This bastard's still in the area. Be extra vigilant."

Hollis's flesh prickled with fear. This was no kid's stuff, that was for damn sure. "Will do, sheriff," he said, with bravado he didn't feel. "On my way to the Flanahans' place now. Check in with you later."

He took a left, heading down toward the lake, then a right, nervously scanning the trees for movement as he did so. The road would take him straight to the farm.

He hesitated. Would Jack be home? It would make all the difference between Hollis either acting like a regular police officer, all politeness and benign authority, or simply taking the opportunity to screw Mrs Flanahan on the living room floor. Their affair had been going on for months. It had started one evening when her husband was over at Dunwin's slaughterhouse and she was all alone. One thing led to another, which led to a whole series of wildly passionate rolls in the hay.

So should he drop by the farm? As usual, it was worth taking the risk, he thought as he drove off along the road.

That woman's pussy was to die for.

"Chloe, my dear. Get these gentlemen whatever they'd like to drink."

Clayden Heinz smiled over at Larry. "With our complements, naturally."

Tom and his boss were perched on stools at the bar of a stylish cocktail lounge. It was pleasingly old-fashioned, like something from a Forties movie, Tom thought. Looked like it should be in black and white. He had really started to tire of Heinz's excessive hospitality: since the kitchens, they had been shown everything from the servants' quarters to the suites to the roof where the view was admittedly spectacular, stretching out across the whole of Crystal Lake. From that vantage point, they had seen the distant waters and spotted vehicles gathered on its banks. Something was going on down there, no doubt connected to what he and Larry had half overhead of Heinz's conversation with the security guy.

At that moment, though, all that mattered was the prospect of free drinks. Tom could be as shallow as the best of them, when he set his mind to it. Besides, alcohol was just what he needed to calm his nerves.

He opted for a simple beer, while Larry predictably chose a far more corporate Scotch on the rocks. As Chloe fetched them, and Larry fielded yet more of Heinz's slimy chatter, Tom glanced around the lounge. Most of the tables and plush couches were occupied, even at this time, just after 5:00pm.

Guests ranged from the archetypal holiday makers—
old people in shorts and sneakers—to suited
business types.

One woman, he noticed, was sitting alone in the
bar's far corner. She was in her thirties, but a looker.
Strangely, even though she was obviously attacking
a cocktail with some gusto, she was dressed in the
Phoenix's staff uniform. Perhaps her shift had finished. There was no celebration in her body
language, however. She appeared irritated as her
eyes flashed around the bar. Tom soon realized that
she was focusing most of her attention on Heinz,
staring darkly at the manager.

Her eyes suddenly locked with his. She smiled
faintly and gave him a subtle beckon with a slight
jerk of her head.

Tom turned away, awkwardly, just in time to see
April entering the bar.

"Hey," she said, crossing to join them and pulling
herself up on a stool. "What are we having?"

Tom took a swig of beer. "An extra large dose of
kiss-ass," he murmured, ensuring that neither Heinz
nor Larry could hear him. "I haven't even seen my
room yet."

Her hand brushed his knee. "Well, you can show
me later, big boy." She frowned and looked over at
Heinz. "Who's that?"

"The manager of this place. Heinz something. Or
Clayden something, I don't remember which."

April said nothing, but Tom saw her eyeing Heinz
with renewed interest. She was so obviously drawn
to anyone in a position of power. He was amazed,
come to think of it, that she hadn't already tried to

get into Larry's pants. Hell, maybe she had and been turned down. Maybe Tom was the next best thing.

He had to face facts: his secret girlfriend was a power-fucker. It was only a matter of time before she moved on to someone further up the ladder. The question was: who would drop whom first?

"Seen Greg?" he asked her.

"Nope. Who cares? I do hope you're not going to let him socialize with us tonight."

Tom sighed. "Greg and I have been friends a while, April. I don't know what the hell's got into the guy."

"I do. And so do you. He's jealous. The little brat's jealous of both of us."

Tom wished he could take issue with that. Instead, he drained his bottle.

The corridor was tastefully lit: all dark reds and patches of shadow. Greg stalked along it like a cat. He had only just realized that this was the thirteenth floor of the hotel. As far as he had been aware, American hotels didn't have such a floor, in order to pander to people with dumb superstitions. Perhaps this was a mistake. Just like the mistake Tom and his prissy little bitch had made, overtaking him on the corporate highway.

Downstairs at the check-in desk, he had overheard the receptionist tell Larry Bruckenheim which room he was in: 1301. The big suite.

In Greg's hand was an envelope, stamped with the hotel's phoenix logo. Inside, was a folded sheet of the place's headed notepaper. He had written a brief note to Larry, anonymously telling him about Tom and April, plus the fact that Tom had been scouting around for a position with Entraxx's bitter publishing rivals, Mainline Inc. The latter wasn't true at all, but this meant little to Greg. He just wanted to see Tom torn down from his high horse.

He bent down and slid the envelope under the door.

The farmhouse came into view as Hollis's police car juddered along the dirt track. Behind it, the sun had begun its decline, superimposed on a gray sky.

Hollis froze as he sensed movement much closer to the vehicle. His foot stomped the brake and the car ground to a halt. He focused on the trees to the left of the track, positive that he had seen someone on foot—someone big—veer off the road and into the woods. It had been a blur, but he had definitely seen it.

Peering out of the window into the green depths, he could see nothing but trees. There were no paths here, just a tangled maze of boughs and trunks.

Hollis swallowed hard, but his throat remained as dry as sandpaper. Was he really cut out for this job? He looked at the spot where he had seen the figure leave the track. Then he looked straight ahead at the farmhouse. He had to make a decision: either drive on and sit in the warm for a while, eating apple pie, and maybe enjoy a roll in the hay with Dolores, or go bag himself a killer in the woods.

His trembling hand rested on the Beretta. He remembered how good he had felt when he joined the local force, how it had made him feel. For the first time in his life, he was going to mean something. He would no longer be a figure of fun, no longer Zeke The Freak—he shuddered at the recollection—and no longer a coward. He would stand up for the law and save lives. Serve and protect.

The gun was free of its holster and resting in his hand. He checked that it was loaded, then he slowly got out of the car, his eyes fixed on those trees.

As he locked the door—wouldn't do to have his cruiser stolen while he was pursuing a suspect—he took one last look at the farmhouse. The sun had sunk further, framing the building with a vivid halo and casting long shadows across the land. They seemed to reach up along the track, as though trying to grab him.

He ducked between two trees, where he had seen the figure vanish. Clutching his gun to his chest with both hands, Zeke Hollis entered the woods.

As usual, Chester Grey had arisen from his deep sleep precisely whenever the hell he liked. That was the beauty of his new life: the country didn't wake you with a throng of commuter traffic, stressful sales figures or a list of a hundred and one things to do. He would never forget what the coronary had taught him a year ago, not while there was the scar on his chest to remind him, every time he looked in the mirror.

He had learned not to sweat the small stuff, or the big stuff. Scurrying around like a rat all your life was no kind of life. Shame it had taken him fifty-eight years to learn this. Fifty-eight years of running his own publishing house: calling the shots, accruing a personal fortune, banging high-class prostitutes.

He would give anything to turn back time, in order to regain his health. Emergency surgery might have stopped him from dying, but it had slowed him right down. Made his raging Marlboro addiction untenable, too. His life was pleasant enough these days—relaxing was practically mandatory for him, under doctor's orders—but he wished he'd exercised a little more moderation, back in the day. Taken a few more holidays. If he'd done that, maybe he'd have less money, but neither might he have suffered that damn coronary. He'd still be smoking the odd cigarette and scoring the odd publishing victory, instead of his son, Dean, running the business, leaving him in a peripheral, godfatherly position.

When he had the chance, however, Chester Grey still banged hookers. Shame he couldn't keep it up for nearly as long as he used to. Still, a guy of his age needed hobbies.

Grey briefly washed in the bathroom, which he had himself installed in the back of this log cabin, then used a straight razor to shave. Dean had protested when Grey announced he would be handling some of the cabin's renovation work himself, but he didn't want to become an invalid. It wasn't like he was lifting logs, for Christ's sake, just a little basic DIY.

He dragged the razor's blade over his skin with quick, careless strokes. He didn't plan on meeting anyone today, so there was no need to go over the top. Then he pulled on his fishing clothes, slapped the green hat on his head and selected a rod from a whole bunch, which rested against the kitchen wall. The shotgun stayed put in the cupboard. He had no stomach for hunting at the best of times, unless the creature was water-based, with fins. The weapon was purely for self-preservation.

He paused to grab a dog-eared crime novel from the bookshelf and shoved it into a deep pocket on the outside of his jacket. He pictured the day ahead: no phone calls, no faxes, no irate book distributors or editors or authors adding to his stress levels and banging nails deeper into his coffin.

Then he opened his front door and came face to face with death incarnate.

Jason operated the saw as soon as the cabin's door swung open. An angry buzz erupted as he jammed the vicious, blurred blade toward Grey, who instinctively presented his fishing rod. Slicing easily through the wood, the buzz saw proceeded through Grey's jacket and into his chest.

Grey's face was rigid with shock, as though the pain hadn't registered. He opened his mouth and the faintest of hisses sounded at the back of his throat.

As Grey slumped to his knees, Jason stooped with him, ensuring that the blade remained wedged in place. Over the giant's shoulder, Grey saw a young cop, standing maybe ten or twelve feet away.

The boy looked terrified. Grey's last thought was how sorry he felt for him.

Every part of Zeke Hollis's body was telling him to turn and run. This guy was huge: almost seven feet tall. And he was holding some kind of fucking saw. This felt like the movies, not the easy country beat that he'd signed up for.

He could tell that the kneeling fisherman was dead. Blood dribbling from a slack mouth was always a clear sign. The victim's eyes were staring at Hollis, swamping him with guilt. Why didn't he stop this murder from happening? He had looked into the clearing and watched this hulking creature's ribs glistening through its back as it closed in on the log cabin. He could have yelled at it, drawn its attention, but no. A civilian was dead because of his dithering fear.

The giant was facing him, chest heaving, one livid eye visible through its mask hole. This was one angry motherfucker. The fisherman fell sideways, taking the saw with him, clutching its handles. The killer seemed unconcerned by this: maybe, thought Hollis, he was bored with the device.

Or maybe he was about to give himself up.

Hollis knew he had to be braver than ever before. Much, much braver.

He assumed the gun toting stance, mentally screaming at his legs to stop wobbling. Then he raised the gun, leveling it at the psycho's heart. At least, where he assumed there was a heart. If this guy was still walking with half of his skin missing, then it did make you wonder about the rest of him.

"Stop right there, man," he said, surprised by how firm his voice sounded. "Get down on the ground. Now."

Jason obeyed neither command. He took one lumbering pace toward Hollis, then another. He was very much upright.

"Stop right there! I don't wanna kill anybody, but you keep moving and I swear I'll shoot."

Hollis knew damn well that phrases like "I don't wanna kill anybody" and "I swear" weren't helping his case as a convincing cop. Neither were they helping him save his own life.

Jason walked on. "Fucking stop!" screamed Hollis.

He squeezed the trigger.

Nothing happened. Something had jammed inside the weapon.

Jason was almost upon him.

Hollis tried to think of what he'd learnt about guns jamming. What did you have to do, in order to make it work? He had no clue. Hadn't been paying attention. So he hurled the useless lump of metal straight at the maniac's mask.

He had always been a decent shot when it came to throwing and the gun hit its mark. It bounced off into some bushes, leaving not so much as a dent. As the psycho rounded on him, Hollis saw fresh blood on the mask. For a second he was mesmerized by it. Then he turned to run for his life.

Too late. Jason gained an iron grip on Hollis's shirt collar with one huge hand and raised the other above the cop's head in a tightly balled fist.

The fist came down like a pile driver, slamming into the top of Zeke Hollis's skull. The impact shattered his spine and collapsed his neck, forcing the head down into his torso.

Jason stood back to view his handiwork as Hollis briefly convulsed, then tumbled to one side. He suffered one last flashback to the school yard: all the kids, standing around him, fingers pointing, their faces contorted with juvenile loathing as they yelled, "Zeke the freak! Zeke the freak!"

If they could see him now.

"Can you drive?" asked Shona, perching herself on the log beside Halo. She was forced to repeat the question, as Metallica's latest album was blaring out of an old ghetto blaster, which sat nearby.

"Yeah. You wanna escape?"

Shona nodded, more than half serious. She looked edgy. As she spoke, she was surveying the undergrowth, which surrounded their demolition zone of a campsite.

"We couldn't do that," said Halo. "For one thing, they'd kill us. For another, we can't leave them out here without wheels."

All around the women, the others were acting as they always did. Like monkeys. For the last half hour, testosterone had flooded the clearing as tents were shoddily erected and beers were "shotgunned". This grim process involved bashing a hole in the base of a can and holding it to your mouth, in order to catch the full force of the intoxicating liquor within. Halo had watched Trey as the paper-thin line between Dr Jekyll and Mr Hyde grew ever more redundant.

Having lit a fire in an old oilcan that had been resting dormant on one side of the clearing, the men were taking it in turns to leap over the thing. Halo and Shona sat there wincing as they attempted ever more elaborate stunts. Sooner or later, someone was going to get hurt. It always happened, on each of the camping trips they had ventured out on. Someone got burnt, or cut, or broken. They would then spend the rest of the month wearing their scars as badges of honor.

Halo looked glumly around the site. It was no more than about thirty feet square and increasingly dark around the edges. What she could see of the sky was shot through with blazing orange streaks as the sun breathed its last. Soon, the fire in this canister would be their only light source, besides a few torches. Halo couldn't believe that she had allowed herself to be brought here, even after what the cop had told them. This would be the last time, she thought. Hopefully not literally.

"Hey, at least you can drink," offered Shona as if reading Halo's bleak thoughts. "I had to go and get myself a bun in the oven just when alcohol was needed."

Halo smiled thinly. For a moment, she considered telling Shona that she was pregnant too. But she couldn't trust Shona not to tell everyone else. She had known the girl for a while and they were fairly tight, but Shona was impulsive and often not the sharpest knife in the drawer. Right then, with the music pumping, it might be hard to impress upon Shona that Halo didn't want anyone else to know about the baby.

So when would she tell Trey? As she watched him dance around the fire, shirtless, spitting beer at his friends, the only sane answer had to be "never". His insistence that they press on with this journey, despite the fact that a homicidal nut bag might be on the prowl, had finally made something snap in Halo's head. It was, she realized, the part of her brain which had continually made excuses for him. Because that's what she did, every time. When he was violent toward her, she would remind herself that he came from a broken home and had a lot of pent up aggression. Not his fault that he couldn't control it, surely? When he refused to seek therapy for his problem, she rationalized this as having been because today's males found it hard to admit to problems.

Oh, girl, you're chock-full of excuses and justifications, she thought, gazing into the fire. You should be running the country.

"So, why ain't *you* knocking back a beer?" asked Shona, snapping her back to reality.

Once again, Halo seized on a good excuse. This time, it was almost true. "Because I'm scared too," she said. "I want to stay alert."

Shona rolled her eyes. "Great vacation, huh?"

"Oh, the best."

The two of them almost managed a laugh, just as the music stopped.

"Hey, where's Duke?" Basket asked, looking around the site. He and Trey had been so busy clowning around, they hadn't seen the big guy go.

Halo felt her whole body tense. Hairs prickled on the back of her neck.

"Did you guys see him leave?" frowned Trey, looking at the women. They shook their heads.

There was a loud clunk that made Halo jump up from the log.

Basket laughed. "It was the tape, Halo, turning itself off."

"He'll be back." Trey shrugged. "Turn the tape over, man."

Basket crossed the clearing to the ghetto blaster that lay on the ground, mere feet away from a clump of bushes.

He bent down to find the eject button.

The bushes split down the middle with a huge rustle and a big, shadowy figure launched itself at Basket. Halo and Shona screamed, clutching at each other. Basket roared with fright as the intruder grabbed his waist from behind and hoisted him into the air.

Trey ran to help, then slowed to a halt. He started laughing raucously. "Fuck, man, you got us good. I'll admit it."

Duke was smiling as he let go of his brother, sending him tumbling down on the ground, all scowls and scuffed pride. "Where's Duke? Where's Duke?" he said, mockingly. "I went to drain the vein, dummies. Better get used to that. It's gonna happen a lot tonight."

As Basket flipped the cassette tape over, Duke grabbed a beer and walked over to the log where Halo and Shona sat. They grudgingly shifted along the length of it, allowing him to sit as their heart rates returned to something approaching normal.

"Did I scare you little ladies?" he asked, wringing his hands together in the fire's heat.

"Oh no," said Shona. "Not at all."

He laughed. "Yeah, right."

There was a pause as he looked around the camp-site, tugging his ring-pull off in one continuous yank. "Of course," he said, "as usual I'm the only guy without a chick. Now, you're girls, right?"

Cautious nods.

"Why do *you* think I don't have a chick?"

They looked at him for a while, not knowing what to say.

"If you had a chick," said Basket, "she'd be a chick with a dick. Get it, Trey? A chick with a dick?" He and Trey slapped palms, chuckling.

Duke glared at them, then continued his interrogation of the women. "Am I pig ugly? Is that it?"

"Yes," cackled Basket, reaching for the play button. "That's definitely it."

"Fuck you. Shut the hell up. At least people can tell who *I'm* talking to."

Basket scowled and activated the tape. Music blared from the ghetto blaster once again.

"Am I ugly?" repeated Duke, louder. The women shook their heads. In truth, he really wasn't ugly. If he'd come packaged with an entirely different personality, either of them might have looked twice.

"You're just an asshole," said Shona. "And you know it."

"True," he said, taking the insult surprisingly well. He always seemed to have a soft spot for Shona: she could say things to him that no one else dared voice.

Another pause as he took a slurp from the beer can and rocked back and forth to the music, making the log jerk with him.

"Hey, Halo. Is there anyone you could set me up with? What happened to your sister? She was hot."

At this, Halo had to think a little. What *had* happened to her big sister? "We fell out, last year when she kicked me out," she said. "We don't speak any more. She still works around here: I heard she's at the big hotel that opened up."

"Right on," said Duke, taking another slug from the can. Then he frowned. "What was her name again? Sheila? Sharon?"

Halo smiled. "Shelley," she said.

By the fifth drink, Shelley was beginning to feel fine and dandy. The figures in the room had become less distinct, but she could barely remember why she had been so pissed off.

Ah yes, Clayden Heinz. Her bastard boss, lover and tormentor. He had left the lounge a while back, no doubt to go find his next piece of cooze. The cute young guy was still sitting at the bar, but his girlfriend seemed to be sitting next to him.

Her mind settled on Halo for a minute. She still thought of her as a daughter. And why not? She had doubled as both of the girl's parents for all those years after their own mother died. Dad had already flown the coop at that point, so Shelley raised the girl all by herself, with help from a succession of boyfriends. So maybe there had been some lurking resentment on Shelley's part, that she had spent so much time looking after Halo's best interests, when she could have been living her own life. That resentment finally exploded, as was inevitable, and out Halo went.

She would patch things up with Halo, one day soon. They may have stood outside Shelley's trailer in the rain that night, exchanging insults as she hurled Halo's suitcase onto the ground, but deep down they were still sisters. That thought was a strong source of comfort to her: the fact that there was one person in this world who she would always be close to, even if they outwardly hated each other, at this point in time. They would make up and everything would be fine.

Shelley had to admit that throwing Halo out had been a good move, purely from her own point of view. On the most obvious level, she had a hell of a lot more room in her trailer. She didn't have to worry so much about her kid sister seeing her bringing men home and she didn't have to spend time looking after Halo. The girl was beautiful and she loved her dearly, but at the age of eighteen she needed a wake-up call: get out there in the big, wide world, or, at least, a different trailer park and gain a little independence. It was just a shame that Halo had apparently moved in with that shady looking character, Trey. It was also a shame that she and Halo hadn't spoken since the bust-up. But there were always downsides to every decision you made in life. Such as bumping uglies with your boss.

She downed the rest of the cocktail. Ah, the hell with it, she thought.

Just as she was about to stand up and head to the bar for a refill, a man slid smoothly down into one of the chairs at her table.

"Do you mind if I join you?" he said.

Shelley sat back and gave him the once-over. He was older—even older than Clayden in fact—but a handsome, suave devil. His suit was immaculate and his eyes sparkled kindly as he peered across the table at her empty glass.

"Can I get you another?"

"Maybe," she said. "I'm Shelley. And you are?"

His smile dazzled her, displaying rows of perfectly kept, whiter-than-white teeth. "Norwood," he said. "Norwood Thawn, at your service."

EIGHT

Darkness was descending over Clear Waters. The sun was handing over to the moon, which now had to contend with thick slugs of gray cloud.

The trees around the former Crystal Lake stretched in all directions, appearing thick and impenetrable in the fading light. A modest town center, which some locals laughingly referred to as "downtown", nestled to the east. To the north, the Phoenix Heights hotel dominated the landscape. It was by far the area's largest building, painfully out of place alongside miles of sprawling greens and browns.

The absence of moonlight, together with the low wattage of lamp bulbs, which lined walkways at ground level, made the lake itself resemble a black gulf. A hole where the forest's heart should be.

In the area covering a mile's radius around the water, the odd camp fire glimmered like a beacon. Not twenty feet from one of these, Jason Voorhees stood silently.

Moonlight weakly illuminated one side of his mask as he watched the scene before him, his huge hands empty by his sides. Through the gnarled trees and bushes, figures gathered around a bright, fierce flame, which snapped at the air. Jason's eye followed them as they moved, dancing around the fire. Not all of them were dancing, however; two sat aside from the group. Jason's gaze fastened on one in particular. Her long dark hair framed a petite face that was being propped up by her fists. She appeared the group's most vulnerable member. Her flesh would rip with ease. Her bones would offer no resistance before they splintered and cracked.

As he watched, his breathing quickened and deepened, his jaw working angrily behind the mask. Besides these intruders, the woods seemed entirely silent and still. Yet he had caused a whole world of panic, simply by standing here. In the earth that surrounded him, a thousand insects swarmed over each other in droves, increasingly desperate to escape his aura. Some were too slow and the evil overwhelmed them, rendering them dead husks in a ready-made grave.

Oblivious to the effortless carnage he had brought about, Jason's eye continued to stare, unwavering, unblinking.

Halo should have become used to the spectacle. Yet the bizarre, primal ritual never ceased to amaze her.

Normally, it would also amuse her. This evening, however, it was merely something to keep her mind off the possibility that the fleeing killer might cross their path. She kept remembering Denzela's prophecy: the storm, the man-child.

"Halo! Have a goddamn beer!"

For something like the tenth time, she gave Duke a firm no, citing the fact that she didn't feel well. Again, he shrugged and turned around to laugh at Trey, who was removing his own clothes for some unknown reason.

Looking back, she was sure Denzela had been talking about Trey. He would have become the storm, if she had told him about the baby. A storm which would undoubtedly try and force her to have it terminated. So maybe Halo had changed the time-line by not telling him. She had Shona to thank for that—if she and Basket hadn't broken their own news, Halo might have already told Trey. The evening would have become even less pleasant.

Trey was naked apart from his Daffy Duck briefs. Halo shuddered. Not because he had a bad body— no, not at all—or even because of that duck's grinning face, but because she knew what he was about to do. The fire still burnt fiercely in the oil drum, yellow and orange flames lapping a good foot above the metal rim. Trey regarded it with a mixture of hunger and determination. Basket and Duke were following his train of thought, no doubt due to man's in-built communication with his fellow man. Perhaps it was done by a type of osmosis, she thought. Testosterone floated through the air and shared idiotic thoughts with other guys.

"What the hell is he doing?" asked Shona, still perched on the log beside Halo.

Trey was staring at the drum, one foot comically scraping the ground like a bull's.

"Do it for metal!" yelled Duke. He and Basket began clapping their hands, repeating the mantra: "Do it!" Trey broke into a sprint toward the drum.

"Trey, don't. Please," yelled Halo. She was too far away to stop him, so that was the best she could muster.

Trey reached the drum and leapt into the air, his legs split like an athlete taking a hurdle. Halo held her breath.

He hit the ground awkwardly, stumbling, then rolling onto his side. Halo could see him grinning, so allowed herself to exhale.

"I know he's your boyfriend," murmured Shona. "But he's a jerk."

"Sure is," said Halo, returning to the log. "I'm just worried about what they're going to do, to top that little performance."

"Naked," cried Duke, as if answering her question. "We've got to do it butt-naked."

The women shared a sigh.

Shelley always knew when she had drunk too much: she started saying too much. Words would begin to fly out of her mouth that would have been much better off tethered inside the part of her brain marked "too much information". This stranger, Norwood, had only joined her ten minutes back and he already knew all about her tryst with the hotel manager. He seemed to be a good listener, but Shelley knew that she was ranting at him, letting off steam. This would be a mistake, as he was one good-looking guy. He surely didn't want to hear all about her dumb heartache, did he?

"So he broke it off with you today, my dear?" asked Norwood, frowning sympathetically. "Is the man going blind?"

Shelley flushed at the compliment, along with the fact that he really did seem interested. Still, she resolved not to keep talking about it. "I think it's best if I forget all about it," she said. "I don't want to burden you with it, you poor guy."

"No, no," said Norwood, gently waggling a fore-finger and pursing his lips. "You, my dear, can burden me all you like."

"Thank you."

"Not at all. Now, tell me. Do you make a habit of sleeping with staff at your workplace?"

Shelley was surprised by this sudden inquisition, but didn't want to let it show. "No, I don't," she said breezily. "That was a first for me."

Norwood examined her evenly. There was some-thing going on behind those lovely eyes of his, but Shelley couldn't decide what it was. Disapproval? Lust? Secrets of his own?

"Good for you, my dear," he finally said, pulling a silver cigarette tin from his breast pocket. "Do you mind if I smoke?"

"Not at all. So what's a fine, cultured gent like you doing in Clear Waters?"

Norwood flicked a Zippo lighter open and drew on a long cigarette until the tip glowed orange. "Why do you ask? Do you see this as a dead end town?"

"Yep," she smiled. "Full of no-hope people, doing no-hope things."

Norwood said nothing. He craned his head back slightly, made an circle with his mouth and exhaled. A smoke ring emerged from between his lips and softly floated upwards. For a second, it hung above the man's head. Shelley briefly thought of her sister, and how she really should get in touch with her. She felt bad about effectively forcing the girl to move in with that jerk Trey.

Norwood's eyes entranced her once again.

Sensing that he didn't intend to make any further comment, Shelley changed the subject. "How long are you here for?"

"I'm not sure. Probably until the FBI catch up."

After a pause, Shelley laughed nervously. Norwood's deadpan expression cracked down the middle and he followed suit, chuckling softly.

Another pause. Shelley took a large sip of her cocktail and threw caution to the wind.

"Which room are you in? They got you in a good one, I hope."

"I'm in a suite on the thirteenth floor."

Shelley rolled her eyes. "Oh, not that floor. The designers made a big mistake when this place was built. Clayden still hasn't gotten around to fixing the room numbers. You're not superstitious, then?"

"Not remotely," he said. "There is no such thing as bad luck. It implies lack of responsibility. Everyone should be made to..." He hesitated, as though choosing words with care. "Everyone should take responsibility for their actions."

Shelley eyed him curiously. "Wow. I can see that you're very serious about that."

"I am," he smiled. "But I also like to have fun. Do you, my dear?"

He leaned in toward her, sucking the tip of his cigarette.

She smiled back. The flush across her face began to spread. Downwards.

Larry Bruckenheim felt like the king of his castle. It was a feeling to which he was well accustomed, except he was no longer in the corporate environment. He could enhance the feeling with a large dose of alcohol. Maybe women, too, if he found a discreet opportunity. Over the years, he'd lost count of the number of loose dames he'd banged in expensive suites, then politely ditched before breakfast. His wife knew nothing.

He finished his second Scotch and ordered another from the cute bartender, whom he had tried and failed to engage in conversation. He had played the usual tricks, of not so casually mentioning that he was an MD, but none of it seemed to have translated into much interest in those gorgeous brown eyes. Ego tarnished, he sullenly looked around the room. The lounge was filling up, mostly with Entraxx employees. He did his best to remember their names, but generally he bluffed his way through with hearty slaps on backs, or suddenly feigning distraction when it came to introducing someone to someone else.

Then he saw her: a woman, perhaps in her thirties, perched on a bar stool on the other side of the room.

Her legs were crossed, making her short skirt ride up to display maybe half an inch of stocking top. Larry was mesmerized by the sight—stockings were his big thing, particularly when they were being used to tie him to bedposts—but made a special effort to wrench his gaze upwards, back to the face. She was quite beautiful. Furthermore, she was looking directly at him and smiling.

Larry smirked and sipped his Scotch. He waited a few minutes, just in case this hot little number was with anybody, perhaps one of the jackasses lined up at the bar, waiting to order, dollars in hand. As if realizing that he was waiting for a green light, she raised her eyebrows. The message was loud and clear: "What are you waiting for?"

Sufficiently full of Dutch courage, Larry left his stool, grabbed his drink in one meaty paw and heeded the siren's call.

Ping! The elevator doors glided smoothly open.

Shelley wasn't about to tell Norwood, but this wouldn't be the first time she'd had sex in his suite. When her and Clayden's fiery, loins governed passion had been at its peak, they had embarked on a tour of vacant hotel rooms, screwing until they collapsed, laughing and glistening with sweat.

She was excited, yet strangely nervous. This new man seemed so respectable that she could barely imagine him having sex. He somehow had the chaste air of a minister, despite his flirty playboy act. It was a direct contradiction, which made him hard to predict and seriously turned her on.

This could be very interesting, she thought.

As Norwood slid his keycard into the door's metal slot, he turned to glance at her. Somehow, she realized, he had managed to give this simple act a sexual overtone. It seemed that the minister's robes were about to come off.

Larry couldn't believe his luck. He had attracted many an envious glance from his Entraxx subordinates as he and Penelope chatted in the lounge. She, he had learned, was a novelist who liked to travel around America, penning her latest sex and shopping blockbuster in a non-stop variety of hotel rooms and restaurants. He'd never heard of her—Penelope Thawn didn't sound familiar at all—but bullshit was his inherent specialty. The woman was convinced that he'd seen her on numerous talk show appearances and even read one of her novels while on vacation in Milan. He would soon have her between the sheets. No one in the company would ever breathe a word, either, on pain of being ejected faster than a drug addict.

"So tell me about yourself, Larry," she said, brushing one immaculately manicured hand against his right knee. "You're the boss of this big company, but what about your home life? Are you married?"

Luckily, thought Larry, he wasn't wearing the ring. The road was clear for some straight up deception. "No," he said, glancing around the room to make sure no one was within earshot. "Never found the right girl, I guess. Plenty of time for me."

Penelope smiled, but for a moment he felt her pale eyes searching his soul. It was an uncomfortable feeling, as though she knew full well he was married and had been testing him. He swallowed hard, wondering whether she had spied the strip on his ring finger where his suntan became altogether more pale.

Damn.

As he turned to pick up his drink, tiny muscles pulsed on either side of Penelope's finely crafted cheeks. When he swung back to face her, she was smiling again. "Of course," she said. "Where's the rush, huh?"

Larry nodded and chuckled. He was feeling unaccountably nervous, but when she replaced her hand on his knee, and kept it there, his momentary unease was forgotten.

"I'm glad you're not spoken for, Larry," she said, with a delicious pout. "I think we should have some fun."

He stared at her stupidly. This was taking him back to high school. No matter how robust his ego had become on a corporate, business level, deep down Larry was always surprised when a woman wanted him.

Shelley gasped as her blouse buttons popped beneath Norwood's clever fingers. For all of this man's classy charm, he had soon dispensed with the pleasantries, once the door to his suite had been closed. Turning to kiss her with a passion that made waves course through her body, his hands had roamed her curves. As they lay on the king-size bed, he nuzzled her breasts, which were bulging out of a black bra, while fingering the clasp on her back.

"Beautiful," he breathed. "Quite beautiful."

Shelley only moaned in reply, as his mouth fastened around one of her nipples.

Larry frowned as Penelope pushed the button marked "13".

"There's really a thirteenth floor? Usually—"

"Hotels don't have them," she said, finishing the sentence for him as the elevator doors glided together. "Is this a problem?" She wrapped her arms around him and pulled herself so close that he could feel body heat through the thin material of her dress.

"Oh no," he said. "Not a problem at all."

His emphasis on those last two words was increased by the fact that her hand had snaked inside his trousers and was doing things to him that made all words irrelevant. Her lips brushed against his neck, making him shudder.

Larry found himself drifting on a sea of delight, only roused from it when a loud *ping* signaled their arrival. "We're here," said the love goddess whom he knew was going to make his year. "Come."

They walked a short distance along the corridor, Penelope maintaining a light grasp on his hand. Then she produced a keycard and opened the door to her suite. Pushing it inwards, she gestured for him to enter first. He found himself in a large living area, typical US suite material, with comfortable, multicushioned sofas and a suitably oversized television set, complete with a VCR.

Behind him, the door clunked shut. It was fun time.

"Take your clothes off, darling," she said, breathing into his neck. "Then I'll take you to the bedroom."

Larry didn't hesitate. He tugged furiously at his shirt as Penelope looked on, a smile playing on her lovely lips. His pants and the rest soon followed, until Larry stood naked in the middle of this strange woman's hotel room. Trying to stand in his most confident, manly pose, stomach in, chest out, he hoped to God that she liked what she saw.

Penelope reached over to him. He thought she was aiming for his hand, but soon inhaled sharply as she grabbed something far more intimate. Then she slowly walked away, tugging him very willingly in her wake.

When they reached the door to what Larry assumed was the bedroom, she once again ushered him in first. He did so and gasped at what he saw on the bed inside.

A couple's lower halves were partially covered by blankets, but Larry could nevertheless see that they were having sex. They lay on their sides, the man spooning into the woman (hadn't Larry seen her in the bar earlier?) from behind. Her eyes were tightly closed, but his were fixed on Larry, hard and cold.

Larry was confused. He was severely turned on, but didn't want this. He hadn't signed on for group sex, just some quality time with Penelope. As he tried to turn away from the bed, her arms grabbed his, holding him firm with a strength belied by her size. "Watch them, Larry," she said. "This is what we'll be doing, very shortly."

He frowned, feeling uncomfortable with the situation and unnerved by the man's gaze. This stranger was smiling, but this wasn't the smile of a happy swinger. If spiders could smile, when flies struggled against the silken bondage of their webs, they would look exactly like this. Yet Larry couldn't take his eyes off the scene.

The woman on the bed had heard Penelope speak and opened her eyes. She looked startled and attempted to pull away from the man, but he held her still, forcibly.

"Come now, my dear," Norwood told Shelley. "Let's not make any snap decisions."

He placed the palms of his hands on either side of Shelley's face. With one smooth movement, he wrenched the woman's head to one side. There was a sickening crack.

Larry's jaw hung low as he struggled to take in the information. Nausea rose fast from his guts as he watched the woman slump back on the bed like a broken doll. Grinning, the man continued to gyrate against her.

"Slut," he said into the corpse's right ear. Then he turned to face Larry. "And shame on you, sir, for watching."

"He's a married man, darling," Penelope called over to Norwood. "He wanted to fuck me."

Larry's legs finally became operational and he turned to run. Penelope blocked the doorway, her eyes possessing a terrible, righteous fire. He instinctively shrunk back from her, but she immediately took a step forward.

"'Till death do us part," she hissed. What happened next was a blur to Larry; it looked like the woman had swung a punch at him and missed. Then he felt the agonizing pain across his throat, the blood running hotly down his chest. The dizzy terror as his brain was starved of oxygen. He slumped to his knees with a splutter, vaguely noting the dripping knife in Penelope's hand before the floor rushed up to meet him.

"Quickly," said Norwood, abandoning the body in his bed and jumping across the room. "Into the bathroom with him. That's a fine carpet and I won't have it tarnished with a sinner's blood."

"I still can't believe the depths to which the human race is prepared to sink," panted Penelope, as they dragged Larry's corpse. "It makes me so mad."

"I know, my dear. But we're doing our best. Look at it like donating to charity. You can never give enough, but every cent helps."

Norwood tugged the shower curtain to one side. The pair wheezed in unison as they heaved Larry Bruckenheim over the bathtub's rim. When they returned a minute later, they were carrying Shelley Harlan's body.

No one seemed to know how the fight had started. Least of all Duke and Basket, who were having it.

Halo was too jaded to join Shona in the traditional chorus of protest. She was beginning to suspect that all this pugilism might be an attention seeking exercise. Intervention never yielded positive results, anyway; by this stage of the evening, the two men were simply too drunk to respond. They were like dogs that had been set on each other, with what remained of their brains having been set to "kill". They were also naked as the days they were born, complete with minor burns attained from jumping over the blazing oil drum.

Halo vaguely recalled that the argument had flared over who had leapt over it the highest. Any excuse would do.

In the clearing, thankfully a fair distance from the fire, the brothers had spent a few minutes taking it in turns to shove each other backward and forwards. Their eyes were glazed and unfocused, their balance unsteady. Yet neither fell over. This was an ugly battle of wills.

Duke threw the first punch, missing Basket's head by inches. "Hey," said Trey, "That's enough. Cool it down, guys."

Halo looked over to see Shona crying. She put an arm around the girl. "Don't worry," she said. "They'll stop in a minute. They always do."

In response to Duke's attempted blow, Basket ducked past the larger man's defenses and swung a fist of his own. This one connected with some force, striking Duke under the chin and practically lifting him off the ground. Time seemed to miss a beat, then Duke stumbled backwards, his balance gone awry. He thudded into the dirt, dazed and instinctively grabbing his chin, slowly working his jaw to check that it still functioned.

"Oh shit," said Trey, turning to Basket, who was staring down at his prostrate brother, clearly ready to fight some more. "What did you have to do that for, man?"

"Baby," said Shona, between sobs. "Please, don't fight no more."

Everyone watched as Duke slowly pulled himself to his feet. He stood up straight, eyes fixed on his brother.

"Come on guys," said Trey, holding his hands up. "No more."

Duke looked around the camp, from person to person, as though seeing complete strangers. Finally he murmured, "Fuck you all." He lumbered out of the clearing. Before anyone could speak, the woods had claimed him.

Basket sat by the fire, his chest shaking as he laughed. "He'll be back, man. Don't you worry. He'll be back."

NINE

Ed Daimler knew that his sense of priorities was all ass backwards. His task was to halt one of America's most brutal killing sprees in living memory. He had no ID on these people; just a fairly flimsy profile at best, together with the belief that they might be heading for Crystal Lake, Clear Waters or whatever the fuck it was called.

Despite all this, he was struggling to focus on the subject. He needed a drink and he was damn horny. These two factors seemed to override the case at hand, which worried him. It also concerned him that his hands were shaking. Luckily for him, van Stadt was at the wheel of their Lincoln Grand Marquis, so he was able to sit beside her with his arms folded, hiding the evidence of his condition. He was praying for the next service station, so that he could visit the rest room and take another life saving gulp.

At least it was the evening and therefore a more respectable time to drink. There was less guilt involved. In some ways, he quite liked the clandestine nature of his booze habit. It reminded him of his short-lived cocaine period, over ten years back. As much as he'd initially liked the rush of the drug itself, he had also got off on the whole process of closing the cubicle door, chopping out the drug, then mastering the art of flushing the cistern at the precise moment he took his illicit snorts. Ultimately, his then wife had put a stop to it all. "Kick the coke or I'm out of here," she had told him. "You've become a jackass."

Daimler smiled weakly to himself, as van Stadt expertly maneuvered through the commuter traffic on this jam-packed highway. Jackie had eventually left him, even though he waved goodbye to hard drug use. The affairs had finally worn her down; she was not a woman to be messed with, and he had messed with her, big-time. When she heaved her suitcase out the door, he had no one to blame but himself.

God, how he wished he had Jackie—or just *a* Jackie—to kick him into shape these days. She would be going through his pockets, then throwing away the miniatures and the mouthwash. She would remind him of what he was supposed to be doing, and the huge responsibilities that came with his job. Most effectively of all, she would tell him how proud she was of him, when he got his act together. Somehow, when Daimler lived alone, the addictive sides of his personality rose to the surface.

Casting another sideways glance at van Stadt's legs—he felt sure that she was fully aware of his attention and was about to reprimand him at any moment—Daimler grabbed the car phone again. "We're supposed to be the FBI," he said. "Can't even get the damn phone to work."

"You sure you're using it right?"

As much as he desired van Stadt, her smug habit of assuming him to be an idiot was starting to wear thin. "Of course I am," he said, eyes boring into the side of her head. "I pressed the right fucking button."

What was he doing? Snapping at his partner. Cursing at her. He felt sweat run cold at the base of his spine. Get a grip.

Van Stadt glanced at him strangely. "Okay, Ed. Look, are you all right?"

He sighed, feeling like a little boy. He just wanted her to stop the car, cradle him to her bosom and tell him everything was going to be fine. Then maybe give him some head.

"Sorry, Mel. I'm fine. Just a little tense. I'm always like this, until the job's done."

He knew full well he was lying. He wasn't always like this, in the least. He was renowned as being a levelheaded professional, reliable and pragmatic. Not some edgy fuck-up liable to bite partners' heads off at a moment's notice.

"Damn it," he said, banging the phone on the dashboard. "Let me try again."

Van Stadt said nothing. She kept her gaze fixed solely on the road as Daimler jabbed the phone's illuminated buttons. "What are you trying to do?" she asked.

"Get through to the sheriff's office at Crystal Lake. At least make them aware that our UNSUBs are on the way."

Van Stadt clearly wanted to reiterate her concerns that he was making a big assumption. He could practically see her biting her lip as she checked the wing mirror, prior to switching lanes yet again. Maybe it was time to cut her some slack. "*Might* be on their way," he said. "I admit, it's a risk. But what else do we have?"

Before she could reply, he found himself with a working phone line. The sheriff's office picked up after more than ten rings and a gruff voice greeted him. Deputy Kenny Ryger.

After explaining who he was, Daimler cut straight to the chase, telling Ryger to get as many men on patrol as possible.

"So we're looking for a couple?"

"Most likely," said Daimler. "Possibly an older couple, almost certainly married. I'm sorry that I can't tell you much more. This won't be much help, but I'm ninety percent positive that these people won't *look* like killers."

"They never do, I guess," said Ryger. "Thanks for the call, sir. I'll make sure the sheriff gets this message. You can rely on us."

"That guy sounded half capable," said Daimler after disconnecting the line. "Called me 'sir', too. Makes a change from the usual territorial pissings we get from small-town forces. You ever get that, Mel?"

She shook some hair away from her eyes. "All the time. I'm a woman, too, don't forget."

Daimler laughed, looking her up and down. "How could I forget?"

The comment was meant to be humorous, but his fractured state of mind made the words spill out in a seedy fashion. Desperate, even.

The car fell silent for the next few miles.

"Fuckin' fuckers."

Duke had no idea where he was going. All he knew was that every step took him further away from the campsite. That was good enough.

Branches and leaves lashed at his face, despite his best attempts to intercept them with his hands. A black canopy hung above him, as trees conspired to block the moon from view.

His head felt heavy, but he had the gung-ho attitude that a run of shotgunned beers always assured. He also had a full bladder and a belly full of hatred for his asshole brother. Struggling to remember what the argument had been about, he came up with nothing, but felt certain that he had been in the right. He always was. He was the older brother with the most experience in everything, whereas Basket knew nothing.

Crunch.

Duke frowned and stopped in his tracks. The sound had come from behind him, between his own footsteps.

He listened for a second, then turned around to look back along whichever path he had carved for himself. He saw nothing. Literally, nothing. No matter which way he faced, he could barely see his own hand in front of his face. For a terrible second, he wondered if he had finally drunk himself blind.

"Basket, you fucker? Is that you, come to give me some more shit? I wouldn't advise it, man."

No answer. Maybe the sound had been an animal, or a branch that he had unwittingly wrenched from a tree while protecting his face.

"Come any closer, and I'll piss on you," he said, breaking into a deep, booming laugh. "Getcha with the ole firehose. See how you like that." He listened again, hearing nothing at all. Then he fumbled with the front of his jeans, tugging the zipper down. Taking himself in hand, he began to emit a powerful stream, which made him sigh with relief. There was a wet pitter-patter as his urine splashed over leaves and cascaded down from one to another.

Crunch.

This time, the sound was closer. Behind him again.

He groaned as he tightened muscles, bringing the flow to a premature halt.

Silence returned.

With a grunt, he once again let nature take its course. Bladder empty, he stood there in the darkness, considering his options. Even through the booze, he had enough sense to know that he would have to return to camp at some point. He might be a stubborn son of a bitch, but he didn't like the idea of sleeping rough in the middle of the woods. No, he might as well head back. He had made his point. He would go back and call Basket an asshole. Maybe even crack open a beer with him and forget all about it. Then he'd continue his top secret mission to steal Shona from the guy.

It dawned on him that he'd lost all sense of direction. How many times had he turned around? Just the once? Twice? More?

He turned to his right, in order to avoid walking into the piss-soaked bushes. Then he broke into a stride, devoting effort to steadying his nerves. Duke was not a man who felt much fear, but some semblance of doubt had begun to gnaw at his bravado.

Something struck him hard across the face and he stumbled backwards, dazed, hitting the ground. There he sat, slowly shaking his head, soon realizing that he had walked directly into a low-hanging bough. He would have to be more careful.

He dragged himself back upright, using a tree for support. His face throbbed painfully. Had he broken his nose? It sure felt that way.

Something fast and immensely powerful slammed into his stomach, bursting effortlessly through his flesh, burying itself deep inside him. He wheezed, his eyes widening but seeing nothing new as the fist moved around inside him. Grabbing. Tugging.

The pain was unbearable. He vomited as the fist was wrenched back out of him. Duke felt something wet and sloppy wrapping itself around his throat, barely registering that it was a stretch of his own gut. He weakly lashed out at his assailant, but to no avail. The reeking tube was tightened around his throat like a garrote, squeezing mercilessly until he slumped to his knees, hands spasming feebly by his sides.

A final, savage blow to the head sent Duke spinning down into the wretched mess that caked the soil.

* * *

"I hope he's been murdered."

Basket lay fully naked on the ground of the clearing, the back of his head propped up on the log previously occupied by Halo and Shona. He held his latest beer over his genitalia, solely because Shona insisted that he did so.

Trey sat cross-legged next to Basket, staring at the oil-drum's flames. He was bare-chested, in jeans. "Shut up, dude," he said. "Shouldn't be saying things like that."

"I mean it, man," shrugged Basket. "I hope he's run into the guy the police were after. That would teach him."

"Dickweed," said Trey. He dropped an empty beer can, which hit Basket on the side of the head.

The women were walking around the campsite's perimeter. Halo felt like a caged animal. When she really stopped to think about it, she had been caged ever since she left her sister's care and moved in with Trey. Her eyes glistened.

"Hey, you okay, girl?" Shona gently rubbed Halo's back with one hand. "What's the matter?"

Halo thought for a moment, then glanced over to check that the men couldn't hear.

Halo turned to face Shona. Once again, she decided not to tell the other woman about the baby. "I don't want to be here," she said, simply.

"You and me both. But let's just sit it out, huh? At least try and make the best of a bad situation."

Halo stared out of the clearing, into the darkness that appeared solid, like it had been painted on to wood.

It's a bad situation all right, she thought. Why can't I help feeling that Duke really isn't coming back?

"I really don't have anything suitable for the woods, darling," said Penelope Thawn, perched on the bed. "I should have planned ahead better."

"Wear what you have on now." Norwood straightened his shirt collar in one of the suite's numerous mirrors. "It's a dry enough evening. If conditions worsen, I shall carry you. How's that?"

Penelope fluttered her eyelashes at him as she stood, reaching for her elegant jacket. "You're so romantic, my dear. Let's hope we can find Jason tonight. I think we'll make a good friend in him."

"You have more faith in our compatibility than I," he said, holding open the suite's main door and waiting for her to step through. "But I'm certainly willing to give it a try. The man *does* seem to be on our wavelength."

"Let's tune in," she said, disappearing out over the threshold.

As Norwood Thawn followed her, he picked up a piece of cardboard from a small side table, then shut the door.

The Thawns strolled off, the "Do Not Disturb" sign swinging gently on their door handle.

"Hey, where did Larry go?" asked Tom, looking around the lounge bar, his vision only slightly compromised by the few bottles he had downed.

Greg, who had contrived to sit himself at the bar between him and April, turned back from ordering yet another large gin and tonic, and smirked. "Why do you ask, Tom? Looking for an ass to park your tongue?"

Tom ignored him and sipped his beer. Then he sighed as Bill Behler, a new Entraxx recruit who was proving even more irritating than Greg, sidled over to join them. As usual, that horribly slick grin was plastered across the kid's face.

"Hey there, cats," he said. For some reason, Behler referred to people as "cats" as if he was some kind of bluesman. He certainly had pretensions to such a status, forcing anyone within reach to listen to his appalling, home-recorded demos. "Did you see who Larry went off with?"

"Nope," said Greg. He didn't like Behler, possibly because the pair of them was too similar for comfort. "But I'm sure you're about to tell us, Gossip Boy."

"I sure am. Larry hit it off with that hot older broad, who was sitting across the room. The two of them started getting pretty friendly, as far as I could tell."

"So what?" asked April, propping her face up with one hand. "Larry does that all the time. All of Entraxx knows it."

"Oh," said Behler, looking genuinely surprised. "Right."

"Thanks for the exclusive, though," laughed Greg. "Go off and spread it around, why don'tcha?"

Behler smiled awkwardly. "Catch you cats later," he mumbled. "A few of us are going down to the woods for a smoke." He threw them the grin of a man who believed marijuana to be highly radical, before slinking off across the lounge.

"Prick," said Greg, spitting the word into his glass.

* * *

Basket was pacing around the fire now, still naked. "He's been a long time," he slurred. "He never takes as long as this. I should go look for him."

"Put some fucking clothes on first, dude," Trey said with a grimace. "You're turning my stomach."

"Stay here, for God's sake," said Shona wearily, looking miserable as she hovered near the campsite's perimeter, rubbing her hands together in an attempt to keep warm. The temperature had dropped dramatically, even though their oil drum continued to burn. "We don't want to lose another."

"How long do we wait before trying to find the police?" Halo said aloud, back on the log, watching the flames.

"Maybe the police already found Duke," said Trey, walking around randomly, waving his arms like airplane propellers. "He was in a pretty bad state, man. They might have arrested him, thinking he was that killer guy."

Basket groaned and fell over, hitting the ground hard.

Trey started to laugh, then saw what had made his friend topple.

Lying on the ground beside Basket was a human head, crudely severed, as though it had been torn from the neck.

From where Halo was sitting, she could see only the back of the head. But it was Duke's. She knew it was Duke's. Trey and Shona were goggling at it, hands cupped over their mouths.

Basket sat up, wondering what all the fuss was about, rubbing the back of his neck, which the flying head had evidently struck. Seeing his brother's dead eyes staring up at him, he howled, hands scrabbling at the dirt as he attempted to put distance between himself and the head.

Shona finally found it in herself to scream, her whole head shaking as she did so. Trey lost a battle with his stomach and bent double, throwing up on the ground.

All Halo could do was sit there and stare at Duke's head, as her worst nightmares were realized. Denzela's words echoed through her brain: the warning of imminent danger, the man who would bring the storm.

In the corner of her eye, she saw movement. Rapid movement. She heard Shona scream again, more urgently this time, as if there was an immediate threat to them. Turning slowly, Halo saw a giant striding purposefully from the woods, seeming to melt out of the black. A hockey mask wrapped around his face, this figure was unarmed but there was no question that he had killed Duke and further intended to kill every last one of them.

Halo's legs felt weak beneath her as she sprang up from the log. She was the closest to the intruder, who was rapidly gaining ground on her.

Jason's hands flexed with the anticipation of ripping the girl apart. He changed direction slightly, heading straight toward her.

"Kill her, Jason," said his mother's voice, deep inside the cobwebbed corners of his mind. "Kill her. She must die, just like all the others."

Jason quickened his pace, raising his arms.

Halo stumbled backwards, eyes wide, the breath catching in her throat. She knew that no matter how fast she moved she couldn't outrun this maniac. She was dimly aware of Shona screaming again and some terrified yelling from Trey, Basket or both. It was like she was in a trance. Her legs were failing her as though their muscles and ligaments had been rendered to jello.

He was so close that she could see one eye through its mask-hole. It blazed with the cruel spite of youth. This was the man-child, she knew instinctively. And it was about to take her life, fulfilling Denzela's prophecy.

Then Trey was standing beside her, grabbing her by the shoulders, forcefully rotating her a hundred and eighty degrees and barking in her ear like a rabid dog. "Run, you stupid bitch! Run!"

The world switched back out of slow motion. Halo took off like a rabbit from a trap, not stopping to look at anything or anyone.

Once a scary mass of the unknown, the trees were offering vital sanctuary. She buried herself in them, ignoring the scrapes and scratches that she was dealt. The only important thing was to get as far as away from the clearing as possible.

Behind her, back at the campsite, heart-rending sounds of terror scalded the air.

Trey roared defiantly as he grabbed one side of the oil drum. The flames lashed up at his face as he strained against it. The drum was now the only thing that separated him from Jason.

"Help me," Trey called back, over his shoulder. He was hoping that Basket would appear at his side, to help him tip the drum, but nothing happened. He and that useless girlfriend of his had deserted the campsite. It was down to him to face this freak.

For a second, he considered turning tail himself and making good with his feet. It wasn't too late: he was a fast runner. But then what? Running through the darkness with this bastard trailing him? Better to try and stop him.

Every sinew in Trey's body stood up to be counted, as he once again shoved at the drum. This time, it up-ended, tumbling away from him and right into Jason's path.

The giant looked down to see his own legs consumed with flame. The lashing inferno had already set about devouring his lower half and was making its way up his huge frame.

"Burn, you motherfucker," breathed Trey, standing back and watching his handiwork. "Burn!"

The flames were savaging Jason's torso, preparing to lap at his head.

Trey's grin faded only when it occurred to him that while this guy was on fire, he didn't appear to trouble him unduly. That's when Trey decided to turn and run. As if sensing that his prey was about to flee, Jason stomped toward him with immense strides, taking one of his arms in a paralyzing grip. Trey gasped at the giant's speed and strength. Jason slung another arm around his back, wrenching the man toward his own blazing body.

Trey shrieked as the fire ate him alive. For a minute, the two figures resembled one blazing torch, Trey struggling feebly. Soon, the intense heat melted his nerve endings and he fell limp in Jason's merciless grasp.

The giant manipulated the blackened, broken corpse like a toy, using it to extinguish the remaining flames on his back. With a barely audible grunt, he tossed Trey's body aside and looked around the empty campsite.

Then his big feet were punishing the soil once again. He was back in the shadows.

MY LIFE PART TWO:
GROWING PAINS

I'll never forget the look in Walter Cusp's eyes, shortly before his fate was sealed. Neither will I forget the reason why he deserved to die. After the relatively pure environment of elementary classes, starting off in middle school felt like being thrown into the wild. It was a source of conflict, both among the other children—who generally fought like rats—and within my own mind.

On one hand, I enjoyed the education. I enthusiastically stuffed my young head with every form of knowledge I could get my hands on. I fed on information like others chewed their precious candy bars. Why, I could practically *feel* the boundaries of my brain expanding, just as fast as the sugar addict's gut. Mr Patterson made the already interesting subject of science a true joy, while Mr Allington attacked his math teaching with a joyous fervor for numbers, calculus and the cold, hard beauty of *the fact* that couldn't fail to rub off on me. To be quite honest, there wasn't one subject at Primetree Middle that I didn't like.

The downside of education, needless to say, was the fact that I had to be surrounded by other humans. I hesitate to describe them as humans, but that was the traditional term for these walking slabs of gristle, greed and sin. All around me, I saw children gorging themselves, fighting and worst of all, at our age, indulging in early experimentation of a lustful nature.

Ironically, I always thought Walter Cusp had been one of the good guys. His family took him to church every Sunday, a tradition he seemed to welcome. During recess at school, he and I would exchange notes from classes we had missed and generally have a meeting of minds. He struck me as a high-minded kid, above and beyond the fleshy, grubby debasement of his peers. Like me, he was eleven years old. Unlike me, he had a mop of red hair, which hung down over his eyes. Irritatingly, he made little effort to brush it away while talking to me, rendering the sight of his eyes quite an occasion. In retrospect, that hair was just a shield he used to hide his true nature from me.

We started hanging out after school. We lived in the same neighborhood; even rode much the same kind of bike. My father didn't mind too much, as long as I didn't lapse on my studies. Besides, he knew that I had been taught far too well to stray from the righteous path.

One blazing summer afternoon, Walter and I were lazing around on the hillside, which overlooked the

Castlebrook shopping mall's forecourt. We could sit there for hours, our bikes splayed out on the hill beside us, watching the ants bustle to and fro from their cars, loading up on the latest vehicles for their gluttony. The mall seemed to shimmer in the heat.

"Look at them," I told my friend, nodding down toward the shoppers. "They're so pathetic."

A pause. "Who?" he asked, speaking through the single reed of grass, which poked out from between his teeth. For an intelligent child, Walter was often very slow on the uptake. Deliberately so, I often suspected.

"Them." I stabbed a finger down toward the forecourt, a hot feeling growing in my stomach. "It's just greed upon greed, Walt."

"I think the mall's kinda cool."

Before I could turn and put him right, as I already had on numerous matters of the world, he sat up, his face suddenly shot through with glee.

"Hey, I made out with Betsy Goldman."

He grinned, expecting the same reaction back. Thinking fast, with the hot feeling inside reaching meltdown proportions, I gave him what he wanted. "Way to go, man," I said, slapping one palm against his. "What, exactly, did you... uh, do?"

"We kissed, and she let me touch her tits. And... other stuff, for a while, before she stopped me."

Right there, right then, I felt like ramming my fingers through Walter Cusp's stupid, wide eyes and tugging out his diseased brain. We were kids. This idiot couldn't even keep his sins under control until he reached his teenage years; not that there was *ever* any justification for that kind of business, outside of holy matrimony.

Instead of killing him, I smirked back, like the average young boy might.

I smirked, filed away the information and consciously cooled that anger in my guts. I would bide my time.

The Weinhard mine system, I discovered in the local rag, was to be reopened. No doubt to be transformed into some gaudy rollercoaster, rather than being used for its original purpose. Anyway, work had already begun.

One day, toward the end of summer, I showed Walter the page that I'd torn from dad's newspaper. We sat on the edge of a fast flowing river, as the horizon slowly dirtied, transforming from pure blue to angry orange. Since Walter made his unwelcome revelation, we hadn't hung out so much. Whereas we would normally ride our bikes two or three times a week, I saw him once a fortnight. Walter seemed puzzled by this change, but at that age you don't ask friends why they've cooled off on you. The slut Betsy Goldman had also cooled off on Walter; hearing that stories had begun to circulate about her virtue, or lack of it, she refused to so much as look at the boy.

Walter stared at the monochrome photograph of the mine's front entrance. "Cool," he whispered.

"Bet there's treasure in there," I said, casually, gazing at the sunset's intense glare.

"Even cooler," he grinned. "Let's go in and get it."

"Don't be stupid," I said, feigning shock, as though the idea had never occurred to me. "We can't do that. *Can* we?"

Walter is walking ahead of me, in a corridor hewn from black rock. The only light comes from our torches. The mine is closed for the night, but has been very badly secured. Two skinny kids like us are making short work of edging past all these hastily nailed planks and signs.

Whenever Walter turns to make sure I'm still there—I'm being unusually quiet, for some reason—I see excitement flickering in his eyes. No, scratch that. Not excitement: greed. The boy is a sinner, both in terms of material goods and pleasures of the flesh. This reminder only serves to strengthen my resolve.

We've ventured quite a way down into the mine, along sloping, low ceiling tunnels, which seem to be solely propped up by thick wooden posts. Every once in a while, a piece of rock will fall from the ceiling and we hesitate, half expecting the whole shebang to come down on our heads.

"How will we know, when we find the treasure?" wonders Walter, still ahead of me, his back shining brightly as it takes the brunt of my torch glow. He hangs a right. Peering beyond him, I see that the tunnel ends, maybe fifteen feet ahead.

Walter's eyesight is less acute than mine, so he keeps walking. I remain at the junction, guiding my torch upwards to study a wooden prop and its relationship with the cracked ceiling.

Walter's voice, which is several feet away, says, "Looks like a blind alley, huh?"

I take a step back, then swing my right foot, slamming it into the wooden post with every ounce of strength I can muster. This kick is so triumphant, it's as if some kind of higher agency is flowing through me.

The post snaps away from the ceiling and I stagger backwards, throwing myself out of the way. The ceiling piles in immediately, as do large portions of the walls. A glimpse of Walter's shocked face, made even more pallid by his torchlight. Then rock and rising clouds of dust replace it.

I pick myself up and inspect the damage. The fallen rock is so dense that I can barely hear Walter Cusp's screams. When I was younger, dad showed me how to bury live rats in the larger size matchboxes. Walter's pathetic mewls take me back to those happy days.

As I make my way back up through the mine, I kick another two posts down behind me, just for good measure. Don't want anyone opening the tomb too soon, after all.

Just over two hours later, I'm back home, my face a mess of soot and tears. A police officer is sitting at our kitchen table, gazing at me sympathetically.

"We were looking for treasure," I stutter. "Walter ran into a wooden post and the ceiling... the *ceiling*..."

I stop short and cry my heart out like the pain is simply too much.

Walter Cusp: you could have been my friend forever. But no. You *had* to go and burn in Hell.

TEN

"It may not be my place to say this, Ed, but..." Van Stadt's voice trailed off. Daimler watched the side of her face, feeling tense as he waited for her to say it. Whatever "it" turned out to be, he would naturally deny everything. He was functioning perfectly well and there was no problem at all.

They would soon arrive in the Crystal Lake area and face the task of searching various motels and hotels. Daimler just wanted to get on with it. He didn't need an inquisition from an agent almost two decades his junior.

The rest of her sentence didn't arrive. He surprised himself by deciding to push her.

"What, Mel? But what?"

"I can't help feeling that your professional judgment is starting to waver. Let's put it like that."

Daimler swallowed. She was right, but to admit it would be a disaster. So he switched to defensive mode. "I've no idea what you mean."

"I can smell the liquor," she said, sending a chill up his spine. "Ed, I've smelt it all day. Why do you think I've insisted on driving? It's not because I enjoy notching up the miles."

The car fell silent again. He wondered whether, if he continued to stare ahead of him, her accusation might somehow be forgotten. Lost in the traffic.

"If you don't want to talk about it, I understand. But it's worrying me. After all, partners are supposed to depend on each other. My life could rest on you being together. And I'm not sure—"

The sentence didn't need a second half.

Daimler cleared his throat. "Look, Mel, it's like this. I'm under a lot of pressure with this case," he said. "To tell you the truth, I've been under a lot of pressure for some time now. You solve one case and along comes another. The better you are, the more police departments need your help. I find it real difficult to turn them down."

To his surprise, van Stadt didn't give him a face full of venom, by way of reply. For perhaps the first time, her eyes showed some kind of emotion. Daimler was unsure whether it was sympathy or pity.

"I can imagine that scenario," she said. "How do you say 'no' when your assistance might prevent a killer from taking more lives? At the academy, they warned us about the dangers of becoming too involved with your work. It's very dangerous, as you know."

Daimler nodded. He looked down to see one of her hands resting on his right thigh.

A small, imaginary electrical current shot through him.

Van Stadt seemed to realize what she was doing, and withdrew the hand. Silence reigned once again.

"It's... a fine line," said Daimler.

Van Stadt nodded. She had switched back to her cool, professional default setting. He looked at her quizzically, wondering what just happened. That was the first time she had ever touched him, since they initially shook hands.

Halo had stopped running. She was lying on the ground, curled up into a fetal position, sobbing into both palms. She had dimly heard Trey's screams and knew only too well what they meant. He was gone, forever. Even though she knew that she couldn't have prevented his death, she remained wracked with guilt. For all his imperfections, he had saved her life back there. She had rewarded him by blindly charging off into the woods.

She wondered if Shona and Basket were safe. Everything had been such a blur when the man-child marched into their lives, that she had no idea what had happened to them. They could have been slain by the giant. Or they might be hiding in the trees, just like her.

The ground felt cold against the side of her face, but she cared little. She was concentrating on trying to control her tears and breathing, in order to make as little noise as possible. Surely, if she kept quiet, the chances of the man-child finding her were remote. She prayed also that the terrible screams in the campsite would have already drawn the police, who would come to their aid.

In the back of her head, there was a horrible fear that, even if the police *did* arrive, the man-child would be too much for them to handle. There was something about the way he moved—and particularly the way that his torn body had obviously been through numerous wars—which told Halo he was no longer human, if indeed he ever had been.

Then it struck her: the legend of Jason Voorhees, the boy who drowned in Crystal Lake, back in 1957. Various scare stories had been doing the rounds for as long as she had been alive, about how he was a grown man, a hateful demon, relentlessly seeking revenge for both his own death and that of his mother. Halo shuddered at the memory of the tale: his mother's head had been hacked off in 1979 by a camp councilor, who then herself was murdered.

This couldn't really be Jason Voorhees. Could it? He was supposed to wear precisely that kind of mask, though, wasn't he?

These thoughts made her shake. She wanted to scream her brains loose: purge all the revulsion from her system. Instead, she had to keep it all in or die. It was a simple enough choice, but the pressure was starting to make her crazy.

All around her, the woods stood silent, as if nothing untoward had happened. Still breathing too quickly—it was starting to make her feel faint—she looked around her. Thin traces of moonlight filtered down, illuminating the odd branch, bough or bush. In some ways, the light was comforting. In others, it was a liability: the more light that surrounded her, the more chance there was of the madman closing in.

The small glimpses of forest were also starting to play tricks with her head: at one point, she thought she saw *that* mask staring blankly down at her. In fact, it was two knot holes in a gnarled trunk.

Slowly, the cold began to register. She had initially been shaking because of the fear. The effect was amplified by the frigid climate, away from the safety of the fire.

Safety—what a joke.

Then she remembered the Camaro, the battered shit heap that seemed, in her mind, to be a golden chariot of the gods. If she could get back to it, she might... No, it was Duke's car and his keys were lying somewhere out among these trees, wherever he had been slaughtered.

She needed to stay there and somehow live through the night. Then, by dawn, perhaps the man-child would have gone, or she could find the keys, or the police would have taken care of everything. Perhaps.

She pulled herself into a tighter ball.

Then she heard the noises. A series of crackling thumps, at once the sound of snapping twigs and disturbed undergrowth.

They were footsteps and they were nearby.

Worst of all, they were getting closer.

Bill Behler's mouth opened wide, his eyes shot through with shock. The knife had entered through the back of his head, the tip poking out through his mouth. The blood-slick blade had wedged itself between two of his front teeth.

This was not the way he had intended the evening to swing. Behler and his two colleagues, whom he referred to as Halverson and McCrimmon, had wandered out of the hotel's bar, through reception and out into the pleasantly lit gloom. Alcohol surged through their blood streams, although Behler seemed the worse for wear, as was generally the way. He jumped up onto the hotel's phoenix fountain and momentarily swung from one of the giant bird's metallic wings, before Halverson and McCrimmon each grabbed a leg and persuaded him to come down. Not a moment too soon, either, as a burly security guard had seen him climbing and was about to reprimand them.

As Behler hit the gravel once again, he looked at his hands, dismayed. Both palms were sore and reddened, the flesh on one having received an inch-long tear. "That thing's sharp," he said, rubbing his palms together, smearing blood between them. "I could sue those bastards."

Garry Halverson, an excessively tall, gruff looking man with an expertly trimmed moustache, slapped him on the back. "Damn straight. You should have the right to swing on that thing like a fucking crazy person, without coming to grief. I say we speak to Mr Soames, tonight. See if he'll represent your case."

"You'll get nae sense out of Soames tonight," said James McCrimmon, a rotund, fair-haired Scot who had made the big move from Glasgow to Philadelphia the previous year. "He was already on the brandy when we left."

"When is he not on the brandy?" said Behler, studying his palms. "The guy keeps that stuff in his desk drawer. Thank God I'm so drunk I can't feel a thing."

"A little bit of the demon weed should help, too," said McCrimmon. "It's a healing thing, man. Natural shit."

As the three men attempted to walk in straight lines, out of the hotel's grounds, they lapsed into debate about exactly which one of them was carrying the dope. Confusion reigned, until Halverson finally discovered the small, green package in his suit's breast pocket. They roared in celebration as Phoenix Heights's well presented drive surrendered to the woods.

"We should go down to the water," offered McCrimmon. "The lake. How far is it?"

"I have no idea," said Behler, steadying himself against a tree, then wincing as the bark chafed his cut palm. "Let's just walk for a while, then get some smoke happening. I don't want to be too far from the hotel bar."

"Good point," said McCrimmon.

The three of them were slowly navigating a well-trodden path, lit at regular intervals by lamps attached to the tops of tall poles. The buzzing of crickets filled the air. Fireflies darted tirelessly around the lights.

"What a beautiful summer's night," said Behler. "We are lucky cats."

At this, Halverson abruptly stopped walking. He was frowning. "Look, Bill," he said, "I think you're a cool guy and everything, but do you *really* have to say 'cats' all the time?"

Behler appeared confused, as though realizing only now that he used the expression. "Wow," he said. "Er, no problem."

"Cool," said Halverson, slapping Behler on the back so hard that the younger man took a few involuntary steps forward. "Now let's smoke some herb."

Within minutes, they located a spot just off the beaten track, which still enjoyed some illumination from nearby lamps. The crickets' clicking was louder here, but none of the men paid it much attention. They were too busy sitting in their triangle, fumbling with papers and their cigarette lighter that didn't work.

"Fuck," said Halverson, shaking the thing in his oversized hand and attempting once again to ignite it. Nothing happened. "Does no one else really have a lighter?"

He watched as the other two men shook their heads. "Shit!" he growled, hurling the lighter to one side. "What does a guy have to do to get a smoke around here?"

"Ask two strangers for a light?"

This male voice did not belong to Behler, Halverson or McCrimmon. They turned to see two people, cutting elegant silhouettes against the lamplights.

"Hi there," said Halverson, as they all placed one hand over their eyes, attempting to get a better view of the newcomers. They didn't look like cops. "Do you, uh, have a cigarette lighter, by any chance?"

A cute giggle revealed that the male newcomer's companion was a lady. The strangers meandered over to join the drunkards, shadows playing over their faces until they were up close. Finally, they sat down, smiling amiably as the triangle became a pentagon.

"I think you guys are having a little smoke," said Penelope, waggling a finger with what the three men assumed to be mock reproach. "What is it?"

"Just good herb, ma'am," said Behler, raising one eyebrow and smirking in a manner which he imagined made himself look desirable. "Just good herb." He looked at his colleagues, to see that each of them was attempting to make eyes with this lady, whether her husband was watching or not. This, he realized, was not a good strategy if they were to gain fire from these people. He turned his attention to Norwood, who was sitting cross-legged, his hands on his knees.

"Are you, er, guys, here on vacation?"

"We surely are," said Penelope, gesturing back over her own shoulder. "We're staying at the Phoenix Heights hotel, a way back there."

"So are we," Halverson told her, blowing her a little kiss.

"Are you coming on to my wife, sir?" asked Norwood, still smiling.

"No, not at all," said Halverson hurriedly. He was clearly so drunk that he imagined that he could blow the kiss without anyone else noticing. "I mean, she is beautiful, but I'm sure she's more than happy with you."

"Indeed she is," said Norwood, fishing around in the inside pocket of his immaculate suit. "But we have an open relationship, gentlemen. If my wife chooses to sleep with any of you later on, she will do so with my blessing."

Three pairs of eyes goggled back at Norwood. "Now," he said, producing a lighter. "Shall we spark up?"

"Can't think of a reason why not," said Halverson, taking the precious device from the older man.

The conversation progressed awkwardly from there, as the joint was constructed. Time and again, the newcomers seemed far more interested in asking questions than answering any which the trio directed at them.

A plume of smoke sailed out of Halverson's mouth after he took the first drag. Then he passed it to Norwood, who also partook.

Penelope was walking slowly around the group, talking as she did so. At first, the three Entraxx men didn't pay much attention—two of them were more interested in exactly when the joint might arrive—but her words slowly started to filter through. She had changed tone, no question.

"How would you say this contributes to your lives, gentlemen?" she was asking.

They exchanged surprised, worried glances. McCrimmon spluttered, then unleashed a rasping cough, holding the joint at arm's length away from his face.

"It's a reasonable enough question, surely," said Norwood, not visibly affected by his own tokes. "Can nobody answer it?"

"Helps us chill out," shrugged Behler, finally. "We all work hard."

"It's hardly natural, though, is it?" said Penelope. "Or, to put it a different way, it's abusing a natural substance to cloud your brain."

McCrimmon turned and handed Penelope the smoking joint. "I'm not being funny, love, but you should maybe try some."

Penelope held it between her lips and drew the smoke in, then blew out. "You're right," she said. "It does relax a person. It's relaxed us, hasn't it darling?"

"Oh yes," her partner smiled.

"So we'll kill you relatively quickly," she said. "Keep the suffering short."

The hazy smoke cloud that surrounded the trio, seemed to act as a time buffer, so that her words took extra long to sink in. There was a muffled explosion.

McCrimmon toppled forward and slammed into the dirt, the top half of his head destroyed by a single bullet. Penelope stood behind him, the barrel of her gun smoking steadily. The joint was still in her hand. Regarding the horrified survivors emotionlessly, she took her second draw on it.

"Right," said Norwood, standing up and brushing himself down. Behler and Halverson saw that he was holding a knife, the seven or eight inch blade shining dully in this light. He gestured to Halverson. "Take this."

Shocked into silence, Halverson took the offered knife by the handle, aware that Penelope was pointing the gun at him.

"Stand behind your friend here," said Norwood. "Now, stick the knife through his brain stem."

Down there on the ground, Behler resembled a petrified statue. He couldn't move or speak. He could barely think about anything other than escape. Yet Penelope's gun could just as easily be turned on him as on Halverson. These people were obviously insane.

Halverson was looking at Norwood. "Stick the knife...?"

"Through his brain stem," Norwood patiently repeated.

"You'd gladly hand him this," said Penelope, holding up the joint. "What's the difference? Both interfere with the brain."

"But that wouldn't kill him," protested Halverson, pointing at the spliff.

"Ah," she sneered. "Short term, long term. Whatever." She moved closer to Halverson and hefted the gun directly at his head. "Now do it."

Halverson was trembling, just as Behler was. He raised the blade in his hand, his wide eyes fixed on the premature bald patch on the back of Behler's head.

"Please," Behler managed to say. "Just let us go. We've hardly seen your faces."

"Sorry," said Norwood. "That changes nothing. Our time is running out. You'll probably be two of our last converts. Wonder who'll play you in the movie, hmmm?"

Another explosion. Halverson jerked away from the gun, one side of his head blackened and torn. He hit the ground with a gasp.

"That's another thing about dope smokers," said Penelope, bending down to take the knife from Halverson's dead fingers. "It takes so long for them to complete the most menial task."

She rammed the blade through the back of Behler's skull.

* * *

Halo devoted every ounce of concentration to remaining still and silent. The footsteps emanated from the undergrowth directly behind her. She had no way of looking back over her shoulder without repositioning herself and making unwise noise.

He's found you, her paranoia warned. He's just toying with you. Run, while you still can. You were stupid not to run and run, in the first place.

Halo tensed her muscles, ready to tear off through the woods if the killer got too close. A hissing whisper broke the silence. She frowned and turned her head slightly, listening hard. It came again.

"Halo?"

This time, she heard. The voice was easily recognizable.

"Shona," she whispered immediately, turning around and standing up, feeling her neglected ligaments creak. "Yeah, it's me, Halo."

Shona let out as quiet a relieved exclamation as possible, as she lurched the remaining few feet to embrace her friend. They clutched each other, both breathing hard. The pungent smell of urine told Halo precisely how scared Shona was.

"Halo, he killed Trey. He killed him."

"I know. I kind of saw it. Where's Basket?"

"Don't know. I heard him yelling. Oh, Jesus Christ. Who is that guy? Do you think he's still looking for us?"

Halo answered both questions with a pained shrug. "I think we should stay here and wait until dawn."

Shona seemed horrified. "Dawn? That's about eight or nine hours away, at the very least. My God,

Halo, I'll either freeze to death or die of fright before dawn."

"Okay. What do you suggest?"

"We go back to the campsite, get in the Camaro and drive the fuck out. I would've done it already, but I didn't have the guts, on my own."

Halo rolled her eyes. As if two pregnant women would have any more of a chance against this bastard than one. Still, at least Shona's plan was proactive. People had spent years telling Halo she needed to be more proactive, to the point where she had to look the term up in a school dictionary. Maybe they had a point.

"What about the keys?" she asked Shona.

"Screw the keys. I can hot-wire."

"You can?"

"Sure. Me and Basket have stolen a car. Or two."

Halo was about to give Shona the third degree, for both stealing cars and not telling her about it, when priorities gripped her once again. She merely nodded. "Fine. We'll try it."

The women each took a step back and bleakly surveyed the surrounding panorama of gray and black smudges.

Halo rubbed her upper arms. "Which way? I'm lost."

Shona was concentrating hard. She pointed behind Halo. "That way. I'm pretty sure. It ain't far."

Halo swallowed hard. "Okay, then. You'd better be right about being able to hot-wire, though."

"Honey, we've done plenty of 'em. Where else do you think we get money? Let's go."

Halo felt as though the woods had tightened like a stricken heart muscle. Overhanging branches seemed designed to ensnare them and scratch flesh, while mangled roots did their utmost to trip them.

Shona walked ahead, acting as a guinea pig for noisy twigs or obstacles, which Halo then did her best to avoid. The pair regularly stopped in their tracks and cocked ears, listening out for irregularities in the woodland soundscape. None came. As they drew closer to what Shona assured her was the campsite clearing, Halo felt thrilled by the thought of escape, terrified by the idea of bumping into the fiend again and nauseous at the prospect of seeing dead loved ones.

Further along whichever twisted track they were negotiating, Shona finally turned to Halo. "We're here. This is the campsite."

Halo took a step to one side, attempting to look past Shona.

She winced as something crunched underfoot.

They froze like prey and didn't move again until they were convinced that the darkness offered no danger.

Over Shona's shoulder was indeed the campsite. The moon illuminated it dimly. Halo shuddered as her eyes began to discern the jagged outline of something burnt in the clearing's centre. Knowing these to be the remains of her dead boyfriend, she wrenched her gaze away.

"Let's walk across," said Shona. "The car's on the other side."

Halo closed her eyes and shook her head decisively. "I can't walk across there. Trey's there. Duke, too. Or *part* of..." She found the sentence too horrible to finish.

For a few seconds, the reality of the situation was vivid to Halo, like a picture coming into focus. Duke's head had been cut off, and Trey had been burned alive. Only God knew what terrible fate had befallen Basket. She hurriedly shook off these thoughts. They were too big for her to take in. Not yet. If they ever got home, she might be able to start dealing with this stuff. As much as it went against her nature, it was time to concentrate on their own lives. All four of them, she thought, snaking a protective hand across her belly.

"But the trees are hard to walk through," Shona was saying, her voice barely audible. "It'll take too long."

"How do you know the killer's not sitting in that clearing, waiting for us? How much of it can we see?"

Halo saw the silhouette of Shona's hand reaching up to clasp her own mouth. She clearly hadn't considered this possibility.

They stood at the campsite's perimeter for some time, peering through the half darkness. Halo felt even more vulnerable than she had, when curled up back there in the undergrowth. At least she'd had cover. Maybe being proactive wasn't always the way to go.

A compromise struck her. "Why don't we just walk around the edge?" she whispered.

Shona thought about this for a second. Then she completed a shadowy nod.

The women stepped cautiously out onto the clearing's edge. They looked at each other nervously, then began to make their way around the perimeter.

Halo could smell charred flesh. She stopped in her tracks and clasped one hand over her eyes. Hot tears dribbled through and over her fingers.

Shona's face was a strange mixture of sympathy and desperation. "Halo, shush," she whispered. "I know how you feel, but we have to be as quiet as we can and move fast."

Halo wiped her eyes and took a deep breath. Shona grabbed her hand and guided her along. Soon, they were on the opposite side of the clearing.

Something moved in the trees above them. A heavy rustle. They looked upwards, their faces ashen and shocked. Birds exploded through the branches and out into the air.

Halo clutched her chest. She could swear that her heart was going to burst loose. Shona tightened the grip on her hand and dragged her along behind her.

"There's the car," she said. "There it is."

Halo managed a half smile as they walked side by side, heading toward the vehicle. They could see the Camaro's profile, no more than ten feet away, on that dirt track, just off the clearing.

As clouds shifted, the moonlight intensified, revealing the dim outline of a man.

Jason's mask glinted like a warning beacon. He was standing in front of the Camaro, his wedge-like feet planted shoulder-width apart.

Looking straight at them.

Halo jumped twice. Firstly, at the sight of him. Secondly, because Shona had broken the silence with an ear-splitting scream. She spoke in a high-pitched babble.

"Jesus Christ! Run like hell. Along the fucking road!"

Shona broke into a sprint, heading toward the dirt track. Halo immediately followed suit, more scared than she had ever been. In retrospect, all those nights when Trey had beaten on her resembled walks in the park.

Jason scanned the women's progress as they ran.

Finally, he strode away from the Camaro, following them along the track. Something sharp glistened in one of his fists.

Melissa van Stadt's head craned back, allowing Ed Daimler to bury his face in her neck, covering it with slow kisses. Her breathing rate increased, her fingernails scratching at his chest through the material of his shirt.

They were in the back of the car, pawing at each other without any regard for who might see them. The truck stop was almost empty, save for a couple of juggernauts. Steam from a trucker's coffee flask curled upwards through one of the windows.

The two FBI agents weren't paying any attention to their surroundings. Passion had detonated: all they could think about was scratching their collective itch. Daimler hurriedly unbuttoned the top three buttons of his colleague's shirt, then ripped the rest. The tiny plastic discs hurtled through the air in various directions, clacking off the Lincoln's windows.

He kissed her hungrily, then slid his mouth down to her breasts, which heaved out of the bra he'd been eyeing all day. She gasped, clutching the sides of his head.

It seemed she was losing control of herself. Good. All Daimler could think about was her. Fuck the case. Fuck everything else in the world. And most importantly, fuck her.

With one spare hand, he undid his pants, easing them down. Then he set about removing the lower half of her suit.

"Oh yeah," she said, opening her eyes. "Take 'em off. I want it."

She lifted her well-defined legs into the air, the pads of her feet curling against the roof. Daimler couldn't wait any longer. Tearing off her black G-string, he fell into the sweetest, most mind-blowing haze he had ever known.

The car phone's loud ring snapped Daimler back to reality. He had been staring out of the window, mesmerized by the white lines that flashed to one side of the Lincoln. His eyes darted around as he cursed to himself. For one second there, he had been *living* that scene. He crossed one leg over the other in an attempt to hide the evidence.

Van Stadt, still at the wheel, was staring at him. "You going to answer that?"

He held the bulky phone next to his head, trying to screw his professional head back on.

"Daimler."

He listened for a whole minute. Van Stadt occasionally glanced over, trying to read his expression. He gave her no clues.

"Great," he finally said. "Fax the pictures and profiles over now. And fax another copy to the sheriff's department at Crystal Lake."

As he deactivated the phone, a grim smile split his face. "There was saliva inside Katherine Banks's mouth," he said. "Dunvey ran a DNA test and he's got a ninety-five percent positive ID."

"Who is it?"

"A female. Name of Penelope Thawn, originally Stanton. She's married, Mel."

Van Stadt shook a triumphant fist. "Knew it."

ELEVEN

"Alrighty, good people of Entraxx. Just to let you know that Ballroom B will be ready shortly. Apparently, there was some problem with the preparation. Typical, huh?"

The big, jovial man with the mass of broken blood vessels on his nose was Cary Carson, the Entraxx bigwig who had assumed Larry Bruckenheim's party hosting duties. After all, the big cheese hadn't been seen for hours. Rumors put it down to him having sloped off with a hot blonde.

Tom Sheridan felt his surroundings shift, as though he was momentarily underwater. He wasn't a great drinker at the best of times, but had sunk several beers. Anything to numb the growing dread he was feeling. It had been a while since he had suffered one of his panic attacks—at least two years back, in a Chicago shopping mall—but anxiety was, for some reason, beginning to well up inside him. It was the feeling that something absolutely terrible was going to happen, even though he had no idea what.

Perhaps it was Greg, he told himself. There was a real confrontation brewing between the two of them, despite his attempts to defuse it earlier in the evening. Yes that's all it was: a tightening of the gut, preparing for conflict. The fight or flight impulse, in advance.

April slapped one palm on his right shoulder, in order to steady herself.

"You drunk, April?" he asked.

"No. Just a little tired."

Great, he thought. Another classic April Mather performance coming right up.

The world thrashed up and down, whipping itself into a blur of greens, blacks and golden yellows. The latter color was provided by the lamps which lined the track.

As she ran, Halo's heart seemed to thump her under the chin. Shona ran ahead. The two of them had been running for a straight ten minutes, aiming simply to cover maximum ground.

The last time they dared to pause and look behind them, had been about two minutes into this insane sprint. Halo shuddered as she remembered gazing back along the track and seeing that mask as the psycho walked into sight around a bend. There was no real urgency in his stride, but his body language bled determination. She and Shona knew that this bastard wouldn't rest until both of them were dead.

Halo thought there must be at least half a mile between them. Then it happened: one moment, Shona was sprinting ahead of Halo, the next, she was screaming in agony as she piled forward into the dirt. Halo narrowly escaped running directly into her friend.

Halo saw that Shona had tripped over a rock that jutted cruelly out of the ground. For a split second, she couldn't resist gazing back along the shaded track. It stretched back a good distance and there was no sign of their hunter.

Shona was clutching her right calf with both hands, face distorted, teeth shining white. "Please don't be broken, please don't be broken..."

"You haven't broken your leg, Shona. That can't have happened. Come on, we've got to keep going."

She grasped her friend's armpits, hauling her upwards.

"Oh fuck," said Shona, saliva dripping onto her T-shirt. "That hurts."

"Lean on me," said Halo. "We've got to move until we find help."

"I don't know how far I *can* move." Shona cautiously tried to take a few paces, as Halo moved anxiously beside her, then screwed her face up again. "Fuck, I must have pulled a muscle."

She turned to face Halo, making direct eye contact. "In these kind of situations, I know that I'm supposed to tell you to go ahead and save yourself. Well, please don't do that, girl. I don't want to die."

"I won't leave you," Halo insisted. "But we can't just stand here."

The trail behind him remained static. No movement. She fully expected the relentless freak to stalk into view. Being sure to maintain her grip on Shona, she looked around them. This wretched track was flanked by much the same dense greenery as they had seen anywhere else. Then something caught Halo's eye: a yellow glow in the near distance. It was so faint that Halo initially thought it might be a torch, but it wasn't moving. With her free arm, she pointed. "Look."

"What do you think that is?" breathed Shona.

"I don't know," said Halo. "But it's not on this damn path. We need to get off. Maybe that's a house. We could use the phone."

"Let's go. I can do this."

Halo practically dragged her friend with her. Shona kept up the pace, her brow dripping sweat.

They headed directly toward the light, leaving the track and experiencing the now-familiar assault of wicked branches and leaves.

"How you doing?" she asked Shona. "My God, your..." She stopped herself.

"My what?"

"Your... baby."

"Oh, don't worry about that."

If Halo's face was not being lashed, she would have thrown her friend a puzzled frown. As it was, she ignored the comment and continued her efforts to support half of Shona's weight, while hauling her through the trees. She felt exhausted, but had no intention of allowing this to stop her. They had to get out of here alive. For a second, she wondered about her own child, then told herself that a little running wasn't about to harm it. Her thoughts turned unwillingly to the maniac. Would he show mercy if he knew they were pregnant? Might be worth trying, if it came down to the wire.

The yellow light steadily grew closer. They would soon be there, wherever *that* might be.

Melissa van Stadt almost managed a chuckle. "Have you used one of these machines before, Ed?"

They were in the forecourt of another gas station. She paced up and down by the Lincoln, while her colleague knelt outside the right-hand door, his upper half disappearing inside. Every few seconds, he uttered a new, frustrated profanity.

"I *said*..." began van Stadt. At this, Daimler withdrew his head from the vehicle. His face shone with perspiration, even though the temperature had dropped considerably.

"I heard what you said, Mel. I can use a fax machine, yes. It's installing the damn thing that's the motherfucker." His head dropped back out of sight. "But, no thanks to you, I think I've done it."

Van Stadt rolled her eyes and folded her arms, leaning back against the car. "Great. Now let's see what these people look like."

A window: that's where the light had been coming from, Halo realized, with something approaching relief. They were approaching a small log cabin.

"That looks good," said Shona, her voice shot through with more than a little hysteria. "Am I imagining things, or does that look good?"

"It does. But is anyone home? There's only one little light on."

"I couldn't care less whether anyone's home or not, as long as there's a phone in there."

"Let's not get too excited," said Halo. Inside, however, she couldn't help but hope."

The green tangle of the woods reluctantly freed the pair and they stumbled across open, grassy ground. "Hey," said Shona as they drew near. "Isn't that the front door? Isn't it open?"

The cabin and its surroundings were bathed in light from some new source. Halo involuntarily covered her pained eyes, causing Shona to slip over. Halo bent down to help her. Then Shona screamed, pointing away from the cabin.

Halo squinted over across the grass to see what looked like a corpse. As she grew accustomed to the light, she saw that the poor bastard was once a cop. Was his head missing? No, it seemed to have rammed down into his body. Flies had gathered, crawling over the discolored flesh. Halo felt sick.

"Oh Jesus," said Shona, as Halo helped her to her feet. "I think there's another one."

Two feet poked out of the open cabin door, their owner out of sight inside.

Shona lowered her voice. "What if *he's* in there? What if he's somehow got here first and is in there, waiting for us?"

"That's impossible. We ran like crazy and he was walking. And I'm no expert, but that body looks like it's been there a while. Let's get inside."

As they slowly made their way toward the front door, Halo spied the security lamp, which had been activated, revealing the bodies.

The corpse in the doorway came into view: a fifty-something man, lying flat on his back in fishing garb. A rod lay beside him in two pieces. What really drew the pair's attention, however, was the circular saw that sat upon his chest, half of the blade clearly buried inside him. His face was purple.

Halo couldn't hold the vomit down any longer. Twisting herself away from Shona, who grabbed the front door's frame, she bent double and emptied her stomach. As she recovered, tears stinging her eyes, Shona followed suit.

"We've got to get inside," Halo said. "Come on. We've just got to step over him."

Shona leant on Halo once again, and they stepped awkwardly over the body and into the cabin's gloom. They stood directly over the corpse. Some insane part of Halo's imagination half expected those eyes to open and the saw to start revving. The light they originally saw had come from one of the rear rooms, and it was no good to them right now. The room they were entering was lit only by the security light outside. Whole sections of it were steeped in darkness.

"Where's the light switch?" asked Shona, searching the wall with an urgency bordering on blind panic.

Halo ran her hand along the wall behind the front door. She found a switch and flicked it. Nothing happened.

"Damn," she whispered, almost not wanting to tell Shona the bad news.

Then the ceiling appeared, lit by intermittently flickering tubes of light, which eventually solidified, revealing the room's entirety. Halo was relieved to see that they were the only people there. Aside from their dead friend, of course.

Shona used various items of furniture as props, in order to negotiate her way around the room. "Where's the fucking phone?"

Halo looked first at the open front door, then the body. She took in a deep breath, positioned herself behind the corpse and stooped over it.

"What are you doing?" Shona was staring at her, momentarily distracted from her frenzied phone hunt.

"We've got to get this door shut," said Halo. "Just ignore me for a moment, would you?"

She bent down and gripped the corpse's hands.

She had held dead hands before—her own mother's, when she had lay there in the open coffin, for what remained of the Harlan family to inspect. She had looked so peaceful, but Halo knew there was nothing left inside. Those hands felt so cold. No doubt they were all the colder because Halo's father had failed to show at the funeral.

Halo shivered, as though the ice was traveling from the dead man's hands and into her blood stream. She held them tight, then lifted the arms from the floor. They creaked like lengths of timber.

Halo pulled them back over the corpse's head, stretching them until they were taut. Then she dug one foot into the floor and attempted to wrench the body along the floor. At first it seemed to be glued to the wood below, then came loose. Halo growled as she yanked with all her strength, trying to ignore sickening details like the mauve flesh wobbling on the man's face and the blood congealing on the buzz saw's teeth.

"I can't see a phone, Halo. No phone."

"Keep looking."

The corpse's feet were inside the cabin, but those big legs still blocked the doorway. Halo stopped pulling and let the corpse's arms slacken. She sucked in a deep breath and renewed her efforts, wincing as another ligament cracked. Was it hers, or one of the fisherman's?

Behind her, Shona was hobbling around the room's perimeter, peering down the walls. "Still nothing. I don't fucking believe it. What a fucking hillbilly."

"Don't speak ill of the dead." Halo said this despite dearly wishing that this guy hadn't eaten so much during his life.

Outside, the security light went off.

Halo paused, looking out at the clearing, which was a monochrome landscape, splashed with only the occasional sliver of blue from the fluorescent lights. The security light must be on a timer, she figured. Comes on, waits a while, then goes off if there's no further sign of movement, like an automatic traffic light.

With one last heave, she dragged the corpse over to one side of the room. Dropping those hands with a sigh of relief, she walked back and kicked the fishing rod's halves out of the way. Then she grabbed the door.

Was someone standing out there, in the darkness? She could see someone.

She blinked. There was only the same empty patch of land, bordered by those damn trees. Halo shook her head and swung the door, clunking it shut. She saw the empty keyhole. She looked at the fisherman, feeling dread at the thought of having to rifle through his pockets. Then she saw the key, hanging from a hook, to the door's right side.

"Nothing in here," said Shona behind her. "I'll check the bedroom, if there is one. Damn hillbilly bastard..." Her voice dwindled behind Halo, as she left the room.

Halo snatched the key from its hook and shoved it into the lock, twisting it. There was resistance and her heart sank. Then, with some determined jiggling, the key sank in another half inch and the lock submitted. A satisfying *thunk* sounded.

Still, thought Halo, would it be enough against Jason?

Jason?

She frowned at herself for having accepted that this was, indeed, Jason Voorhees. Yet when she really came to think about it, he fitted every single description of the legendary killer. Hopefully, not including his inability to die.

She turned and looked around the room, taking it all in properly for the first time. It was clearly designed for one occupant, as the rocking chair suggested. A heavy wooden dining table held one used coffee cup, a single plate and other china items. A set of bookshelves ran along the west wall, displaying well over a hundred dusty spines. A small, dormant fireplace occupied the east wall, while a tiny kitchenette had been clumsily installed into one back corner.

The two windows were criss-crossed with bars. A couple of firm tugs on one suggested that they didn't open. It was a matter of security, she judged, to stop people precisely like them breaking in. Not that such precautions had prevented the cabin's owner from dying a terrible death. Perhaps it was a bad idea to turn this place into a fortress. They were sitting ducks in here. If Jason could find them. Hopefully, they had given him the slip.

She wondered whether there was a rear exit.

"Halo," yelled Shona, sounding alarmed. Halo flinched, almost having forgotten that she was not alone here.

She ran to the back of the room, pulse pounding, and was faced with two doors. One hung open, revealing an empty bathroom. The light that had signaled them to the cabin was a single bulb, dangling naked. Halo grabbed the other door's handle and pushed.

The bedroom was tiny, with one window, barred like the others. Shona stood wide eyed by a cupboard, clutching what looked like a long, black metallic tube in one hand. As Halo calmed down and walked across the room to her friend, she saw that Shona was holding a double-barreled shotgun.

She winked at Halo.

"This could be useful."

"This will definitely be useful."

Daimler hefted the length of glossy fax paper in one hand, staring intently at the two faces, which stared back at him. Beside him, van Stadt was backing the Lincoln into the parking lot of a compact, rundown motel named Sunny Climes. They had reached the edge of Crystal Lake and, on

Daimler's insistence, "We're going to stop at every damn motel until we find them."

Daimler looked again at Penelope and Norwood Thawn's faces, shaking his head. Such respectable-looking folk. The pair had married only six months ago. She was a socialite from a rich background, while Norwood had been a sixth grade teacher until he was fired, a month ago. According to reports, he had gone nuts, beating one boy in front of the rest of the class. The kid's crime—blasphemy.

The car's engine died. As van Stadt undid her seat belt, he snuck in a quick glance at her breasts. Perk of the job. And mighty perky they were, too.

They exited the vehicle and walked across the pot-holed concrete, which passed for the Sunny Climes' parking lot. Silence hung between them like a curtain. Daimler could tell that van Stadt considered this kind of hands on, door-to-door investigation to be beneath FBI agents, but he didn't much care. Whatever got the job done was wholly appropriate, as far as he was concerned. Besides, the Crystal Lake sheriff's department also had the Thawns' mug shots, and would be conducting their own search. The noose was tightening.

Still, this was set to be one long night.

Fax paper dangling from one hand, he yanked open the motel's front door.

Five minutes later, the pair was back out in the parking lot. Daimler marched back to the Lincoln, while van Stadt shook her head behind him, hands buried deep in the pockets of her long leather coat.

* * *

"So how the hell does this thing work?"

Shona held the weapon uncertainly, its polished barrels glinting like the tears that hugged her cheeks. Shortly after making her discovery, Shona had further noted that this room didn't have a phone either. She had collapsed on the bed, her body wracked with sobs. Halo hadn't known what to do. So she merely leant the shotgun against the wall and sat quietly beside Shona. It wasn't as though she felt that great herself. There came a point when each of them had to maintain their own reserves. Halo surprised herself with this last thought. Such self-preservation was usually alien to her.

Shona was sitting up again, a certain degree of determination back in her eyes. She had clearly never handled a shotgun before, but then neither had Halo. "I don't even know if the damn thing's loaded," she said.

"Just pull the trigger and hope for the best."

"I guess so. How difficult can it be?" Shona leveled the shotgun across the room and cautiously snaked a finger inside the trigger guard. An imaginary light bulb appeared above her head. "Halo, why don't you take the buzz saw, from the dead guy?"

Halo screwed her face up. "Ugh. Can't face yanking it out of him. It was bad enough, holding his damn hands." She decided to change the subject. "What did you mean earlier," she asked, "when you said not to worry about the baby?"

Shona looked at her in a matter-of-fact manner. "I'm not really pregnant."

In any other circumstances, Halo would have been shocked. As it was, with their very lives threatened, a little bit of deception didn't seem so outrageous. Still, she was curious.

"Why did you say you—?"

"Basket's been screwing around on me. I figured that, if I told him I was pregnant, he might come to his senses and stop fucking other women."

Halo's eyes widened. "Or he might have run a mile."

"Oh, never. He always talked about having a kid. He..." Shona stopped, as though realizing she was referring to her boyfriend in the past tense. "My God, I can't believe he's gone." She clasped her temples.

Halo wasn't listening any more. She was gazing over at the bedroom's single window. The curtains weren't entirely drawn. Through the gap, Halo could see that the security light was back on.

"Stay here," she told Shona, who looked up at her alarmed, sensing the tone of her voice.

"What's wrong?"

"Nothing, I hope. But that light's back on, outside. It could be anything. A deer..." Her words came out sounding a great deal more optimistic than she felt.

"Or the cops," offered Shona. "They've got a man down out there, after all."

Halo nodded and left the room. Back in the living area, she realized that they should have kept the lights off and lit candles or something. Still, too late now.

Someone, or something, was out there. Fear ran an icy finger up the length of her spine.

She noticed something dark resting on the kitchenette's surface, appearing out of place beside the shiny cutlery. Darting over, she reached for it.

Her hand came back grasping an eighteen inch machete by the handle. It was an ugly blade, afflicted with rust but patently still sharp enough to do the job. Tiny splinters present along its length suggested that the cabin's owner had used it to chop wood.

The muscles in Halo's arm tensed with the effort of supporting its weight.

She returned to the middle of the room and listened hard. Absolute silence. The sound of nothing was so intense that it almost seemed unnatural. Halo's guts told her that something bad was going to happen. Not even the comfort of clutching a fearsome weapon seemed to ease her dread.

"Hey," hissed a voice, which made her jump half out of her skin, even though it clearly belonged to Shona. "Wait for me. I don't wanna be alone in there."

Halo's friend was leaning against the back wall. The shotgun appeared huge against her small frame. Halo placed her forefinger against her lips, then to her right ear. Using the shotgun as a crutch, Shona made her way to Halo's side. Then they listened: nothing, apart from the sound of Halo's heart beating a steadily rising rhythm. She became so conscious of it; she began to wonder why Shona didn't hear it too. No doubt, she was listening to her own.

Shona wiped her face and turned to Halo, about to speak.

She was cut short by something banging hard against the other side of the door. Despite their best efforts, the women yelled, their nerves cranked too high to suppress the shock.

Shona leveled the shotgun at the door, wormed her finger through the trigger guard and stopped breathing. Halo crossed the floorboards and tugged desperately at a window latch. If Jason really was trying to get in through the front door, they would sure as hell need an alternative escape route. That shotgun mightn't even be loaded.

"Who's there?" called Shona.

Silence for endless, dragging seconds.

A second impact broke the lock with a loud crack.

Halo gasped as the door crashed inwards, revealing Basket standing in the doorway, wide-eyed and covered in blood.

Unable to stop herself, Shona fired the shotgun. The noise punched the women's ear-drums, while the recoil sent Shona stumbling back into the rocking chair.

For a split second, Basket seemed suspended in mid air by invisible wires. The blast sent him hurtling back a distance of ten feet, landing on the grass. The top half of his head, they saw, had been removed by the buckshot's onslaught. Only a jerking jaw remained. A long, deep gash, no doubt rendered by Jason, ran diagonally from his left shoulder to his right hip.

Shona lowered the shotgun and cupped one hand over her mouth, unblinking. She rocked back and forth in the chair. "I saw him, but I was already pulling the trigger," she told Halo, pleading to be understood.

Halo nodded, but she was dumbstruck. She was struggling to think practically. "Let's get out of here, Shona. Right now. Don't even think about what just happened."

Shona was pointing at the door, somehow managing to look even more appalled. Halo was about to repeat her instruction when she followed Shona's gaze.

Jason Voorhees.

His hulking frame entirely blocked the doorway.

Shona shrieked as Jason entered the cabin. His tattered and charred clothing was splashed with blood, both faded and fresh. In his hand was a vicious-looking tent spike, which she guessed had been taken from their campsite. It looked as though it had been dipped in red paint.

The killer's shoulders pumped, his breathing audible even through the mask. He remained mere feet from the doorway, blocking his prey's exit.

Jason looked first at Shona, who was struggling to her feet, wrestling frantically with the shotgun, and then slowly turned to regard Halo. The fluorescent lights rendered his eyeholes impenetrable circles of black and lent his mask an unholy glow.

Time slowed. Halo gripped the machete's handle harder than she had ever held anything before. The women stood apart, forming a triangle with this maniac. He would have to choose which of them to attack first.

Jason stood at one end of the dining table, Halo at the other.

Her thought was eclipsed by another explosion, heralding Shona's second shot.

The blast struck Jason dead centre in the chest, driving him backwards, out onto the porch.

Despite holding little hope for success, Halo seized the end of the table and yanked it upwards, surrendering the china to gravity's pull. It smashed against the floorboards. When the table was vertical, Halo stood between its legs and pushed it over to the door, barricading Jason out. The table was, after all, roughly the same size as the entrance. But it wasn't going to work. She knew that.

Jason shoved the table away from the door with phenomenal force, sending Halo flying across the room. She landed awkwardly, crying out as her lower back made equally raucous complaints. The machete was no longer in her hand: she had no idea where it had ended up.

"Oh fuck," breathed Shona as Jason reappeared, tossing the table aside like a minor irritation. It hammered off a wall and landed on the floor, narrowly missing Halo.

The shotgun hung in Shona's hands: even she knew that there were only two barrels.

Halo watched Jason striding furiously toward Shona. She made a decision: for the first time in her life, she wasn't going to take this shit. No, she would fight back. She would show him. Trey was a bastard, but he didn't deserve to die. Neither did she, Duke, Basket or Shona.

She would show this murdering fuck.

A glance to her left revealed that the machete lay within reach. In a second, its reassuring weight was back in her hand.

Shona shrieked as Jason rounded on her, the tent spike held aloft in one fist.

As Halo ran toward the maniac's right, every cell in her body blazed with fear and anger. She swung the machete with a grunt. To her amazement, it sunk lengthways across Jason's neck.

Jesus. Have I cut his head off?

Shona shrieked again, this time with a hysterical jubilance. Thick black slime oozed from Jason's wound and the tent spike clattered on the ground. His fists opened and closed erratically.

Halo tried to pull the machete's blade out. It stuck fast.

She opted to release the handle, to distance herself from Jason.

The women stared at each other as Jason swayed, then slowly reached up to grab the embedded weapon.

"Run like hell!" said Halo, seeing in Shona's eyes that she would be up to the task, pulled muscle or not. Adrenaline was a great instant Band-aid.

The pair scrambled for the door.

For a split-second they were stuck in its mouth, side by side, resembling dumb cartoon characters. Then they burst out into the open air like champagne corks, their lungs sucking in breaths that they had never expected to take.

Jason's head jerked and twitched as he tugged the machete.

It came loose. More black slime gathered at the neck wound, oozing its way over his shoulder. He turned the machete around in his hands, gazing intently down at it. He firmly gripped the handle with his right fist. Then he walked out of the door, leaving small black dots on the floorboards.

TWELVE

For a while, they stood unnoticed on the campsite's edge. The young boy was the first to spot them. No more than six or seven years old, he was running around the small area clutching a toy airplane, whooping as he made it swoop through great arcs in a make-believe blue sky.

His mother was mousy and middle-aged, her brown hair strangled in a bun on top of her head. She watched him like a hawk, occasionally issuing a warning that he had strayed too close to the modest fire, which they had stoked.

Beside her sat a bespectacled man who looked like an accountant. Nevertheless, they both appeared relatively athletic. A mound of bicycles bore testament to their respect for the endorphin. On the man's knee bounced a girl too young to ride a bike of any description, her face red enough to match her short locks of hair, which sparsely patterned her head.

"Hello," said the boy, staring blankly at the two newcomers who stood on the threshold of his family's space. He uttered the greeting without judgment or suspicion, but curiosity was present in his tone. He had stopped running, but continued to make his airplane perform silent, spectacular feats.

The newcomers stared back. Shadows from the fire danced on their faces, making them distorted and unclear.

Behind the boy, the father stood up, bringing the little girl with him. He peered over the flame, assessing the potential threat.

"Hello, right back at you," said Penelope Thawn.

The father visibly relaxed. "Do we have visitors, Jack?" he called to his son, smiling. Then, with polite concern, "How are you guys doing?"

"We're fine, sir," said another voice, male. "A little cold, perhaps. Mind if we join you by the fire for a minute?"

The parents exchanged glances. They relaxed further, upon seeing that the visitors were well dressed, people of distinction.

"Sure," the father said. "Come on in."

The pair advanced and stood beside Jack. Norwood Thawn grinned down at him. "Is that a Messerschmitt?" he asked, pointing down at the toy.

"Don't know," Jack shrugged. "It's just a plane."

"Just a plane," chuckled Norwood. "Ah, the glorious simplicity of youth." He reached out and ruffled the boy's hair. Then the newcomers walked over to the fire, extending hands to be shaken and offering their names. The father's name was Clark, while the mother was Molly. The little girl's name was left unannounced.

The newcomers sat by the fire, Penelope pausing only to check that the ground wasn't overly unclean. Having completed his airplane piloting duties, Jack joined them by the fire.

"You guys having fun?" asked Norwood, smiling. "Family holiday?"

Clark placed one forefinger on the thin piece of silvery metal that held his spectacle lenses together and pushed them back an inch along his nose. "Sure is. We've been coming here for a while now. Couple years."

"You haven't been put off by all the local stories?" asked Penelope. As she spoke, she leant forward and stared at Molly's hands. The woman was oblivious to this attention. "Jason Voorhees, for instance?"

"Ah," said Molly, with a dismissive sweep of the palm. "Every place has its scary legends, don't it?"

"Yes," said Penelope, "but what if Jason Voorhees isn't a legend? He's still around, isn't he?"

Clark rubbed his chin with one hand, while balancing the child precariously on one knee. "Is he? Can't say I'd heard about that. Has it been in the papers?"

"Well, it's more of an opinion than anything else," said Penelope. "I just wouldn't want you good people to come to any harm."

Jack looked up at Clark. "Who's Jason Foordeed?" Clark merely placed a hand on Jack's shoulder and laughed softly.

A pregnant pause formed in the air.

Penelope pointed to Molly's hands. "That's a beautiful ring. You guys been married long?"

Clark slung an arm around Molly and squeezed her shoulder. "Almost ten years, this fall. Pretty good, huh?"

Penelope grinned. "And are these both your kids? I mean you had them together?"

Seemingly unaffected by the directness of Penelope's question, the couple nodded. "For our sins," laughed Molly, inclining her head toward Clark's.

"That's fantastic," said Penelope, holding her hands up by the fire and rubbing them together. "These days, the family unit has taken quite a bashing, hasn't it?"

"Yep," nodded Clark. "I believe in family. Always have, always will."

"Good man," said Norwood, slowly rising to his feet. For a second, the family saw flames reflected in his eyes. The little girl started crying, for the first time.

Norwood turned away. He stooped and extended a hand that Penelope took, gracefully standing back up.

"Thank you for your hospitality," said Norwood, waving farewell. "We must resume our stroll."

"Good night," smiled Penelope.

Clark, Molly and Jack bade them goodnight. Then, still hand in hand, the Thawns walked off into the darkness.

Halo and Shona had been running for less than two minutes when one fact became painfully clear: adrenaline could only carry a wounded party so far.

Shona began to hobble wildly and Halo feared she might fall.

They had charged along a narrow trail, which sat behind the log cabin. This path didn't benefit from any strategically placed lamps and was lit solely by the moon's dim pallor. Halo hoped to God that Jason hadn't seen them head off in any particular direction. That would dramatically increase their chances of survival.

She stopped running and grabbed Shona. "Take a few seconds," she told her. "We've got a few seconds, at least."

"The pain's back," said Shona through gritted teeth. "It's real bad again."

"Just breathe," Halo urged, gripping her friend's shoulders. "Catch your breath at least, and we'll run again. We have to. We can rest when—"

"When we're dead?" asked Shona, choking up. Her eyes glistened in the dim light.

"Hey. Don't even say that, you hear me?" Halo squeezed those shoulders. "We're not gonna die."

Beside them, the bushes burst open with a fierce crackle. Jason stomped out onto the path, the machete in his grip.

He moved with formidable speed, grabbing Shona's hair and yanking her toward him. Halo's instinct was to hold on to her friend and try to pull her away, but common sense, and his sheer strength, ultimately forced her to let go. She backed away, her legs like marshmallow.

Shona's hair was tangled in Jason's bulky fist. She screamed as he forced her head back against a tree.

Halo screamed too, overcome by the raw horror of what she was seeing. She turned away, eyes blistering with tears, and stared off along the trail. Once again, she felt the painful sting of cowardice.

Jason raised the machete and slammed it down through Shona's left shoulder. Halo saw this, then glimpsed her friend's arm hitting the floor, red and jagged at the shoulder. That was enough for Halo: she ran.

As Shona cried out in agony, feebly struggling against him, Jason rammed the machete through her stomach. She howled even louder and spat blood on his mask. Red rivulets slowly made their way down the surface: her last act of defiance.

Jason twisted the machete inside Shona, but she was lifeless. As if frustrated by the lack of reaction, Jason yanked out the machete with one mighty swing. Shona slumped down the tree like a discarded puppet, head lolling on her shoulders, sightless eyes glinting. Jason turned his head to see the dim and distant figure of the other girl, the one he really wanted.

Halo felt she'd handled the situation pretty well, up until this point. Hysteria was in control. Her brain insisted on playing her a loop of a scene in which a masked maniac hacked off Shona Brinkley's arm. God only knew what he had done to her next.

She was running so fast that she feared it might take her a full minute to slow down and stop. Yet stopping was not on the agenda. Of all the terrible things she had seen Jason do—she had accepted that this was the same Jason Voorhees she once laughed about—moving quickly did not rank high among them. He could muster a swift, purposeful stomp. But he was surely a tortoise to her hare.

And who won *that* race? She banished the thought from her mind and kept her limbs pumping, hot blood filling her like fuel. She hammered along the track, barely touching the ground.

She had lost all sense of direction, not that she had much in the first place. She and Shona had been content to be driven out here. Hell, they didn't even know where the lake was.

Ahead, the track blended into an open area where trees were less plentiful. In the distance, there was the solemn glow of lamps. Despite the speed at which she was moving, Halo could see that they formed a symmetrical pattern from top to bottom, like the paint patterns they used to make at school.

There was water ahead—it was the lake.

Speak of the Devil...

Jason cut through the stillness like a saw through flesh. Exposed bones carrying an unholy gleam. Chain clinking harshly as it bounced against his chest. The machete jutted cruelly up from his fist.

Once in a while, Jason's head jerked to one side, attracted by rustling in the bushes, or some distant coyote howl. A wind was rising, as though Mother Nature was riled by his very existence. The few leaves that had surrendered early to the imminent fall began to dance in the air.

Jason pressed onwards, an unstoppable force.

He walked this trail with purpose, but no sense of haste. As though he knew that, no matter how far or fast this girl ran, he would find her in the end.

When Halo arrived at the lake's edge, it had resembled a vast black blanket. With the wind, it began to ripple, betraying its liquid state. Crystal Lake lapped at the banks, which hemmed it in, as small wars of physics were fought on its surface.

Halo was cursing herself. She had turned up here, just in time to see a vehicle's taillights, pulling away from the lake. Maybe they belonged to a police car. Either way, it had done her no good. Even though she knew that making noise would help Jason home in on her, she couldn't resist yelling like a mad thing, running along the full length of a brightly lit jetty and jumping frantically around. When she finished, her throat was sore and her spirits diminished even further. Once again, she was alone in the woods with a psychotic killer.

Crystal Lake curdled and splashed beneath her feet, as though mocking her. Wind tugged at her clothes.

Halo looked back at the dark woods. They appeared dormant, but she would be the very definition of a sitting duck if she stayed on the jetty much longer. Opting to make her way around the edge of the lake, she ran back over the wooden planks.

"Fuck!" She ground to a halt, halfway along the jetty, at the sight of two people on the bank. They blocked her path back to terra firma, but Halo was relieved to see their faces etched with concern.

"Is everything in order, my dear?" asked Norwood Thawn, hoisting a theatrical eyebrow. Halo's first impression was that he had a kind face. Hopefully, he and this dainty looking woman could help her. Please, God. Let them help.

"We heard you yelling," added Penelope, reaching out for Halo like a concerned mother. "Such language! What's happened?"

Halo felt tears bubbling forth, but shook her head, as if ordering them to simmer. This was no time for hysterics: this was a time for very direct communication. With every second that passed, Halo could vividly picture another of Jason's huge steps.

"I'm being chased by a murderer," she said, running to join them and receiving a hug from Penelope. "He's killed all my friends and now he wants to kill me. We have to move."

As Halo waited for the couple's reaction, she caught something strange in their eyes. They were looking at each other, as though somehow pleased by the news. Then the look quickly reverted to one of extreme concern. Halo shrugged off her observation; she must have somehow mistaken their shock for something else.

"Very well," said Norwood, placing a cold hand on her back as the three of them began a brisk walk along the water's edge. "I'm Norwood and this is Penelope. Let's go back the way we came, to our hotel." He pointed in the direction of Phoenix Heights. "Then you can call the police."

"We have to be so careful," said Halo, her eyes darting around. "This man... I think he's Jason Voorhees."

Once again, Halo had the bizarre feeling that something unspoken was passing between her new acquaintances.

Gusts of wind dive-bombed the trio, attempting to knock them off course. The Thawns flanked Halo, each taking hold of an arm. Together, they fought the bluster. It occurred to Halo that she could cover much more ground on her own, but she welcomed the company. Besides, if they knew the best way to head, that was more than half the battle. Until now, she had been moving almost randomly.

"I can't believe this is happening," said Penelope, finally. "You say he killed everyone with you? I'm so sorry. How dreadful!"

"Everyone," nodded Halo, each of the following words grazing her soul. "My friend Shona, her boyfriend... My boyfriend too. Trey."

"Really?" said Norwood, looking astonished. "Oh, my dear, you must be devastated. I can't offer enough condolences."

Halo began to crumple under the weight of delayed grief. "He never knew..." she began, a lump swelling in her throat. "He never knew that he was going to be a father."

"A father?" asked Penelope. "You're pregnant? And not married?"

Halo frowned at this shift in the woman's tone. It seemed wholly inappropriate to the situation. "Yes," she said, seeing Penelope's disapproval. "Well, I hope I still am. I wouldn't be surprised—"

Halo felt Norwood's hand leaving her arm. His fist crashed into the back of her skull, sending her reeling down into the dry mud of the bank.

Too surprised and agonized to speak, Halo clutched her head and rolled onto her back, staring up at the couple. Appearing to tower above her, they returned her gaze with contempt. Leaves hovered in the air around them.

"Filthy whore," said Penelope. "Couldn't wait until wedlock like decent folk, eh? Stand up."

Halo looked numbly up at this woman's face, so full of scorn. Then she lowered her eyes and saw the gun. The big, yawning muzzle was pointed at her head.

"Get up!" screamed Penelope. Norwood leaned in and roughly grabbed Halo's arm, manhandling her until she stood upright.

"Thanks for telling us about Jason," he said. "We've been looking for him."

"What are you, cops?" asked Halo, looking from one face to another. She was desperate to make sense of this insane situation.

Norwood and Penelope spontaneously laughed. "I suppose we are," smiled Norwood, pursing his lips.

"Now, hold still," said Penelope, moving over to stand behind Halo. She wrapped one arm around her throat, sufficiently tight to keep her immobile. Halo then felt the cold mouth of Penelope's gun resting against her right temple. She could smell metal and spent gunpowder. Beside them, the waters continued to roll.

"Right," said Penelope. "Let's reach out to Jason. Give him a little goodwill present, to break the ice."

Halo could see Norwood standing to her extreme right. He looked concerned. "For the last time, darling, are you sure about this? I—"

Penelope cut him off. "I'm absolutely sure. You think we're just going to come all the way up here and decide not to complete our mission? Norwood, this was meant to be. I've dreamed of this very moment. Jason Voorhees is one of us. He kills for the same reasons as us."

"If it's meant to be," said Norwood, nodding solemnly, "I can't argue with that."

A pause, as Norwood took a deep breath. Halo swallowed hard, hating the fact that at any second, Penelope could pull that trigger and extinguish her life. There was something truly loathsome about this pair: perhaps it was their deception. Jason might wear a mask, she considered, but at least you knew exactly where you stood with him.

Tears made their way over her cheeks.

"Don't worry," said Norwood. "You'll soon be dead."

"You're insane," Halo managed. "You think Jason won't kill you too? He kills everybody."

Pity shone in Norwood's eyes. "Penelope and I will be spared," he said, patiently. "You, on the other hand, are a sinner. You will be redeemed."

"Call him now." Penelope's voice was guttural, shot through with expectation.

Norwood faced the woods and outstretched his hands. "Come, brother. We have come to seek you out. Look, we have captured the girl for you. She's all yours."

The three of them listened hard.

"Please," whispered Halo, "let me go. He'll kill all of us." Either her words were lost on the wind and unheard, or the Thawns chose not to respond.

"Come, join the Redeemers," hollered Norwood, maintaining his Jesus Christ pose. "We will kill as one. Come, brother. Come to us, Jason Voorhees."

A leaf fleetingly plastered itself to the left side of Halo's face, then pirouetted away. She knew exactly how it felt, to have no control. Story of her life. It seemed her very imminent demise.

"There he is," breathed Penelope, directly behind Halo's ear. "He is beautiful."

Halo struggled to follow her captor's gaze.

"Don't move." Penelope tightened her grip, preventing Halo's head from turning.

Because of the way Penelope held her, she couldn't see Jason. Yet she could feel his presence, a brooding malice close by. She pictured him standing at the edge of the woods, blank eyeholes staring out of the darkness at these two fanatics. And at *her*.

As far as Halo could tell, Norwood was standing between them and Jason. His hands still appeared to be outstretched, welcoming the psychopath. Halo wondered who was the more insane.

"Join us, brother. Are we not all doing the same work? Cleansing the flock?"

Penelope swung ninety degrees, bringing Halo with her, so that they both faced Norwood. Beyond him, moonlight managed to break through the wood's cover, settling on a dirty white slice of mask.

Norwood turned and looked at Penelope, smiling. Then he swung back to face Jason. "Only today, we have vanquished some sinners. A morally bankrupt corporate giant, over at the Phoenix Heights. A slut, masquerading as a receptionist..."

Halo's eyes almost popped out of her head. "What?" she bellowed, despite Penelope's best efforts to shut her up. "A receptionist? What was her name?"

Norwood kept his back to her. "If we band together," he continued grandly, "we can rid the world of filth. Together, we will be invincible."

Halo's face contorted with rage. "I *said*, what was her name?" she yelled.

Norwood glanced irritably back at her. "She was a whore," he said. "That is name enough."

"Bastard." Halo struggled hard against Penelope's chokehold, only to receive a blow on the temple, from what felt like the gun's butt. Stars clustered before her eyes and she fought to stay focused. The hatred and fear made it easier.

"Keep still or I'll blow your head off," Penelope told her, voice hushed so as not to interrupt Norwood's speech.

As far as Halo could see, Jason had yet to move a muscle. His immobility made him appear part of the forest.

Norwood started walking toward him.

The flask angled upwards from Ed Daimler's mouth as he sucked thirstily on its contents. Van Stadt watched him with barely concealed disgust.

They were standing outside the Home From Home motel. The receptionist didn't recognize the names, the pictures, anything. Same story as all the other Crystal Lake establishments they had tried so far.

Daimler pulled the flask away from his mouth and grimaced as the last of the whisky went down. "God,

I needed that," he said, throwing a half smile at his partner. "Don't tell, will you?"

Van Stadt laughed at him, her eyes alive with astonishment. "Don't tell? Are we in elementary school here, Ed? What the hell's the matter with you?"

Daimler wiped his mouth with his forearm. "Here's the deal. After this case, I'm going to take some time off and sort myself out. I've gone too long without a break. It's... taken its toll."

Van Stadt folded her arms and leant back against the home from home's east wall. "You don't say."

Daimler gave her his best smoldering stare. "Do you think it's affected my looks, Mel?"

Again, the astonishment.

"Would you date me?" he persisted, throwing in another smile. That way, if she took offence, he could half convincingly claim he was kidding.

To his surprise, she avoided his gaze. Color crept into her cheeks.

"What?" he asked, cocking his head to one side, to try and see her eyes beneath that hair.

"We're partners," she said, finally, pushing past him. As she did so, a friction seemed to pass between them. At least, it seemed that way to Daimler.

He slid the flask back into the inside pocket where it lived, then followed her back to the car, with an intrigued look plastered across his face.

Six feet: the distance that separated Norwood Thawn and Jason Voorhees.

Norwood was desperately trying not to show it, but he felt unnerved. Perhaps it was Jason's unearthly countenance. Or the way his rock-like fist grasped the blood-caked machete. It was hanging by Jason's side, but Norwood knew this could change at any moment.

Still, he had faith. Both spiritual, and in his own ability to sway others.

"What say you?" he said, careful to keep his voice steady. Perhaps this giant was like a dog. He might smell fear. Maybe that's how he operated. "Will you join us?"

Norwood swallowed hard. Was Jason Voorhees *really* like them?

His own concealed blade felt cool and sharp against his wrist. He really hoped he wouldn't have to use it.

An ominous silence froze the scene, punctuated only by the clash of wind and water. Halo's breath was coming fast and shallow and her head was light. It was like watching a painting. The man standing before a monster. Nothing moved.

Jason drew the machete up behind his head. Behind Halo, Penelope gasped.

The blade swung down toward Norwood's head. Penelope screamed so loudly that Halo's ears experienced whiteout. She saw Norwood ducking to one side and the weapon slicing through the air, mere inches from his left ear.

Jason walked toward Norwood, piling through him, like a truck striking a barricade. He swung his free arm into Norwood's upper body, knocking him to one side like trash. He hurtled through the air, rolled down a narrow slope and lay motionless at its base.

Still deafened, Halo was spared the full extent of Penelope's second scream, but she could feel it rippling through her.

Jason walked purposefully down the bank, toward the two women.

THIRTEEN

"Jason, what're you doing? Norwood and I are your friends. The only people who *understand* you."

Penelope's cries did nothing to delay Jason's approach.

Halo knew she would rather die from a bullet to the head than be slaughtered by Voorhees. So the choice was easy enough to make. If it didn't work, at least she would die quickly.

In one fluid motion, she lowered her chin, then shot her head backwards, feeling the grim snap of bone and cartilage as the back of her skull pulverized Penelope's nose.

She fully expected the gun to blow her to kingdom come, but Halo had caught Penelope by surprise.

Looking up to see Jason still advancing, a mere four or five steps away, Halo decided to push her luck. She grabbed Penelope's wrist, angling the gun away from herself. Again to Halo's surprise, Penelope yielded the weapon to her. Escaping the older woman's clutches, Halo dashed away along the lakeside, slipping on the mud, then regaining her footing. She didn't look back. This was a lesson she had swiftly absorbed: never look back, never slow down, never stop. Philosophies that might as well be Jason's own.

Penelope had briefly lost consciousness. Incredibly, her legs hadn't buckled. By rights, she should be on her back in the mud, but she had somehow remained vertical. As she reconnected with the real world, her broken nose sent pain signals to her brain. Her mouth and chin were slick with her own blood. Furthermore, her hostage had escaped with the gun. Yet these facts all seemed secondary to her very pressing, immediate situation.

Crystal Lake was behind her; directly before her stood Jason Voorhees. His shoulders rose with great, shuddering heaves, then fell like lead weights. The man's raw intensity had her pinned, like a butterfly.

This wasn't the Jason Voorhees she had dreamed of. This was an abomination from another world. Should she run? No, it was too late. The mud was sucking at her heels, making any kind of high-speed movement impossible. Besides, she could handle this.

Stealing a glance over at her husband's body, what looked like miles away, she choked back tears. Another glance, in the opposite direction, registered the distant figure of that little bitch, making good her escape.

"There's no need for any more violence, not between us," she told the abomination, aware of the coppery taste at the back of her throat. "It is the others, the unclean we need to... concentrate on."

She felt her insides burning. The words were coming out all wrong. She always considered herself Norwood's intellectual equal, but he was the best when it came to attitude changing oration. Still, look where his skills had gotten him this time.

Jason's sole response was a slow cock of the head toward one shoulder. That eye continued to sizzle.

"Can't we come to some kind of... arrangement?" said Penelope, presenting her trembling lower lip in what she hoped was a seductive gesture. Then she slowly reached out with one hand, maintaining eye contact with Jason, as though approaching a frightened animal. She held two heavy links of his neck chain in her palm, smelling both the rust and the bodily decay that lurked behind it. Still, there was something about this behemoth that she found weirdly attractive. This, she knew, was partly why she had brought poor Norwood here.

Jason's eye widened. Penelope couldn't tell whether this denoted more rage or anticipation. She decided to risk it. Releasing her limp hold on the chain links, she trailed her palm down his chest, over his stomach, all the time feeling the cold moisture of rancid flesh, between what remained of his charred clothing.

Jason's shoulders continued to work, his chest heaving.

Her hand reached his groin. Still staring at his eye, smiling at the man, desperate to placate him, Penelope slowly licked her lips.

"Jason, darling. Can't we—"

She fell to her knees very slowly.

"Can't we work together?"

Jason glared down at her for a long moment, as though unable to believe what he was seeing. Then he inverted the machete, holding the handle in both fists like a medieval knight.

Penelope gazed up to see the blade hanging downwards, suspended above her face. Beyond its gleam, she saw Jason's evil eye, telling her that she was about to leave the planet.

"No!" she shrieked. "Pl—"

Jason slammed the machete into Penelope's mouth, then down through her throat and gullet. Two spurting slits forced her neck open as if it were ripe fruit.

The machete continued its inexorable journey earthwards. Finally, its handle rested against Penelope Thawn's blood-red lips.

The wind slowly abated, as Jason Voorhees wrenched his weapon back out. Penelope's body collapsed into the mud.

As though appeased by this sacrifice, Crystal Lake's waters became still.

Halo ducked behind a tree, finally out of breath. The mud on the bank had made running seriously hard work. Suddenly remembering she carried a gun, she rolled the jet-black device over in her hands for a moment.

Seems pretty easy to operate, she considered. There's a trigger here, which makes bullets come out here. Don't know what the tube on the end does, but it probably doesn't matter. How hard can firing a gun be?

She sat there for several minutes, examining the gun, attempting to calm herself, taking some much-needed rest. All the time, her senses remained alert. Surely it was impossible for a man of Jason Voorhees's dimensions to silently approach? Then again, she would put nothing past him.

Halo set off, her back drenched with cold sweat. When was the last time she had eaten? Drunk? Her throat felt like she'd been gargling broken glass, while her stomach felt decidedly raw. She briefly considered her baby's safety, before turning her thoughts to her sister. Was Shelley really dead?

She was running in the general direction of the Phoenix Heights hotel: that much she had gathered from the Thawns, back when they were pretending to be angels of mercy. Halo didn't believe in vengeance, but she would make an exception for that pair: she sincerely hoped that Jason had killed them both. Judging by the way Norwood had hit the ground and the horrible noises she'd distantly heard from Penelope, Jason had indeed done what he did best.

Halo had never been to the Phoenix Heights hotel, but she would find it. If she had to run until dawn and beyond, she would discover the truth. There were, after all, at least two or three female receptionists at the hotel. There was still hope.

Even though Norwood's revelation had churned her guts and made her head spin with potential grief, at the very least she had a direction in which to move. Every cloud had a silver lining, no matter how thin.

She was well away from the lake, flanked by trees as her feet hammered into the ground. Every once in a while, she was tempted to look back over her shoulder, but always managed to resist.

Then the track came to an end. A dense, jagged mountain of fallen trees seemed to reach out around her like a claw. She could either climb over, or head back to the last junction in the path.

The decision was quickly made for her. Jason emerged amid a flurry of leaves, back along the path. He looked even more enraged than before, stomping toward her with unusual speed. It seemed that he wasn't used to his victims being so damn resilient.

Halo wasn't about to stop. She slammed into the tree blockade, as though tackling an obstacle course, scrambling up from one fallen bough to another. She moved so fast, with such determination, that the bark scraped a thin layer of skin from her palms.

The blockade, from her new, heightened perspective, appeared to be the result of an unfinished lumberjack session. The trees had been clumsily hacked down, but the truck had yet to arrive. Or maybe the lumberjacks had seen Jason and ran for their lives. Very wise.

Without stopping to think, Halo leapt across a five-foot gap, making it with inches to spare. Steadying her balance, she felt a swift rush of elation at having made the top of the pile. The only thing to do was...

Jason was looking up at her, on the other side of the blockade, ten feet below her. She blinked once, twice, three times, but he was still there, like a bad dream that wouldn't quit.

Screwing her face up, Halo lent forward and vented her anger. "Fuck you!" Pointing the gun down at his mask, she squeezed of three shots, gasping with exertion. Each of the bullets caused a tiny explosion on his upper torso, but nothing that evidently caused him much concern. She hurled the weapon at his head and leapt back across the gap with agility she didn't know she possessed. Then she scrambled down the tree pile, far too quickly. A wooden spike scratched her upper left arm, cutting through the material and drawing blood. Shrugging off the sudden jab of pain, she took the final jump, back down to the pile's base.

Halo's lungs felt hot as she launched another sprint, this time reaching that damn left junction and taking it, speeding along its narrow, sporadically-lit length.

Behind her, she heard Jason burst out of the trees. No need to turn around: she knew it was him. She could hear his feet on the ground.

Muddling her way through a series of large bushes that marked the path's end, Halo was shocked to find herself on the edge of a campsite. Seized by panic, she instantly took in details: a small water pot suspended over a burning fire. An expensive looking tent.

Dear God, she thought. People. Two adults and two children. Please, no. Not the children. Surely, he wouldn't...

The family's collective breath caught in their throats as Halo appeared, flapping around, eyes wide in the middle of a blood flecked face, framed by chaotic hair. Their little boy's toy airplane broke the silence by clattering on the ground, also serving to galvanize Halo's mouth into action.

"Run!" That was the most concise speech she could muster. Then, as she hurled herself across the site and out the other side, she screamed, "He'll kill us!"

No sooner was she back on the narrow path, zooming past a parked, empty camper van, when horrible screams rose into the night air like demons. These were the most horrendous sounds she had ever heard, even taking into account Trey's death throes. Unimaginable agony endured by both old and young. The ungodly sounds of people being torn apart.

Then nothing but the whirr of crickets.

Jason tugged open the flap of the big tent, his machete dripping red. It was empty. No one left to destroy. He threw the flap back at the tent to which it belonged. As the hulking killer strode across the still campsite, his right heel landed inches away from a lifeless, outstretched hand. A small cluster of diamonds gleamed balefully on the ring finger.

In one swift movement, Jason's heel reduced the toy airplane to pieces, shoving it into the ground. He didn't stop to look down at what he had obliterated. It was of no interest. The point was to kill, not conduct post mortems.

Spying a path that led out of the campsite, Jason stomped off along it, the machete slicing air by his side. He stopped dead by the camper van and listened for a few seconds. His head jerked left, then the rest of his body followed suit, moving in that direction. He lumbered around the van, casually regarding it. Then, seemingly satisfied that Halo wasn't hiding behind it, he continued along the path.

Great exhalations steamed out through mask holes as Jason pursued his prey.

The path soon broadened out revealing a large, open clearing, dotted with the thick foliage of tall trees. This area was barely illuminated, the moon having all but disappeared behind the smothering gauze of clouds.

Jason walked into the middle of the clearing. He drew to an abrupt halt, and once again seemed to taste the cool night air. Searching for signs of life.

The mask's uppermost leather strap looked like it was digging into Jason's very skin. Almost like it was a living part of him.

Halo could see this with terrible clarity, because she was clinging to a bough, halfway up one of the trees in the clearing. Her arms ached with the exertion, but at least this was giving her legs, and that painful hip, a well-deserved break. After bombing out of that campsite, exhaustion and an all-consuming nausea had overwhelmed her. Fighting a groundswell of panic, while simultaneously remembering the campsite family's shocked faces, she had been forced to change plan. Running wasn't working out so great. Hiding might be a better option, if she did it well enough. After all, if Shona hadn't found her deep in the brush, back by their original campsite, Halo might still be hidden there— still terrified, but in far less danger, perhaps.

Poor Shona, she thought. No, don't think about her. Don't think about any of it. Concentrate instead on keeping that puke inside your craw. No matter how badly that stuff wants out—and it does want out real bad—you have to keep it in. Or die.

Those precious few feet below, Jason resembled a stone statue. Halo wondered whether he could hear her insides bubbling and groaning. She wished those damn crickets would whirr louder.

The killer's head moved to the right, making her jump. She froze, hugging the tree like a life preserver.

Jason's head slowly returned to its forward position, then continued scanning to the left. Halo's body was threatening to take matters into its own hands: if she wouldn't permit this vomit to come out then her system was going to do it for her. Halo's vision swam queasily, as cold sweat layered her forehead.

Morning sickness seemed to be a myth. Looked like it could strike at any time. As if to prove the point, Halo's guts went into spasm. Her eyes widened as her mouth filled up.

Norwood Thawn was no drinking man. He had never touched a drop of the demon drink, champagne aside, on his father's express orders. Virgil Thawn had not only been a man to obey and fear, but a man who spoke perfect sense.

Norwood imagined that this was how the world's worst hangover might feel: splitting headache, further pain stretching from the nape of his neck, down over his right shoulder. Perhaps only the mud caked on the side of his face didn't reflect the average drinking aftermath.

For some time, he had no idea where he was. He groggily rose to his knees and found himself gazing dumbly out over a lake.

Head still throbbing, he leant down and scooped up some water with one hand, rubbing it over his face. Blobs of mud came loose, disappearing into the lake. After scrubbing hard, Norwood took a moment to examine his own reflection. It was hard to tell in this light, but most of the mud appeared to have gone.

He looked down at his suit. That would be harder to deal with. It had cost him five hundred dollars. Perhaps a good dry cleaning company might be in order. He would consult the telephone book when they got back to the hotel.

Penelope. The name zapped through his head like a lightning bolt. Where in tarnation was she?

His neck muscles protested loudly as he attempted to turn his head. Instead, he was forced to stand and revolve his entire body. Then he saw her. The bodily husk which once housed his beloved wife was lying on the muddy shore. His face devoid of expression, Norwood stumbled toward her.

Penelope Thawn grinned up at him.

At least, it appeared that way. Her eyes were wide and the corners of her mouth no longer existed, having been hacked through. This grotesque maw was four or five inches wide, revealing shattered teeth and a red stub of tongue.

Norwood's eyes drifted to the ruined throat, then down to the open, bloodstained stomach, where something sharp had either come out, or been inserted. It no longer seemed to matter which.

Ten whole minutes passed as he stood. Motionless. Emotionless.

Then Norwood Thawn underwent a transformation. His fists tightened, his eyes bulged with feral rage and the tendons in his neck stretched like taut ropes. He leant back and roared until all air had evacuated his lungs.

Thawn scrambled across the bank and found a large, heavy rock. Bending at the knees, he jammed his hands beneath either side and hefted it loose from the sucking mud.

Still carrying the rock, he marched back toward his wife's corpse.

Her pallid face grinned on.

Halo tried desperately to hold the vomit down, clutching her chest, eyes screwed shut. Trying to ignore the foul taste. Willing the stuff to stay down.

A flash of fear accompanied the knowledge that some body reflexes wouldn't take no for an answer. Another contraction at the back of her throat heralded the liquid's return.

This time, she threw up into her cupped palms, but it was a futile gesture. Gazing downwards, she saw splashes of her vomit landing on Jason's left shoulder.

The silence was so absolute that he couldn't fail to hear, maybe feel, the impact. His head jerked to the side, then his entire body spun around. The mask wrenched backwards, and his terrible eye once again transfixed her. The effect was so terrifying that she parted her hands, unleashing a measure of viscous puke, which tumbled down and splattered against one side of Jason's mask. He shook his head violently like a mongrel dog, sending globules flying left and right.

He stepped forward and grabbed the tree, his huge arms wrapping around almost two thirds of the trunk.

Her head still spinning from nausea, Halo briefly wondered whether he was going to try and shake her out of it. Surely he couldn't be that strong? This trunk had to be at least four feet wide.

She wiped her mouth with the back of her hand, then rubbed both palms against the rough bark of her main bough. All the time she was desperately thinking about what the hell to do next.

So, it seemed, was Jason.

Having tested the trunk's strength, he took a step back, never letting Halo out of his sight. The pair of them stared at each other for some time. Cat and dog. Then Jason swung his right arm upwards. As he did so, the machete rose behind his head.

It was a truly sickening crunch. So was the next. And the ones after that. Norwood Thawn's eyes sparkled with hateful insanity as he repeatedly lifted the rock above his head, then brought it down onto his wife's torso.

When he had finished, ten blows later, Penelope Thawn's chest was a gaping cavern of red mush, gray lung and splintered bone.

It was the bone that Norwood was after. Digging around in the cavity, his face distorted by base savagery, he tugged at rib after rib, examining each in turn. Some he discarded, sending them skimming across the lake's waters; others he placed in a small pile beside him.

When the process was complete, he gathered four of the jagged ribs in one hand. Together, they roughly formed a single, vicious point.

Norwood reached down and grabbed the crucifix, which was attached to Penelope's bloodied throat by a thick cord. Tugging it loose with one swift wrench, like a cobra's strike in reverse, he set about using the cord to bind the bones together.

The tree shook as Jason's blade took another bite out of it. Halo held on all the more tightly. When she dared look down, she saw him leaning back, swinging the machete in a terrifyingly wide arc and slamming it into the tree trunk. Having destroyed another few inches of wood, he tugged the weapon loose and continued the process without so much as a pause for breath. The whole act was tireless. Robotic.

She wanted to scream, but feared that it might encourage him to chop faster.

If this was the movies, she told herself, someone would arrive seconds before the tree was set to topple. It would be a cop. The father from the family campsite, seeking revenge for his slaughtered brood. Or even Trey, who miraculously hadn't been burnt to ash at all. Whoever it was, they would kill Jason and sweep her off into the sunset. The End.

But this wasn't a movie and Halo knew that no one would come.

Still, she realized, there might be no harm in trying.

The first time she attempted to call out into the thick night, her dry and bitter throat betrayed her. Then necessity took hold and she became the classic damsel in distress, practically deafened by her own foghorn voice.

"Help me! For God's sake, help! He's going to kill me!"

The only answer was another loud *thunk*, from below.

"Anyone, help me! Please, help me."

Her yells melted into a despairing sob, as another *thunk* made the whole tree shake. Jason had to be nearly halfway through already.

As she looked around at the other trees, an idea struck. Wiping her eyes, she tentatively reached up and sought purchase from a higher branch. When it didn't bend, she stretched and grabbed it with commitment, heaving herself up. By her reckoning, there was at least another ten feet of tree to climb. And if she could get up there...

Thunk. Everything trembled again, more so this time.

Halo continued to scale the tree, aware of the need for speed but equally wary of losing her footing and plunging to the ground. She wouldn't last long, dazed in the dirt, looking up at the business end of that machete.

Thunk. Halo gasped as the whole tree shifted, bending to one side. She glanced desperately around her.

The trunk steadied and centralized once again. Yet Halo knew it would begin to topple at any moment.

At least fifteen feet above the ground, she looked up again, searching for the next viable move.

Thunk. Next, a loud *crack*. Halo knew the trunk had finally given in. Time to move.

Issuing something like a battle cry, she ran along the nearest bough, moving in the opposite direction to the tree itself. Her escape route rose as the tree fell. Her foot landed on a thick knot toward its outer extremity, before launching her away from the tree and upward.

FOURTEEN

"Shock me."

Sheriff Daniel Claymark had snatched the phone from its cradle and stood with it wedged against the side of his head. A handful of subordinates watched him nervously from their positions around the extensively wood paneled station. He was horribly caffeinated, and fully expecting more bad news.

The day had started badly for this relatively young sheriff, with the discovery of the two police divers. Those murders had leaked out to the media immediately, but the sheriff had done his damndest to ensure that those two dead, very dead, campers Bobby Dremmer and Gina Levene weren't announced. Not yet. So far, so good, on that score at least. Everything else was very bad.

Two hours ago, he had learnt that Officer Hollis's vehicle had been found abandoned by a roadside, over by the Flanahan farm. Two further officers, Mahler and Kemp, had been sent to investigate the area. Mahler had radioed in, breathless and clearly in shock as he quietly described the massacre that had taken place at the farmhouse. The whole family had been wiped out. Much the same MO as the divers and the campers, in the sense that sharp objects and a great deal of ferocity had been involved.

Then Mahler and Kemp checked on Chester Grey's cabin and found not only Grey himself but also Hollis. Claymark was finding all of this hard to take in. When he took the job, a mere six months ago, he never expected to have to deal with Jason Voorhees again, as the legendary Sheriff Garris once had. Of course, Garris had paid with his life, courtesy of a snapped spine, but Voorhees had supposedly wound up dead. Or was he? The killer that was stalking Crystal Lake was either someone appropriating Jason's methods, the big man himself, or the FBI's two puritanical butchers. Either way, Claymark might as well place an order for a new batch of body bags and tags.

He could barely believe what was happening. Thus far in his reign, he had become accustomed to dealing with the occasional domestic, the odd robbery. Maybe a bar room brawl might pop up, every now and again, to distract him from his latest mug of coffee. Hell, he almost welcomed them. Given the number of kids who visited every summer, Crystal Lake wasn't the most challenging of districts to police.

"We've found more dead campers, sir," said Mahler down the phone line, his distinctively lazy tones irritating Claymark as usual. "Or, at least, parts of dead campers. One guy's been burnt. Another one, well, we've found only the head. We're going to continue to comb the area."

"More dead campers," sighed Claymark, his dry eyeballs flitting around the room at the grim faces. "Love it. I fucking love it!" The last two words were bellowed, accompanied by the crash of the handset striking the cradle.

Claymark turned to his deputy, Ken Ryger, a cold-eyed man who carried a pump action shotgun around everywhere, as though expecting life-threatening conflict at any given moment. He called it the Key, because it was useful for blowing stubborn doors open.

Ryger was engaged in a phone call of his own. Seeing that Claymark wanted his attention, Ryger cut the call short and made obedient eye contact with his superior.

"Do we have that copter in the air yet, Ken?"

Ryger nodded and smiled. "It just went up. With a shooter onboard." His eyes gleamed.

"I need you to keep in contact with those guys. Besides looking for Voorhees or these Thawns, we have to evacuate any campers still in those woods."

Ryger nodded again. "Sure." A man of few words. He looked quite happy, thought Claymark. Perhaps he was looking forward to using that shotgun again. There was a time when Claymark had suspected that Ryger might use it on *him*, when he leapfrogged the old coot to get the sheriff gig. After all, when you were deputy sheriff, where else was there to go?

Claymark turned to his PA, Amy Bright. "How's the search of motels going? Are we keeping the FBI happy?"

Bright shrugged, exuding her usual indifference. "Well, we're lookin', all right. No Norwood or Penelope Thawn found yet, though. The pictures have circulated."

"And where are those wonderful FBI agents?"

"They're conducting their own search."

"Great. Probably visiting the same places as us. Nice to see that they're so trusting in our efficiency."

Bright shrugged again.

Feeling his stress reach epidemic proportions, Claymark reached for the coffee jug once more.

As she hurtled through open air, gravity sucking hungrily at her, Halo groped blindly with both hands, desperate for something. Anything. Behind her, she heard the cracking and groaning of the tree she had abandoned. Something struck her in the face and her hands seized it, finding bark and bough and leaves. She opened her eyes and found herself clinging to a new tree. She could hardly believe she'd made it.

A tremendous eruption seemed to shake the woods. Halo realized it was her first tree's colossal weight hitting the earth.

Determined not to look down, she concentrated on swinging herself toward the trunk, searching with her feet for a bough below. Nothing presented itself, so she made her way monkey style along the heavy branch, sweat running into her eyes.

Upon reaching the trunk, she allowed herself a whole minute to breathe, eyes closed. In through the nose and out through the mouth. All the time, listening out for Jason. The fat crunch of his foot-steps. The whistle of his machete through the air. Most of all, the *thunk* of the blade in her new tree's base.

None of these sounds reached her.

Finally, she opened her eyes, her heart slowing from a frantic techno pace to more of a strident tribal drum.

Then she allowed herself to look down. At the wreckage of the tree, which had fallen away from her.

Where was Jason? He was nowhere to be seen. Halo blinked. Was she simply missing him? Was he standing there in the shadows, looking up at her, silently taunting?

Narrowing her eyes and concentrating, she peered down. In the process of leaping to this tree, she had descended a few feet, so the ground was now a mere ten below. If he was there, she should be able to spy him.

Then movement—a slight shift in her field of vision. Where was it? She stared into the gloom, until it happened again.

Then she saw Jason.

He was lying on his back, directly beneath the fallen tree. It had landed along his body's length, very effectively pinning him down and resting on the right side of his head. The movement that Halo had detected was one of his fists. It was flexing, stretching, trying to reach something.

She didn't need to see the glint of metal in order to deduce that it had to be his machete.

Galvanized by this turning of tables, Halo began to make her steady way down the tree, every muscle and fibre aching from the exertion. When she neared the ground, she swung out on a bough, dangled for a second, then let herself drop the remaining distance with the limited grace she could muster.

She had been planning to make good her escape, but a new thought seized her: Jason Voorhees was trapped. He was technically in her power. *She* could do anything to *him*.

Thoughts of violence almost never came to Halo, but self-preservation was oiling the wheels. What if she ran away, but he simply managed to shift the tree and give chase once again? She was a stone's throw from him. At ground level, she could see his hand more clearly. Opening, closing. Reaching out. Halo walked slowly toward the spot where Jason lay.

"Yes, Ms Bright. I know."

Daimler threw a weary glance at van Stadt, while he continued to speak to the sheriff's PA. "You told me that you'd call if you found anything. I'm just calling to say that we've now checked all the motels. I think we now need to turn our attention to the hotels. Maybe our perps have finally decided to spoil themselves and live the high life."

While Bright repeated her mantra about the lack of police resources—after all, it seemed they already had one killer on the loose—Daimler sipped from a foam cup. "I understand. I've understood, each and every time you've told me that stuff. That's why we're here: to help. We need to work together. Can you fax me a local hotel list, please?"

He swiftly wound up the call and sighed. This Bright character was anything but her namesake.

The agents had parked outside the Budget Inn, the last motel on the list. A steady stream of rundown vehicles drifted in and out of the small lot.

"Shall we play 'spot the hooker' while we drink our coffee?" said Daimler, never really expecting a response from his way too sensible colleague. He consulted his watch. "Eleven. The night is still young."

"You sobering up, now?"

"Yes, thanks Melissa. Didn't we drop the alcohol conversation, oh, about fifty miles back?"

"Stop drinking and I'll stop bitching about it," she offered, a mere hint of a smile playing along her lips.

"Oh, this is just way too much fun."

The fax machine emitted a loud click and began to whirr.

He may have been rendered immobile, but Jason Voorhees was no less unnerving. Halo stood at what she trusted was a safe distance from his prone body. From this vantage point, she could discern his mask and most of his left side. As evinced by his active hand, he was still conscious, even though some of the tree's weight ensured that the left side of his head was flat against the dirt.

Halo placed her hands on her knees, peering at the mask. Sure enough, that terrible eye was looking straight at her. Through her, it seemed. For a moment, she thought she heard a child's voice, somewhere inside her head. Calling to her for help. Drowning...

Halo knew it was Jason. With a shudder, she shrugged off those plaintive cries and scanned the surrounding area. It didn't take long to find what she was looking for: the machete was lying a few feet to her right, thankfully well out of Jason's reach.

Halo moved over and grabbed the heavy wooden handle, wincing as she felt the slime that clung to it. Was this human gore? Pieces of his own flesh? She tried not to think about it. The point was she had the machete again and therefore the power.

She swallowed hard, wondering what to do next. If she was really going to kill him, then how could it be achieved? She tried to remember what Trey had said about the British SAS aiming for vital arteries, but realized she had never listened to the poor guy's macho babbling.

The thought of stabbing someone, even Jason Voorhees, made her feel faint.

"Why..." she said, addressing him, having no idea of how to finish the sentence. She finally settled for "Why?"

No answer arrived. Jason simply continued to watch her, with the steadily resentful gaze of an incarcerated lion. Waiting for the right moment to strike or escape, she thought. But he couldn't, could he? That tree must weigh a ton.

She felt a surge of hatred for this monstrosity, as his victims flashed through her mind. It struck her that she was in a position to stop the carnage for good. Right here, right now.

"I could kill you now," she murmured. "I could kill you."

No answer. Just that unblinking stare.

Frustrated by his lack of response, Halo raised her voice. "Do you understand?"

The terrified faces of dead people continued to parade before her mind's eye.

Trey, Duke, Basket, Shona. All the other poor souls whose names she didn't even know.

As though acting on their pleas for retribution, Halo tightened her grip on the long blade and took a step toward Jason. She positioned herself carefully, so that his vile claw couldn't reach her, no matter how hard it spasmed and shifted.

Jason remained silent, even as the machete hovered by his mask. Even as the razor-sharp end positioned itself inches from his right eyehole.

The blade tremored almost imperceptibly.

The child's voice returned to her head. Louder, this time and far more effective in playing with her emotions. Like every man, this horrendous killer was once a small boy. Life had done this to him: turned his soul sour. Hadn't it?

Halo gasped as tears rolled over her face. She knew that she should kill him, no matter what had happened to this man, in order to rot his soul so comprehensively. Yet the act was far beyond her ability: killing simply wasn't in her DNA. It wasn't even a matter of murder being wrong, period, she just couldn't physically do it. Again, she tried thinking about Trey, Duke, poor Shona and the others, but even this failed to spur her to end Jason's life. Hayley Harlan was simply not the killing kind.

As she pulled the blade away from Jason's face, he unleashed a low growl. His hand shot out, attempting to grab her ankle, but missed by a good measure.

Halo stepped back as the whole tree juddered. It was a spasm of rage. Unmistakable. She retreated again, still holding the machete. The tree shook again. This time, she could see that Jason was writhing beneath it, trying to move that incredible weight. Halo suddenly wished she had killed him. Would her own sense of decency prove her undoing?

There's still time, she thought. Step back in and finish it, for everyone's sake.

Another violent jolt made leaves rustle along the tree's length.

Halo shook her head. As she did so, Jason became motionless and gripped her with his foul gaze. The child's voice was no more: it seemed he was done with the mind games. Right there and then, she understood that he would stop at absolutely nothing, in order to end her life. Him being pinned to the ground beneath a huge tree merely granted her a temporary stay of execution.

As she swung on her heels and ran on hollow legs, Halo wondered why her mercy had so enraged him. Was it because he resented the power she had momentarily held over him? Or was it because some part of him wanted to die?

Not really important, she told herself, the machete cutting effortlessly through the air as she gathered speed. One of her hips was killing her.

Back over her shoulder, rumbles and crackles continued to denote Jason's systematic bids for freedom. It didn't take long for the realization to dawn: even though she was running away from him, those sounds were getting louder.

Eventually, they stopped altogether. Had he given up, or was he free again? Halo tried not to think about it.

"Why don't you just go home to your girlfriend, Kip? I don't want you hurling inside this goddamn car."

Kip Mahler glanced ruefully over at the man he grudgingly referred to as his colleague. Lyle Kemp had been part of the sheriff's modest force for far longer and had obviously seen way more corpses. Either that, or the bastard had no soul.

Mahler's flesh felt loose and clammy on his bones, as though seeing all the death and devastation today had somehow transformed his physical make up. He hadn't eaten since breakfast and didn't believe he would ever eat again. Having seen all that dead meat, hamburgers were sure off the menu. Yet none of it seemed to even scrape the surface for Kemp the tough guy. He went about his duties with that stoic, tobacco-chewing calm as though rescuing another cat from an old lady's tree.

"I'm not going home, Lyle. All this shit today has just sickened me, that's all. We can't all be robots, man."

Kemp shot him an irritated look, his thick moustache bristling. "What's that s'posed to mean?"

Mahler let silence do the talking. He scanned the trees, as they hummed along this dirt road. The same kind of road that Hollis had been patrolling, he realized. Hollis hadn't exactly been a friend of his, they were too busy competing for the next rung up the station ladder to socialise—but he had been a fellow police officer. What happened to Zeke could just as easily have happened to him.

Still could, he reminded himself. That was about the only reason to be glad of Lyle's company. At least the man's unnaturally level head helped keep Mahler a few notches below the freak-out level.

He drew in a deep breath and closed his eyes.

"Holy shit!" yelled Kemp, stamping on the brakes.

The vehicle came to a swift halt. Mahler's head jerked forward, the tip of his nose squashing against the glass of the windshield.

What the hell was going on?

This, Halo noted, was the second time a car had almost killed her that day. The shock of narrowly escaping death subsided and she realized that she had found a car. A cop cruiser, in fact. With living, breathing cops inside it. They would help her. Standing directly in front of the vehicle's grill, she could dimly see two silhouettes inside.

"Help me."

"Oh my God," said Mahler, removing his nose from the glass. He told himself that, if he survived this night, he would always wear a seat belt. "She's holding a fucking machete, Lyle."

He turned to see Kemp coolly regarding the mad-woman outside. Her mad eyes and hair. That bloodied face. The huge blade, caked in red.

"Looks that way," he casually grunted, leaning back in his seat and tugging his Colt .45 from its holster.

* * *

Feeling very much the rabbit in headlights, Halo wondered why these cops weren't dashing to her assistance. Were they bloated with too many donuts?

"Help me," she repeated, louder this time. Then she looked anxiously around her, scanning back along the thin path from which she had emerged.

The driver's side clacked open. The first thing Halo saw was a gun, resting on the door's upper rim and pointing straight at her. Then two beady eyes behind it. A hint of moustache.

"Put that thing down," said Kemp. Halo was initially shocked by his cold, authoritative tone, then remembered the machete. She lowered it.

Those beady eyes rose, peering over the car hood.

"Drop it, ma'm. Let go of the handle."

"Listen," stuttered Halo. "There's a killer after me. I think its Jason Voorhees. He could be—"

Kemp's voice hardened. "I said, drop it. Do it now, or I'll blow your goddamn skull wide open."

Halo bit her lip. She regretfully released the handle and heard the weapon strike the ground.

Content with this, Kemp stepped around the car door. Halo didn't like the look of him, but at least he was a man of strength.

"Please," she said. "We should get out of here. It's Jason Voorhees."

"I'm sure it is." The tone was warmer now, but patronizing. "I'm Officer Kemp. Tell me who you are."

"I'm Hayley Harlan. Listen: I met two more killers, by the lake. I think..." Her voice faltered. "I think that one of them might have murdered my sister. Can we go to the Phoenix Heights hotel?"

Kemp didn't respond to the request. He simply walked over to Halo, placed an uncaring hand on her back and firmly guided her around to the car's left-hand rear door. "Let's just get you to the sheriff's office, miss. There's plenty time for other concerns."

Halfway into the car, Halo froze angrily. "She's my *sister*. Shelley Harlan. I need to know if she's okay."

"First we need to ask you some questions. Establish who you are."

Halo sighed and heaved herself inside the car. There was no part of her, which didn't ache. Heart included.

The younger, kinder-faced cop smiled her way. "How you doing, ma'm?"

Halo flinched as the car door slammed shut beside her. Looking out of the window, she saw Kemp pulling on a pair of surgical style gloves.

"For fingerprints," Mahler informed her, sounding for all the world like a kid playing at being a cop.

"Mine will be all over the handle," shrugged Halo, her dread and irritation mounting. "That's pretty obvious. But it belongs to him."

Mahler's face darkened. "Him? You mean..."

Halo nodded grimly.

Kemp stood at the front of the car, bathed in the headlights. He bent down, partly out of view. Then he came up frowning.

Mahler frowned back at him, through the windshield.

"Jason Voorhees," said Halo, pointedly. "Can we get going, please?"

Mahler was still staring at his partner. Kemp spread his hands, as though confused. He opened his mouth. "Hey, Kip. I can't find the damn—"

Then his mouth wasn't there anymore. Neither was his head.

Halo shrieked so loudly, she could have sworn that something snapped in her throat. Mahler just sat there, goggling at the jet of blood that was spurting from his colleague's neck stump, spraying the windshield like rain. For a surreal moment, the body remained standing like a puppet, swaying gently. Then the knees buckled and it fell out of view.

Jason Voorhees stepped into Kemp's place, like an actor taking his mark on a floodlit stage. In the headlights' glare, he glowed with a new intensity. He was once again clutching the machete.

To Halo's dismay, Mahler had frozen rigid. He seemed to think that Jason operated on the shark principle: don't move and he won't attack. "Drive the fucking car!" she yelled, her mouth inches from the cop's ear. Her left hand found the door handle.

Mahler looked over at the driver's seat, still dazed. Then he snapped out of his fugue. Scrambling over the gear stick and dropping into position, his hand reached out for the ignition.

"Fuck," he said, his voice rising an octave. "Keys... Out there in Lyle's pocket."

Outside, Jason was bending down in front of the cruiser.

"Let's get out and run," yelled Halo, amazed that she was now calling the shots. What kind of cop was this guy? "Go!"

The world outside the car shifted dramatically.

Halo felt her center of gravity moving and quickly realized that it was the vehicle, not the surroundings, which were tilting. She peered out through the

gore-splattered windshield to see that the hood was
rising up Jason's body.

"Oh God," said Mahler, his voice now female oper-
atic. "He's gonna flip us!"

Halo frantically twisted her car door handle and
felt the exit pop open an inch. Then everything spun
around.

Jason rose stiffly to his full height, bringing the
cruiser up with him. He watched, entranced, as the
metal box swung into the air, slowly becoming a vertical structure, resting on its back bumper. Screams
issued from within, like kids on a fairground ride.
Momentum did the rest. The police car teetered,
then continued to tumble backwards. It landed on
its roof with a savage rending of metal and glass.

Jason waited for the screams to continue. None
came.

MY LIFE PART THREE:
SEEKING REDEMPTION

I obviously have no idea what kind of impression you've formed of me thus far. Diaries are very much a one-way medium. I guess that when my actions come to light, they will speak for themselves and these diaries will no doubt be discovered. Maybe published. But I'm no serial killer.

Hey, I'm not stupid. I don't want to go to prison. Who's going to spread the good word, if I'm behind bars? I'm just a person with certain beliefs, who will act on them when the opportunity presents itself. Yes, that's it: I'm a creature of opportunity.

I'm also a Redeemer. Yes, that's with a capital "R." You see, there is more than one of us. I discovered this when I moved to the big smoke. If you move in the right circles, you'll eventually find like-minded souls.

That's how I met Levin. Never knew whether that was her first name or second. Didn't really care, to tell you the truth. We more importantly shared an outlook on life. Number one: there were rules. Number two: certain people had no regard for these rules. Number three: certain people needed to learn the hard way.

To look at her, you'd never know that Levin was so hardcore. She was a mousy little thing in her mid-twenties, so delicately structured that you'd swear a good gust of wind might carry her clean away. She never seemed to eat, but we both enjoyed the odd beer. My father used to disapprove of my mother's drinking, but this was one of the few areas in which he and I disagreed. I didn't see alcohol itself as a sinful substance: it was overdoing it that deserved punishment.

Levin and I originally met in some bar or other, both reading books about morality, getting to talking and swapping notes. I never felt attracted to her and sincerely hoped the feeling was mutual.

One fateful Friday in Rotolo's bar downtown, Levin sank more beer than usual. We both did, but I was born with the ability to remain pretty sharp, no matter how much I drank. It was a blustery winter's night, with empty tables outnumbering the patrons. Out on the street, a stray newspaper sheet billowed around, controlled by the gale's fickle whims.

We had been talking about forms of worship for a while. I had been arguing that personal beliefs were enough, and that you didn't need church or a community. Levin disagreed: quietly at first, then, with added liquor, quite vociferously. "You don't know what we..." She corrected herself. "What I have."

My ears pricked at this. I was curious. "What do you mean, 'we'? Do you attend a group?"

Levin smiled and shook her head, then fidgeted with one side of her woolen beanie hat, as she always did when agitated. She glanced awkwardly over at the neon rest room sign and started to shift in her seat. "I'll be right back," she said. "Another beer?"

I quickly reached out and covered her spindly hand with my own. My tone was firm. "Don't avoid the question. What did you mean?"

Levin tried to pull her hand away, but I exerted a grip, hurting her ever so slightly. She winced and looked at me imploringly.

"I can't. Just forget about it, okay?"

Never having had a talent for forgetting, I flat-out refused to do so. Over the next half hour, I refused to let Levin and her supposedly full bladder leave the table. I mentally bludgeoned her until the whole truth seeped out.

The heavy trap door was tugged opened for me, revealing a metal ladder, which descended out of sight.

This was it. I was finally about to attend a gathering of the Redeemers. For some time now, I had been positive that an underground movement existed somewhere in America: people with similar ideas to myself. Surely Levin and I couldn't be the only ones with the right view of morality?

My path to the Redeemers' secret chambers, since that night in Rotolo's, had been long and winding.

For two months, Levin would report back on her progress toward getting me in. They weren't accepting any new members, she repeatedly told me. I repeatedly told her to keep trying.

Levin had given me a sketch outline of this clandestine sect. They were like-minded souls: people who believed in standards, but were far from being armchair moralists. No, the Redeemers would take very direct action from time to time. All members were sworn to absolute secrecy. If their behavior in the world at large led to their arrest, they would expose the sect at their peril. One member, Levin believed, had led the authorities to one of the high priests, who had committed suicide upon their arrival. The loud-mouthed traitor was subsequently bludgeoned to death in prison by an inmate who had been financially compensated by a mysterious third party.

All in all, it was just my kind of club. Some people drift through life, turning a blind eye to the wretched life choices made by others. They choose to ignore the evils that men and women do, because it's so much easier.

Not me. I intend to make a big difference with my life. That's why I persisted for so long, until finally Levin came back bright-eyed, carrying the news that I had finally gained the Redeemers' trust. I could attend a gathering of the Redeemers in a week's time. I wouldn't be allowed access to all of the chambers in use at this soirée, but I didn't care. There would be time for that.

So there I was, gazing down that trapdoor, imagining what might lie below. Levin stood beside me,

along with Mr Buenos, the owner of the restaurant.
He was clearly sympathetic to the Redeemers' cause,
as they held regular meetings beneath his establishment. Either that, or he took the money and couldn't
care less what they were doing down there.

Levin and I had shown Buenos our ID—amethyst
stones on black cords around our necks—and he had
opened the portal. I gestured for Levin to go first; for
some reason my heart was fluttering about my chest
like a sparrow. Then I followed her down into the
darkness.

When he was sure my head was safely out of the
way, Mr Buenos wedged the trapdoor back into
place.

FIFTEEN

Tom had never seen Greg looking quite this drunk.
The man had been knocking back the firewater all
evening, as though the bar closed at regular hours
and Entraxx's celebrations wouldn't stretch on
through the night. He was red in the face and
swaying around the room, slapping people's
backs.

Tom was quite drunk himself, having lost track of
the number of beers he'd consumed in this lounge.
It had been a long night, and he felt beat. He would
hit his bed early, if the promised Entraxx festivities
didn't commence by midnight.

Tom took another look at Greg and groaned. The
man was making his way across the room, toward
him and April. As he moved, he held the backs of
chairs like crutches. He locked eyes with Tom, like a
bull seeing a red rag.

"Oh, please get rid of him," said April, clearly inebriated herself if her distorted speech was any indication. "He's putting a real crimp on my night."

Tom sighed heavily as his new nemesis drew closer. Perhaps, he thought, he could feign a coronary. Or maybe a real one was on the cards.

Halo was woken by moaning. It dragged her back to consciousness, out of the thick, moist cotton wool, which seemed to fill her skull. She had no idea where she was, but it wasn't good. The moaning. What was it? She opened her eyes and saw her own legs, crunched up below her. No, they were above her. She was upside down. Then it all came flooding back.

Oh God, she thought. I'm in the police car. Jason flipped it. The weight of my own body is pushing my head down like this. It's full of blood. And that moaning is coming from the cop in the driver's seat.

Moving her head from side to side—the neck was sore, so sore—Halo saw shards of broken glass lying on what had been the inside of the roof. Both the side windows had been broken in, their metal frames buckling in the process, narrowing what might have otherwise been viable gaps to crawl out through. Halo felt a stab of anxiety as she realized that the doors probably wouldn't open either.

She had at least been fortunate that the roof had been strong enough to resist being entirely crushed, otherwise her spine might have snapped like a twig.

"We've got... to get out." The murmur came from the cop, who seemed semi-conscious. Gazing past her own contorted body, Halo could see his head, bent to one side against the roof. Or the floor, as it had become.

She shushed Mahler and he fell silent.

Please God, thought Halo, let Jason assume that we're both dead. Let him stalk off into the distance and live unhappily ever after. Let—

"Get me out of here," Mahler said. "I don't wanna die. I have a girlfriend, a mom, a dad..."

Halo surprised herself by becoming riled. There was something about this guy's rampant self-pity that provoked her. "If you want to get out of here, then shut the fuck up," she said, her voice sharp as steel, aware that the aggression was so unlike her. It angered her to think that Jason Voorhees could do this to people; not only tear them apart physically, but distort their personalities. She hated that bastard beyond anything in the world.

The cop persisted, freaking out. "I can smell gas, you dumb cunt. The whole fucking car could blow."

Halo hadn't noticed the reek, but it seemed horribly plain. Somewhere behind her head, she could also hear a slow, steady drip.

As Halo focused on escape, the cop continued to babble, still at an unwise volume. "We'd be fine if it hadn't been for you running out of the goddamn woods. Jesus fucking Christ, I'm not ready to die."

Halo gingerly cradled the door handle in her palm. It resisted movement, remaining stiff.

Even as her heart sank, Halo remembered. Just before Jason had turned them over, the door had popped open.

Abandoning the handle, she placed her flat palm on the door itself and shoved. Something cracked along the length of her arm, making her grimace.

The door grudgingly admitted an inch of weak light, indirectly provided by the cruiser's head-lamps, which were still on.

"Is your door open?" asked Mahler. "Mine won't move. You've got to get me out of here."

"I won't help you, unless you're quiet," said Halo, knowing that she was bluffing; she would be com-pelled to rescue him, even if he assembled a philharmonic orchestra inside this damn death trap.

"I've had enough of being told what to do," he blurted, voice now louder than ever. "You open my fucking door, right now. I've got a gun in here and I'll shoot you, I swear to God."

Trying her best to ignore him, Halo shoved at her own door again. It opened wider.

Her smile faded as it slammed shut again. A pair of horribly familiar feet became visible, out through the ruined window. Big, black, flecked with the blood of innocents. Halo's stomach danced.

"What are you doing?" yelled Mahler, unable to see that Jason had returned. This, she thought, was a small mercy.

Jason's feet moved away along the car. Halo twisted her head slightly and saw that he had stopped by Mahler's window.

Oh no. She had to tell him. "Jason's right outside your window. Use the gun!"

Then she watched, a captive audience, as Jason's bony knees landed heavily beside the vehicle, one by one, along with a dull flash of steel.

Mahler wailed. He was writhing in his cramped space, struggling to grab his firearm.

Jason slid the machete blade through the open window, positioning it across Mahler's throat. The cop's wail rose in volume and pitch.

Halo began to hyperventilate, feeling wholly unable to stop herself. Her whole life had spun out of control and death was laughing in her face, too.

Mahler's histrionics were cut short by an unspeakable gurgle. It intensified as Jason drew the machete back and forth, as though sawing wood. Halo closed her eyes and desperately concentrated on regaining her breath.

The gurgling ceased. A tiny part of Halo's mind—a part she didn't like to believe existed—spoke up: silence at last.

She twisted her legs around on the ceiling, attempting to change her position. At the moment, her head was dangerously close to the window.

Jason's hand shot into the car and grabbed her throat, with the speed of two consecutive frames of film. Halo spluttered and choked, fully expecting to die in seconds.

The hand around her throat was ice-cold. There was no doubt that Jason Voorhees was dead. He had been worm food for decades and reeked accordingly.

So why wasn't *she* dead yet? The grip, she realized, was only tight enough to hold her in place, staring at the makeshift roof of her cage. It wasn't even interrupting the oxygen flow to her brain.

Then she was being moved like a doll, her head slowly twisted to the left by that gelatinous fist. Was he going to break her neck? She knew it would rupture like a twig, in his grasp.

No. He was turning her to look at him.

Jason's mask filled the buckled window frame. She was tempted to close her eyes, but decided she may as well suck in all the sights this grim world had left for her.

Halo had a full view of his rancid, deformed eye socket.

The man-child. Yes, this was him, all right. This was the first opportunity she'd had to examine him up close and personal, albeit fully involuntarily, and she saw a child consumed by hatred and vengeance.

That explained why she wasn't dead yet, she knew, feeling sick to her soul. Earlier, she had wielded absolute power over Jason. He had been helpless, at the end of his own blade.

Payback would be a bitch.

When the machete's tip appeared in the window frame, alongside Jason's head, it came as no surprise. What Halo said next surprised her greatly.

"Bring it on, you sack of pus," she croaked. "An eye for an eye."

The obscene metal edged inside the vehicle.

She could have sworn Jason was smiling behind that damn mask. The thought angered her. If she was going to die by this bastard's hand, she wanted to know that she had at least scarred him, somewhere deep inside.

She drew her lips back over her teeth. "Bring it on, motherfucker. And I bet you did fuck your mother, didn't you? That's why you're so fucked in the head."

Jason's grip tightened on her throat. The machete point drew closer, only inches away.

"You were so busy fucking your mother, in fact, that you forgot to take swimming lessons, huh?"

The machete twisted, as though Jason was ensuring it was on a direct collision course with one of her eyeballs. Halo squirmed against his grip, but it was sheer iron, and tighter, cutting off her air.

Halo only hoped that she would black out before the blade did its work.

"Vengeance shall be mine." Norwood Thawn repeatedly muttered this phrase while charging through the woods, his shirt drenched with blood and sweat. His once sculptured hair was a wild, random mop. The makeshift bone knife jutted out of his right hand, like an extension of his person.

He was swiftly tracing his and Penelope's steps, back to the hotel. Here, he planned to regain their Pontiac and use it to hunt down that unholy wretch Voorhees. Having said that, he was also open to the possibility of stealing the first automobile to cross his path.

To think that he and Penelope—oh, sweet, dear Penelope—had placed so much trust in Jason. Norwood had questioned Penelope's faith, but she was generally right in such matters and he had been loath to stand in the way of her wishes. Poor, sweet Penelope—she reached out to what she thought was a fellow believer and was crushed. Jason Voorhees was a wolf in wolf's clothing, after all.

"Vengeance shall be mine," Thawn snarled again, as the wind whipped his face.

As the trees around him thinned, he saw headlamps lighting up a small road which crossed through the woods, up ahead.

Grinning manically, he attempted to restore his persona. Could he ever become the deceptively charming Norwood Thawn of old? Probably not, he realized. Not less than an hour after his beloved wife had been butchered like some base animal.

With this in mind, he decided to play the very genuine role of grieving husband. Norwood tucked the knife into his inside pocket. Then he stumbled onto the roadside and waved his arms.

It occurred to him that he hadn't waited to see whether this was a police car. As the headlamps considerately dimmed, he was relieved to see that it wasn't.

The wheels slowed rapidly, ploughing through the dirt beside him, then coming to rest.

Norwood looked suitably devastated. It came naturally to him.

The vehicle's passenger window rolled down. A hand emerged, clutching a semi-automatic pistol.

"Hey there, Norwood," smirked Ed Daimler, leveling the gun at Thawn's chest. "Where's the wife?"

When the shot sang out, like some blissful angel, Jason's machete was about to burst Halo Harlan's left eyeball. Instead, the blade jerked to one side, scratching her left cheek with its very tip. Halo could smell gunpowder, the same kind she'd smelt back in the log cabin, and knew Jason had been hit by a shotgun blast.

Machete and mask vanished from the window as Jason stood up. He walked away.

Drip, drip. The splash of gasoline.

Suddenly, this mysterious cavalry didn't seem quite so beautiful. If a shot hit the vehicle, she'd quickly meet her maker.

Seeing no reason to hesitate again, she twisted herself around, ignoring all pain which ensued from protesting limbs, so that her feet touched that left-hand door.

With all her might, she slammed both heels against it. The door flew open hard. Outside, Halo could hear someone yelling at Jason, their Southern twang evident.

"Now you stay right there, son. I don't know what you're doing with that cruiser, but I don't like the look of you one bit."

Halo began to drag herself out through the doorway.

"Stop right there I said," the voice continued. "Or I'll shoot to kill."

Don't miss, thought Halo. Please don't miss and hit the car.

She scrabbled at metal, plastic and anything else that gave her a hold.

"Stop!"

The shotgun fired again.

The car didn't explode, but it did shake violently, absorbing some kind of impact.

Finally scrabbling free, Halo saw that Jason had been struck by the blast, staggered back and lay sprawled across the car's up-ended rear bumper. Beyond him, in front of a small pick-up truck, stood a handsome old man with young eyes and long white hair. He looked like some kind of country singer.

He was looking at her imploringly. "I had to do it. He wouldn't stop walking, like I told him."

Halo cupped her hands over her mouth like a loud-hailer. "He's not dead yet. Shoot the car."

Even as she spoke, Jason was stirring, raising him-self off the bumper.

The newcomer set about reloading the weapon, snapping it in half and fumbling with a cartridge. He cursed under his breath.

"Quickly," she urged. "Before he—"

At the sound of her voice, Jason's head swung to face her. The blast appeared to have struck his chest, removing a chunk out of his mask's chin portion and revealing some of his jagged teeth. Despite appearing to be a mess of bullet hits, burn damage and other miscellaneous wounds, he was frighten-ingly steady on his feet.

The old man clunked the weapon back together and hurriedly took aim.

Jason walked away from the police car.

Halo ran toward the trees and launched herself into a dive.

The old man fired.

The blast gunned into the cruiser's exposed under-side, hitting the gas tank.

The police car tore apart; a fiercely expanding ball of light, heat and thunder. Fire lashed out in all directions and pieces of metal showered the sur-rounding area, hammering into the old man's pick-up, the road and the trees on either side of it. Churning black smoke mushroomed.

Halo landed heavily on one side of the road, clumsily attempting to adopt the fetal position. Flame lashed her legs and she cried out. Scurrying further away from the road, she rolled down a slope amidst dirt and leaves.

The blast had subsided, but the fire raged on.

Halo wanted to lie down there in the relative safety of the trees, but was afraid to. The last she had seen, Jason was standing right next to the car when it blew. But she wasn't sure exactly what it took to dispose of him.

As she unsteadily righted herself, it struck her that she might be on fire and she frantically patted her legs, back and front. Her jeans had blackened, but the skin below felt okay. She'd live... for now.

What about the old man? Halo dearly hoped that he had survived the blast. She took a deep breath and began to make her way back up the gentle slope.

Deputy Ryger's chair creaked in protest as he swung around in it. He jabbed a positive thumb in the air. Cradling the receiver under his numerous chins, he reported to Sheriff Claymark.

"Those feds have found one of their killers, Sheriff. He was running around in the woods. They just ran into him."

Claymark raised an eyebrow and nodded. "Swell. That's one good thing today, at least. They gonna bring him in?"

Ryger addressed the phone. "You gonna bring him in?"

Ryger nodded vigorously at the sheriff.

"Okay," said Claymark, to no one in particular. "Make sure our finest cell is ready. We have a distinguished guest on the way."

"See you shortly." Melissa van Stadt deactivated the phone, careful to keep her concentration on the road.

Beside her, Ed Daimler had his gun trained on Norwood Thawn's perspiring face. Thawn was still panting as though having completed a marathon. Both his hands were cuffed to a metal pole, which ran behind the back seat, making him sit awkwardly.

"So I'll ask you again," said Daimler. "Where's Penelope?"

While Daimler was concerned about Penelope still being on the loose, the simple act of apprehending Norwood had sent joy coursing around his system. As always, it was way better than any drink or drug. Sadly, this feeling wasn't readily available in pharmacies, bars or even crackhouses. You had to track down and apprehend a felon on America's Most Wanted list, in order to experience it.

"I think," said Norwood, attempting to regain some composure, "that you'd better save the interview for whichever shit heel station you're taking me to. With a damn good attorney present."

"Mr Thawn," said van Stadt, "I think you'd better find yourself a miracle worker. You were carrying a knife made from human bone and you're covered in blood. I'll wager that none of it belongs to you, either."

At this, Norwood's eyes misted over. "No," he said, sadly. "It doesn't."

His bottom lip began to tremble and he averted his face from van Stadt. When his sobbing began, the two agents stole a curious look at each other. This wasn't quite what they had anticipated.

SIXTEEN

As Halo neared the top of the slope, the gas fumes threatened to overcome her. She changed direction to avoid the noxious heat. Then she peered out at the scene she had left behind. The fearsome blaze continued to suck oxygen. Looking at the smoldering debris which surrounded the cruiser, Halo hoped to see Jason's torched corpse.

Nothing. Perhaps he had been blown to smithereens? In Halo's heart she knew this wasn't the case. At least, until she found hard evidence that he was dead, she would assume the worst.

There was no sign of the old man. Halo surveyed his pick-up. Chunks of blackened, twisted metal dotted the ground around the battered old vehicle. A whole heap of these chunks had landed on the back of the truck itself and sat there, sizzling and smoking.

Halo had to concede that she knew nothing about the power of such explosions. Just about the only ones she had ever seen had been on movies and TV shows: everyone knew that those were as far removed from reality as you could get. In *The A-Team*, for instance, grenades propelled people over bales of straw, who then picked themselves up, unblemished. Maybe a little shaken. She and Trey had watched an episode once and it had made him real mad. "Where's the fuckin' shrapnel?" he'd shouted at the screen.

Halo could feel every scar and bruise, both outside her body and inside. It was clear only adrenaline and the sheer bloody-minded will to survive were keeping her standing. Right now, she could so easily crumble into a heap and pray for death.

Finding a vantage point behind a thick tree, she drifted into a trance, staring into the fire. She wondered whether she would have fought this hard to live, if she hadn't known she was pregnant. If not, was that healthy? How much was her own life worth? She was starting to think it was worth more than before. Now that Jason had tried to deny her right to exist, it seemed all the more precious to her. You don't know what you've got, until it's almost—

A big hand slapped on her shoulder, gripping the bone.

Halo was yanked out of her contemplation, as if propelled by a bungee cord.

She turned to see the old man, her savior. His face had been rendered half black, like some kind of cartoon character after a dynamite blast. Ash clung to his beard like snow. He sealed his lips with one forefinger.

Halo nodded and tried to calm herself down.

The old man's eyes were darting around, surveying their immediate environment and stealing the odd glance at the inferno. He leaned over to Halo. "I'm not sure if he's gone."

"Neither am I."

What she wanted most, besides being whisked magically out of Crystal Lake, was a big hug. There was something paternal about this guy, but this really didn't seem the right moment to seek fatherly reassurance. Still, there was no harm in a pleasantry or two.

"My name's Halo. Thanks for getting involved: anyone else would have just driven on. He was about to kill me."

"My name's Rick Hunter and it's my pleasure. Hell, that guy looked just like... uh..." He scratched his head.

Halo lowered her voice, as if the very recital of the name might conjure up its owner. "Jason Voorhees?"

Hunter nodded, frowning. Then he shook his head. "Can't be. I've been hearing about that kid... That man... for decades. He was supposed to have died in the Fifties, for crying out loud. He's an urban legend."

"Not any more. This is the real deal. I've already put a machete in his neck and seen him shot. I've shot him myself, goddammit. And now this. He keeps coming back."

Hunter placed a gentle hand on her back and briefly squeezed her to him. Then he hefted his shotgun in one hand.

"One slug left, that's it," he said with a weak smile. "We need to get to that pick-up, real quick, you hear me? He may well have been blown to tiny pieces by that big bang, but I wouldn't bet my gold discs on it."

Halo wanted to ask what he meant, but the situation took priority. They turned their attention back to the pick-up.

"Here," said Hunter, grabbing her hand. "Take the keys. Just in case." Halo felt the warm metal of a key ring being pressed into her palm.

"No, don't do that," she protested. But Hunter firmly shook his head. "Just in case," he repeated. "Now let's go. Real quick and quiet."

The very moment they crept out on to the road, Halo expected Jason's all too familiar frame to lurch out of the darkness, machete poised behind his head.

The only sound came from the flames, which were starting to recede. Their footsteps made little or no sound, imprinted as they were into the road's dirt surface.

Halo realized that Hunter's truck was facing the smoldering police car. Once inside his vehicle, they would have to turn around in order to escape the scene. All the more opportunity for Jason to attack.

She clutched Hunter's arm. He jumped, just as she had on the slope, then realized it was her.

"Why don't we get away on foot?" she whispered. "I've got a really bad feeling about getting in that thing."

Hunter considered the suggestion. "We're too far away from anything," he decided. "We need these damn wheels."

Halo tried to cast aside her fears. She let herself dream that maybe Jason had been killed in the explosion. After all, there had to be a limit to his indestructibility.

Or even if he was alive, perhaps he had staggered off into the woods, wounded and looking to regenerate.

Clunk. Hunter pulled his truck's door open.

Halo expected Jason to burst out from the shadows inside, but nothing happened.

Hunter gestured for her to enter the passenger's side.

Halo took one last look around and saw what she had been dreading.

Something was moving in the fire. Shifting. Altering.

"Come on," urged Hunter, behind her.

Halo continued to stare. Then she realized that it was only the cruiser's frame transforming, molded by the intense heat.

The engine revved and the headlamps blinked into operation, half-blinding Halo.

In the driver's seat, Hunter frantically waved for her to join in. A "What are you waiting for?" look was plastered across his face.

Halo ran to her side of the pick-up and tugged open the door. She felt like she was dancing on a razor's edge. Any moment, she was going to fall.

The moment her backside hit the seat, Hunter spun the wheel. He backed the pick-up against the side of the road. Then moved it forward again.

It wasn't enough. With a grunt, Hunter backed the pick-up a second time.

Halo gripped the sides of her seat. She was seeing things in the darkness. Every cluster of branches, every configuration of leaves, it shape shifted into hockey masks before her paranoid eyes.

The pick-up lurched forward. Halo didn't have to look at her knuckles to know they were white.

Then the pick-up was back on the road. Halo studied her wing mirror, watching the fire shrink into the distance, as though waiting for the catch. She pondered whether she would ever be able to live a normal life again. Would she always be waiting for Jason to pop up?

Then she remembered Shelley.

"I have to go to the Phoenix Heights hotel. Could you take me there?"

Hunter arched an eyebrow, then shrugged. "No problem, Halo. Which, by the way, is a very pretty name."

"Thank you." Halo rubbed her sore eyes. When they opened, she noticed that it was nearing midnight. Time flies when you're fighting for your life, she noted.

"I'm sorry," she added. "You've done more than enough already. It's just that I'm really worried about my sister."

"Like I say, we'll go straight there. I know a good route. We'll both have to speak to the police. You also look like you need an ambulance, missy."

"Oh yeah, I'll do all that stuff, once I know whether Shelley's really dead."

The truck's speed was reassuring. Every turn of the wheel took them further away from Jason, she told herself, unfolding her arms and trying to relax.

All around them, woods were starting to give way to open fields. Just the sight of open space made Halo's stomach loosen a knot or two.

"You a musician?" she asked, remembering the gold discs.

"Used to be. Now I'm a producer." A smile triggered crow's feet at the corners of his eyes. "I'm too old to tour, these days."

"Where were you going tonight?" she asked, closing her eyes.

"Went hunting today. I was on my way home, couple miles out of Crystal Lake."

"Hey, talk about living up to your name." Halo didn't agree with blood sports, but felt she owed him some interest. "Sorry for interrupting your journey. Did you get anything?"

"A few birds and whatnot. They're in the back, but they're probably barbecued by now, with all that junk."

Halo actually allowed herself a laugh. She couldn't remember the last one she'd experienced. It felt so unnaturally good that she didn't want to stop. The laugh ended up sounding hysterical, though, so she regretfully cut it short.

"You've had a terrible shock," said Hunter, as Halo twisted around in her seat. "You'll need good care."

"I know," she said, pressing her face against the window that looked out over the back of the pick-up and the dark road beyond. She wanted to see if Hunter's poor dead birds were visible, amid the debris. "I just need to keep going for a while..."

She had planned to end the sentence with the word "longer", but it never came. Instead, her mouth stayed wide open.

HATE-KILL-REPEAT

There, among the warped lengths of metal, the half-rolled tarpaulins and—yes—the dead creatures, was a hockey mask, gazing impassively up into space.

Dryness spread through Halo's mouth, then down her throat. She feared she would turn to stone, that very second, merely from gazing upon the mask.

Was it just a mask?

Blown off of Jason's head by the explosion?

She sensed Hunter's concern. "What's wrong?" he asked.

Her mouth moved: a futile gesture. Her brain was not up to formulating words. All of its energy was concentrated on watching the mask.

Then it began to rise.

In horribly timeless slow motion, Jason Voorhees raised his top half like the blade of a penknife. His malformed head rose smoothly and inexorably, until it was level with hers.

Halo watched powerlessly as Jason yanked his machete free of the junk.

Without taking her eyes off him, she murmured. "He's on the back of the truck."

"What?" Hunter's brow furrowed. He checked the wing mirror and saw nothing. Then a glance back over his shoulder delivered the goods.

"Well, fuck me."

"What the hell are we going to do?"

Jason pulled himself toward them, machete in one fist. Crawling like some giant cockroach.

"Hold on to something, real tight," said Hunter. "Do it now."

Halo thrust the fingers of her right hand through a plastic handle near the ceiling. She had no idea what to do with the other hand, so braced her entire body, pressing her feet firmly under the dashboard.

Jason's fist punched in the back window.

Glass shards whipped the side of Halo's head.

Hunter slammed down the brake, practically standing on it. Halo gritted her teeth, determined not to vanish through the windshield. The truck jerked violently, reaching a whiplash halt.

Jason soared over their cabin, down over the hood and bounced along the road like a lump of clay, in front of the truck. He had initially struck the ground head first. Anyone else would have died instantly. Yet Jason Voorhees was not anyone else.

"Run over him," Halo yelled.

Dazed from the emergency stop, Hunter pulled himself together and gunned the accelerator. The truck groaned in protest as it took off, rather slower than either of them would have liked.

By the time it hit Jason, it was traveling at no more than ten miles per hour. Still, thought Halo, the vehicle's weight alone had to damage him.

The truck rose into the air as one front wheel clambered over Jason's left hip, chest and right shoulder.

"That should do it," breathed Hunter. "Let's get the hell out of here."

Halo was already gazing through the space where the back window used to be, one knee crunching painfully on tiny fragments of broken glass which had sprayed her seat.

"He's not on the road," she shouted. "He must be under us!"

Before Hunter could react, a terrible raking noise came from somewhere beneath them. Then, with an ear-splitting rending of metal, something burst upwards.

Hunter's face twisted in agony. He howled as his groin soaked with blood.

Transfixed, Halo sorely wished she could do something to help, but was also aware that he had lost all control of the wheel. She reached over and gripped one side of it, attempting to keep it steady. Nevertheless, they were drifting off the road.

Her new friend's face had turned purple. His tortured roar stopped for a second, only to be replaced by an even louder, more miserable cacophony.

Halo couldn't take any more. Spying a stout wooden fence bordering a field to their right, she spun the wheel in that direction.

The truck crashed through the fence, landing on the ground beyond with an almighty judder. Halo looked through the window and saw that Jason had finally lost his grip. He lay tangled in the spiked remnants of the fence: possibly even impaled. She couldn't see. All she knew, was that the filthy parasite had been prized from the truck.

As they bumped and bounced across the field, Halo would have been jubilant, were it not for the fact that the man she had briefly known as Hunter was dead. Decades of life extinguished in the space of one minute. Slumped to one side, his face was ghastly, his foot still jammed against the accelerator.

Halo brought the wheel back around, directing them back toward the road. The truck burst back out through another section of fence. This time, Halo took the impact in her stride, like a rodeo rider.

One mile later, she stamped on the brakes as smoothly as possible, considering that she wasn't in the driver's seat. Then she jumped out, ran around to Hunter's side and struggled with the effort of removing him from his own vehicle. There was, she noticed, a jagged hole in the seat where the machete had penetrated upwards. Halo winced.

Sweat dripped from her face as she laid Hunter in some grass by the roadside, as gently as her ebbing strength would allow. She would send people to collect him, she told herself.

The machete had fallen out, under the truck. It was partly bent, and covered in disgusting gore, so she hurled it far into the bushes. Then she scrambled back inside the vehicle and drove on. Hunter's seat was slick with his blood and the sound of his pain still seemed to echo in the confined space.

Yet Halo was beginning to feel numb. Her brain had somehow managed to accept witnessing the slaughter of a good man. The experience had been filed away. Repressed. Priorities had taken over. She had to find Shelley, dead or alive. Inside, Halo felt cold and hollow.

That scared her more than Jason Voorhees ever could.

SEVENTEEN

Sometimes, Clayden Heinz liked to simply stand back and admire it all: his little empire. Cradling a glass of Scotch on the rocks, he sucked on a Gauloises cigarette and gazed up at the behemoth that he had built. Almost literally, he had certainly been involved in the hotel's long renovation, at every stage. Planning what in his eyes would be the perfect place to stay. An establishment that would bring new respectability to the area, and more importantly, money. The area had a few hotels dotted around, sure, but nothing like this.

Heinz allowed himself to appreciate the beautiful phoenix fountain, which constantly jetted water up in majestic arcs. By this time of night, it was illuminated with powerful submerged lamps, so that the water appropriated the golden glow of fire.

His focus shifted lazily to the building itself, panning from window to window, along each and every floor. Some were blacked out, curtains drawn. Others emitted dull light.

He was in love with the place, more so than he had been with any lousy piece of skirt. Thirteen gorgeous floors, almost two hundred sexy rooms. The kind of facilities that other hotels could only lust after. Heinz issued a self-satisfied snort.

It had been a hell of a day. The business with Shelley for one thing. Then the scare with a supposed murderer running around. Or was it more than one killer? With all his usual running around, Heinz had failed to ever get the full story. Perhaps Bluestone would bring him up to speed later.

His watch sounded, as it always did on the hour. Another day over.

Hopefully, by daylight tomorrow, the police would have caught this latest Jason Voorhees wannabe. Heinz didn't care, provided it didn't harm his business.

He took another sip of Scotch. As he swallowed, his ears pricked. Was that an engine approaching? Sounded like it was moving fast.

He stood up from the fountain, trying to listen over the endlessly surging water, which gushed from the metallic bird's mouth, into the huge bowl below.

Sure enough, it was an engine. And it was getting closer. He could hear the spin of wheels on gravel. His gravel. The special 2.5mm limestone chips which he had personally selected from a glossy catalogue.

Perhaps this was a last minute visitor, unexpectedly finding him or herself at a loose end. Often happened on a Saturday, but why all the rush?

Lights came into view as the vehicle entered the hotel's grounds. Heinz wrinkled his nose: it was a dirty, run down pick-up truck.

The truck screeched to an abrupt stop by the fountain. The door opened immediately to reveal a young woman who looked like she had been through several world wars. Heinz recoiled at the very sight of her: the tangled, matted hair (was that blood in it?), the scratches on her face, the torn clothing. She was running—well, limping—toward him.

Heinz's human side—the one which had started to erode at the age of ten, when his mother left home—knew that he should appear shocked and sympathetic. He should usher this girl into the safety of his establishment.

In reality, all he could think was: why here? Of all the places they could have driven to, why did they have to come to his precious outpost?

Halo reached him, staring furiously at the metallic nametag, which clung to his suit's breast. "You the manager?"

Her eyes were beautiful, but diamond-hard. "I... I am. Can I help you, miss?"

Halo's words came out like a toppling domino chain. "I need to check on my sister. Shelley Harlan. Is she here? Is she still working here?"

There it was again: Greg's bony, white knuckled forefinger, prodding Tom in the chest.

"You've really changed since you became the big man," said Greg, his eyes focused on no one in particular, even though he was clearly talking to Tom. "We used to be good friends."

Tom placed his drink on the bar behind him and held both hands up in protest. "I thought we still were, until today. Greg, man, why didn't you talk to me about this before? We're supposed to be having a good time."

"You're not approachable any more. All you seem to do is sit in your office, writing memos. Ah, fuck it."

Greg swung his hand through the air. As he did so, his drink splashed over his glass's rim, down onto the carpet.

Tom could feel April's irritation, both at Greg for being such a jerk, and at him for not doing something manly, like beating Greg to a pulp. April always struck him as the kind of girl who would go out with security guards, or something. In fact, he'd seen her making very obvious eye contact with the hotel's own head of security, earlier that night. Not that he cared all that much.

This was an issue he really needed to face: what exactly *did* he care about, these days?

Greg's voice faded away, but his lips kept moving.

Tom tried to look at himself objectively. In just a few years, it seemed that he had changed dramatically, and not all for the better. Where was the emotion in his life? The passion? Sure, he and April had good sex but when that was done, they had nothing much to talk about. She just lay there smoking cigarettes and the pair of them small-talked as though they had just met.

Greg's finger prodded him again, but he barely noticed.

"See? You're not even fucking listening to me, right now. Asshole."

"Greg, will you leave us the hell alone?" April piped up.

Greg turned on her, eyes blazing. "Who asked for your opinion, April? What do you care? Everyone knows you're only fucking Tom because of his position."

Tom slammed his bottle down on the bar. "That's enough," he said, noticing nonetheless that April didn't deny Greg's accusation. Worst of all, he couldn't care less. What had happened to the old Tom Sheridan? He shook his head, lost in his own wilderness of the soul. He needed something new and doubted it was going to come from Entraxx.

Greg was glaring at him. Challenging. "How do you plan to stop me, tough guy?"

"Ladies and gentlemen." This was Cary Carson, standing once again in the center of the lounge, clinking a fork against a glass. Tom snapped out of his self-analysis and tried to pay attention, glad that Greg had been momentarily silenced. "Apologies for the delay, but it's now midnight, and you shall go the ball. Follow me through to—"

Suddenly, Carson's voice was overlaid with another, louder and far more urgent. A woman's voice, out in the reception area, sounding very upset.

"Is she here, or not? I have to know immediately."

The reception area disturbance had distracted Carson. "You can, uh, bring your drinks with you," he said, trying to keep his clip-on grin straight. Then he turned and peered anxiously through the glass of the lounge's double doors.

Leaning back on his stool, Tom did the same. He could see a mop of messy hair, standing by the reception desk, coupled with a finger that was doing a lot of pointing. Might this person be related to Greg?

"Her name is Shelley Harlan. No, I've already spoken to your dumb manager outside. He told me she's been fired, but doesn't know if she's still in the building."

Then the girl's face became visible and Tom recognized her instantly, despite the drastic change in her appearance and attitude.

April was frowning at him. "It's that girl," he said. "The one with the rednecks this afternoon."

April gave him a mock excited look, then dropped it like a stage curtain. "I couldn't give a tiny rat's ass," she said, spitting each word in his face. "This whole night sucks."

Tom stared at April for a moment, finally realizing a lot of things about his girlfriend.

Greg was trying to look out into the reception, but Tom imagined he was seeing two of everything. The bar lounge was starting to empty out now, as over a hundred Entraxx drones clutched their drinks, preparing to relocate and dance the night away.

Halo's voice drifted back in from reception again. "Fine," she yelled. "I'll find her myself." Tom saw her marching toward the double doors, so wasn't at all surprised when they burst inwards, knocking one Entraxx suit off balance and causing his drink to be deposited on a female colleague's lap. Tom gulped.

People shrank back from this newcomer, who looked as though she had been raised by gorillas.

Some of them even outstretched arms to protect those behind them, in a heroic gesture. It was as though they fully expected this woman to produce an Uzi and go postal.

Halo adjusted her voice to a slow, even and perfectly audible snarl. "Has anyone... seen... Shelley Harlan? The receptionist?" Her eyes jerked demandingly from person to person.

Carson was staring hard out at reception, clearly outraged that hotel security had yet to intervene and cart this problem away.

Tom made his way through the crowd, jostling people aside. He smiled nervously at Halo.

"Remember me?" he said. "We met earlier today."

Halo nodded neutrally. "I remember."

"Why do you need to find your sister?"

"Because..." Halo began. Her bottom lip began to quiver, but she pulled herself together with an angry gnash of teeth. "Because," she said, more mechanically, as though trying not to think what these words meant, "I think she might have been murdered."

"Oh my God," he said. "I'm so sorry. Don't worry, I'll help you look." Around him, the lounge was rippling with dismay at this talk of murder.

Halo nodded thankfully at Tom. Feeling as though he was taking his life in his hands, he stepped forward and lightly embraced her. She felt like an oak mannequin.

"What are we all waiting for?" said a familiar voice, just behind Tom. "So Tom's got a new chick with a sister who might be dead. What the fuck? Let's get drunk."

Tom's blood boiled. Releasing Halo, he turned around slowly to see Greg, just as he had expected and feared.

Greg shriveled in the heat of Tom's wrath.

Throughout the lounge, you could have heard an Amex card drop.

"I think you've had enough," said Tom. Then he leant back and punched Greg in the face.

His former friend tumbled against people behind him. They flinched away from him, ensuring that he struck the plush carpet with full force, groaning nauseously.

April appeared next to Halo, whose arm she prodded. Halo glared back.

"She's not really your new girl, is she, Tom?" April slurred. "If so, I can't say much for your taste."

All around them, colleagues were expressing hushed surprise that Tom and April were together in the first place.

"She's not my new girl, April. But you're not my girl either. Sorry."

April squealed and raised a hand to slap Tom. Halo grabbed the other woman's wrist, fixing her with a threatening gaze. April broke loose and stomped out of the room, hands cupped over her mouth, unleashing sporadic roars of outrage.

"Okay," said Halo, turning to Tom. "Are you done? I need to find my sister."

"Sure. Let's go."

Cary Carson stomped into the spot which Greg had once occupied. Giving Tom the evil eye, he waved for everyone to leave the room. "Come on,

folks. Nothing to see here. Head on through to Ballroom B. Down there on the left."

People barely moved, entranced by the spectacle. Greg lay on the ground between their feet,
clutching his face, unaided by anyone.

"What the hell are you doing, Sheridan?" Carson
demanded, his nose even redder than usual.

Halo spoke up. "Probably what he should have
done a long time ago."

Tom looked at her, then back to Carson. Still
stoked with adrenaline from throwing his first
ever punch, he ground his jaw uneasily.

Carson glared at Halo as if he wanted her to
crumble to dust, right there and then. "When I
want the opinion of trash," he said, "I'll ask for it."

Tom raised his fist. "You know nothing about
this woman. You want a knuckle sandwich too,
you old corporate cocksucker? Shove your stupid,
dull, dehumanizing company up your flabby ass."

That was OTT, he thought, even as he said it.
But it should do the trick. There was no going
back.

Carson looked stunned, as did many of their
audience.

"That goes for all of you," Tom added, casting a
withering glance at random faces. "Standing there
with your mouths open when someone seriously
needs help. Let's hope your weekend hasn't been
spoilt, huh? Have a peachy fucking night."

He placed a trembling hand on Halo's back and
guided her out through the double doors.

A burly official was marching up to meet them.
Tom recognized him as the hotel's security chief.

Walt Bluestone stood with his hands on his hips. He ran a distasteful look up and down Halo, who glowered back. "I heard there was a commotion in there," he frowned, nodding toward the bar. "Anything to do with you people?"

Clayden Heinz had seen a shadow, out the corner of his eye. He gulped back the last of his scotch, then crunched the remaining chips of ice between his teeth. Still holding the glass, he approached one of the thick clumps of trees which made Phoenix Heights appear even more palatial.

As financially rewarding as hotel management had been for him, Heinz's heart had always been with security. If he had been born bigger and stronger, that's the job he would have done. The idea of people trusting you to protect them, while paying you handsomely, attracted him greatly.

He liked to keep track of his own security team's movements. Vicariously grab a piece of their action. He knew he checked up on them more often than the average hotel manager might. Bluestone had tried to subtly tell him so, on more than one occasion, but Heinz feigned ignorance and continued to join his guards for strolls around the grounds. Maybe some of them thought he was gay.

Nearly at the trees now, he could hear a faint crackle. Radio static? Must be one of the guards. Bored and tipsy, Heinz wandered into the darkness which skulked between the trees. The gravel gave way to soft earth, making him wish he wasn't wearing his new Guccis.

Fishing around in his pocket, he produced a key fob, which doubled as a tiny torch bulb. He activated it with his thumb and it emitted faint light. Just enough for him to avoid bumping into things.

He heard another crackle, nearby. He followed it, his heart thumping. This was the life, he thought.

A huge figure loomed over him.

Norwood Thawn had stopped crying about a mile back. Ed Daimler figured he was fair game for questioning. Damn the rules. It had been a long day and Daimler felt hard done by. Mean-spirited. He wanted to toy with this fucking psycho.

"So what's this little spree been all about?" he asked, looking down the gun's barrel at Thawn's red, puffy face. "God stuff?"

Thawn looked at him, as though he was scum.

Maybe I am, thought Daimler. But I'm no killer. At least, I only kill people who try to kill me.

Seeing Thawn's lips remain tightly sealed, Daimler felt even more playful. He couldn't resist provoking the captive some more. He felt like a cat with a cornered mouse. Why not jab a couple of paws at it?

"That's fine," he murmured, smiling at Thawn. "No need to talk. I think I've got you all figured out, anyhow."

Thawn's eyes flashed with indignation. Daimler laughed to himself. Thawn was a bright guy. The very thought of being so easy to decode must really make him mad.

"Really?" Thawn finally said, disdainfully. "Well, aren't you the good little agent. Quantico will be pleased. Until they realize you're talking out your ass."

"Am I? You don't even know what I think yet."

"I know that you know nothing about me."

"I'm a profiler, Mr Thawn. Just like my colleague here. Our job is to build up a picture of what goes on in the sick, twisted psyches of fuck-ups like you."

Again, anger in those blue eyes. Daimler was getting the rise he wanted.

"We've seen your 'work', if you could call it that," he continued. "To be honest, it doesn't take even a man of my experience to unravel your moral fabric."

Thawn looked away, staring out of the window. Yet his brain was ticking.

"And it is all about morals, isn't it?" Daimler pressed. He adopted a child-like voice. "'People don't behave the way I want them to!' Boo fucking hoo."

"Ed," said van Stadt. "Aren't you supposed to save this stuff for—?"

"I don't care," he told her. "We've traveled a long way to catch up with our guest here. I wanna get some value out of him." Then he turned back, adjusting his gun so it was trained on Thawn's left eye.

"So where does all that hate come from, Mr Thawn?"

Silence. Blurred trees zipped by.

"I asked you a question," said Daimler, as calmly as he could manage. Images of the victims were flickering through his mind. He would have dearly loved to pistol-whip Thawn, right there and then. Smash in his face and see how righteous he felt then. "Answer me."

A gentle smile spread across Thawn's lips, as if he knew the tables had turned. Daimler couldn't legally make him talk, so this fed was the one most likely to wind up frustrated by the one-sided discussion.

Daimler decided to play a trump card. "We've done some checking up on you," he said, trying to maintain a cheery disposition, as irritating for Thawn as possible. "Son of an evangelist, back in Ohio. Now there's a shock, huh? Did he interfere with you, perhaps?"

Thawn exhaled sharply, turning his eyes back to Daimler. He looked like a snake, posed to strike. Except Daimler knew he couldn't.

"Ed, that's too much," said van Stadt, in the process of taking a left turn. "Calm it down."

"Mel, I'm perfectly calm." Daimler grinned at Thawn. "So did he? No, perhaps not. You would have enjoyed that too much."

Beside him, van Stadt rolled her eyes.

Ping! Tenth floor. The elevator glided open after what seemed like an eternity. Halo was up here under sufferance. Her new ally, whose name she still didn't know, had blustered his way around the security meathead, then bustled her off swiftly toward the elevators.

"If you don't stop pushing me around, I'll break your jaw," she told him, as he waited for her to step out on to the tenth floor's red patterned carpet. "You don't seem to understand what—"

"Look, I understand that you're extremely worried about your sister. But running around the reception area shouting isn't going to achieve anything. What's your name, by the way?"

"Halo. I don't care what yours is." In reality, she did care. But now was not the time for pleasantries.

Those things hadn't gotten her very far in life. Besides, she'd wasted enough time already, hadn't she?

"Oh, swell. Anyway, we need to be a little more subtle about this."

Tom paused outside one of the doors that lined this lengthy corridor and fumbled for the key. As he twisted it in the lock, a muffled clunk signaled their right of entry.

"Having said that," he muttered over his shoulder as he led the way into the room, "we should also call the police."

"Not yet," said Halo, roundly ignoring the lavish splendor of Tom's spacious room. "Shelley first, then the police."

Tom had the phone receiver in his hand as he turned to face her. "But don't you think the police would be useful in finding her?"

Halo folded her arms defensively as she paced around the room. "I'm worried they'll think I'm crazy. I mean, I'd have to tell them that I've been chased around Crystal Lake by Jason Voorhees."

Tom stared at her. "Why would you tell them that?"

"Because it's fucking true," she snapped. "The bastard killed everyone that you saw me with today. He almost killed me several times. And if you don't believe me, I'm going straight back downstairs."

"Okay, okay. I believe you. So, do you think Jason killed your sister?"

Halo made herself relate the story of her meeting with the Thawns, as patiently as she could.

When she had finished, Tom looked incredulous. He replaced the phone handset and fell into a sofa. "My God. So they definitely said they were staying here?"

She nodded.

Tom thought for a moment. "Did you get their names?"

"First names. Norwood and Penelope."

"Okay," said Tom, reaching for the phone again. "Let me try something."

Clayden Heinz was dancing on broken glass. The sudden appearance of Tyrone Finton, one of Walt's bigger boys, had made him drop the tumbler. In the aftershock, he stumbled around, standing on the damn thing and smashing it.

"Fuck it," he said. "Thank God these Guccis have tough soles."

"What are you doing in here, Mr Heinz?" asked Finton. He had reacted professionally to the sudden surprise, but the bunched muscles on either side of his jaw suggested that he wished he could strangle the little jerk.

Heinz felt a twinge of embarrassment. Then his ego took over, and he flushed with indignation at being questioned by one of his own grunts. "I heard a noise," he said. "I thought I'd take a look. You got a problem with that?"

"With respect, sir, I do. That's the kind of thing we should be taking care of. Especially on a night like this, with killers on the loose."

Heinz nodded, saying nothing. He knew the grunt was right. "So why are you in here... Fenton, is it?"

"Tyrone Finton, sir. I saw rustling in these trees. Turned out to be a family of raccoons."

"Ah," said Heinz, as the pair threaded their way back out onto the gravel. "Pesky little varmints, huh?"

Back among the trees, somewhere in the darkness, they were being watched.

EIGHTEEN

The FBI's new captive stared morosely out into the darkness, as if willing his wife's face to appear, somewhere out there in its depths. He wrung his hands together, as best he could in the cuffs.

Daimler had decided to ignore his prisoner for a while. No longer holding Thawn at gunpoint, he was chatting to van Stadt: a somewhat one-sided conversation. While Daimler felt bloated with the triumph of finding Norwood, his colleague stony faced.

"Once we've dumped this jerk," he said, "would you let me buy you dinner?"

Van Stadt turned her head slightly in his direction. That expression, he thought, could wither a dick at forty paces. Yet her frosty veneer was all part and parcel of the attraction. He wondered if they would ever get it on. Earlier that night, he had thought that the pair of them had reached a kind of understanding.

They had been flirting, hadn't they? Or was it just him? Had he lost all sense of perspective?

He suddenly felt impotent and stupid. Gripping his gun, he swung back to Thawn.

"What's to stop me from killing you now?"

Thawn raised an unimpressed eyebrow. It was van Stadt who spoke. "Ed, if you don't stop this, I swear I'll report you."

Daimler bared his teeth. Why couldn't she get the message? This was unorthodox, sure, but it was about saving lives. They had to find Norwood's wife, before she continued the couple's work.

"Nothing," he told Thawn, answering his own question. "There's nothing to stop me."

"Oh, really?" said Thawn. "I had assumed the question was rhetorical."

Van Stadt opened her mouth, but Daimler raised a finger before she could speak. She scowled at the road, which was now flanked by huge fields.

"I'll shoot you and say you tried to resist arrest," smiled Daimler.

Thawn shrugged. "Then you'd never find out why we did it. What's your name, again? Ed?"

"Never mind what my fucking name is. All you need to know, is that I'm the guy who's going to drastically redecorate the back of this car, unless you tell me where your murdering bitch of a wife is."

Thawn tugged furiously at his bonds. Daimler realized he had hit a sensitive area, but wasn't sure why.

"You really want to know, Mr Big Shot?" asked Thawn, looking even more feral than when they had picked him up.

"I'd like nothing more in the whole, wide world."

"She's dead."

Van Stadt issued a gasp. Daimler frowned at her. "Really, Norwood? How did she die?" he asked.

Thawn's voice vibrated as he began the sentence. "She was murdered... by Jason Voorhees."

Daimler laughed uproariously, slapping the butt of his gun against the head of his seat.

Thawn studied him with contempt.

Daimler's face was red. He wiped his eyes. "Jason Voorhees! Now, I had a feeling the two of you would come up here looking for that myth. But, let's get this straight. You're saying that not only did you find Jason, but he killed your wife?"

Thawn nodded gravely. "That's right," he said, eyes locked with Daimler's. "He killed her, and you too will die, very soon."

Daimler blinked. He cupped his free hand behind one ear. "Excuse me?"

Thawn went back to staring out of the window.

Tom replaced the handset with a sigh. He had tried a scam with the switchboard, pretending to be an old friend of Norwood and Penelope's. It was their wedding anniversary, he told the receptionist and he wanted to have a bottle of champagne delivered to their room. Did she have any guests by those names?

She didn't. He had failed, miserably.

"Of course," he said, looking across at Halo, who was still pacing relentlessly around the suite's living area. "They'd hardly stay here under their real names, would they? I say we call the cops."

Halo thought about this for a full lap of the suite, then threw her hands up. "I guess we have to."

Less than a minute later, Tom was talking to another receptionist, this time, at the local sheriff's department. He told her the bare essentials: his friend had been attacked and her sister was missing. And no, they didn't have Shelley Harlan's phone number or even the damn address.

He slammed the phone down. Behind him, Halo awaited the news.

"Done. They're coming over. Why don't you clean up a little?"

In his time, Ed Daimler had shot five men dead. Wounded two. FBI agents tended to kill fewer than street beat cops, simply because feds were less hands on. The FBI figured out a serial killer or killers' profile, gave the local police an outline of their man (it almost always was a man, which was why Penelope's involvement here intrigued him) and stood back with their arms folded, like spectators at a firework display. Yet Daimler always seized any opportunity to get in there, to get his hands dirty. Use his gun, if necessary. Perhaps he really did have a death wish.

Was he really going to make the total six? He considered this as he peered along the barrel at Norwood's loathsome face.

"You really want to do it, don't you?" said Thawn, eyes twinkling as if some new energy was flowing through him.

"No, Ed doesn't," said van Stadt. "*Do* you, Ed."

"No, I don't," said Daimler, insincerely. "I really don't. But I might have to, Mr Preacher Man, if you don't tell me the truth about Penelope. Jason Voorhees, my fucking ass!"

"It's the truth. We did go looking for Jason, but we made a grave error. He killed her and almost killed me, too."

Daimler's eyes narrowed. For a moment, he considered it. What if Thawn was telling the truth?

In an instant, Thawn's face became a shocked mask. He was staring past Daimler, out through the car windshield.

"It's him," he breathed, hoarsely. "It's—"

Daimler was about to congratulate Thawn on his performance when his colleague yelled, "Whoa!"

Daimler followed Thawn's line of sight in time to see that the car was speeding directly for a giant of a man, or a thing, standing in the middle of the road.

The entire bathroom was spotless, shining white. Halo emerged from the glass shower cubicle with a fresh towel wrapped around her, the tiles cool beneath her feet.

Doing something so superficial as bathing had been difficult, but it undeniably felt good. As she stood under the warm jetting water, it had been hard to register that something nice was actually happening to her. She had washed the blood from her body, then tenderly held her abdomen for a while, wondering how her unborn had fared, amid all this madness.

She climbed back into the same clothes, which she had left piled up on the toilet seat. It made washing seem a little pointless, but she didn't have much choice. As she pulled each garment on, her muscles resisted painfully. She also noticed just how many holes and rips her clothing had accrued.

Outside in the living area, Tom was knocking back another cup of coffee. "Need to sober up," he said, as if it needed explanation. Then he looked at her strangely. "You look..." He paused, breaking eye contact, as if he knew his thoughts were inappropriate. "...even better."

An awkward silence descended on the room.

"How long will the cops be?" she finally asked, renewing her pacing routine.

"It's a small town," shrugged Tom, replacing his empty cup on the table. "Probably about five minutes."

Van Stadt swore at the top of her lungs as she violently swerved the Lincoln. Daimler shielded his face with both hands. His gun's muzzle pushed against the vehicle's roof. Thawn gazed hungrily out at the beast that slaughtered his wife. Jason Voorhees didn't move a muscle. Covered in blood, vomit and grime, he resembled nothing so much as a huge scarecrow that had been somehow transplanted from field to road.

The Lincoln missed Jason's left side by what looked an inch, thundering on past him.

"Who the fuck was that?" roared Daimler. "What was that mask?" He scowled at Thawn. "And don't say it was Jason Voorhees, you prick."

Thawn had twisted around in his seat and was staring through the back window, watching the giant get smaller and smaller.

"You okay?" Daimler asked van Stadt. She nodded, despite looking winded.

Thawn began thrashing around, yanking at the cuffs, unhinged. "You have to let me out of here! I have to go back and take my revenge."

Daimler stared at the man, shocked to realize that Thawn was starting to convince him. He didn't sound as though he was trying to tell him and van Stadt what to do. The man was pleading.

"You can lock me up forever afterwards," Thawn persisted. "But please take me back there and give me the knife. Otherwise, I'll never rest."

Daimler peered past Thawn's frantically moving head, back along the road. Whoever they had narrowly missed was long gone. He gritted his teeth.

"Well, Norwood, old friend, perhaps you don't deserve to rest. Not for what you've done."

Thawn was about to retaliate when the car lurched. One corner lowered, bumping against the ground. Daimler gripped the back of his seat, looking at van Stadt for answers.

"Oh great," she gasped, as they slowed. "We got ourselves a flat."

Halo still didn't know what to say to the man who was attempting to bring some sanity to her ordeal. He was good-looking, she knew that much, and there was an instant bond between them. She could feel it and was unusually confident that he felt it too. Yet the timing couldn't possibly have been worse. It was so wrong, in fact, that she was consciously repressing her attraction to this guy. Almost to the point of being cold toward him.

Perched awkwardly on the air conditioning unit, over by one of the big windows, she decided to soften a tad. At least, show some interest in him.

"So, I guess you lost your job, huh Tom?"

Over on the sofa, Tom clutched his forehead, eyes shut. "Too much damn caffeine," he murmured. "Uh, yeah. I lost my job. But who knows? It could be the best thing that ever happened to me."

"Sure looked that way. Didn't think much of your friends in the bar, there."

"So how you feeling?" he asked.

She shrugged. "I'm breathing. Hopefully, so's my baby."

Tom's eyes doubled in size. "You're pregnant?"

Halo laughed grimly and lightly patted her belly. "Well, I was this morning. Hard to tell, after all the shit we've been through. But I think the little guy's all right."

"You know the gender?"

"Nah," said Halo. "Just a feeling." She flashed him a smile much brighter than she felt. "I think your girlfriend was pretty pissed at you."

"She's not my girlfriend any more, like I told her."

Just making sure, Halo told herself. But why was she thinking like this?

Still human, came her own answer. I'm still human, thank God.

She casually glanced down through the window. "Hey, looks like the cops have shown up."

All those storeys down at the ground level, a swirling red light eased its way into the premises.

It had come as no surprise to Daimler that he was the only agent here who knew how to change a tire. Women were so keen on equality, he considered, until it came to practical, greasy fingered concerns.

Then they were more than happy to sit back and let men take over.

The Lincoln had rolled to a lazy halt, halfway along a road, which dissolved into the night, both east and west. Tall cornfields barricaded them in. These made Daimler nervous. If Thawn were to escape, he'd have ample cover in which to lose himself.

But Thawn was here to stay, Daimler told himself. He was still handcuffed to the back seat; Daimler had checked, only a few minutes ago, before dealing with this wheel.

To keep himself entertained out in the cool night air, Daimler opened a back door, so he could talk to Thawn while he worked. Van Stadt remained silent in the driver's seat. She had clearly decided to wash her hands of the whole affair, which pleased Daimler. His antagonistic techniques would be a whole lot more effective, without her bleating. The "good fed, bad fed" routine could only go so far.

"You know how to change a tire, friend?" he casually asked Thawn, while pumping the jack with his foot. The spare wheel sat on the ground beside him. "Or is that beneath a highfalutin intellectual like yourself?"

Thawn sniffed.

"Thought so," grinned Daimler. "What was it you taught as a teacher, again? Back in Ohio? Anything to do with religion, by any chance?"

Thawn shifted in the back seat, presenting his back to Daimler.

The agent took his foot off the jack. Gripping the butt of his gun tightly, he leaned into the car and rapped it hard on the nape of Thawn's neck.

"Ahhh!" The prisoner's natural urge was to rub the point of impact, but his cuffs made this impossible. "You..."

"Come on Norwood, say it. Call me a mother-fucker. Say it. You may as well—you're a fucking hypocrite. Think you're on the moral high ground? What about murder, huh?"

Norwood shook his head, still dazed by the blow.

"What I want to know," continued Daimler, "is whether you know you're being hypocritical, or whether it's a blind spot in your moral fiber. These are the little things that interest me. The kinds of details that will help me hone that bestseller, one of these fine days."

"Go fuck yourself," spat Thawn.

"Yes!" said Daimler, triumphantly. "That's more like it. That's the spirit." He banged his palm against the Lincoln's bodywork and began to pump the jack in earnest. "So are you gonna stick to your story about Penelope being dead, and that being Jason Voorhees we just saw on the road?"

Thawn nodded. "I certainly am. If I were you, Eddie, I'd watch your back."

Daimler laughed off the suggestion.

Seconds later, when Thawn was looking else-where, he stole a look back along the road. The dark surface showed no signs of movement, although it was hard to tell once the blackness took over.

Corncobs caught his attention, as they drifted lightly on their stalks.

Daimler felt as though he was being watched. His eyes darted from one stalk to another, and in between.

Jesus. Was that a footstep behind him?

After a while, he shrugged off his paranoia. The sooner he changed this wheel, the sooner they'd have Norwood Thawn safely under lock and key.

Tyrone Finton allowed a relieved sigh to whistle out from the gap in his front teeth, as he watched his boss walk off across the gravel, toward the newly arrived cops: Sheriff Claymark and his dumbshit deputy.

Finton hated cops. Ever since the day he had been refused a place on the force, he had decided that they were scum. Still, on this occasion he was pleased to see them.

For the last half an hour, he had endured Heinz's fawning bullshit. Question after question: did Finton never get bored, patrolling these grounds? (Real answer: "Hell yeah." Actual answer: "Not at all, Mr Heinz.") Did he feel uncomfortable with carrying that subtly concealed firearm? What was the most violent situation he'd ever been involved with?

Heinz was a freak. The next time the man came up to talk, he would tell him to fuck off, job or no job. He was here to provide security, not wild stories for Clayden Heinz to jerk off over.

Hands reached out from the shadows of the trees behind Finton. They seized the sides of his head so tightly that they felt automated, like production line clamps. Immense pressure caused his skull to collapse in on itself. Finton's eyeballs dribbled down over his face like runny eggs. Jason's hands shifted from the Finton's head, roughly grabbing his torso and easily hauling the corpse back into the darkness.

Less than fifty feet away, Clayden Heinz extended a genial hand, as he ushered Sheriff Claymark and Deputy Ryger toward the hotel's entrance. Seconds after they disappeared inside, a shrill alarm bell sounded.

NINETEEN

"Sweet fucking Moses, I don't believe this. Not again." Chuck Waylon was talking to himself. His head jerked up from a shelf in a store cupboard, just off the sprawling kitchen area where he reigned supreme. Telltale spots of white powder remained on the shelf's lacquered, wooden surface. Moistening a forefinger with his mouth, he ran it over the cocaine and then rubbed it into his gums.

The fire alarm had sounded when he snorted the second of two five inch lines. In his paranoid state, he had momentarily thought that his Class A drug use had in itself triggered the siren, but quickly checked himself.

As neurons pinballed around his brain, Waylon yanked open the door, revealing four chefs standing around, looking at each other, keen to shift the blame.

"Who set it off this time?" said Waylon. "Come on, tell me."

The solution was staring him in the face. The youngest trainee, Jamie Woods, stood at a hob, eyes lowered in shame. Gray smoke was rising from his pan of burnt steak, hitting those damn ceiling sensors. The smell of roasted onions soared through the room. Woods's face reddened as all eyes descended on him. "It was me," he nodded. "Sorry, chef."

"That's right," barked Waylon. "Sorry, chef!" He felt that familiarly bitter taste at the back of his throat, wondering whether everyone could see he was wired to the gills.

The blaring alarm echoed throughout the building. Waylon hated it with a passion: it interrupted their work and broke the whole beautiful flow of his kitchen. "How the hell did you manage to burn that shit? Where's your mind, boy?" He slapped the side of his own head to underline the point.

Double doors leading toward the hotel's main restaurant burst open. Walt Bluestone strode through, typically on the money. His eyes darted around for signs of flame, then met Waylon's gaze. "'Nother false alarm?" he said, wearily. "How wonderful."

"We need to talk." Waylon held open a side door for Bluestone. As the security chief disappeared through it, Waylon ordered his chefs to regain control of the situation. He then closed the door behind him and joined Bluestone in the cold, stonewalled delivery corridor.

The bigger man spoke into his walkie-talkie, giving someone the go-ahead to deactivate the alarm. "Burnt steak, yeah. This is getting real old."

"It sure fucking is," said Waylon as Bluestone shut off the connection. "This new system sucks, man. I'm anticipating a lot of business tonight, in the restaurant and then all night through room service. If the alarm keeps sounding every time there's a little smoke, we're going to hell in a hand-basket. We'll be screwed. Do you understand me?"

Bluestone frowned. "You high, Chuck?"

Waylon stopped mid rant, like a deep-sea diver coming up for air. Jesus. Could Bluestone hear his heartbeat? His mouth felt almost entirely numb.

"Yeah, I am," he sighed. "It's a long shift, Walt."

Bluestone glanced left and right along the corridor. Then he leaned in toward Waylon. The chef instinctively flinched back against the wall.

"You're damn right it's a long shift," said Bluestone, eyes alert. "Tonight, I'm going to be here until at least dawn, leading the troops. Can you give me some too? It's blow, right?"

Waylon rubbed his chin. He didn't have much coke left, but sorely wanted to stay on side with Bluestone. So it was worth it. Besides, Waylon's dealer was on his way with some more.

"No problem," smiled the chef. "I'm happy to do you the favor."

Bluestone nodded his appreciation. "Thanks, man."

As Waylon pulled the coke wrap from his pocket, he checked his watch, seeing that it was later than he'd imagined. Mike Costa would be arriving shortly.

* * *

Cary Carson rapped another fork against a glass, to secure everyone's attention. The Entraxx attendees were spread around a long ballroom, which reeked of fresh paint. Yellow paint too, for some reason. Polished off with gaudy chandeliers, it wasn't the classiest of chambers they could have chosen in which to dance the night away, but it had plenty of chairs and tables, a slick-looking DJ who spun fine tunes and its own well-stocked bar. That last one was the real draw.

Shortly after Carson had finally managed to have the lights turned down relatively low, the atmosphere had been punctured by the fire alarm's shrill, urgent blare. At first, his people paid little attention and continued to get in line for free drinks at the company's expense. Then everyone had started to wonder: was this really a drill? Maybe it was real.

The hum of their speculation had died down, upon hearing Carson's clinking glass. The DJ killed the music.

"Okay, guys," said Carson, wondering where in the blazes Larry Bruckenheim had gone. "This may still be a drill, but that siren's gone on a while. I suggest we leave calmly through this door…"

As he pointed toward an arbitrarily selected exit, the fire alarm halted. A ripple of laughter and applause washed over him.

"Ah, there we go," he said, racking his brains for something funny to say. "Well, I guess this is a real case of—"

Music blared through the PA once again, drowning him out. Carson stood awkwardly, grinning, as his underlings turned away from him, lost once again in wine and song.

Tom opened the door to see a gleaming star-shaped badge, attached to a surprisingly young sheriff. Beside him was a fat man holding a shotgun, the end lowered against the carpet. Behind both was the greasy individual whom Tom remembered as being the hotel manager.

"Did you call us in?" Ryger asked Tom, with a bluntness bordering on impatience. Claymark frowned at his subordinate.

Tom nodded and opened the door wider, to reveal Halo sitting on the back of the sofa. With one look at her, Claymark and Ryger seemed to understand that this was no joke. The sheriff turned to Heinz. "We'll take it from here, sir," he said.

"But... what's going on?" Heinz persisted, as though the whole thing was an inconvenience. "I think I should know."

"You'll know, as soon as we have the information," Claymark assured him. "Now, go about your business and, as I say, we've got the ball now."

Heinz threw poisonous glares at Tom and especially Halo. "Absolutely, sheriff. I should add, however, that the lady there isn't one of our guests."

Claymark held him with a steady gaze. "Thank you, sir," he said pointedly.

Heinz walked off along the corridor, like a rocket powered by pure indignation. Tom managed a thin smile as he watched him go. "You'd better come in," he told the cops, stepping back into the suite.

* * *

"Why we stopping in here, Mikey?"

Michael Costa ignored his dumb brother, as he steered the Porsche into the Phoenix Heights's grounds. The honest answer, of course, was that they were there to deliver some snow to the hotel's head chef. Johnny probably wouldn't understand what cocaine was, even if Michael told him the truth.

At eighteen, Johnny was seven years younger than him—not to mention twice his weight—but sometimes he genuinely suspected the kid had been born missing a gene or three. For one thing, he was always so fucking cheerful. And he always asked questions. Worst of all, he still insisted on wearing that hat with the comedy propeller blade on top. The sooner he got Johnny hooked on mind-numbing narcotics, the better.

The Porsche cruised smoothly around the back of the hotel, where golfing flags poked up from the ground like sentinels. There was only one security guard in evidence, but he simply waved the vehicle onwards, recognizing the driver as a friend of Chuck Waylon's. Everybody knew what was going on, Costa was sure. But as with all his clients, no one really cared. So long as Chuck kept the kitchen running just fine, he wouldn't feel any heat from management.

"Why are we stopping, Mikey?"

Costa ground the Porsche to a halt, creating small explosions of gravel. "To deliver *Gremlins 2*." He jabbed a finger in Johnny's general direction. "You stay here for five minutes, all right?"

Johnny frowned. "Okay. So you're delivering *Gremlins 2*, huh?"

"That's right." Costa smiled. He slammed the car door and patted his jacket pocket as he headed off toward the hotel. "The new batch."

Maybe the coke was messing with his emotions, Waylon wasn't sure. But he was starting to feel sorry for Jamie. The kitchen was once again running like clockwork, just the way it should. Still, the poor kid was looking devastated at having caused the alarm.

"Look, Jamie," he said, lowering his voice as he stopped by the trainee's workstation. "You shouldn't have burnt the steak. But the fire alarm's way too sensitive. We're dealing with it. Just don't feel too bad about it, huh?" Jamie's fresh face brightened a shade, as Waylon dealt him an encouraging slap on the back.

"Hey," he suddenly told Jamie, lowering his voice to a whisper. "You like blow? Coke?"

Jamie looked simultaneously aghast and intrigued. "Never tried, chef" he mumbled.

There was a barely audible rap on the glass panel of the door, which led to the delivery corridor. Waylon spun around defensively, then winked conspiratorially as he registered that the newcomer was his man. Well accustomed to Michael Costa's covert visits, the other chefs paid no attention as Waylon darted over to the door. Opening it, he waggled a finger for Jamie to follow.

Cheeks flushing, the young chef did as he was told.

Johnny Costa wondered when Michael was going to let him see *Gremlins 2*. He'd sure liked the original.

He undid his seat belt, spun his propeller blade and looked out across the open grounds that sprawled back behind the hotel.

He drummed pudgy hands on his upper thighs, starting to hum a Guns N' Roses tune.

Detecting movement, out there on the golf course, he casually squinted through the windshield and saw that someone was walking over the grass. Squinting harder, he could see it was one of the hotel's security team.

Someone lunged through the open window and grabbed him by the head, knocking his hat to the floor of the car. Too shocked to make a sound, Johnny scrabbled at the attacker's wrist, finding no purchase in what felt like thickly caked slime.

Before he could do anything about it, some dark giant was pulling him headfirst through the window. His belly momentarily halted his exit, before an insistent wrench snapped something inside him and he tumbled out onto the gravel, groaning loudly.

Jason raised one foot into the air, then brought it down, shattering Johnny's windpipe like frail plastic.

Jamie's body language betrayed his nerves. He stood against the rest room's damp wall, clutching it like a safety blanket, watching as Michael Costa used a credit card to separate piles of cocaine on the top of a closed toilet seat lid.

"What's the matter, Jamie?" Waylon chuckled. "There's nothing to be afraid of here. You've had a bad night. This stuff'll cheer you up." He wondered if the kid thought that he and Michael had ulterior motives and intended to molest him, here in these cramped confines. As a matter of fact, Waylon wouldn't mind having his way with Jamie. That, he knew, was the real reason why he was being so generous to the kid. Still, forced entry certainly wasn't his style and coke never did him many favors in the bedroom department.

He swallowed hard, looking forward to hoovering up his share. Costa snorted his first, using a rolled up dollar bill of some denomination. Probably a fifty, knowing Mike. Waylon sometimes thought he was in the wrong line of work. Why was he a user, not a dealer? It was pretty damn obvious who got the better quality of life. Then again, in recent months, Mike had become both. Never get high on your own supply, as the saying went.

Costa vacated the cubicle, revealing four lines left on the toilet seat. He sniffed and gestured for Jamie to enter. "All yours, kid."

Jamie hesitated. Waylon wondered again what the chef thought would happen, once he entered that small space. Maybe he really was terrified of the drug. That wouldn't last. "Go on, or I'll do all four," he grinned, pointing inside.

"Fuck it," said Jamie, a smile creeping across his face. He prized himself from the wall, took the rolled up note from Costa and entered the cubicle, bending over the seat.

"Just do two lines, though, huh?" laughed Waylon. "Good kid. We'll make a junkie of you yet."

"Hey, stop right there."

Jason had been striding across the golf course when the cry came from across the dimly lit grounds. The giant stopped dead and searched slowly, systematically for the one who dared challenge him.

A security guard was advancing on Jason from the shadows. While he had a gun in his hands, it wasn't pointing at the intruder. Not yet.

"Could you identify yourself please, sir?" The voice was etched with fear.

Jason stood motionless, his empty hands glistening red. Getting a better look at the intruder as he drew nearer, the guard raised the gun.

Grabbing a nearby golf flag, Jason wrenched its metal pole from the ground. Then he hurled it like a spear. The pole pierced the guard's stomach, emerged through his lower back and sunk into the earth behind him.

The guard spluttered, coughing blood as he leant back against the pole, sliding a few inches down it. He raised the gun again. Upon him, Jason snatched the weapon and threw it to one side. The terrified guard opened his mouth, only for it to be smothered by one of Jason's hands. Forcing his fingers between the guard's teeth and gripping hard, Jason yanked downwards.

Snap.

The man's lower jaw snapped off and hit the grass, followed by thick swathes of blood.

Waylon enjoyed watching Jamie's face change as the drug zoomed ravenously through his system. "Goddamn, boy," he said, slapping his back. "Your whole head has lit up like a Halloween pumpkin."

"Whoah," said Jamie, struggling to blink. "This feels pretty immense."

There followed minutes of inane babble. Waylon was used to this. It never ceased to amaze him how a topic seemed so intensely important while you were on the crest of a wave, only to fade along with the narcotic effect. No sign of it ebbing yet, he could tell. This was good shit.

Finally, Costa slapped Waylon's palm. "I gotta go," he said. "People to see."

"Brains to fry," grinned Waylon. He turned to Jamie. "Let's steam back in there, huh?"

"Jesus," sighed Jamie. "I'm not sure I can work like this."

"The hell you can't. Now let's go."

Jamie grabbed the door handle first. Then he hesitated. "You sure this stuff is safe?" he asked edgily, addressing neither of them in particular.

"It's not gonna kill you," said Waylon.

Jamie nodded, reassured. He twisted the door handle and ducked through into the delivery corridor.

Jason slapped a palm over the back of Jamie's head and propelled his face toward the wall. It splattered against the stone with a crunching squelch.

"What the fuck?" gasped Costa, next out of the door.

As Jamie slid down the wall, his face left a wide, wet smear of red, like a paintbrush.

Jason grabbed Costa by the throat and rammed two fat fingers into his eye sockets. The dealer struggled pointlessly against Jason's might, shrieking as blood spurted down over his face.

Waylon couldn't believe what he was seeing. He looked from Jamie's corpse to Mike, who was already a lifeless rag doll in Jason's hands.

This murderous freak was blocking the corridor to the outside world. As Jason threw Michael Costa to one side, the chef ran the short distance to the kitchen door and piled through it.

His chefs glanced around, expecting the latest rant, drama or both. Their casual attention turned to alarm as they saw the horror in their manager's eyes.

He waved his arms madly.

"Get the fuck out of here, all of you!"

TWENTY

The door crashed out of its frame and thundered to
the floor, narrowly missing Chuck Waylon. His chefs
cowered as Jason Voorhees entered the kitchen.
Waylon was already dashing to the room's opposite
side, cursing the fact that Jason was blocking the
double door exit. Why hadn't he run straight
through them?

Jason moved quickly. Another two big strides
brought him across the whole room to Bryan Kelser,
another trainee chef. Seizing the terrified man with
one hand, Jason reached up to grab one of the
butcher's knives, which hung in a shiny row on the
wall. Trapped on the far side of the kitchen, Waylon
and his remaining two chefs shouted in protest,
while looking desperately around for something to
save their own necks. Waylon wielded a meat
cleaver, while Skipper hefted two small pans of

boiling water. Leah held an electric carving knife that buzzed in his hand.

Jason powered the wide blade down into Kelser's forehead. It gouged through skin and skull, swiftly turning his lights out. Jason flung Kelser to one side. The young chef folded over his own workstation, the knife still embedded in his skull.

The killer returned his attention to the various sharp objects on offer. He began to walk along the row, prompting the chefs to move along the other side of the long table that divided the kitchen lengthways.

Snatching a small knife from a stretch of marbled work surface, Jason whirled around, sending it flying through the air. It struck Leah in the chest and he gasped, falling sideways, still clutching the carving knife. Skipper shrieked in agony as the whirring blade sliced through his left knee on its way down to the floor. He dropped the pans, which hit the tiles, the contents of one striking Leah full in the face.

Skipper seized his ruined kneecap, cartilage oozing between his fingers. Beside him on the ground, Leah's face sizzled and bubbled.

His coke high somehow enabling him to focus, Waylon looked behind his stricken workmates and saw the entrance to the freezer room. It was a huge metallic door, which they always called the bank vault. A small, square, thick window was embedded in its centre, allowing you to see how much stock lined the shelves, without freezing your ass off.

An idea struck Waylon. Every nerve end in his body felt alive. This was a matter of do or die.

Turning around, he deactivated the lock with trembling hands and pulled open the door with a concerted, vein-popping heave. A gust of freezing air struck him.

Waylon grabbed the agonized Skipper by the arms and pulled him backward into the freezer room.

"What the fuck you doing, man?" he yelled.

"Saving the hotel," said Waylon, distractedly. He wasn't looking at Skipper as he spoke. He was watching as Jason stalked around that long kitchen table, quickly approaching them. He was now holding the kitchen's biggest meat cleaver. Over a foot tall, it was so polished that the overhead lights shone brightly from its surface.

This was the vital moment, Waylon knew. Would this fucker take the bait and enter the freezer, or would he?

Time to find out. Waylon held the freezer door open. Inside, Skipper was dragging himself along the floor, trying to get out, his face a horrified mask.

As Jason stomped toward the door, Waylon released it and darted around the table again. The door was designed to close automatically, but slowly. That way, idiots were less likely to lock themselves in.

Jason swung to face Waylon.

Oh fuck, he thought. I'm dead. Get out of these double doors.

Then Skipper wailed from inside that small room, effectively signing his own death certificate. Jason's head jerked back toward the freezer chamber, just as the door was about to close. Jamming one fist into the gap, Jason easily prized open the portal and disappeared inside.

Skipper hollered blue murder.

Seizing his chance, Waylon ran over and pushed the big door shut with a wheeze. Through the window, he could see that Jason was paying no attention. He was holding Skipper up against the only patch of wall that didn't have shelves, and chopped into him with that huge blade.

Bloody froth piled out of the kid's mouth and his eyes rolled skywards, as though his spirit was only too keen to leave its shell.

Waylon activated the lock and heard heavy bolts glide across, between door and frame. This damn thing was heavy duty.

No more noises from inside. Skipper was history.

Waylon took an involuntary step backward as Jason's mask filled the freezer window. He heard thumps and clangs from within.

Jesus, he's trying to knock it down, Waylon thought. But he can't. Can he?

Thinking as fast as his mangled mind would allow, Waylon backed toward a wall-mounted telephone. Stabbing two buttons in rapid succession, he speed dialed Walt Bluestone's pager.

Then the chef stood by the double doors, waiting and watching as the monster in his freezer room doubled its efforts to escape. All around, wrecked corpses littered his spotless kitchen.

"Time out, it's recap time," said Sheriff Claymark. He and Ryger were sitting on one sofa, Halo and Tom on the other. Ryger's shotgun was propped up against the wall beside him. "You were chased by Jason Voorhees, and a couple called Norwood and

Penelope tried to kill you. Is that what you're saying?"

Halo nodded, trying to quell her contempt for the disbelief in Claymark's voice. She fixed him with hard eyes. "That's exactly it."

She groaned. It was just as she'd told Tom. They weren't going to believe her. Why had she bothered? Why hadn't she just gotten the hell out of town, maybe taking Tom with her?

"Sounds about right to me," the sheriff said finally. "The FBI have captured one of the couple, and the other was just discovered on the bank of the lake, dead."

"Good," murmured Halo.

Ryger gave her a surprisingly hostile look. "Was that anything to do with you?"

"Hey," interrupted Tom, frowning. "That's a great way to talk to a woman who survived three killers in one day, man."

Ryger ignored him. Tom glowered, balling a fist under the table.

"I told you," said Halo. "Norwood and that dead bitch grabbed me. Jason appeared and I ran off, after he threw Norwood across the bank. I just wanted to live." She stood up, her frustration now boiling over. "Now can we please establish whether my goddamn sister is alive or dead?"

"They're working on it, over at the station," said Claymark, intending to reassure but failing badly. "Trying to contact her at her home address."

"Can we look in the Thawns' room, here in the hotel?" asked Tom. "If they did, I mean... if they..."

"Call reception," Claymark told his deputy. "Find out which room they were staying in."

April held her head in her hands, leaning forward like an airsickness victim. The tears on her face shone different colors, as disco lights revolved overhead.

"I just can't believe he did that to me. Right in front of everyone in the company."

Sitting at a table next to her, Greg stroked the girl's back. "The guy's a jerk, April. At least you know that now. You can move on, huh?"

She convulsed, letting loose another agonized sob, which evaporated amid the sounds of MC Hammer. "I'm so fucking embarrassed, Greg. All I want to do is go to my room."

Greg continued to work her back, feeling the strap of her bra through the thin fabric. "Okay, if that's what you really want to do, we could do that."

April sat up straight, shrugging away his hand. "I meant alone, Greg." She eyed him suspiciously. "You wouldn't be trying to hit on me, minutes after my boyfriend ditched me, would you?"

Greg held up his hands. "Hell, no! I just meant I would walk you up there."

He fidgeted in his seat and took another glug of beer. He watched the hot young things on the dance floor, women he had been fantasizing about all year long, shaking their stuff. If April wasn't willing, then perhaps busty Raynor from advertising might be.

"So, uh, you want to go up?" he asked.

April shook her head and wiped more tears away. "I don't know what I want, Greg. Get me another drink, would you?"

Greg rolled his eyes as he got up to hit the bar again. So now he was stuck with a girl who wasn't interested, so no other woman would approach him. The sooner he could get April tucked up in bed, the better.

Not for the first time, Waylon wondered why he was still in the kitchen. The killer's masked face had remained in that window, looking straight at him for the past five minutes. Were there two eyes or just the one? He had no intention of getting close enough to find out.

Every now and then, two mighty, simultaneous thuds sounded as the imprisoned hulk slammed fists against it.

As much as Waylon was trying not to look at the corpses, he was desperate to avoid eye contact with his captive. It was like trading stares with a crocodile at the zoo, which you knew damn well was dying to gnaw your bones.

Crash. Waylon jumped like a gazelle.

The double doors had burst open behind him.

Walt Bluestone walked in, glassy eyed, still buzzing on the coke. "What is it, Chucky boy? Got another line for..."

The remaining words seemed to tumble from the security chief's open mouth, down to the blood slick tiles. His eyes became cold steel as he surveyed the carnage: two dead bodies. Waylon was thankful that Walt couldn't see the two in the side corridor, plus Skipper in the freezer chamber. That might induce cardiac arrest in the man.

Then Bluestone's pistol was out and flashing in the glare of the kitchen lights. It was in Waylon's face.

"What the fuck?" he protested as Bluestone glowered along the barrel at him.

"What the fuck happened?" Bluestone barked. Waylon could see that his finger was on the trigger. Itchy. Why did he have to choose this night, of all nights, to give the guy some blow?

"Hello?" said Waylon pointedly, desperately trying to rein in his sarcasm. It would be highly unwise to push Bluestone over the edge. He gestured toward the freezer door.

Bluestone got his second big shock of the day as he saw the bloodied hockey mask behind the glass. "You've gotta be fucking kidding," he breathed.

Lowering the gun away from a grateful Waylon, he took a step toward the freezer.

"Careful, Walt. I've seen what this motherfucker can do. He's strong as all hell, man."

This information didn't seem to sink into Bluestone's head. He was still staring at Jason, as though disbelieving the evidence provided by his own eyes.

"Who the hell is it?" he said.

"How the fuck should I know? I sure as hell didn't invite him over to sample our canapés."

"You called the cops?"

"Uh, no. I thought I'd call you first. Hell, I don't know what I thought." Waylon realized he was welling up. He never usually felt emotional while high on blow. It must be masking a whole world of pain. He cupped a hand over the lower half of his face and leant back against the wall.

"How'd he get in there?" asked Bluestone.

Waylon composed himself. "Well, Skipper fell inside and he followed—"

"Skipper's in there?" interrupted Bluestone, furiously. "Oh my God, we've got to get him out."

Jesus, thought Waylon. Walt and Skipper were friends. Why the hell did I tell him Skipper was inside? "I'm pretty sure he's dead," he added. "That bastard killed him. I heard screams, then they stopped."

Bluestone wasn't listening to reason. He had raised his gun to the window, pointing directly at Jason's head. "Okay, motherfucker. I'm going to open this door. One false move, and I swear that mask won't offer any protection against the bullet which I *will* put in you."

Fear swept through Waylon like a whiteout. "Don't do it, Walt, please! Look, I'm calling the cops. We'll let them deal with it." He turned around and snatched the phone from its cradle.

"Our team's more efficient than those damn bumpkins. If Skipper's in there with this prick, I want him out now."

"I told you, Skipper's fucking dead."

Bluestone wasn't listening. Still pointing the pistol at Jason, he raised a walkie-talkie to one ear: a crackle of static.

"Sir?"

"Kramer, where the hell's Finton? Can you get everyone over here to the main kitchen room? Clear out any restaurant guests, too. We have a code red situation."

"We sure will, if you let that thing out," said Waylon. Bluestone shushed him and continued to speak into the device.

"Immediately, do you hear? We have dead men in here. Yes, you heard me right. Get here now."

"Okay," chirped Waylon as Bluestone broke off the line. "See you on Monday."

In a flash, the pistol was pointing at him again. "Oh no you don't. The cops will need to speak to you, about what the hell happened. Stay put."

"Fuck you. Don't point that thing at me again."

Fire blazed across Bluestone's face. "I'll do what the fuck I like! Now call room 1010 and let the sheriff and his lard-ass deputy know what's happening."

Thin white layers were beginning to form over Jason's considerable surface area. His mask had become crystallized beneath a latticework of ice flecks, which spread and solidified. His exposed ribs and spine carried similar marks of frost. The blood on his long blade had already frozen hard.

Behind him on the ground, partly buried beneath a toppled mountain of burger buns in cellophane, Skipper's pale face was also starting to gather ice. His open wounds glistened as the cold ate away at them.

Jason had no interest in the contents of the freezer, nor in the man he had butchered. He merely stood observing the two living, breathing vessels outside, as they threatened him and argued.

He had all the time in the world.

One man in the background was holding a phone to his ear. The bigger man was pointing the gun again and shouting through the glass.

More men were entering the room behind him, four of them, all with guns.

Child's play.

The biggest of the walking, talking bags of blood and bone was reaching for something on the other side of the door.

Familiar sounds, muffled and mechanical. The sounds that Jason had heard when he was first imprisoned in here.

The door was about to open again.

Kill. Kill. Kill...

In room 1010, the phone rang loud and clear. The handset rattled on its cradle and a red light flashed on its electronic display. No one was there to hear it.

It stopped dead.

Waylon slammed the phone back on its cradle and ran out of the double doors. Bluestone and his men didn't see him go. They were too busy staring at the behemoth which was slowly lumbering out of the freezer room, age-old joints cracking in its right arm as it raised its glistening blade.

Bluestone took another step back, his men repositioning themselves to accommodate him. They were all painfully aware of the ricochets, which might result if all five guns fired at once in this relatively confined area. Nobody wanted to shoot. But this thing just wasn't following orders.

"Last chance," yelled Bluestone, with all the stony authority he could muster. Yet the hysteria in his voice unnerved his men. "Stop moving or die!"

Jason took another step forward. Raised his blade some more.

Bluestone fired first, the blast loud as an atom bomb, drilling through his and the others' eardrums. The bullet punched into Jason's chest, where his heart should be.

The giant took a half step backwards. Then a whole step forwards.

Shocked by the lack of response, Bluestone fired again. So did his men. Muzzles flashed to his left and right, spent bullet shells flying.

Small explosions of dark green slime burst out of Jason's chest. One slug struck his forehead, having burst through the very top of his mask, chipping and blackening it.

Like a beast goaded one too many times, Jason launched into a frenzy. His blade slammed downwards, cleaving Bluestone's skull in half, right down to his neck. Blood splattered the security chief's men as he went down.

One guard broke off from the pack and vanished through the double doors, his face contorted in fright. The others fired again repeatedly, experiencing what they imagined must be combat shock.

More oozing slime marked the bullet hits. Jason staggered back further this time, falling against the freezer door's bulky frame. Immediately heaving himself upright, he made a vicious sideways swipe which removed most of one man's head, slapping it wetly against a white wall.

The remaining guards roared in horror as their second colleague collapsed. As Jason forced himself upon them, frenziedly swinging the weapon and carving off chunks—ears, arms, shoulders, a flap of scalp—they fired wildly. Blindly.

Two consecutive bullets hammered into gas ovens with brightly burning hobs. Another split open a pipe that ran up the length of one wall.

Whoosh.

There was a low, primal *boom*, like hell's own fireplace coming alight. Within seconds, the kitchen was consumed by rolling, orange flame.

TWENTY-ONE

"You know, Thawn old buddy, I think I got it all figured out."

"Well, please do enlighten me."

Daimler's brow was dripping with sweat, much of which was probably down to alcohol. He finally had the new tire in place, after a painfully difficult job. Either he was fatigued or this damn thing was warped. In the front of the car, van Stadt was talking to someone at the sheriff's office, over the phone. Explaining the delay.

Tightening the lug nuts, Daimler glanced in through the side door where Thawn was still sitting. Of course he was. Where else would he be?

He grinned at the seething killer. "Yes, I've got your profile down. I know the real reason why you killed all those innocent people."

Daimler watched Thawn carefully. The captive was rolling his eyes. "Innocent? You'd hardly call all that detritus innocent. Sexual deviants, filthy drug users... Not one of them was an upstanding member of society."

The FBI agent laughed, shaking off a stray drop of sweat that had infiltrated his left eye. "And you, Thawn. What are you?"

A pause. "Another rhetorical question, Ed?" Thawn sniffed.

"Damn right it's rhetorical. You, Norwood Thawn, are a stone cold killer. Whatever happened to 'thou shalt not kill' in that mind of yours, huh?"

Thawn's smile actually succeeded in chilling Daimler as he spoke. "Except..."

Daimler tightened the wheel another notch. "Except," he repeated, unimpressed. "So that's the best you can do? Your get-out clause? Making exceptions for people you consider unclean? Ever heard of a little guy called Adolf Hitler?"

No reply. "Well, let me tell you something. I think it's all an excuse. Wanna know the real reason why you hate those people so much?"

Thawn was studying the roof of the car disinterestedly. The man's arrogance infuriated Daimler. He was sorely tempted to shoot him in the kneecap, right now: flip his attitude one hundred and eighty degrees. If van Stadt hadn't been there, he would have done it already. That girl was such a goody two-shoes.

"You hate them," he continued, "because they're free. You were brought up by that extreme father of yours, with a whole list of things you weren't supposed to do. Brainwashed, beyond the regular tenets of religion. I tell you, I've got no problem with religion when it's regular and caring and raising money for charity. But your father, by all accounts, he was something else, wasn't he?"

Thawn was looking at him again. It was a raw, hateful look.

"So when you reached a certain age, you must have looked back on your life and seen all the missed opportunities. All that repressed fun. And you hated anyone who had lived a normal life: screwing like rabbits, smoking the odd joint, drinking themselves sick."

Daimler could see he was pulling wires, changing gears in Thawn's head. "And that's why you really hate them. You wish you could be them. You'd always wanted to act on that resentment, but you needed a spark. Meeting a like-minded sicko like Penelope was the trigger."

"Shut up!" roared Thawn suddenly. "You piece of scum."

"Whoah there, Mr Stones In Glass Houses," grinned Daimler. "Looks like I'm right, huh? Got you all riled up."

"Ed," called van Stadt from the front. "Just spoke to the sheriff's people. They found a woman who claims to have been attacked by Jason Voorhees and abducted by the Thawns tonight."

Thawn raised an eyebrow, his face still hot with temper. Then he smiled again. "She won't last long, if Jason's after her," he said.

"Be quiet," van Stadt told him. "Besides, she's with the cops at the Phoenix Heights hotel. She'll be safe now."

"There's our lead witness," said Daimler triumphantly, slamming his palm against the roof over Thawn's head. "Like jail food, Norwood?"

Norwood Thawn chuckled. "As I said, my poor deluded agents, she's a dead whore walking."

The hotel's fire alarm sounded again, as Jason Voorhees thundered through the kitchen's double doors. Flames clung fiercely to his shoulders and what remained of his clothing. He continued his stride as though they were mere irritations.

Behind him, the kitchen was an inferno. Fire lapped vigorously at the ceiling, constantly fed by the gas supply. Blackened heaps of flesh cooked steadily on the floor.

A huge billowing fireball seemed to follow Jason, setting the double doors ablaze and blooming along the corridor behind him.

At the other end of the corridor stood the security guard who abandoned his colleagues. He leveled his gun at the steadily advancing demon and squeezed off a couple of rounds. Most missed Jason entirely, as his hands were shaking.

Jason shrugged off the two bullets that had sunk into his torso and walked on, still on fire.

Once again, the guard turned and fled.

Halo, Tom and the two cops stood in the corridor outside the Thawns' suite.

"Damn fire alarm," mumbled Tom, as the klaxon continued to sound. "Must be malfunctioning. How many more times today?"

Halo knew he was talking for the sake of talking. Everyone had become very silent with the grim anticipation of what they might find inside Room 1306.

Deputy Ryger looked nervously at his superior. "Could be a real fire, Dan."

"For the last time, Kenny. You'll call me sheriff and like it. And I very much doubt the hotel's on fire."

Halo wasn't really listening to any of them. The alarm seemed distant, a mere irrelevance. She was staring at the door that separated the four of them from the truth about her sister.

Tom tried to lure her gaze away from the door. "You all right?" he said awkwardly.

Halo shook her head. "Not in the least," she breathed.

Without thinking, Tom gently pulled her to him. "You don't have to do this," he said.

"Yes I do."

"Yes she does," echoed Ryger. "We have to ascertain—"

"Ken, shut the hell up," said Claymark, talking over him. "Look, let's not get carried away. We're not even sure we'll find anything. As far as we know, your sister might be fine and well at home." He turned to Ryger. "You got that key?"

Ryger nodded and opened the door.

The DJ had shit for brains.

"Ritchie Valens," Greg yelled at him. "That's right. You got the song or not?"

The DJ shrugged. "Maybe," he said. "I've got a 'best of' record."

"It'll definitely be on that," Greg assured him, slurring his words. "It's one of the best songs ever."

No one in Ballroom B was paying the fire alarm the slightest bit of notice. Even Cary Carson seemed happy to accept it as yet another drill, or mistake.

Greg was feeling happier. With every new drink April knocked back, she became significantly friendlier. He was enjoying being the shoulder to cry on. Give her another half an hour, and she would almost certainly want to fuck him. Even if it was only to get back at Tom, it was still sex, wasn't it?

He swung his arm around her, cupping his hand over one bare shoulder. The party was in full swing. The free alcohol, which showed no signs of abating, meant that very few people could even say "inhibitions" let alone have any. Alice Cooper was pumping through the PA—something about a man behind a mask—and even the most reserved office goons were pretending they were sixteen again. Ever-shifting lights painted the walls various colors.

It had also occurred to Greg that, after the inevitable two-day hangover from this party, back in Corporate World there would be an empty chair where Tom Sheridan once preened himself. Maybe he, Greg Spiner, might finally land the job he deserved. Life wasn't so bad.

An old guy—from accounts, he vaguely recalled—bumped into Greg's chair. Clutching margaritas, he apologized to Greg, grinning stupidly. Greg nodded tolerantly and the jerk went on his way.

April was yelling in his ear. "Is it me, or is this music too loud?"

"Nah," he laughed. "If it's too loud, you're too old."

April slapped him playfully. Greg smiled to himself. Playful slaps were very good signs. Soon, he'd be playfully slapping her ass.

Out of the corner of his eye, he saw some unusually fast movement. Looking over, he did a double take.

Revelers were falling over each other, stumbling away from the entrance doors. The music drowned out anything they were saying, or yelling, but their body language spoke of mounting fear.

Greg knew why that might be. He turned to April and pointed toward the panicked corner. "Look, Tom's back. He's drunk and he wants a fight. Well, it's time for a rematch."

"That doesn't look like Tom," she yelled, as he stalked off toward the entrance doors, rolling up his shirt sleeves.

Greg pushed his way through the crowd, feeling like a car on the wrong side of a freeway. He laughed at the petrified people who bustled past him, babbling unintelligibly.

"You fucking cowards," he snorted. "It's only—"

He stopped in his tracks.

He was on the crowd's far side, watching a huge man hack through a woman's throat with a glinting cleaver. The whole scene looked all the more unspeakable for being lit with garish disco colors. The blood that poured from her arterial vein flashed from red to blue to green. Smoke gushed from the killer's clothes, as though they had been on fire.

Greg went to flee, but a big hand grabbed his shoulder, yanking him back to face the aggressor.

"Fu—"

Before he could finish the expletive, the top half of his skull was hacked clean off.

Sailing through the air, it landed on the DJ's turntable, knocking the needle aside and revolving on the vinyl.

Mass terror became Ballroom B's new soundtrack, as Ritchie Valens's "Ooh! My Head" scratched to an abrupt halt.

The smell said it all: Norwood and Penelope Thawn's suite reeked of death. Halo was grateful that Tom stayed close to her. But she felt overwhelmed.

"Here," he said, giving her a handkerchief. "Bunch it over your nose."

She did. Then she watched as Claymark and Ryger searched the living area, pulling out drawers and opening the closet. When the bathroom was the only remaining possibility, Halo's stomach felt like it was filled with iron.

The cops vanished into the room.

Halo heard the *clack-clack-clack* of a shower curtain being dragged along the rail. Twin, deep sighs. A disgusted exclamation. Her flesh crawled. She remembered snapshots of her time with Shelley. Growing up as sisters; Shelley telling Halo what their father had been like; Shelley assuming the maternal role when cancer took their mom; and finally Shelley having had enough of Halo and kicking her out. Yet nothing could change the fact that they were sisters. Blood. To the end.

Halo wanted to see for herself. Yet, as she tried to walk, the world spun hazily around her. Very quickly, without even realizing she had fallen, she found herself looking at the ceiling. Tom's anxious, blurred face appeared for a second, then faded to black.

April was floundering in a human sea. Panic had spread through the ballroom with lightning speed. Not even Carson had attempted to quash it with one of his well-oiled speeches. He was fighting for his life with utterly selfish vigor, just like the rest of them.

Most of the ballroom's floor was littered with corpses, limbs and organs. Jason stood in the middle of the room, facing April and many others, the entrance doors far out of reach behind him. One senior excutive had tried to make a run for it, but had been cut to ribbons with the swinging cleaver.

The remaining Entraxx employees cowered away from this murderous intruder. A door marked "Fire Escape" was housed in one wall behind them, but it was failing to open, despite increasingly frenetic attempts to force it.

People were wrenching each other aside, in order to get further away from Jason. People were tripping over heads and limbs. April felt something squelch beneath her right heel. Looking down, she glimpsed a deformed face swimming in gore. She screwed up her eyes and unleashed a pitiful squeal.

Then Jason began his final attack, wading into the crowd. Hacking at anyone within range, he systematically reduced Entraxx employees to meat. April saw Cary Carson raising a fistful of dollars in a last-ditch attempt to make this madman see reason, only to lose his entire arm with one swish of steel. After a second blow to the waist, Carson keeled over in two separate halves.

Moving as one, the crowd urgently pushed against the fire escape door. Fists hammered on it until they were bloody. Fists hammered into the faces of fellow humans. Fists were hacked off and drifted on the river of blood, which formed a chaotic current around people's feet.

All the time, those disco lights continued to flash red, blue and green.

April shrieked as Jason decapitated the woman behind her and pushed the body aside.

Then it was her turn.

Jason swung the cleaver into April's stomach until it burst through her back. Then he lifted her into the air, throwing her over his right shoulder. Falling from the blade with a final screech, she hit the floor head first.

Jason removed two more heads with one long, sweeping arc. With his spare hand, he crushed someone's throat, making blood gurgle out over his wrist.

Then something gave way, at the back of the crowd. The fire escape burst outwards and less than twenty survivors piled through it, tumbling forwards, driven by their own momentum.

Directly into a blazing inferno.

Jason stopped for a long moment and watched them writhe and squirm in the flames.

Then he made his way back through the human debris.

After he had gone, the entrance doors swung back into place.

The furnace beyond the open fire escape door was scattered with motionless, unrecognizable bodies. The alarm continued its shrill blare.

Party over.

"There," said Daimler, kicking the wheel which had given him so much trouble. "Now, let's get you safely locked up, Mr Thawn. Don't suppose you like gay folk, huh? Well, there'll be plenty where you're going."

"Come on, Ed," called van Stadt. "It's heavens knows what in the morning."

"I know. Couldn't resist a little more taunting."

Thawn smiled back. "You think you've got it all worked out, don't you, Edward Daimler?"

The agent nodded, resting his arms on the window frame, looking in at his prey, like a sadistic child studying an ant in a bottle. "When it comes to you, I certainly do. Show me those cuffs again."

Thawn yanked his wrists upwards. Daimler reached in and tugged on the chain which separated the man's bounds. "Yep. You're good to go—to hell."

"Have you had a good life, Ed?" Thawn asked. A creepy tone pervaded his voice, and Daimler instinctively pulled his hand back. Whether he wanted to admit it or not, this man had finally succeeded in frightening him. Daimler considered himself to be fairly hardened to the world. As far as he was normally concerned, the only thing that scared him was the thought of losing his mind, or becoming a full-blown alcoholic. People didn't usually frighten him.

Maybe it was Thawn's vicious intellect. Or those eyes. Or the fact that there were probably so many more people out there like him.

"I've had a great life, thanking you kindly," said Daimler, grabbing the front passenger door's handle. "Why do you ask?"

"It's just good to know," said Norwood Thawn, a strangely benign expression on his face. It was almost as though he felt sorry for Daimler.

Now why would that be?

Daimler opened the door and climbed inside, his eyes fixed on Thawn. Anticipating some kind of move.

But Thawn didn't move. He merely spoke. "If it's any small consolation, Ed, much of what you theorized about me was correct."

Daimler frowned, feeling puzzled and afraid.

He turned to van Stadt. Saw the black hole in the end of her gun, pointing at his face. Her eyes were frozen pools.

"Mel? What—?"

"Thanks for the dinner invitation," she said brightly. "But I'll pass."

His smile died.

Van Stadt fired the gun and the Lincoln filled with Ed Daimler's brains.

MY LIFE PART FOUR:
FINDING REDEMPTION

It took several more rungs to reach the ground than I had expected. Once at the ladder's base, I found myself standing next to Levin in a dark, brick walled chamber. Piles of crates hugged the walls, presumably containing alcohol for Mr Buenos's restaurant. A golden glow spilled in through the room's one open doorway. Beyond this arched portal, I could hear the hum of lively chatter.

Levin turned to me. "You ready?" she asked. "You're sure about this?"

I nodded.

"And you won't let me down?"

I shook my head, getting impatient.

"Okay," she said. "Let's go."

We walked through the doorway, entering a surprisingly bright and plush room. Animal head trophies stared blankly down from the walls.

Chandeliers were dotted along the ceiling's considerable length.

I'd be lying if I said I wasn't surprised by the people here.

Roughly two hundred in number, they were mostly middle-aged, wore suits or ball gowns and mostly looked like doctors, bankers, lawyers and accountants. Our entrance attracted curious glances from only a few; the rest continued chatting while sipping at champagne glasses which were periodically refreshed by one of the waiting staff.

"These are the Redeemers?" I whispered.

Levin frowned beside me. "What did you expect?"

"I don't know. Why didn't you tell me to wear smarter clothes?"

"It's unimportant. Not everybody does."

I looked around and saw that she was right. People in jeans and T-shirts were dotted around the room, a few of them even in their late teens. On the face of it, there appeared to be little common ground between some of these people.

Levin slid her hot hand into mine. "Come. I want you to meet somebody."

She led me through the crowd. I exchanged knowing smiles with various members, as their faces flashed by.

We reached the far side of the room, where Levin found who she was looking for. Dressed immaculately, he initially stood with his back to us, talking to a tall man in a parka jacket.

Levin waited patiently for a moment to catch his eye and intervene. Finally, he turned to greet her. "Ah, good evening, my dear. Levin, isn't it?"

Then he extended a hand to me. "Norwood Thawn."

I took the hand and shook it firmly.

"Melissa," I said. "Melissa van Stadt. Pleased to meet you."

Norwood and I hit it off so well that Levin eventually wandered away, latching onto someone else. We discussed the importance of moral values, and cautiously danced around the issue of when it was correct to enforce those values. Eventually, I felt the need to establish the Redeemers' power structure.

"So," I said, sipping from a champagne flute. "Are you the head of the Redeemers?"

"Dear me, no," laughed Norwood. "For one thing, you should know that this isn't the movement's only chapter. We're fast becoming worldwide. All entirely underground, naturalment."

He paused to politely acknowledge a passing member, then resumed his flow. "If there is a leader in this group, though, it's a lady named Penelope. She coordinated our first get-togethers. Of late, she has also become my fiancée. We are to be married."

"Congratulations," I said, with a sincerity I didn't honestly feel. Ever since the man's eyes locked with mine, I had been bewitched by his handsome presence. It was wrong of me, but I couldn't seem to help it.

"You shall have to meet her, when she arrives. I'm sure she would love to see a new recruit."

The conversation went on, and I revealed that I was about to leave town and undergo FBI training at Quantico, Virginia.

"Really?" he said, arching an eyebrow. His face darkened a shade. For a moment there, I thought he was about to call someone over to have me forcibly ejected from the premises. "Levin didn't mention that. So you'll either be a valuable ally to us, or our worst enemy, hmm?"

My head felt light from the champagne. "Oh, believe me," I said. "If ever I can help you, or any of this order, I will. We're thinking very much on the same page."

Norwood chewed this over and nodded. He was smiling again.

"To unity," he said, raising his glass to clink mine.

"To unity."

A week later, Levin committed suicide.

I found the body in her apartment, several days after she died. She had overdosed on pills and the lion's share of a whisky bottle.

I was shocked, until I prized the scrawled suicide note from her rigid right hand.

"Can't stop feelings for other women," it read. "Especially Mel. This is against everything which I believe. If I can't stop this unclean lust within myself, then I must stop everything."

And so, she did. A righteous and noble act.

I went on to Quantico, feeling highly subversive as I wormed my way through the course. Sure, they checked my history, but there was nothing untoward to be found, apart from a few traumas: my mother going missing and never being found, a school friend dying during an ill-advised adventure.

So long as I passed all the tests and said the right things, there was no way they could see me as anything other than a model applicant. That's the beautiful thing about the human mind: you can keep things hidden inside it, which no one else can access.

My mask remained firmly in place.

TWENTY-TWO

"Well," said Norwood Thawn, "You sure took your time."

Melissa van Stadt was using a handkerchief to wipe as much of the mess from her face as possible. It came off in thick globs. "I said I'd look out for you," she sighed. "Just didn't expect it to happen within a year. I thought I might as well let Ed change the tire, to save us the job. You know, I wasn't at all sure that you'd recognized me."

"Oh, I never forget a pretty face." He considered those words. "Or a cliché."

If the compliment was making van Stadt blush, then it was hard to see through all the blood. "All day, I must admit, I was praying that it wouldn't come to this," she said. "I was hoping that we wouldn't find you. But of course, that goddamn alcoholic had to go and be the master profiler."

"Yes, didn't he," Thawn said, studying the pulp that had once been Edward Daimler's head. "Well, who's laughing now? Anyway, if he was abusing the grape, then he deserved it on general principles. I just wish you hadn't shot him inside the vehicle. This is truly disgusting."

Van Stadt nodded as she wiped her face harder, using the wing mirror as her guide. The Lincoln seemed like a tiny point of light in a galaxy of black. A thought struck her.

"So, were you telling the truth about Penelope?" she asked.

Thawn nodded, exhaling heavily. "Jason killed her."

"I'm so sorry for your loss. And for the Redeemers."

"And as I said, I will kill him. Can I get my knife back, from the trunk?"

"Sure," she said, pressing a button that prompted the trunk to pop up. "Go get it."

There was a pause. Norwood coughed. "You need to unlock me first."

Van Stadt slapped her forehead, smearing it with blood again. "Of course! I'm sorry." She turned around and crawled through the seats, with the key in one hand. As she twisted it in the handcuffs' lock, their faces were inches apart. She could taste his breath.

"Norwood," she said. "Penelope may have been cruelly taken from you, but you'll never be alone. The two of us should... stick together, you know?"

Thawn looked at her strangely for a second, then smiled. "That's right." As the handcuffs fell away, he flexed his hands and rubbed the indentations on his wrists. "What was your name again?"

"Melissa. You can call me Mel. I'll give you my number. Maybe we should meet up, when it's safe."

"Thank you. I'd like that." He clambered out of the Lincoln and dragged Daimler's headless corpse out of the passenger seat. Then he walked to the trunk and undid the plastic forensics bag which held his precious weapon.

The vehicle hummed and vibrated as the engine coughed into life.

As Thawn weighed the knife in one hand, he stared coldly over the roof and beyond, off along the road.

The Phoenix Heights's one remaining security guard was running toward Clayden Heinz in the foyer, along with several guests who had no intention of stopping until they were safely off the premises. Some had suffered bloody wounds. Others carried serious burns, their clothes smoldering. Most of them had ignored the fire alarm, until it was almost too late.

Heinz was panic-stricken. Five minutes ago, he had seen his head chef running through the foyer at full pelt, his white uniform splattered with blood. Heinz had called out, demanding to know what was going on, but Waylon vanished through the front doors, out into the night.

"Meyer," barked Heinz, seizing his unfeasibly tall guard by the shoulders, panicking even more when he saw the haunted fear in the man's eyes. "Tell me whatever's happening is under control."

"It's Myers, Sir. And—"

"Who gives a fuck what your name is?" Heinz said, screaming to make himself heard above the surrounding pandemonium, sending spittle flying into Myers's face.

The security guard struggled to deliver the necessary information to Heinz. "We need to evacuate the building immediately. Not only do we have a real fire, but an intruder killing people. He's taken out most of our team, including Walt. And I can't reach Finton or Brookes on the radio. I'm afraid I ran from the kitchen, sir. This killer seems to be wearing heavy-duty bullet-proof equipment. We could barely touch him."

Heinz looked as though he was about to die, right there on the spot. His face was bright red and his eyes danced madly. More mayhem rang out around them.

"What the fuck are you saying?" Heinz demanded. "Who is this killer? Take him down!"

Myers opened his mouth to answer and choked.

Heinz stared at him indignantly. "Speak, you idiot!" he cried.

Blood dribbled, then poured out of Myers's slack mouth.

Heinz watched horrified as a cruel metal spike burst out of the security guard's stomach. Myers slowly fell to the floor, revealing Jason standing behind him. Jutting from Myers's back was a golden pole with a restaurant menu attached to the other end. All around the foyer, terrified guests bolted toward the outside world.

Heinz tried to do just that, but collided with a party of his own guests. He shoved a young girl aside, sending her spinning against a wall.

The girl's father growled and raised a fist to punch Heinz.

Jason tugged the pole out of Myers and hurled it like a javelin into the back of Heinz's head.

The hotel manager spun around theatrically, eyes lividly bloodshot, the spike's tip where his nose once was, making him resemble some surreal caricature. He slumped face down on the floor, the restaurant menu jutting out of his head. The shocked father grabbed his daughter's hand, ushering the whole family out through the glass doors.

A new wave of people poured out into the foyer, some from the elevators. Jason raised his meat cleaver in greeting. Many turned and ran back toward the flames.

"Come on, missy, you've got to wake up."

"Get the hell off of Halo. Stop slapping her!"

"Don't tell me what to do, boy."

"Ryger, just shake her. That's an order. We don't slap civilians, remember?"

"Yes, sir."

Halo's eyes snapped open, to see a huddle of faces above her. "I'm awake," she protested.

"There's something going on downstairs," said Tom, stroking her face where Ryger had struck. "We need to leave the building."

Halo sat bolt upright on the bed. "But what about Shelley? We can't leave her here."

"Miss Harlan," said Claymark kindly, "I'm afraid your sister is dead."

"Yeah, sure, I know that," said Halo, impatiently. "But we can't leave her. She'll be lonely."

Claymark and Ryger exchanged worried looks. Tom placed a hand on Halo's shoulder, which she shrugged off. "Come on Halo, we need to leave. There's definitely something going on downstairs. Listen: the fire alarm is still going and you can hear people screaming. This ain't no drill."

Halo jumped off the bed and rounded on the three men with wild, cloudy eyes. "Let me tell you, boys," she said. "There'll be some goddamn screaming in *here* if you expect me to leave my big sister."

Hack. Chop. Slice. Jason made light work of the constant flow of guests attempting to leave. Most were too preoccupied with their lungs being full of smoke to notice him, until it was too late. Bodies littered the foyer, almost all missing one or more limbs. What remained of the reception staff lay on and behind the front desk.

A middle-aged man charged into the foyer as a human fireball. His limbs flailed as he blindly ran toward Jason. Sensing movement, the giant turned and the man ran directly into the cleaver blade. With a barely audible cry, he fell back off the blade, then collapsed on to the ground, still burning, but motionless.

Whether Jason Voorhees realized it or not, this was his first ever mercy killing.

An old woman leaning against a Zimmer frame appeared at one end of the foyer. Upon seeing Jason, she made alarmed wheezing noises and tried to increase her speed.

The giant stomped toward her, raising the cleaver.

Ping! Jason turned to the direction of the noise, in time to see one of the elevator doors open. Leaving the old woman to speed-hobble toward freedom, he strode instead toward the middle-aged couple who had emerged from the elevator carriage, dragging bulky suitcases behind them.

"Jesus!" cried the wife. "Who the hell is that?"

A matchstick dropped from one corner of her husband's mouth. "He ain't no friggin' fireman, honey. Back in the elevator!"

The pair abandoned their cases and backed into the golden carriage, stabbing frantically at the buttons.

Then they begged for their lives as Jason advanced on the closing elevator doors.

Norwood extended his hand. "Give me the gun."

Driving beside him, Melissa van Stadt passed over the weapon. Thawn held it in his right hand for a while, rubbing his forefinger over the trigger.

Then he handed it back. "That handles the finger-print side of things. I snatched the gun from you, blew Ed's head off..."

"Held me at gun point and made me drive you to the hotel. Then tied me up."

"You want to be tied up?"

"Well, otherwise you'd have to kill me."

"That's true. I am a murdering fiend, after all."

Van Stadt smiled affectionately. "You've just been doing the right thing and you know it. I'd do anything to support this cause."

She placed her hand on his for a moment, then pulled it away. "In fact, I already have. You're not the only Redeemer I've helped out of trouble."

"Really?"

"Oh yes. This job allows a great deal of travel."

"I'm sure."

"Are you entirely sure you want to go to the hotel?"

Norwood wrapped his hand around the full circumference of his knife's base. "Oh yes. I thirst for vengeance."

Van Stadt glanced at the weapon, as though seeing it for the first time.

"Are those... Penelope's bones?"

Norwood nodded gravely. "Appropriate, don't you think? She'll be killing Jason herself, in effect." He pulled a metallic silver case from a pocket.

Van Stadt didn't look convinced. "If this Jason is as strong and unstoppable as you say he is, shouldn't you be getting out of town? I'd hate to save your liberty, only to see you lose everything."

"I have no choice," Norwood said quietly. "She's in my head, telling me to do it. I must do it. If I can, I'll silence that little whore Halo, too."

Opening the silver case, he pulled out a cigarette and placed it between his lips. A search for his Zippo came up with nothing. "Got a light, my dear?" he said.

"I don't smoke," said van Stadt, frowning at the very idea. She drove on.

Ping! An overweight Mexican businessman sighed with relief as the elevator finally reached his floor, the twelfth. He had begun to worry after five minutes of the fire alarm first sounding, then investigated and seen smoke billowing out of windows below. He wanted out, as quickly as possible.

Fuck taking the stairs; the effort would probably kill him anyway.

As the elevator doors glided open, his reflection was replaced by a nightmarish vision. The carriage was mostly filled by Jason Voorhees, who stood amidst what looked like an afternoon's work at the slaughterhouse. The entire floor of the elevator was awash with blood, in which the chunks of two dismembered corpses drifted.

Before the businessman could run, Jason was upon him, swinging steel down into the man's heart. Blood sprayed Jason's mask as he wrenched the cleaver up through his victim's shoulder with a resounding crack. He was dead before he hit the floor.

Smoke issued from beneath the elevator. The light inside the carriage flickered uncertainly. Ignoring all of these signals, Jason lumbered off along a long corridor lined with doors, some of which hung open.

He rotated left and crashed through a locked door, sending it hurtling down to the ground. Slashing the throat of a screaming young blonde wrapped in a towel, he immediately departed the room and walked on.

Smashing through another door, he found a couple asleep in bed. Before they knew what was happening, he had decapitated one and chopped the other to pieces.

Then he moved on, looking for more life to crush. One life in particular.

* * *

Tom was beginning to despair: Halo had lost her mind. He cast his thoughts back to his college psychology class. What did they call this? Denial. Yes, this was textbook denial. Halo was talking like his Alzheimer's riddled grandmother, an empty smile plastered across her face. Her brain had erected a stone wall against reality.

Claymark was using the phone, directing a helicopter to change course and head this way. Tom hoped he was merely allowing for the worst-case scenario.

Ryger peered down, out of the window. His rugged features registered alarm. "There's smoke down there. We gotta go."

Tom grabbed Halo's shoulders. "Hear that? We could all die if we don't leave now."

Halo stared at him dumbly. Grinning.

"Sure." Cupping a hand over her mouth, she directed her voice toward the bathroom. "C'mon, Shelley. Time to skedaddle!"

The fire had devastated most of the ground floor. The intense heat had ignited the wiring, which serviced most of the building, causing it to melt, burn and spread. Many guests had been burnt alive in their rooms, or suffocated by the black smoke that was sweeping along the corridors.

The fire alarm had stopped, the system having been compromised by the very blaze it had been designed to detect.

Residents piled down the external fire escape in their undergarments, few of them pausing to help the less actively mobile. As too many people attempted the descent at once, several toppled over the edge, plunging to their deaths.

Fire engine sirens wailed in the distance, but the local department's efforts would be an operation in damage limitation at best.

The hotel was dying.

If there was one thing Rosa Mendez hated about living in this place, it was the noise you heard, late at night. Sometimes, it was difficult to sleep. And she was fifty—she needed that rest.

Her room was the hotel's smallest, she knew. After all, she was a cleaner and she got to clean most of the other rooms on a daily basis. She had a bedroom and a tiny bathroom. The limited space was made bearable only by the fact that her bed swung neatly back up into the wall when not in use.

She was lying on it and getting annoyed. The damn fire alarm had been bad enough—thank God it had finally stopped—but she could hear guests shouting. She was used to a little chatter, out in the corridor, or through the surprisingly thin walls between rooms. But people were running riot out there. Was a party going on, in one of the rooms?

As more wild noise cut through the night, Mendez switched on a side lamp, heaved herself out of bed and wrapped a nightgown around herself. Heading over to the door, she peered through the spy hole embedded in the wood. Through the lens, she saw the usual distorted image of an empty corridor. Perhaps the door opposite was ajar, but it was difficult to tell.

A distant, rowdy yell made her curse. She grabbed the door handle and wrenched it open, her bare feet padding out onto the carpet.

The opposite door was yanked open from within and Jason stomped out, seizing a horrified Mendez by the shoulders. Her mouth affected a silent scream as he dragged her back into her room and threw her across the bed.

Quickly surveying the possibilities, Jason grabbed the foot of the bed. He wrenched it upwards and back against the wall. Only the cleaner's head, arms and feet were visible at either side of the bed.

Placing a gore caked boot against the bed's upright base, Jason grabbed one of her hands, one of her feet and pulled them toward him. Mendez howled as a sickening crunch signaled the ruin of her spine.

Jason released her and marched out of the room. A thick cloud of smoke drifted behind him, like a silent companion.

Shortly, another splintering of wood and rending of metal was followed by more screams.

"Here you are, Mr Thawn. That'll be ten dollars."

Van Stadt had pulled the Lincoln up halfway along the driveway that served the Phoenix Heights. "I thought it would be safer for you to get out at a safe distance here, rather than driving right up to the front doors."

"Good point, Melissa." Norwood Thawn turned and studied her face: her deep blue eyes; the expression that spoke of admiration, maybe even worship.

"Here's to unity," she said.

"Unity," nodded Thawn.

"Okay, tie me up," she said. "Perhaps you could punch me too, or something? Whatever looks more convincing."

A pause.

"How about this?" asked Norwood, casually.

His bone knife flashed across the car's confined space. Its jagged prongs plunged easily through van Stadt's shirt and into her chest.

She gasped and spluttered, eyes wide.

"Convincing enough, do you think?" said Norwood, his face hardening. "Here's your last thought on Earth: my wife is irreplaceable. No one will ever replace her. No one will *ever* replace her." He emphasized the last "no one" by driving the weapon deeper into the FBI agent's body.

As Melissa van Stadt's breathing faded, she was a picture of disillusionment. Norwood watched until the light in her eyes seemed to dwindle, then yanked the knife back out, splashing more blood against the windshield.

He grabbed the gun from van Stadt's holster. Then he climbed out of the car and darted along the driveway, keeping as close to the trees as possible.

The familiar sight of the hotel soon came into view. Norwood peered up at it. Was that smoke coming out of the windows? Some of the rooms also had a glow which very much resembled fire.

A shadowy figure was running toward him, past the fountain, over the gravel. Closing fast.

He gripped the knife in one hand and the gun in the other.

The figure—a man of roughly his own age—kept running. Thawn realized he was simply escaping the grounds.

Thawn chuckled to himself and once again let his eyes wander up the hotel's distressed front face. Jason was definitely here, but not for long.

"That's it. We're going. Right now." Tom grabbed Halo's hand and yanked her across the suite's carpet. To his surprise, she offered no resistance.

"Bye, Shelley," she yelled, over her shoulder. "See you in the bar, later."

Claymark and Ryger anxiously waited by the door. "There's no smoke up here yet," said the sheriff. "But it's only a matter of time. Depends how strong this place's firewalls are. We need to take the fire escape down."

The four of them ducked out into the empty corridor, Claymark leading the way.

"Why not the elevator?" asked Tom.

"You don't use 'em in a fire," said Ryger, as though he was an idiot. Tom bristled. He didn't like this fat fuck.

He kept a tight grip on Halo as they all broke into an urgent jog, following the corridor as it twisted from side to side.

"Is that the fire escape?" Tom heard Ryger ask his sheriff, pointing to something at the corridor's far end.

"Looks that way. Let's get to it, Ken."

Seeing the fire escape spurred everybody on, except for Halo, who ran leisurely, like a tired child being led.

Tom yelped. Halo was squeezing his hand so hard that he feared the bones would shatter.

She stopped dead, forcing him to do the same. Tom watched the cops run ahead, oblivious that he and Halo were no longer behind them. "What is it?" he said, desperate to get out of this damn building.

Halo appeared to be in the grip of an asthma attack. "He's here," she gasped. "I can feel him."

Tom stared at her. "Jason?"

A huge crash like a thunderclap seized both their attentions. They turned to see Jason Voorhees smashing up through the floorboards in a haze of cracked wood and smoke.

Landing on his feet in front of the hole, he stood between the cops and the fire escape.

TWENTY-THREE

Halo felt as though she was waking up from a nightmare. Except it wasn't over yet. As Tom looked on, she snapped back into survival mode. Everything came back to her—even Shelley's death—but the need to live outweighed all other concerns.

"Let's go back," she snapped at Tom, who was struggling to process his first sight of Jason Voorhees.

"Back?" he protested. "But the only way out is the fire escape. And we can't—"

He was interrupted by a blast from Ryger's shotgun, which ploughed into Jason's stomach, throwing him off balance. Even from this distance, Halo and Tom physically felt the thud as he hit the floor.

Halo heard Ryger say, "That oughta do it," but she knew damn well that it wouldn't. Nevertheless,

Jason presently lay flat on the carpet. For a moment, she entertained the idea of dashing past him, to get to that fire escape.

Then he sat up, making the cops yell in surprise and swung his cleaver blade clean through both of Ryger's legs, just above the knee.

The deputy's upper half fell backwards, his divorced legs toppling like skittles. He fired the shotgun again, whether by accident or design, and this second salvo pumped into the ceiling. Plaster rained down on Jason and the two men, one of whom was lying on his back, screaming for mercy as Jason stood over him.

Claymark was yelling something, locked into the gun-leveling stance. But it did no good. Jason trod over what remained of Ryger's body, popping his stomach, left shoulder and head like water balloons.

"Come on, sheriff," Halo cried. "You can't stop him."

With a cry of anguish, Claymark took her advice and came running back along the corridor. It was his turn to manifest shock symptoms, as the three of them charged away from Jason. "Why doesn't the man die?" he repeatedly babbled, shaking his head.

Two corridor bends later, Jason was no longer in view behind them.

"Maybe we should try the elevator," said Tom. "It might still work."

"I doubt it," gasped Halo, "but let's see."

The golden doors came quickly into view. Tom pressed the call button three times in sharp succession.

To their surprise, the doors slid open, revealing an empty, blackened shaft.

"Oh, great," said Claymark, peering down. "I can't even see the goddamn elevator."

"You two go ahead," said Halo, nodding along the corridor. She looked back anxiously over her shoulders. "I wanna try something."

"What?" said Tom. "What do you wanna try? Let's just keep running."

"Go ahead," she repeated, voice firm. This time, Tom and Claymark submitted and moved off along the corridor.

Halo stood in front of the elevator, facing back the way they had come.

As inexorable as the changing of the seasons, Jason turned the corner. Upon seeing her, his pace quickened and he hoisted the cleaver.

She suddenly paused to wonder exactly what it was that she wanted to try. Was she going to jump aside at the last possible second and let him fall down the shaft? Or drag him down there with her?

She had little time to decide: Jason was closing in.

His head cocked to one side, as though he was puzzled by Halo presenting herself to him. She hoped he was too pig ignorant to be suspicious of such an easy kill, after a memorably long chase. She desperately wanted him to break into a run. That would help. Then his momentum might carry him over the edge, down into the black.

But Jason Voorhees did not run. Then he was upon her, swinging that chopper down in a wide arc, which threatened to bisect her.

Somewhere along the corridor to her left, she heard Tom yelling. He was watching.

She ducked aside, feeling the sharp blade cleave hairs from her head. The force behind Jason's swipe had unbalanced him; all his weight was leaning forwards. Reaching up with both hands, Halo grabbed the chain around his neck and swung him with all her might.

He didn't move. Regaining his balance, Jason looked down at Halo and prepared to deliver the coup de grâce. Then, for no reason immediately apparent to her, he tumbled forward and disappeared into the shaft.

Halo sat up, stunned, to see Tom and the sheriff standing there. "Teamwork," said Tom, sharing a high-five with Claymark. "We shoved him in there good."

"Thanks," said Halo, her eyes lingering on Tom's for a second. "I was almost hamburger there." With something approaching a smile, she picked herself up and peered down into the shaft's gloom, as steeply as she dared.

That was all she could see. Gloom.

Tom and the sheriff joined her. Claymark's face was still flushed. He still appeared traumatized by this indestructible being. "But will that kill him?"

"I don't have a clue," said Halo, from over Tom's shoulder. "But it should get him away from us for a while. Now we just need to—"

The words evaporated in her mouth, as the rasp of metal on metal sounded. A series of heavy thumps and jolts followed. Jason Voorhees began to clamber back out of the elevator shaft with a series of hoarse grunts.

They backed away from him. Halo slapped her hand on the back of Claymark's wrist, as he went to tug his gun from its hip holster.

"Don't waste your bullets," she warned. "God, the fucker must have been hanging on. Let's run!"

Already, Jason was blocking the route back to the fire escape, so once again they were forced to move in the opposite direction.

As the trio darted around a sharp bend, Halo spied an open room door and impulsively hurtled through, followed by Tom and Claymark. Once they were inside, she closed the door and locked it.

"What are we doing?" protested Claymark, as he looked around a spacious suite, which judging by the possessions scattered around had been abandoned. "We shouldn't lock ourselves away."

Halo fiercely shushed him. "If Jason walks past," she hoarsely whispered, "we can leave and head back to the fire escape. Otherwise, he'll chase us forever. He doesn't stop. This is our only chance."

Crash: the sound of a door being broken inward back out in a nearby corridor.

Claymark opened his mouth to speak, but Halo shushed him again, listening keenly. Angered, the sheriff made his way over to the door with exaggerated tiptoe steps and carefully moved his eye over the spy hole.

Halo and Tom watched him nervously, barely aware that they were still holding hands.

Claymark shook his head, signaling that he could see nothing.

Halo could feel heat gathering in the floor beneath them. Tom was feeling it too, judging by the way he was squeezing her hand.

One of the room's walls caved in, sending plaster and lumps of brick hurtling through the air. Jason forced his way through the new hole, incandescent with rage.

Claymark hurriedly opened the room's door and stepped through it. Jason walked across the carpet, toward a frozen Halo and Tom.

Standing in the open doorway, Claymark fired twice into Jason's shoulder. The giant glanced at Claymark, but was in no mood to be distracted.

Claymark fired again, this time hitting Jason's left ear. The killer roared at this, clutching the side of his head. Straightening again, Jason finally changed plans and headed for Claymark.

Halo dragged Tom across the room and through the hole in the wall. As they charged straight through the adjacent room, jumping over a freshly slain guest, they heard a pained yell from outside.

Back out in the corridor, they saw Claymark crumpled and broken on the ground, begging for his life as Jason towered over him.

"No!" cried Halo, her voice commanding rather than pleading, as Jason raised the cleaver again.

There was no mercy. The blade chopped down through Claymark's skull, ending his torment permanently.

Halo and Tom sprinted off along the corridor, conscious that they were finally positioned between Jason and the fire escape. The corridor was noticeably smokier and it was becoming harder to breathe.

Ryger's mutilated body signaled that the fire escape was imminent. It also signaled that they were about to see the hole through which Jason had entered from the floor below.

Holding hands, they leapt with perfect timing, sailing over the gap. Halo glanced downwards, seeing a horrendous well of fire, smoke and mangled metal. As they landed together on the other side, the fire escape door seemed to rush up to meet them. Tom shouldered it open and they felt the heady rush of the fresh night air, contrasting drastically with the smog they had left behind.

With sharp intakes of breath, the pair saw that roughly nine levels of fire escape directly below them were missing. Down most of the gap's length, the brickwork showed damage where the fire escape structure had been ripped loose. The entire seventh floor gaped open like a mouth, as though it had been blown outwards.

Way down on the ground, they could see a large, twisted pile of blackened metal and wrecked people.

Halo and Tom had nowhere left to run.

He knew it was insanity. Running up the stairs of a burning building went against the kind of rational thought for which he prided himself. Yet Penelope's voice was loud and clear in his head, spurring him on. The Great Redeemer, his eternal wife, telling him what to do.

Climb on, my darling. Do not falter.

Norwood had one shirt cuff pressed over his nose and mouth, as he ran up the stairs, through the lung-sucking fog. His legs felt weak, but he knew he could not allow them to fail him. He must go on. Two levels down, the knife had fallen from his grasp and skidded along the floor. Crawling on hands and knees, coughing, he had regained the weapon and vowed never to release it again.

Arriving at yet another level, he saw a huge number seven on the wall. He grabbed the next banister and worked his way up it.

Jason turned a corner and resumed his relentless stride toward Halo and Tom. They were back in that terrible corridor. Between them and Jason lay many doors, but Halo didn't like the idea of hiding in another room. It hadn't gotten them very far. And besides, the bastard would now see where they went, smoke or not.

"Oh God," said Halo, watching Jason march. "Let's go back outside and jump."

"Hey," said Tom, pointing at a door marked "Stairs". "This goes up to the roof. The manager showed me. Go."

Halo wasted no time in grabbing the handle. Running through, she heard the door slam shut behind her. Immediately missing Tom's presence, she spun around and saw him on the other side of the door's reinforced glass pane.

Smiling, he blew her a kiss. His voice sounded muffled. "Someone's got to hold him back."

"Come on!" she cried, now pleading more than commanding, "Come with me!"

Tom shook his head grimly.

Halo heard something on the stairs below. Was it movement? Feet on stone?

Peering downwards, she saw only dark, swirling smoke. When she looked back at the glass square, Tom was gone.

Norwood felt as though there was no oxygen left in his brain. He could barely think straight. The smoke had become thinner as he climbed, but the accumulative effect was devastating. He leant against a wall, beside the number ten.

Climb on, my darling. Seek vengeance.

"I can't," gasped Norwood. He slumped to the ground, finally submitting to the lack of oxygen.

He felt himself drifting away.

Tom had wrapped himself around a bulky soft drinks machine. With Jason no more than a few big strides away, he pulled it off balance and rode it until it struck the opposite wall, blocking Jason's path.

"That should slow you down," he said, covering his mouth and shifting from foot to foot. God, the heat.

Jason reached the machine and stopped. He and Tom silently regarded each other.

"Would you like a Coke?" said Tom.

The machine vibrated as Jason seized it with both hands.

Tom trembled. "Diet Coke?"

Jason tipped the machine sideways. It fell on Tom, crushing the lower half of his body against the ground and pinning him down. The weight was immense.

Tom raised his one free hand as Jason walked around the machine.

"Please," he said. "Don't hurt her. Just don't hurt her."

Jason's cleaver powered down. Tom wailed as three of his fingers struck a nearby wall.

Jason raised the weapon again as smoke swirled around him.

"Jason!" The voice was Halo's.

"Come on, I'm still here, mother lover!"

"What are you doing?" called Tom, fighting the red-hot agony in his mutilated hand with every syllable. "Get out of here!"

Jason lumbered off, swallowed up by the smog.

"No!" roared Tom. "Come back, you fucking—" His mouth filled with smoke.

As she clambered up the stairs to the roof, trying and failing to forget about Tom, it struck Halo that the area might be locked off. After all, unless you had a swimming pool or a restaurant up there, hotel proprietors weren't so keen on guests walking around on their roof: getting drunk, falling to their doom.

The route upwards was surprisingly complex: a maze of corridors, stairs and assorted maintenance equipment. She eventually reached a set of bulky double doors which didn't even have handles, just one long bar. She tugged it and pulled it and pushed it, until it gave way and the doors opened outwards.

Halo emerged from a corrugated iron hut positioned in the center of the roof's surface, which was vividly illuminated by spotlights and dotted with ventilation pipes and generators. Hardly anywhere to hide.

All around sprawled the vista of Crystal Lake, shrouded in places by smoke that drifted up from the hotel's pressure-cooking carcass. Already, even up here, Halo could feel the heat of the tarmac as she walked out on to it.

Behind her, the doors crashed open.

She saw Norwood Thawn, falling down to his hands and knees on the ground by the metal hut. His body heaved as he fought for air.

Halo raised the shotgun.

TWENTY-FOUR

Chuck Waylon stood amid the chaos that had broken out in the hotel's front grounds. He was watching the place burn. Fire flashed out of almost every window, right up to the twelfth floor. Every few minutes, there was a very audible crash from within the building, presumably as a section of floor collapsed.

He had seen most of the fire escape come loose under the weight of so many trying to climb down it. He had heard those people's dying cries as the structure plummeted to the unforgiving earth. Goddamn them, if they'd only calmed the hell down and waited.

What remained of the hotel staff had made a half-hearted attempt to round up guests and count heads, trying to do it by the book. Yet everyone knew that all that sensible, official stuff didn't count for shit, once there was a real emergency. It was like the safety instructions on an airplane—once the ocean was rising up to the meet the aircraft, it was every man for himself and screw the rest.

His first instinct after speeding through the foyer had been to run until he was out of the county. Then curiosity got the better of him. If the Phoenix was going down, he wanted to see it, and he wanted to be told that the fruit loop in his kitchen was dead. Otherwise he'd have to sleep with one eye open for the rest of his days.

Two fire engines and six ambulances cast flashing lights around the scene. Distant sirens confirmed that more were coming. Corpses littered the gravel, often tripping medics and firemen as they tried to do their jobs. The living showed few signs of gratitude for having survived. Groans of pain echoed all around him; people with bloody gashes, or missing limbs, bawled like babies as they were eased into ambulances.

Waylon knew he should be helping. Lifting one end of a stretcher or something. But, like so many of the guests, he felt content to stand there, with a silver sheet wrapped around him, pretending to be in shock. Matter of fact, he didn't need to pretend. The cocaine made a reliable self-diagnosis difficult, but he knew that when this was done, he'd need a damn good therapist.

"I'm Zell Rayner from *WCX News*," said someone to his right, shoving a branded microphone under his nose. "Sir, what has been your experience here tonight?"

Waylon eyed Rayner darkly. Then he placed a bloody palm on the newsman's face and casually shoved him away.

* * *

"Where is he?" said Thawn, standing, his face taut with the effort, his clothes blackened. He coughed into one hand. Halo saw that the other gripped a bizarre knife. "Where's Jason?"

Halo grimaced. "Shut up, you fucking bastard. You killed my sister."

Thawn seemed indifferent to the news. "Oh, did I? Which one was she?"

"She's the one you're going to die for." Halo tightened her finger on the trigger.

"Have you turned the safety button off? It won't fire if you don't press it."

Halo gritted her teeth.

"Oh, and hold it against your shoulder. Otherwise, the recoil might knock you off the building. We can't have that now, can we?"

"I doubt the owner had time to put the safety back on," said Halo. "Why did you kill my sister? The receptionist."

Thawn took two steps away from the metal hut, toward her. Halo held her ground. "Look," he said, "I'd love to discuss this with you in depth, but answer me this: where's Jason?"

Halo nodded behind him. "Coming up the stairs right now."

Thawn rotated a full circle, shrewdly scanning the rooftop. "For a moment there," he said, "I thought that was one of those 'He's behind you' ruses."

He started walking around one side of the metal hut, his back now to her. Halo followed him, keeping the gun trained on him.

"Stop right there," she shouted. "Where the hell are you going?"

"To climb up on this thing," said Thawn, still presenting his back to her. "I want to get the element of surprise on that monster."

Halo found herself laughing. "Monster? You are so deluded. You're just the same as him. Pure evil, full of hate."

Thawn ignored her. He was reaching up the metal hut's sides, searching for hand and footholds. "Don't suppose you'd like to give me a leg up?" he said, wrinkling his nose.

"Fuck you," said Halo, with such force that spittle lashed her chin.

"Ah, come on," he protested. "Whatever little score you think you have to settle with me, we both want Jason dead, don't we? So let's work together. You hit him with that thing when he comes through the door. Then I'll finish the job."

"I'd rather die than work with you."

"Then kill yourself," he grumbled. "Right now, I don't have time for this. I need retribution, with or without you." He found a foothold and heaved himself up the rough surface with a clang.

"And what about *my* justice? *My* revenge?"

Thawn stared down at Halo from the hut. "We can deal with that afterwards, if we really must. It doesn't matter to me. I'm looking forward to being reunited with my wife." He glanced at the sky.

Halo uttered a harsh, mocking laugh. "I don't know where you think you're going, mister, but it sure ain't heaven."

Thawn fixed her with an exasperated stare. "Just get ready."

Halo's head was spinning. As much as she hated to admit it, she and this fucker did share the same goal. Survive and kill Jason. The man-child who had disposed of almost everyone she knew. Including Tom. She bit her lip and ran back in front of the entrance, positioning herself.

Smoke gushed from underneath the doors. She wondered whether the fumes might finally have overcome Jason. Surely that wasn't possible, after everything she had seen him survive?

Thawn had positioned himself at the peak of the hut's roof, hunched up like a gargoyle, clutching that knife. There was no part of her body that didn't want to raise Ryger's shotgun and blast him off that perch. Yet if he was going to help bring Jason down, his death could wait a few minutes.

Halo was also tempted to dash to the roof's edge and see what was happening down below. She resisted, keeping her eyes fixed on those doors. Trying to forget that she could feel the ground's heat through the soles of her sneakers.

An almighty rumble split the air behind her. Seeing that Thawn looked alarmed, she spun around and saw that a portion of the rooftop was no longer there, having collapsed. A jagged hole, ten feet square, gaped up at the stars. Fire and smoke belched through its new outlet.

"Jesus," she breathed, horribly transfixed by the sight. How long until the whole building went down?

"Hey!" The voice was Thawn's, strained and urgent.

She spun again in time to see him falling through the air toward Jason, who was standing in front of the metal hut, the doors slamming shut behind him. Jason was entirely black, including most of his mask. Having heard Thawn's warning, Jason started to turn around.

Thawn landed on the giant's back with a thud, hugging Jason's neck, his feet gripping the killer's waist. Jason swung violently, attempting to dislodge the aggressor. Some kind of gun struck the ground beside the two men; it must have tumbled from Thawn's pocket, Halo vaguely noted.

She cursed herself for missing a chance to sink a slug into Jason. Leveling the shotgun at his chest, she rested the butt against her shoulder. That would be the only advice she would ever accept from Norwood.

Thawn was wasting no time. As Jason thrashed wildly around, he leant back like a bronco rider, his right hand in the air, clutching the bone knife. Then with a snarl, he slammed it down.

The sharp points disappeared into the top of Jason's skull. With a strangled grunt, Jason fell to his knees. Turning the cleaver around in his hand, he slammed it up and back over his own head. Thawn gasped hoarsely as it sank into his stomach.

As Halo looked on, Thawn thumped his fist down on top of the bone knife. In reply, Jason twisted his upper body so dramatically that Thawn was sent hurtling off the cleaver. He landed awkwardly, something breaking inside him.

Halo saw another portion of the roof caving downwards. There was no time to study it properly: she was about to blow Jason's head off. He was still on his knees, grabbing at his skull with both hands, trying to pull the blade out. Looking down the barrel, she fixed the mask in her sights. Then, she squeezed the trigger. Despite Thawn's advice about recoil, the force of it still took her by surprise. She tried to regain her balance, but ended up on her back.

Jason was still kneeling. No damage.

"Fire again!" called Thawn, weakly, clutching at his stomach wound.

Shaking his head, as though shrugging off a bad hangover, Jason rose yet again, the bone knife still protruding several inches from the top of his head.

Crouching, Halo struggled to reload the shotgun. The fact that she had no idea how to do so, was a problem. How did they do it on TV? She reached below the barrel and found a tubular handle with finger grip texture. Wrenching it back toward her, she mouthed a silent "Yes!" as the spent shell exited, courtesy of a slot on the weapon's side. She presumed that another shell had simultaneously clicked into position.

Would it be the last?

Jason walked toward Thawn, who was struggling like an overturned beetle. He flicked his wrist and a small blade appeared in his hand. He attempted to hurl it at Jason, but his arm had been broken. The blade fell uselessly to the ground.

"Shoot!" Thawn screeched. "Fucking shoot!"

Halo aimed the shotgun at Jason.

She paused, frowning, as Jason threw his cleaver to one side. It clattered on the ground and lay still.

Jason reached down toward Thawn with his bare hands.

"No!"

Halo fired. Jason's head exploded.

At least, Halo thought it had. When she recovered and looked clearly, she had merely blown the protruding part of the bone knife to smithereens.

Thawn was crying deliriously as Jason seized hold of his upper body, tugging in opposite directions.

He was going to tear the man apart.

"Help me!" he cried, reaching out for Halo. "Shoot again!"

Halo's heart pounded. She couldn't let anyone die that way.

Then she remembered a snapshot of her dead sister, back in the good old days. The two of them, taking turns on a tree swing in their backyard. It was a simple image, but it gave her strength. Or froze her sense of humanity. Either way, she wasn't about to lift a finger to help Thawn.

As the man's shrieking reached a horrendous peak, Halo reloaded the shotgun slowly. Methodically.

Smoke from the hut was rapidly engulfing the two combatants. Jason appeared to tear a thick ream of flesh from Thawn's torso, making bile bubble out of his mouth.

"Kill me," he begged, his voice glottal and slurred. "Kill me!"

"Sorry," said Halo. "You're not worth the ammo. Send my regards to your wife."

The man's vocal agony reached new heights as Jason lifted him into the air by his feet.

Suspended upside-down, above a massive hole in the roof, Thawn bared his teeth at Halo, his face bright red, dripping with his own blood. A maze of intestines bulged from his torn belly. "You're next," he gargled.

Jason released the feet and he tumbled into the abyss.

Norwood Thawn was burning in hell, just as he deserved. Yet Halo's limited sense of triumph was short-lived. Jason returned his attention to her, most of his jet-black body glistening with blood.

The giant searched for his cleaver on the ground. In the spot where it had been, a gaping hole pulsated with heat and light. The hotel had swallowed the weapon.

Jason straightened and focused on Halo again.

She was already running, over to what she believed was the front of the hotel, praying that the ground held up beneath her. Maybe, just maybe, if she made herself visible on top of the roof, someone might see her and work miracles.

Steaming, bubbling heat seemed to surround her: it was like moving across the base of an awakening volcano.

Jason's footsteps landed close behind her, but the roof was crumbling at his feet. He swayed on the edge, as a wide portion of stone, its underlying rubber membrane and an entire ventilation unit melted into the abyss. He stepped back, shaking with rage.

Halo resumed her dash toward the roof edge.

Waylon felt the crowd surge around him. Most of them were looking upwards, walking backwards, away from the building, in order to secure a better view.

Zell Rayner jabbed a finger skyward for his cameraman's benefit. "There's someone on the roof!" He was keeping himself off the screen, while a flunky attempted to wipe blood from his face. Waylon regretted daubing that stuff on Rayner: it would probably make that jackass think he was some kind of war correspondent. He'd probably win a damn award.

The crowd gasped as they peered up at the roof's lone figure. The cameraman trained his sights on her. "It's a chick," he muttered in Rayner's ear.

"It's a female," Rayner announced into the microphone, irritably shrugging off the flunky, now that most of the blood had been cleaned away. "There is a woman trapped on the roof. Can the fire department save her?"

Next to him, a fire chief overheard the question and sadly shook his head.

One front section of the hotel came loose. Tumbling to the ground in a shower of metal, glass and stone, leaving fire trails in the air, it sent onlookers scattering in all directions.

Halo waved her arms. A weak ripple of crowd noise floated up to reach her. She knew it was useless. What did she expect? The fire engine's ladder wouldn't reach this height, and neither could she jump off the building, down into a conveniently stretched out blanket. She checked on Jason's progress. He had navigated the latest hole in the roof. There were no obstacles left between them.

She considered jumping into one of the holes. A horribly inviting prospect, as it would rob Jason of the pleasure of killing her. Yet once again, her womb seemed to warn her not to.

Halo pressed the shotgun's butt against her shoulder and aimed at Jason's mask.

He walked toward her, hands still wet with Thawn's life essence.

Halo fired. As she did so, her brain panicked. She was standing with her back to the edge of the roof. The recoil might—

She found herself falling backwards, frantically swinging her arms to quell her momentum and releasing her grip on the shotgun. It was gone in an instant, striking the side of the roof and clattering out of sight.

"She's about to fall!" shrieked someone in the crowd, giving rise to collective hysteria, edged with morbid excitement.

"Keep the camera on her," whispered Rayner to his man. "This is TV gold."

The fountain's water exploded upwards. Deputy Kenneth Ryger's shotgun had landed.

Halo regained her balance and darted away from the roof's edge. Jason was further away, having been thrown back by the blast, but she couldn't even tell where she had hit him. He was covered in wounds, but none seemed to have any effect, barely even slowing him down.

The night air seemed to move, as smoke brought it to life. The heat was so fierce that Halo couldn't stay in the same place for too long. Just as well, as Jason was closing in again. Backing along the roof edge, she winced as the ground behind her gave way. There was nowhere left to run. She was fenced in by burning caverns in the ground.

Jason was so close she could hear him breathe.

Flashing lights caught her attention. She looked over and saw a helicopter, suspended in the darkness at roof level. The craft's rotor chopped through the air, the word "POLICE" emblazoned across its sleek body.

"Nobody move," said a distorted, amplified voice. "Sir, we have in you in our sights. Surrender immediately."

"Yeah, right," Halo muttered, concentrating on not falling backwards. She felt dizzy.

Just stand upright, she told herself. That's all you have to do.

Jason kept walking. A shot rang. Jason's chest squirted blood, which hit Halo's sneakers. Another shot carved him a new mask hole. He reacted as though swatting flies.

Halo's heart sank. Was this all they were packing? They needed a fucking bazooka. She prepared to die. After the day she'd had, it almost felt like a relief.

"There's clearly some kind of conflict, up on the very edge of the roof," said Rayner, in full live news drama mode. "A huge male is advancing on the woman, while a police helicopter opens fire on him. Either they missed, or he's wearing some kind of body armor. This is terrifying to watch. Nobody knows yet whether this man was responsible for the hotel fire, as the cause has yet to be established. Rest assured, *WCX News* is staying right here until we find out."

* * *

Halo did her best to fight Jason off, as he grabbed at her head. But what, really, was the point? Nearby, the helicopter ducked and swerved, attempting to find an angle for another shot. "Stand away from the female," the voice commanded.

Halo blinked as she saw a gun rammed against the right side of Jason's head. It fired, sending chunks of flesh and dark blood hurtling out of the other side. Then it fired again, blowing more of Jason's brains off the side of the building.

Jason released Halo and turned to see Tom clutching the smoking gun, which Norwood had dropped. He was bare-chested and covered with soot, his shirt wrapped around his wounded left hand. Halo gasped, but had no time to celebrate his reappearance.

Having suffered these close range blasts, Jason finally appeared unsteady on his feet. Tom fired again, taking off another piece of Jason's head.

"Sir, hold your fire," ordered the helicopter. "We have this situation under control."

"The hell you do," Tom yelled, his voice hoarse, as Jason turned on him. A fist drove into Tom's shoulder, sending him flying back into the fog.

"Tom!" Halo cried, praying he hadn't tumbled down into one of the roof's many holes.

She doubled up in excruciating pain as another punch struck her abdomen. Her mouth opened and closed, desperately seeking air. In a single, wretched instant, she felt the sure knowledge that her baby had died within her.

Halo's eyes narrowed and her flesh pricked all over. A war cry began in her gut, traveling up through her body, swiftly gaining force and volume until it finally soared out of her mouth.

"You *motherfucker!*"

She threw herself at Jason, grabbing him by the head, ramming her fingers into his eyeholes and feeling the cold flesh yield to her fury. She hammered on the jagged bone, which still pierced the top of his head, slamming it deeper into his skull.

He grabbed her sides, squeezing her with a crippling force.

She could feel he had been weakened. She could feel his blood on her fingers. She could feel his pain and she wanted him to feel more. Most of all, she wanted this vessel of sick, pointless hatred to die.

Still clinging to his head, she exerted her weight on him. Driving them both toward the edge of the roof.

"You've taken your last victim," she screamed. Blood pounded hotly in her head as she urged them both toward oblivion.

Jason took another step backwards, finding only air. Then he and Halo were toppling together, falling off the roof.

For a split second, Halo was riding Jason Voorhees, gazing down at the flashing lights and the people below. She felt strangely detached. Maybe it was because this was the right thing to do. The sight was strangely beautiful.

Then it all changed. There was a sudden tightness around her throat. She was suspended in the air, as if captured by a freeze-frame, while Jason's body fell away from her, down toward the ground.

Her backside landed on the side of the roof. Then she was dragged backward across its rough surface.

She felt that tightness around her throat again, which she realized was the result of the neck of her T-shirt being bunched up and pulled.

"Jesus," said Tom, behind her. He sounded crazed. "I only just grabbed you. What were you doing?"

Halo stared blankly at the point where the roof's edge met the night. She was cradling her belly with both hands.

"Ending it."

As Jason plummeted, there was stunned silence at ground level. Jaws hung low, eyes didn't dare blink and *WCX News's* cameraman struggled to follow the giant's descent. The more nervous spectators scampered for cover.

Jason hammered onto the fountain with an almighty crunch, landing across the phoenix sculpture's wings. His body was impaled in eight places along their spiked peaks, while the bird's majestically upturned beak pierced his guts. One wing's wicked peak had plunged through his mask and out through the back of his head.

Cries of horror rang out. Some began screaming uncontrollably, as if this was one shock too many, tipping them into madness.

"He's hit the fountain," said Rayner, feeling unable to do anything, other than state the blindingly obvious. "The water is still flowing, over him, washing away the blood. So much blood."

The fountain's large basin slowly began to turn black, as Jason's bodily fluids were recycled through the system. His body remained still, as the water gushed over him from ruptured head to foot.

Chuck Waylon stared at him, hardly daring to blink, waiting for this big bastard to slowly, methodically drag himself from those great metallic points.

He didn't.

Waylon punched the air and felt around for the small coke wrap in his pocket. Time to celebrate.

Halo and Tom waited as the helicopter drifted toward them. Inside, the shooter stowed away his rifle and wrenched open a side door as the craft rested one leg on the side of the building. The roof shook beneath the pair, yet neither appeared alarmed. They had already made their peace with death, several times over, so any further life was simply a bonus.

Halo gripped Tom's hand, intertwining her fingers with his. "You know, someone told me this was going to happen," said Halo, vacantly. "A psychic. She said that the wings of destiny would save me."

She nodded down at the fountain. "Looks like she was right."

Tom felt too weak to comment. His makeshift shirt bandage was dripping with blood, his skin an ethereal white. He nodded gravely and stood back, allowing Halo to clamber aboard the helicopter first.

Once in the air, they watched as the entire hotel caved in on itself. Five minutes later, there was no roof left to stand on.

Bright light scythed through the black. Fatigued nurses were tugging at the ward's curtains, ushering in the sun's long rays.

Halo blinked. She drew one hand up from beneath the sheets, using it to shield her eyes. Every single part of her ached, despite the painkillers.

Around the ward, she could dimly make out other beds. She remembered everything after leaving the hotel roof in short, sharp flashes.

Watching the hotel collapse. The temperature inside the helicopter seeming to drop as it flew over Crystal Lake. Being given heavy sedation, once she was stretchered into the hospital. Repeatedly asking after her baby when she was woken up. Being told the cold, hard truth. It was no news to her, but desperately painful to hear spoken by someone else. She appreciated the honesty, nonetheless.

She also remembered worrying that Tom was going to die, especially after realizing what had happened to one of his hands. He had passed out in the helicopter, as she sobbed into his shoulder.

Where was he?

Her neck creaked with the effort of turning her head. She slowly focused in on Tom's face, in the adjacent bed. His upper body was visible; a drip had been attached to the back of his left hand and an IV bag hung from a nearby metal post. His right hand was securely bandaged and an oxygen mask obscured half his face.

But he was alive. That in itself was a mercy.

She remembered more of Denzela's prophecy: "There'll be a great new arrival, but you'll also experience great loss." Once again, the woman had been correct: just not in the way Halo had anticipated. She would have to find her and thank her.

Tom's eyes creaked open like coffin lids. Seeing her, he gamely attempted a weak smile.

"So, are we dead yet?"

Halo shrugged. Tom reached over with his mummified hand. Halo wrapped her own hand around as much of it as she could.

Tom unleashed a chuckle that exploded into a raw, hacking cough.

"We'll have to change beds," he said. "I'm a little short of fingers this side."

Then Halo was crying. And laughing. Emotion exploded out of her in a tidal wave, as she gripped that bandaged lump.

Man, what a brutal comedown. Waylon shielded his eyes against the sun and checked his watch: 7:30am.

He had been up for what remained of the night, bolstered by his magic powder. For the last hour, though, his sense of buoyant confidence had crumbled away, bit by bit, leaving him nervous, paranoid and more than a little shaky.

Guilt bloomed quickly within him: the fire had, as far as he could gather, started in his kitchen. Worst of all, though, was what he had done to Skipper. The kid's awful wailing continued to reverberate inside his tortured brain.

As if starting his life long penance right there and then, Waylon had finally helped load the burnt and mutilated into the backs of ambulances. Someone from the sheriff's department, who would be asking him follow-up questions later today, had interviewed him. He had finally granted an interview to a steely-eyed Zell Rayner, relating everything that had happened in a lengthy, amphetamine fuelled rant. After ten minutes, Rayner had to forcibly stop him talking.

But whatever he had been doing, Waylon had kept one firm eye on Jason Voorhees. He now knew the man's name, as various folk had been bandying it about for the last few hours. Having spent most of his life in Chicago, Waylon had only vaguely heard of the legend, and struggled to absorb everything. So what was this Voorhees? How did he withstand so much damage and still live? What was his secret? Did he do PCP?

The fountain's water basin was jet black. Water continued to pour over the impaled giant. It was a bewitching sight: mythical bird met mythical killer, head on. Waylon drew limited comfort from the fact that, no matter how bad his own comedown felt, Jason's had been infinitely more damaging.

The fire engines were long gone; the blazes had died at around five, leaving the Phoenix Heights hotel a hollow, charred mass of twisted girders and brick.

The living had all been ferried off to hospital. Body bags had been zipped up and removed.

Which only left Jason Voorhees.

Waylon was standing by the fountain, as four medics jumped into the basin, up to their knees in the foul water, climbing up to grab strategic areas of Jason's body. They were instantly drenched.

"Need a hand?" he asked them.

The medics looked at him for a moment, then the most senior looking shrugged. "Sure."

Waylon leapt into the water and positioned himself under Jason's head. "You know, this bastard tried to kill me last night," he said. "Took down most of my team."

The senior medic wasn't listening. He was yelling at someone, off in the distance. "Hey, Scotty. You worked out how to turn this damn water off yet?"

Waylon looked at what remained of Jason's face. At the metal spike which split through the mask's centre, then out of the back of his skull.

"This oughta do it," called a voice in the distance.

Waylon drew back a fist and smacked the top of Jason's head. "Fuck you," he said. Then he spat on the mask and watched his phlegm dribble down its filthy, dented, cracked surface.

The fountain's water thinned and then stopped altogether.

"Okay," said the senior medic. "Push him upwards, after three."

Everyone nodded. Waylon placed his hand under one of Jason's shoulders.

"One... Two..."

The twitching of fingers on Jason's right hand went unnoticed.

"Three..."

Those fingers balled into a fist.

"Do it!"

MY LIFE PART FIVE: THE RESURRECTION

I knew nothing, until I woke up in hospital, full of tubes. Apparently, I had been comatose for four days. Which would account for all the dreams that had been swirling around in my head, and now left stains like fresh paint. The most memorable saw God and the Devil engaging in epic combat with each other in the heavens, hurling bolts of translucent energy at each other. At one point, they both had Norwood Thawn's face—God displaying the man's charmingly benign side, the Devil his infinite darkness. Finally seizing each other with great fury, they fought for several minutes as the elements around them were thrown into chaos. Clouds darkened and winds raged. The sun and the moon became replaced with glowing hockey masks. Then the pair tumbled from the sky and plunged into the depths of Crystal Lake.

When Jason Voorhees rose up from the burning, blood-red waters, machete in hand, with horns protruding from his misshapen head, it was very obvious which side had won. It's not so obvious, the more I start to think about it, which side I am actually on; especially after the business with Daimler. The best I can do is to follow my beliefs, just like any other fallible human being.

It took a while for the memories of killing him to come flooding back. The process was surprisingly guilt ridden, I must confess. As much as Ed Daimler irritated and offended me, bringing his life to a halt brought me no great pleasure. Then there was Norwood, repaying my kindness with the worst kind of treachery.

That knife—was it Norwood or Penelope who had stabbed me, in effect?—had missed my left lung by a quarter of an inch. Thankfully, the hotel fire meant that emergency services soon found me, bleeding to death in that brain splattered Lincoln and carted me off in an ambulance.

So why did I still love him? That's right: love. I'd never felt it before, considering the inner chambers of my heart to be locked off zones, but there was something about this man that made me hear wedding bells.

Of course, it was all academic. Norwood Thawn had been incinerated in that hotel. His body had not been recovered, strictly speaking, but neither had at least fifty of the guests and four members of staff. It was as if they had ceased to exist, reduced to ash. No doubt, many of them were first hacked to death by that devil Jason Voorhees, before the fire erased them entirely.

That little bitch, Hayley Harlan—nicknamed Halo, which was a joke in itself—had already related how Norwood and Voorhees had fought on the roof. I really had to fight to hide my emotions as her interview transcript was read out to me: the heinous details of his evisceration, the way in which he was dropped into the flames.

How Norwood would have hated to learn that his nemesis Voorhees had somehow survived his fall from that roof, eventually reanimating as five people attempted to remove him from that fountain. Killing two of them within seconds, Voorhees had reportedly wrenched himself from the metal phoenix's spikes, jumped down to ground level and strode away, heading toward the woods and, more specifically, the lake. I was sure that *WCX News* were kicking themselves for not hanging around any longer. What legendary, if largely unbroadcastable, footage they would have captured. Still, WCX cameras had immortalized Voorhees tackling Harlan on that blazing rooftop and those scenes had been networked for all their considerable worth. Harlan and her new boyfriend had become quite the celebrities, for squaring off against this fearsome slayer and living to tell the tale.

So have I, for that matter. I've become the plucky new FBI recruit who witnessed her partner having his head blown off by a puritanical serial killer and was subsequently stabbed and left for dead, after being forced to drive him to the Phoenix Heights. Certainly not the way I planned it, but the results have been satisfactory. Everything truly happens for a reason. This whole sorry affair has even produced results for a girl named Tina Shepard and her boyfriend, whose cases are apparently being reconsidered, given that Jason Voorhees actually appears to exist.

Hayley Harlan? She can wait. She'll get hers, just the way Norwood Thawn would have wanted. No, it's Jason Voorhees who needs to pay, and as quickly as possible. I know what you're thinking: Norwood tried to kill me. So why avenge him? Well, sometimes love knows no reason. And even if Norwood had his faults—such as attempting to end my life—his cause is something from which I shall never waver.

That's why I was glad to be summoned to Washington DC by the FBI's directors. As I approached the Hoover Building, shielding my eyes against the sunlight that glinted off its crushed dolomite limestone, I could easily anticipate what they wanted to know.

Sure enough, I was consulted about Jason Voorhees. I sat in a long meeting room, flanked by the FBI's big brass. They offered their condolences for my former partner to whom I nodded bravely (it was like being interviewed by the cops about Walter Cusp, all over again, like taking candy from a baby) and told them Ed was a damn good man. Well, what was the alternative? Ed was a pathetic alcoholic with old-fashioned attitudes and way too much testosterone? That rather assuaged my guilt; the fact that I had at least ensured that the FBI would never learn of the downward spiral their darling Daimler had been riding.

Then they began asking questions about Voorhees. I hadn't actually met him, they knew that, but Norwood Thawn had. What, if anything, had I learned about Clear Waters's now very real killer? The public was calling for action to be taken, and the district's mayor was desperate to rid himself of this perennial bugbear, once and for all. The tourist trade had unsurprisingly died a terrible death. Perhaps worse, people were evacuating Clear Waters, loading up and rolling out in their droves.

"What," asked the FBI's director, "do you think might be the best course of action, as regards Jason Voorhees?"

Six pairs of eyes drilled into me. An expectant silence consumed the room. Inside, I positively hummed with the thrill of all this power. My fingers traced the outline of the scar on my chest.

"I'm so glad you've asked," I said, fixing each of them in turn with a confident beam. "I have a plan which will finally allow us to trap Jason Voorhees. Then send him straight to hell."

ABOUT THE AUTHOR

As Jason Voorhees is his favourite slasher movie icon, Jason Arnopp is pretty damn happy about having written his first novel, *Friday the 13th: Hate-Kill-Repeat*. An obsessive collector of horror movies and webmaster of www.slasherama.com, he writes about film and TV for a variety of magazines, including: *SFX*, *Heat*, *Doctor Who Magazine*, *Word*, *Metal Hammer*, *Classic Rock*, *Closer* and *The Dark Side*. In a past life he worked on UK rock magazine, *Kerrang!*, travelling the world interviewing rock stars and receiving at least one death threat. He has written two music biographies on Slipknot and The Darkness, but has become bored with most modern music. He'll stick with Eighties trash metal, thanks very much.